The critics on Anita Burgh

'A blockbuster . . . an excellent reading experience'
Literary Review

'The mix of suspense, romance, humour and good old heart-tugging pathos is irresistible'
Elizabeth Buchan, *Mail on Sunday*

'A blockbusting story of romance and intrigue'
Family Circle

'The perfect beach book'   *Marie Claire*

'Its crafted writing keeps you hanging in there until the last page'   *City Limits*

'Sharp . . . wickedly funny'   *Mail on Sunday*

'Ambition, greed and manipulation add up to a great blockbuster'   *New Woman*

'You won't be able to put it down'
Good Housekeeping

'A well-written contemporary story that has all the necessary ingredients to make a great read – and it is!'
Oracle

'Anita has the storyteller's gift'   *Daily Express*

'Sinister and avaricious forces are at work behind the pious smiles . . . Gripping!'   *Daily Telegraph*

'A sure-fire bestseller'   *Prima*

Anita Burgh was born in Gillingham, Kent, but spent her early years at Lanhydrock House in Cornwall. Returning to the Medway Towns, she attended Chatham Grammar School, and became a student nurse at UCH in London. She gave up nursing upon marrying into the aristocracy. Subsequently divorced, she pursued various careers – secretarial work, as a laboratory technician in cancer research and as a hotelier. She divides her time between Gloucestershire and the Auvergne in France, where she shares her life with her partner, Billy, a Cairn terrier, three mixed-breed dogs, three cats and a bulldog puppy. The visits of a constantly changing mix of her four children, two stepchildren, six grandchildren, four stepgrand-children and her noble ex-husband keep her busy, happy, entertained and poor! Anita Burgh is the author of many best-sellers, including *Distinctions of Class*, which was shortlisted for the Parker Romantic Novel of the Year Award. Visit Anita Burgh at her website: www.anitaburgh.com.

By Anita Burgh

Daughters of a Granite Land 1: The Azure Bowl
Daughters of a Granite Land 2: The Golden Butterfly
Daughters of a Granite Land 3: The Stone Mistress

Distinctions of Class
Love the Bright Foreigner
Advances
Overtures
Avarice
Lottery
Breeders
The Cult
On Call
The Family
Clare's War
Exiles
The House at Harcourt

Tales from Sarson Magna: Molly's Flashings
Tales from Sarson Magna: Hector's Hobbies

THE STONE MISTRESS

Daughters of a Granite Land

BOOK THREE

Anita Burgh

ORION

An Orion paperback

First published in Great Britain in 1991
by Chatto & Windus Ltd
This paperback edition published in 2001
by Orion Books Ltd,
Orion House, 5 Upper St Martin's Lane,
London WC2H 9EA

Second impression 2002

Copyright © Anita Burgh 1991

The right of Anita Burgh to be identified as the author of
this work has been asserted by her in accordance with
the Copyright, Designs and Patents Act 1988.

A CIP catalogue record for this book
is available from the British Library.

ISBN 0 75283 759 1

Typeset at The Spartan Press Ltd,
Lymington, Hants

Printed and bound in Great Britain by
Clays Ltd, St Ives plc

For Mic Cheetham and the Isle of Mull

Part I

Chapter One

1

It was hot. The atmosphere in the crowded room was thick with cigarette and cigar smoke. The waiters worked using a semaphore of their own invention. The beat of the orchestra throbbed relentlessly. The crooner gamely tried to be heard above the rattle of crockery, the persistent popping of champagne corks, the shouting which passed for conversation here. The small central dance floor was packed with couples who clung to one another as if to wreckage as they swayed and inched their way around the maple floor.

A woman entered, pausing at the top of the flight of steps which led into the main body of the room. There was a ripple of applause which she graciously acknowledged before descending and slowly making her way between the close-set tables. The head waiter fussed in front of her, clearing a path as if for royalty. She was accompanied by four young men, all grinning proudly at being one of this evening's chosen. She paused for a moment to greet the diners at one table, standing with hand on hip, her thigh thrust forward provocatively, her back elegantly arched. Seeing someone else she recognized, she swooped towards him and bent to bestow a kiss, laughing confidentially. She glanced about the room waving at other familiar but less important faces, here and there in the throng. The party reached their table. With sinuous grace, the woman edged her way between table and banquette. The waiter flicked open her napkin, making it crack like a sail, and laid it reverently on her lap. Glasses appeared, menus were consulted.

Francine Frobisher leant back against the buttoned, red

velvet banquette. She slipped a cigarette from a heavy gold case, placing it with exaggerated slowness into a long ebony holder, which she then stroked gently. She looked slyly at the man sitting beside her, laughing when she saw the excitement in his eyes. As she placed the holder in her mouth, four lighters clicked. She looked from one to the other of her companions, deciding who she would graciously allow to light her cigarette. She chose the man she had laughed at and the others turned despondently away.

Francine had chosen this man for several reasons. He was American and she liked their uncomplicated enthusiasm in bed; she did not know him, something that always added delight to any encounter; he was young, and the older she became the more she appreciated youth; but most importantly of all, she had chosen him because with his black hair, grey eyes and his slightly crooked and sardonic smile he had reminded her immediately of Marshall Boscar. Marshall was the only man she had ever loved, or rather Francine imagined she had loved, for it was unlikely she had ever cared for another human being with as much dedication as she devoted to herself. Francine had coupled with a battalion of men, but none had affected her as Marshall had. Marshall had been a challenge and one which, as soon as she had thought him conquered, had slipped through her fingers. Now he was dead and would never be hers.

Francine came here to the Garibaldi Club most nights after the show. It suited her: close to the West End theatres, with good music, passable food and a sophisticated clientele who never did anything so crass as to ask for her autograph. And it was always crowded like this, making conversation difficult, which also suited her. She never wanted to talk for some time after a performance, preferring to watch and take her time over deciding who would share her bed that night.

At forty-four most women of her generation were resigned to widening hips, grey hair and wrinkles marring

4

youthful beauty. But not Francine. Nature had been kind, for she had good bone structure and a perfect pale complexion which complemented her fine blonde hair. Her eyes were of a stunning green, as dark as the holly. But she, grasping these gifts, had never taken them for granted and over the years had worked hard at maintaining her beauty with a regime so rigid it would have defeated most women. Francine deserved to look the way she did. And she had been rewarded, for her appearance had, in no small measure, assured her position as a famous West End musical star.

For the sake of her companions it was fortunate that conversation at the Garibaldi was difficult for, apart from her performance and her beauty, Francine had no other interests and thus nothing of note to say. She did not read books, only scripts. The daily newspaper was opened only at the gossip page. Magazines were flicked through for the pictures of current fashions which she studied with professional care. She never went to the theatre to watch others, the only music to which she listened was on records of her own singing.

Europe was at war: men were dying in their thousands; women were being widowed, children orphaned; Jews were being slaughtered; fear stalked the world – and all of it passed Francine by. For her, tragedy was a broken nail, a blemish on her skin, an ill-fitting frock. To Francine, war was a bonus for it brought full houses, desperate for her magic which enabled them to forget their tribulations for a few hours.

Her companion leaned over and whispered in her ear, 'Would you like to dance?'

'No, thank you,' she mouthed back. The dance floor was too crowded. Francine liked to dance only when she was certain she would be noticed.

'Would you like to go somewhere else?'

She shook her head. There was no point. She had been everywhere else; this place suited her best.

Two women, in their early twenties, escorted by a

slightly older, tall, slim, uniformed man with a face more interesting than handsome, ran lightly down the red-carpeted staircase. The head waiter scuttled officiously towards them, bowing obsequiously – here was a client not famous like Francine, but possessing that other quality important to men of his trade – wealth.

'Alphonse, how's your family? Safe, I hope. Have you a table for us?' One of the women smiled appealingly at him, not waiting to hear his answer. 'Just a tiny table?' She was petite, fair haired. Her hazel eyes, flecked with gold, were large and expressive. Her face was of such fine-boned beauty that it invariably turned all heads when she entered a room.

'But of course, Lady Copton. For you there is always a table.' Alphonse bowed, snapped to attention and began to flap his hands at the other waiters as if irritated, but in fact his actions were alerting them to the importance of this customer. Her companions hardly warranted a glance from him as they followed Juniper Copton.

'You order, Jonathan.' She put down the large menu, as if weary of making decisions.

'But I don't know what you want,' Jonathan Middle-bank said reasonably. His mind was already racing, wondering how on earth he was to pay for this in the event that Juniper did not pick up the bill. It was a faint risk, she always insisted on paying, but there had been times when she had been known to wander off, completely forgetting her guests and the bill.

'Something light, and champagne. What about you, Polly?'

Polly, Countess de Faubert et Bresson by marriage, but who preferred her maiden name of Frobisher, was in complete contrast to Juniper. She was tall, with sleek, almost black hair, and brown eyes, the colour so deep that they appeared fathomless. Her features were strong rather than delicate, and her expression suggested an intelligent, serious nature. Polly looked down at the menu. She was not hungry, she drank little, she found the smoky atmosphere of the night club oppressive and was already wondering what she was doing here. Even as she thought this, she knew the answer. Juniper had insisted on her coming and when she did that few could resist, least of all Polly.

'I'm not very hungry. A sandwich perhaps and some soda water,' she said eventually.

'Polly, really! This is a celebration. You've got to drink champagne. I insist. Order the best, Jonathan. At least have an omelette, Polly.'

'Very well.' Polly resignedly shrugged.

'Don't you want to celebrate?' Juniper persisted.

'Of course.' Polly was lying, for she saw no cause for celebration. Certainly not because she had returned from a month in Devon, nor that Jonathan Middlebank had looked them up on a forty-eight-hour pass from the army. In fact she felt acutely uncomfortable in his presence, doubly so with Juniper there. She liked Jonathan, she always would: you couldn't love someone as she had loved him and be left with no feeling, not if you were Polly. She had long ago forgiven Jonathan and Juniper for deceiving her, for she was incapable of holding a grudge. No, her unease was caused because, try as she might, she could not forget that it had happened.

'So tell me all about the great escape from France,' Jonathan said, once the wine and food had been ordered.

By now Juniper had evolved a ripping yarn of her and Polly's exploits in France, escaping just ahead of the German army of occupation. Polly had listened to the performance before, but she still had to admire the easy way Juniper could turn the fear and nightmare of those three weeks into a long joke which, already, had Jonathan doubled over with laughter.

While they chatted, their heads close together the easier to hear above the hubbub, Polly looked about the crowded room and wondered how people could be so unthinkingly happy when the life they knew was disintegrating fast. Or was it bravado? Suddenly her body

7

went rigid. In a break in the dancing, across the room she saw her mother, Francine. Her pulse began to race and her hands felt clammy – her usual reaction on seeing her mother. For Francine had honed to perfection the trick of reducing the grown-up Polly to a gauche schoolgirl with just a couple of her well-chosen, cutting sentences.

Polly sat undecided what to do. If she crossed the room she knew she would return humiliated. If she did not, and Francine saw her, then she risked an abusive row that would leave her feeling wretched for days when she finally went to visit her mother, a visit that was already overdue.

'Excuse me. I'm just going to powder my nose.' She had to raise her voice for the others to hear. She slipped away from the table and made her way to the cloakroom to repair what little make-up she wore. If she was to speak to Francine with her immaculate grooming, then a repowdered nose was essential.

'How is Polly?' Jonathan asked, suddenly serious, as he watched her edging diffidently through the crowds.

'She's fine. Her husband's dead, you know,' Juniper said conversationally.

'In the fighting?'

Juniper chuckled, a husky low laugh which was a delight to hear. 'Good Lord, no! Not Michel. He was at his château with his mistress – no doubt cowering away from the Germans. He was scurrying down to the cellar to get wine, tripped over his dressing-gown hem and broke his rotten neck.'

Jonathan looked up, shocked at Juniper's evident amusement.

'You needn't look so po-faced, Jonathan. You know damn well what a heel he was. Michel was an unspeakable sadist to poor Polly and made her life a living hell. I'm glad he's dead. I'm only sorry it was instantaneous. Apparently he didn't know anything about it.'

Jonathan shuddered involuntarily. Hearing such news in Juniper's beautiful low voice, with its faint trace of an American accent, somehow made it seem more horrific.

Surreptitiously under the table, Jonathan touched wood. He was far too superstitious, and these times made one far too vulnerable, for him to be able to speak ill of the dead.

'You know what you should do, Jonathan, my darling: you should step in quick, and ask Polly to marry you and make up for lost time.'

'She wouldn't have me. I can't say I blame her, not after . . .' He looked away, embarrassed.

'Rubbish, that was all my fault, I seduced you. Don't say you've forgotten already – hardly complimentary to me.' Juniper chuckled wickedly which only increased Jonathan's discomfort.

'I was sure she would have met someone else by now. Someone suitable.' He wanted the conversation to move away from past memories which still, after all this time, shamed him.

'She had. Andrew Slater – an absolute sweetie. She met him in Paris soon after she'd run away from Michel. But he's no use, he's missing, presumed dead. You should grab her before someone else does. Come on, Jonathan, admit it, you've always been potty about her.'

'Oh Juniper, you're incorrigible . . .' He shook his head in resigned amusement at her flippancy. 'I doubt if Polly thinks he's dead. She'll hope for ever, I know Polly. Now would be the worst time to try anything.'

'Of course she thinks he's alive. I've told her it's silly, wasting her life waiting for someone who won't come back. After all, how many of the men left behind after Dunkirk do you think survived?'

'Precious few.'

'Well, there you are then,' Juniper said matter-of-factly.

'She'll still need time to get over him.'

'In wartime? There isn't time. I wouldn't.'

'No, Juniper, I guess you wouldn't.' Jonathan smiled at her honesty about herself. It made even her most shocking statements acceptable.

She flicked open a heavy gold powder compact and

inspected her face. Apparently satisfied by what she saw, she clicked it shut with a snap.

'Let's dance,' she said.

'You know me, Juniper. Four feet . . .' He smiled apologetically.

'Gee, I know such boring people.' She pushed him affectionately. 'Got any pennies? I'm going to telephone, call up reinforcements who care to dance.' She laughed as she kissed him lightly on the cheek, then slid from behind the banquette and made her way up the stairs to the telephone.

Far away in the street an air-raid siren wailed, unheard by the crowd in the Garibaldi who continued to laugh and dance.

A waiter wound his way through the crush to the band and whispered in the conductor's ear. Billy 'Hot Feet' Jackson tapped his baton loudly on the music stand and was rewarded by a measure of silence.

'There's an air-raid alert, if anyone's interested,' he said laconically. The crowd laughed.

Francine's companion jumped to his feet and held out his hand to her. She shook her head and smiled.

'Shouldn't we go to the air-raid shelter?' he asked anxiously.

'What for?' She shrugged. 'They smell disgusting. Have you just arrived in London?' He nodded. 'Ah well, then you don't understand. The sirens are always going, but nothing happens. Even if they did come they wouldn't bomb us, they'll only kill the poor around the docks. Do sit down and stop fussing.'

The momentary lull in the tumult was coming to an end. The more nervous had slipped away. The orchestra struck up again and the racket in the club was quickly back to its normal fortissimo.

Polly, her shiny nose newly powdered, lipstick replenished, stood at her mother's table waiting for a chance to speak. A couple of Francine's more neglected companions looked up at her, their eyes registering appreciation.

'Hullo, Francine,' Polly said shyly. She knew better than to call her 'Mother' in front of her admirers, that would never be forgiven. 'You look well.'

'Good God – Polly! Have you grown? You look even taller. I thought you were in France. What are you doing here?' This was Francine's greeting to the daughter she had not seen for over four years.

'I got out, and . . .'

'How long have you been back?'

'July. We docked at . . .'

'What month is it now? September? How sweet of you to rush and see me.' Francine's eyes were flashing menacingly.

'I was going to call tomorrow.'

'Well, telephone first, it might not be convenient,' Francine said coldly.

'Of course.' Polly turned away with relief, she'd got off quite lightly.

'Are you sure you're not still growing?' Her mother had the parting shot.

Those five storeys above them heard it coming, the high-pitched scream of the bomb as it hurtled towards them as if knowing it too was about to die. Far below, 'Hot Feet' had just announced, to tumultuous applause, that the new crooner would sing 'A Nightingale Sang in Berkeley Square'.

And then all hell erupted as the high explosive smashed through the floors of the building and nosedived into the dance floor. The flash momentarily blinded, the blast sucked air from lungs, the din burst eardrums. And everything disappeared in a choking cloud of brown dust.

There was total silence. Then in the pitch dark the sounds began – the screams, the moans, the cursing. God, Jesus, mothers were called for, begged for, wailed for. The raw notes of agony filled the air instead of night-ingales in Berkeley Square.

Polly regained consciousness in a dark, choking world filled with demented cries. For a moment she had no idea where she was, or what she was doing sitting on the floor in the noisy darkness, her nostrils full of a strange acrid smell. And then she remembered . . .

'Mother,' she called, and then louder to make herself heard over the cries around her. And louder still, until she too was screaming that one word: 'Mother!'

Francine was sitting on the floor propped up against the wall. The banquette lay heavy across her legs, furniture was piled around her, trapping her. She was aware of a heavy weight in her lap, but felt too disorientated to be curious about it.

'For Christ's sake, whoever you are, stop that bloody caterwauling. Your mother can't help you now,' Francine said sharply into the dark.

'Mother, is that you?'

'It's Francine Frobisher,' came the cold reply. Even in this situation Francine refused to admit to mother-hood.

'Thank God, you're all right,' Polly found herself saying with genuine feeling. 'It's Polly, I'm over here.'

'A lot of use that is. I can't see where "over here" is, you fool.'

'Are you hurt?'

Gingerly Francine felt her face with her fingertips and could have wept with relief when she felt no blood.

'Apparently not. But I'm trapped.'

Polly scrambled in the direction of her mother's voice, but found her way barred by the heavy banquette. She tried to lift it, coughing and spluttering from lungs choked with dust.

'Oh, for God's sake, Polly, stop fiddling about. Leave it to the professionals. Make yourself useful – find my handbag and give me a cigarette.'

'I don't think you should smoke. What about the gas?'

'You always were such a pessimist,' Francine said irritably.

'If you're all right then I've got to find Juniper.' Polly began to inch away.

'I shouldn't worry about her, she's indestructible.'

Moving was difficult. People lay everywhere, some moaning, some chillingly still. The debris of shattered furniture impeded her and she was afraid of hurting the wounded by blundering into them.

'Help me . . .' a voice croaked, a voice choked with blood. 'Please help me . . .'

Polly turned towards the sound, feeling gently with her hands. She made out the shape of a piano and beneath it a hand which grabbed at hers in desperation.

'The pain . . .' the voice said.

'Help's coming.' Polly held the hand tight. 'Are there any men here?' she called out, knowing that she could not budge the heavy piano by herself, and trying to keep the panic from her voice. She sat clutching the hand, feeling helpless and close to tears.

'I got engaged tonight . . .' the croaking voice said with difficulty.

'That's marvellous. When's the wedding?' Polly forced herself to sound bright.

'Special licence – three days . . .' And then the piano moved a little and the woman groaned, a blood-chilling sound of agony. 'Stay with me . . .' she managed to say.

'I'll stay. It won't be long, I promise. Don't talk, try to conserve your energy.'

In the darkness, Polly sat and talked to the stranger. She told her about the flat in Paris, about Andrew and her fears for him, of Hursty her cat named after Hurstwood her childhood home in Devon – anything she could think of.

Across the rubble a thin shaft of light pierced the gloom and then another, picking out the shadowy form of a looter scrambling over the bodies as he plundered the jewellery of the dead. A voice bellowed, 'Bugger off, scum.' The man disappeared into the murk like a rat slipping behind a wainscot. Voices shouted out words of comfort. People were told not to panic, to hold on. In the street above they could hear the wail of sirens.

It was nearly half an hour before a fireman reached Polly. His torch swept over her.

'Please get more men to move this piano, there's someone in dreadful pain here,' she called, shading her eyes from the beam as she looked up at the black bulk of the man looming over her. He moved his torch to right and left until it rested on the face of a pretty young girl. Her blue eyes were wide open, staring unblinkingly at the light. From her mouth trickled a thin line of blood as red as her hair.

'Help her, please. She's been so brave,' Polly begged urgently.

'God love you, she's dead,' the fireman said, gently prising free Polly's hand. She began to shake, jerking convulsively, her mouth gasping for breath. The fireman wrapped a blanket around her. 'Ben, over here – shock.'

'My mother . . . my mother's over there . . .' Polly said through chattering teeth.

Again the beam of light arced through the dust-laden air. It passed over the dead to where Francine sat propped against the wall, like an elegant rag doll.

'You took your time,' she said.

'Cor, love a duck,' the fireman exclaimed. Francine looked down into the pool of light he was pouring on to her lap. The heavy weight she had felt was the head of her young American companion.

'Oh look, he's ruined my frock,' she said tetchily, pushing at the head, which rolled away, and frowning at the bloodstains on her dress.

'There, there, love, don't take on,' said the fireman kindly, assuming she was in shock, too. She was not. She meant it.

Polly refused to climb into the ambulance.

'Look, I'm not hurt. There are plenty who are,' she insisted.

'Shock can be a nasty thing.' The ambulance driver was equally firm.

Polly held her hand out in front of her. 'See, I've stopped shaking. I'm fine.' She shrugged off the blanket and folded it neatly before handing it to the man. 'I've friends to find.' She turned away from the open door of the ambulance, feeling dizzy and sick, but she chose to ignore both.

'Looks to me as if you could do with a very large brandy.' Polly heard the familiar voice, even now still bubbling with laughter. She hardly dared turn in case she was dreaming. But there was Juniper. Despite being covered in dust, plaster in her hair, and with the heel of one shoe broken, she still managed to look beautiful. Wordlessly Polly fell into Juniper's arms and then, only then, did she allow herself to cry. 'Hush, sweetie. It's all right.' She held Polly close.

'You're safe, I can hardly believe it – the side we were sitting – it's not there any more . . .' Polly's tears made rivers in the dust on her face. She wiped at them with the back of her hand.

'Look at the mess you're making.' Juniper mopped at Polly's face with a clean handkerchief. 'Of course I'm safe. I said this war was going to be fun.'

'Oh, Juniper, how can you say such a thing?'

'Very easily – I just said it. Such excitement! Here take a swig.' She was holding out a silver, crested hip flask.

'But where were you?'

'I'd nipped upstairs to the telephone. I was in the middle of a conversation and whoosh . . . I was flying across the foyer like Tinkerbell.' She giggled.

'Jonathan?' Polly asked, as she took a mouthful of the brandy.

'He's fine too. His dignity's a bit dented – he was trapped in the Gents' loo.'

'Where's he now?' Polly was laughing too and she could feel the brandy seeping warmly into her veins.

'Helping, like a good scout. God, we both look like tramps. Look at your frock.'

Polly looked down to see that the front of her yellow taffeta dress was split from hem to waist. She pulled the remnants around her.

'I don't think anyone is going to take much notice, Polly,' Juniper said kindly. 'But take my wrap if it saves you embarrassment. I'm going to get you home.'

'But my mother . . .'

'Your mother left ages ago.'

'Which hospital did they take her to?'

'They didn't. I can't imagine your mother in a public ward, can you? She refused to go, and then one of her admirers happened to drive past in his Bentley and whisked her away. Everyone was most impressed,' Juniper said ironically. 'Come on, home and no arguments. We're only in the way here.'

Somehow, in the mêlée, Juniper managed to find a taxi. Once back home, in the relative safety of Juniper's house, Polly felt a tiredness so heavy that it was an effort to put one foot in front of the other. Juniper by contrast was excitedly buzzing about the room, unable to sit still or to stop talking.

Polly refused more brandy, but sat thoughtfully sipping the Ovaltine the cook had prepared for her. She was thinking about her reaction to her mother's safety in the bombed night-club. Polly did not like her mother and could not remember a time when she had, so, she had assumed that she felt no love either. But her reaction this evening belied that. In those few moments she had felt real fear that her mother had been killed. Perhaps her mother might have felt the same about her. It would be nice if she could build a better relationship with Francine. Maybe it would help to fill the void left by her father's untimely death.

'What are you looking so serious about?' Juniper seemed finally to have run out of steam.

'I was thinking about my mother and how I reacted when I thought she had been killed. I don't like her, but back there I think I found I loved her,' Polly said, puzzled.

'Blood is thicker than water. Look at us . . .' Juniper helped herself to more brandy. 'We prove that.'

Polly did not reply. She had decided, since her return from France, to stop discussing with Juniper this notion she had that they were sisters. Juniper wanted them to be and would accept no argument against it, whereas Polly, deep inside her, knew that it could not be true, and did not want it to be. She had loved her father, Richard Frobisher, in life; she had no intention of denying him now he was dead.

'I think I'll go up to bed, if you don't mind. I feel very tired.' She stood up and began to walk to the door with legs that felt as if they were weighted with diver's boots.

'But it's early . . .' Juniper complained.

'Not for me it isn't.' Polly shut the door firmly.

Polly was woken early by a white-faced Juniper shaking her.

'Polly, wake up. I'm leaving for Scotland immediately.'

'Scotland?' Polly said blearily.

'I just received a telegram from Caroline. Harry's ill. I must go to him.'

'Of course you must,' Polly was instantly awake. 'Poor little fellow, what's wrong?'

'A fever – they can't get it down. Oh Polly, I'm so afraid.'

Polly was already out of bed and slipping on her dressing gown. 'Would you like me to come with you?'

'There isn't time. I've a taxi waiting. If I'm lucky I can catch the early train.' She kissed her. 'I'll telephone as soon as I have news. Oh Polly . . .' Juniper looked with anguish at her.

'Children do this sort of thing. Try not to worry. He'll probably be right as rain when you get there.'

'Do you think so? Honestly?'

'Honestly.' Polly gave her a quick hug. 'Now run, or you'll miss that train.'

From the upstairs window, Polly watched as Juniper ran helter skelter down the steps of the house. Although she was sorry the little boy was ill, she was pleased by Juniper's reaction to the news. Juniper had always claimed she felt nothing for her son, Harry, but maybe she was about to find out differently, just as Polly had last night.

Later that morning Polly sat beside her mother's bed. She had just suggested that, when Juniper returned from Scotland, she would ask her whether Francine could move in with them. 'Safety in numbers,' she had said lightly. She was not prepared for her mother's reaction to the sensible idea.

'You must be mad, Polly. Me? Living under the same roof as that woman? Never. And you're a fool to trust her. Little whore!' Francine spat the words out venomously.

'Mother!' Polly looked up with a start, astonished.

'If only you knew what I do.'

'What don't I know?'

Francine was torn: she would have liked to destroy her daughter's relationship with Juniper. It would be so easy to tell her about Juniper's attempt, when a mere slip of a girl of seventeen, to seduce Polly's father – the sainted father Polly would never hear a word against. How Francine would like to destroy that adoration. But she said nothing, for to do so would have been to admit that a young girl had almost succeeded in usurping Francine's position in a man's bed – an unheard-of event.

'I'm not prepared to say,' Francine said icily.

'But you shouldn't be here alone.'

'I'm not alone. I've Clara with me.'

'Clara might leave you.'

'Rubbish, she's too old to go gallivanting off to find war work. I'm lucky to have her, some of my friends can't get a maid for love nor money.'

Polly tried hard to look sympathetic, but feared she had failed. The lack of a lady's maid was not high on her list of priorities.

'My frock was ruined last night. Brand new, too. Clara says nothing can be done with it. It's crêpe, you see.'

'We're lucky to be alive,' Polly said shortly, unable to understand Francine's preoccupation with a dress.

'I've always been lucky,' Francine boasted.

'Sixty-four died. I shudder to think how close to death we were.' Polly shivered anew at the memory of the previous night. She put her hand on the coverlet, inching it towards her mother's hand; she touched it gently. 'I felt so close to you last night, Mother . . .' she began diffidently.

Francine moved her hand away abruptly, as if stung, 'Sixty-four? I wonder how many of them I knew . . .'

The shrill ringing of the telephone interrupted her. While her mother launched into a dramatic account of the bomb at Garibaldi's, Polly wandered over to the window and looked down into the street below where workmen were clearing up debris. Idly she fingered the criss-cross of sticky paper stretched across the glass as protection against blast. She had come with muddled ideas of building bridges between herself and Francine. But when she walked into the room, if she were honest, she had to admit that she had felt nothing again. Had shock played tricks with her emotions last night? At least she had tried to talk to her mother. And if she did not want to know, what else could Polly expect? Francine had never been a mother in the true sense of the word; she had always been too self-absorbed to have any time for maternal feelings. She had happily left Polly's upbringing entirely to her husband, Richard. So why had she thought Francine could change?

Francine replaced the telephone receiver and rang for her maid to order tea. Polly turned from the window to see her mother studying her manicure intently.

'We had a memorial service for your father,' Francine said abruptly.

'I'm glad.'

'His body will never be found now.'

'Probably not,' Polly replied with difficulty; she could not speak so easily about him.

'What on earth he was doing in an aeroplane over the Channel with war about to begin, I've never understood.'

'I think he was crossing to France to find me.'

'Oh Polly, hardly. What on earth gave you that idea?' Francine chuckled with disbelief – the very idea that anyone should put themselves out for Polly. Lacking Francine's dramatic blonde beauty, Polly had been a bitter disappointment to her. Francine had never been able to appreciate Polly's different style of beauty.

'Seen that old hag, your grandmother?'

'Not yet. I want to find war work in London. When I know what I'm doing, I'll go and see her.'

'You'll have a hard time finding anything. Everyone is volunteering. There are women all over the place who have been waiting a year now to be called upon by the authorities.'

'I had hoped to join one of the women's services. But they don't seem interested in me.'

'You should be relieved. The uniforms are dreadful. No shape, and itchy too. No, you're better off out of all that – so unfeminine. Mind you, it'll be a problem finding anything else. It's not as if you're good at anything, is it?' Francine looked at her slyly.

'I drove a lot in France, taking supplies to the front. And I can type quite well, I worked on a magazine in Paris,' Polly replied calmly, with no intention of rising to her mother's goading. 'I hoped I could be of use doing something like that here.'

'But nothing happens here. The government whips us all up into hysteria and then nothing happens.'

'It did last night.'

'Ah! Just one night. They won't be back.'

Polly did not know whether to be impressed by her mother's courage or rather, what she feared was probably nearer the truth, to despise her stupidity.

'I'd have thought you'd rush off to Berkshire at the earliest opportunity.' Francine was admiring her nails again as if uninterested in Polly's reply. Polly knew better. Much as Francine hated her mother-in-law, Gertie Frobisher, she could never resist finding out as much as possible about her.

'Grandmama's not in Berkshire. Her house has been requisitioned by one of the ministries. She's staying with Juniper's grandmother at Gwenfer in Cornwall.'

'God, how awful. She might as well be on the moon, it's so far away from civilization,' announced Francine, who had never once visited that county.

The telephone rang and Francine launched into another enthusiastic phone call. She waved her hand at Polly in an unmistakable gesture of dismissal. Polly slipped quietly from the room.

Before leaving the flat she went into what had been her father's study. She sniffed the air, but could find no familiar scent of him. Instead the room was full of the smell of oranges from the crates stacked against one wall. She looked about, amazed. The room was a wartime treasure chest: crates of champagne, two large drums of cooking oil, tins of ham, caviare, tongue, salmon, tinned fruit. Her mother might pretend she did not give the war a thought, but she had certainly prepared for it.

Polly sat in her father's chair, put her cheek against the cool leather and longed for him. She wondered whether there would ever be a time when she would not have this ache inside her. She stood up and looked around the room as if for the last time, then collected her coat and gas mask case from the hall and let herself out of her mother's flat.

She did not know why she had bothered to come. Nothing had changed, least of all her mother.

Sunday in London was normally a quiet day; not today though, there was activity everywhere. Moving about was a slow process. The streets were full of rubble, potholes riddled the roads, there were bomb craters at every turn. The previous night's raid, London's first, had been venomous.

Polly's way was blocked by a barricade across the road, stolidly guarded by a policeman.

'No entry, miss – fractured water main.'

Three houses had been hit, their fronts ripped off but their contents still in place. A bed teetered from one floor, one leg dangling dangerously into space, a painting on a wall was askew, a staircase led nowhere, but otherwise everything was intact. An open wardrobe door showed a neat row of clothes hanging, tea was set on a table, a chamber pot stood under a bed. They looked like giant dolls' houses but from which the dolls were absent.

Out of curiosity Polly joined the large crowd standing at the barrier. Some were clutching bundles of clothes, some had nothing. One man held a bracket clock. A little girl, her face streaked with dirt, clutched a rabbit in a cage. A shout rang out as workmen raced for their lives towards them. Halfway down the row of houses the front of a five-storey building collapsed almost lazily into the road. Everyone ducked their heads and shielded their eyes from the dust that swooshed towards them with the speed of an express train.

The dust settled. The crowd stood staring stoically at the devastation. There were no tears, no hysteria. London was in chaos, ruins everywhere, people had died and Polly's mother thought it all unimportant.

Polly continued walking across the battered city. Above her the sun shone on the barrage balloons that floated like gigantic, amiable, prehistoric monsters. They had been such a comfort to see, making everyone feel safe. But last night they had failed them. From her mother's flat in

Mayfair to Juniper's house in Belgravia was normally a brisk twenty-minute walk, but this morning, due to detours, fallen masonry and craters, it took over an hour.

She let herself in and made straight for the telephone. What she had seen last night and today had made her even more determined to help. Even though it was Sunday, she began to call everyone she knew who might help her to get work – any work – anything to be useful.

3

The dim blue light in the railway carriage was too dull to read by, one could only think or sleep, but Juniper was too uncomfortable for the latter. The carriage was packed: seats for eight were filled by ten, two soldiers stood between the seats, hanging on to the luggage rack on which a young boy had been placed. On top of the bags, surrounded by parcels, one of which looked suspiciously like a black-market ham, he slept peacefully.

Humanity en masse smelt, Juniper concluded. She fumbled in her handbag to find her scent and gave herself a surreptitious dab of Joy.

'Sorry, miss, we are a bit high.' One of the soldiers grinned at her.

'No, no it's not that . . .' She smiled apologetically in the way of one who has been caught out.

'We haven't washed for days, you see, miss.'

'Poor you,' she said with no expression, and opened her magazine pretending to be able to read it despite the poor light. She did not want to talk to the soldier, she did not want to talk to anyone. She moved in her seat, trying to manipulate an extra inch or two for comfort, but in doing so lost precious room to the fat woman sitting beside her whose body seemed to ooze into whatever space was available.

Juniper could not even look out of the window. With the strict blackout the blinds were pulled down and would have to stay that way. She had been travelling for two days. Yesterday, Sunday, she had spent an uncomfortable night in the station hotel at Newcastle. She had been on this train for hours and still she had no idea where she was and when they would arrive in Aberdeen. The train would stop for ages at a time in sidings, with no explanation for the halt. The stations they passed had no names. The signs had all been removed for security; she could be in the middle of Siberia for all she knew.

Now another night loomed. At this rate . . . God she was bored! She wished she had not come now. What had made her? Duty, she supposed, and she smiled at herself in the dim light. Duty was not a word that she, or anyone else come to that, would normally associate with her.

She certainly was not rushing to Scotland from any maternal feelings, she did not have any. One of the most sensible things she had ever done, she congratulated herself, was to arrange for her childless brother-in-law and his wife to bring up her son. The night she had presented Harry to them, she now realized, she had acted out of anger and spite and a need for revenge on her husband. Inevitably, her action had shocked everyone, most of all her own grandmother. No one seemed able to understand or to believe that it was possible to be a mother and not feel great love for one's child.

Her son did not even know her now. When she had last seen him, the boy had greeted her with a marked lack of interest. To Juniper the child's behaviour was perfectly logical. Why should he take to this stranger? He was only two and it was unreasonable to expect him to remember her, or like her. She had not much liked her own mother, Grace, a fat and discontented woman, but with reason she now realized. She shook her head almost imperceptibly. She did not like to think about her mother. There were many things from her past that Juniper preferred not to dwell on.

Now Harry was ill and like a fool she had fought her way on to the first train for Scotland and the discomfort of third-class travel and she did not really know why. She looked moodily at the rings on her fingers.

Once she had loved, been full of it. She had loved her father, Marshall, and her grandfather, Lincoln Wakefield, totally. But both, in different ways, had betrayed her. She had experienced an intense feeling of betrayal when she discovered that her father had not only been sleeping with Francine when courting her mother but years later had rekindled their affair, leading undoubtedly to her mother's suicide. And Lincoln, the man she had loved above all others, had thought to be the kindest man in the world, she had found to be a ruthless tyrant. She had also loved Alice, her grandmother, and still did, but not as she once had, not with the unquestioning love of a child. And no woman could have loved her husband as Juniper had loved Hal Copton. Anything he wanted she had given him, but he had shattered her trust and she had felt the ice form about her heart. There had been other men, too many for comfort, she thought, but she had loved none of them. She was beginning to wonder if she would ever love again . . .

The train lurched to a halt.

'Aberdeen,' a voice yelled.

Juniper jumped to her feet, crashing into the soldier who had tried to talk to her.

'No need to panic, miss, this train isn't going any further.'

She sat down again, feeling silly, and waited patiently for everyone else to collect their parcels, bags and cases. As she watched the odd assortment of packages being taken down from the rack, she wondered if it was war that made everyone travel in such disorder. Or was this how people usually travelled in Third Class? She would not know, used as she was to first class travel, with armies of porters, her matching baggage safely stowed away in the guard's van with someone else to supervise its unloading. If this was normal travel, she hoped this wretched war would end soon. It was horribly uncomfortable.

At last she was on the platform, her one case and bag

beside her. The ice-cold wind lashed in from the North Sea, boring into the very marrow of her bones, and she pulled her fur coat about her. Dear God, who could survive in temperatures like these.

'Juniper!'

She swung round at the sound of her name.

'Leigh,' she exclaimed with surprise at the sight of her brother-in-law pushing through the crowds towards her. 'How on earth did you know I'd be on that train?'

'Polly told us which one. I've been calling the station at regular intervals. You're only ten hours late – not bad at all.' Her brother-in-law was laughing, and just for a second she saw her husband Hal in his face and felt alarmed by the pleasure she felt at the resemblance.

'You've the car. What about petrol?' she asked, pleased to see Leigh's old Morris in the station car park.

'I get a special allowance since I'm a bigwig in the Home Guard!' He shrugged disparagingly as if apologizing for not being in the army. 'I'm not cheating, I had to come to Aberdeen today for a meeting,' he added hurriedly.

'My darling Leigh, I didn't for one moment think you would cheat. You're the one person I know who would be incapable of that.' She gave her husky laugh and gently laid her hand on his arm.

The small Morris car inched its way through the black night, lashed by horizontal rain. Leigh sat hunched over the wheel peering into the darkness, the road ahead illuminated only by the tiny slits in his headlights, all that the blackout allowed.

'A foul night, isn't it? But we should be all right, I know this road like the back of my hand.'

'I've never understood that remark. I don't know the back of mine.' Juniper peered out of the window and flinched away as the branches of a small tree whipped the car. 'There's a ditch looming rather near, this side,' she said as nonchalantly as she could manage.

'Sorry.' He pulled the car to the right and they moved sedately along the centre of the road.

'Why on earth do you live up here? It's the back of beyond.'

'I've grown quite fond of it. There's a beauty and a peace here that's lacking in the south and the people are marvellous.'

'But it's so cold.' She pulled her fur closer and wished she had worn boots instead of high-heeled court shoes.

'Good God, Juniper, this is nothing. It's only September. You wait for the winter, then it's really cold.'

'You should move south in the winter like the birds.'

'Birds can build nests, we haven't the money.'

'But Leigh, I thought whoever had care of Harry had the money from your father's will.' She turned in her seat to look at him.

'It didn't work out that way, Juniper. Hal fought it – and won. You were in France; there seemed no point in bothering you.'

'Leigh, I'm so sorry, I'd no idea. I thought it was all cut and dried. I'll arrange more money for you.'

'Dear Juniper. You're too generous for your own good. I wouldn't dream of taking any more from you for Harry's keep.'

'I wish your brother shared rather more of your character, Leigh.' Juniper spoke pleasantly enough, but Leigh looked at her sharply, wondering if he would see cynicism in her face. He did not, but he reflected that she had every right to be cynical where his brother was concerned. She had made him a generous allowance when many women in her position would have left him to fend for himself.

'Any news on your divorce?'

'Yes. I got my decree nisi last week. That's what kept me in London. I'd meant to go to Cornwall as soon as I got back from France.'

'I'd expected you to have problems with the divorce. I couldn't see Hal giving up easily. Did you see him?'

'No, his evidence was written. He's scuttled off to America, undoubtedly with his lover and undoubtedly to escape the inconvenience of this war. It wouldn't suit him at all, would it?' She laughed. 'The judge was none too pleased; I thought he was going to set the case back, but since I was the one suing . . .'

'You were a brick not to bring up his homosexuality in evidence. The scandal would have finished us as a family.'

'What? And have him sent to prison? I couldn't have a smear like that attached to our son, could I? No, he did the usual thing, a woman in a hotel in Brighton. I bet she had a boring night!' They both laughed. 'Hal's asked for more money, you know.'

'The louse. You won't give him any, of course?'

'I already have. What's the point in continuing to fight? I really can't be bothered. It's only money after all.'

'That's a rich woman speaking. Who got custody?'

'I did. It's automatic these days for the mother to get the child, an improvement on our parents' time. And there can't be a judge alive who would regard Hal as a suitable parent – I didn't keep quiet about the gambling, you see.'

'I have some bad news on that point, Juniper. My mother says she's going to apply for custody. I thought you should be warned.'

'She *what?*' The words exploded from Juniper. 'Over my dead body. Why does your mother always have to interfere? Our arrangement works perfectly. You and Caroline are happy, Harry's happy, I never need to worry . . . On what grounds, for goodness' sake?'

If Juniper could have seen his face clearly she would have realized the degree of embarrassment he was suffering. He had to take a deep breath before he replied.

'She wants you declared an unsuitable person.' He coughed. 'Morally.'

'Me?' Juniper laughed, but it was an empty, tinny sound. She stared into the relentless night. It would seem that her loathing for her mother-in-law was not to be allowed to fade. Early in her marriage she had discovered the manipulation the woman had used to ensure that her eldest son married an heiress. At the same time she had also discovered what an expensive relative she had acquired. Juniper had bought her a house in Kent, a flat in London, and paid her bills, and still did. And this was the result. Well, she thought, they would never see another penny from her, ever. She would engage the best lawyers, she would drag the name of Copton through the mud rather than allow that woman to influence her son. She would hurt her, God how she would hurt. She would make the old woman regret her interference. She would . . . her mind was racing with anger. She looked across at Leigh, his profile barely discernible in the gloom. She huddled into her fur coat, then suddenly relaxed, smiled to herself and stretched like a cat.

'Is there a pub near here, do you know? I need a drink,' she said suddenly, as if the previous conversation had not taken place.

'I think there's one in about two miles. We might get a meal too. It won't be much. You know this area, hotels are pretty primitive.'

'I need a brandy, I don't care about the food.'

When they reached the inn, it was impossible to know from its shuttered windows if it was open or not. Leigh pulled up the collar of his jacket and helped Juniper from the car, sweeping his greatcoat about her shoulders trying to shield her from the downpour.

The innkeeper and clients of The Dunoon Arms had never before seen anyone like Juniper. She stood in the middle of the public bar, her blonde hair plastered against her scalp, her face wet with rain, her fur coat glistening with damp, and still looked beautiful. She smiled at the two old men who were hogging the best of the peat fire – that smile had broken the heart of many a man. When Juniper smiled it was as if it were just for you.

'If you wouldn't mind my having just a tiny bit of the fire. I'm so cold and wet.' The two gnarled old Highlanders creaked to their feet, insisting she should sit as close as possible to warm her 'wee self'.

Leigh returned from the bar with two large brandies. 'You said you didn't mind about food, so I've ordered the same for both of us: soup and salmon. Will that do?'

'Sounds lovely,' she said, downing her brandy in one. She coughed against the unfamiliar harshness of cheap spirit and held up her glass. 'Another one?' The expression in her large hazel eyes was one of innocent pleading. Wordlessly Leigh took the glass and returned to the bar.

They had been fortunate. Inns in Scotland could be a hit-and-miss affair, Leigh had warned her, but here the vegetable soup was hot and delicious, the bread rolls freshly baked and the salmon perfect. The apple pie that followed was sublime.

'That was one of the best meals I've ever had,' she said, patting her flat stomach and draining the last of the wine in her glass.

'A brandy with coffee?'

'What about another bottle of that wine? It was delicious.'

'Another? Wine is in short supply, they may not have another. And, good God, I wouldn't be fit to drive a mile further.'

'Do we have to? It's lovely here, warm, secure. It's as if there's no war going on, as if we've stepped back in time.' Juniper stretched comfortably, basking in the warmth from the aromatic peat fire.

Leigh looked doubtful.

'We could phone Caroline. I'm sure she'd prefer you were safe in an inn somewhere rather than pushing on in this awful weather,' she persisted.

'Perhaps you're right. That's if they've got a telephone. You're not in London now. Maybe they haven't got letting rooms; lots of these simple inns don't, you know.'

'Oh, do ask, Leigh. Please do,' she looked at him eagerly for all the world like a little girl, he thought. A little girl he did not want to disappoint.

He went back to the bar and consulted the owner. Yes they had two rooms, they would put hot-water bottles in the beds immediately and, yes, he was lucky, they did have a telephone, the only one for miles he was told proudly. And yes, they had the wine; there was not much call for wine in these parts.

Five minutes later he returned to Juniper with another bottle of the claret she had enjoyed so much.

'Caroline agrees with you, Juniper; she thinks we should stay. She says the weather is even worse up the glen.'

'See. I'm always right,' and Juniper kicked off her shoes and wriggled her toes in the warmth from the flames.

Two hours later she was shivering in her bed. The hot-water bottle was already lukewarm. If she moved too quickly her flesh touched the ice-cold sheets. A draught howled under the door and another seeped in through the closed window. She was fully awake. She wriggled on her fur coat which she had put over the bed as an extra cover, and sat and waited. She waited until all the sounds in the inn had ceased, then she slid from the bed, quietly opened the door and crossed the creaking landing to Leigh's room. She opened the door stealthily and paused, listening for the regular breathing of a sleeping man. Silently she lifted the covers and slipped in beside him.

'Leigh,' she whispered, 'Leigh, I want you to make love to me.' Her hand slid over him and she began to kiss his body with small, moist, biting kisses. Leigh moaned with pleasure.

'Juniper, how lovely to see you.' Caroline raced down the moss-covered, crumbling entrance steps of the huge mansion and flung her arms about her sister-in-law, as Leigh saw to her luggage.

'It's lovely to see you too.' Juniper kissed Caroline on both cheeks; over her shoulder she saw Leigh shuffling nervously on the steps, looking shiftily from right to left. Oh Lor' thought Juniper, he's going to confess. She had known he would, she had relied upon it as part of her plan. But not yet, not now while she was still here for Juniper loathed scenes. She frowned at him, willing him to remain silent, but he looked away.

'How's Harry?' she said brightly.

'I feel a fraud getting you to come all this way. He's much better, up and about. The fever's completely gone.'

'Oh good. But this is a lovely excuse to be with you two,' she beamed at both Caroline and Leigh who, to her annoyance, appeared to be blushing. 'And London was crushingly boring,' she added quickly to stop Caroline looking at her husband.

The house was even colder inside than out. She refused Leigh's offer to take her coat and buried her hands deep into the pockets.

'So this is the Coptons' Scottish pile?' she said, looking about the sparsely furnished entrance hall. A collection of stuffed animal heads leered down at her, moth-eaten and dusty. 'Gee, don't they give you the creeps?' she yelped, startled.

'I'm rather fond of them. I've called that one Sebastian.' Caroline pointed to the particularly large head of an antlered stag, even more tattered than the rest. 'I like to think that the rest of their bodies were all waiting in heaven for when the various Coptons who shot them got there, and that they then kicked the living daylights out of them.'

'Do Coptons go to heaven?' Juniper asked gaily. 'Aren't they all too evil?'

'I sincerely hope that Leigh will be there.' Caroline smiled back.

'Of course, Leigh's different, isn't he? Leigh's a good Copton,' Juniper chuckled. Leigh avoided looking at her and bent to tend the feeble flame as it gamely tried to catch the damp logs. But at least it was a fire. Juniper crossed towards it just as a cloud of acrid smoke gushed out. She stepped back quickly.

'I told you, Leigh, it was useless attempting to light that

one, the chimney's too damp. Everywhere up here is damp, Juniper, it never seems to stop raining. But the fire in the drawing room is better. And there's a good one in your room. But you'll be wanting to see Harry. Come.' Caroline held out her hand and led the way up the impressive oak staircase, past long lines of dour-looking Lords Copton. Leigh had excused himself and disappeared in a rush into his study on the ground floor.

Harry was in his nursery with a young bright-faced Scottish nanny. He took one look at Juniper and burst into tears.

'Oh dear,' she said to Caroline. 'I should never have been a mother, I just knew I'd be a disaster.' She was laughing but to her surprise she realized it was to cover up a sudden flash of pained disappointment.

4

Why?' The door of the bedroom was flung open and crashed against the wall. An outraged Caroline stormed across the room and roughly shook the sleeping Juniper.

'What's going on?' Juniper asked, dazed with sleep.

'That's what you're going to tell me.'

'What's the time?' Juniper asked blearily peering at her watch. 'Good God, it's two o'clock.' She levered herself up in the bed. 'Caroline, what do you mean waking me up at this goddam time?'

'I repeat, why?'

Juniper shook her head, trying to get some sense into her fuddled brain. Not only was she half asleep, but at dinner she had had far too much to drink. But through the fog of sleep and alcohol, she remembered.

'Oh dear,' she said, fumbling on the bedside table for a cigarette.

'You can say "oh dear". You bitch, Juniper. How could you? Why?'

Juniper inhaled deeply and looked at Caroline's

tear-stained face, her puffy and red-rimmed eyes, and felt a flicker of irritation. If there was one thing Juniper hated it was being made to feel guilty; it was not an emotion she was comfortable with.

'I don't know,' she said finally, a shade petulantly.

'You don't *know*?' Caroline shrieked, making Juniper wince. 'You go to bed with my husband and you sit there and say you don't know why you did it.'

'We'd had a lot to drink,' she said lamely.

'You're always having too much to drink, does that mean you're always leaping into bed with other women's husbands?'

'Don't be silly, Caroline.' She put her hand up to her head and longed for this scene to end.

'Do you love him?'

'That's even sillier. Of course I don't.'

'I suppose I should be relieved by that. I'm not. That I could understand. You terrify me, Juniper . . . You're cold and calculating. You selfishly take whatever you want with no thought of the consequences . . .'

Juniper sighed and looked down at her hands. She supposed she should feel sorry for Caroline and ashamed of her actions, but she did not. It had been a spur-of-the-moment plan to get back at her mother-in-law. But, even if she hadn't planned it, she had been cold and lonely and he was there – it would still probably have happened. She could not understand this fuss.

'He didn't exactly push me out of the bed,' she said defiantly.

'You bitch, Juniper. It's different for a man. The responsibility is with you.'

'Rubbish. He didn't have to do it. He wanted to as much as I did.' She wanted to hurt Caroline, and then when she saw the tears in her friend's eyes she wished she hadn't. It was cruel and unnecessary. 'I'm sorry I said that.'

'No, you shouldn't have said it and you shouldn't have slept with my husband either.' Caroline was sobbing.

'You're right, of course. Will you forgive me?' Juniper looked up wearily.

'Never. I was one of your best friends – one of the few real friends you had – and you've destroyed that. I want you out of my house.'

'What, now? In the middle of the night? How the hell am I supposed to get to Aberdeen?'

'I don't know and I don't care.'

'What about Harry?'

'What do you mean?' Fear flashed across Caroline's face.

'Presumably you won't want him here, reminding you of me?'

'Why upset the child? He isn't involved . . . It's not his . . .' Caroline's hand shot to her mouth as she realized what she had almost said.

'It's not his fault he's got me for a mother. Is that what you were going to say, Caroline?' Juniper asked in such a calm, quiet voice that it made Caroline even more afraid.

'I love him, Juniper. I love him as if he were my own son. You wouldn't take him? Would you?' Despite her anguish, she despised herself for pleading with this destructive woman.

Juniper studied her for what to Caroline seemed an age. Many thoughts flashed through her mind. Uppermost was the idea of retaliation for being screamed at in the middle of the night. But then she hated petty people and wouldn't that be petty in the extreme? The boy was happy here and what on earth would she do with him in London?

'No, I won't take him. But Caroline, I'm not leaving now. I'll go in the morning – first thing. Now, if you don't mind, I'd like some sleep.' And she turned away from Caroline, plumped up her pillow and lay down, closing her eyes.

Caroline stood speechless, looking down at the woman she had once pitied, whose son she had taken into her home and loved as if he were the child she could never have. Because of Harry their lives were inextricably entwined. She could not afford, ever again, to show the extent of the hatred she now felt for Juniper. If she did, she risked losing Harry for ever.

'Goodnight,' she found herself saying and loathed herself for the normality, the politeness in her voice.

'Goodnight, Caroline. I'm truly sorry.' Juniper's reply was muffled by the pillows.

Juniper did not see Leigh in the morning. When she eventually appeared with a throbbing head it was to find one of the estate workers waiting for her with the battered Morris. She popped into the nursery to say goodbye to Harry who accepted her kiss with a turn of the head almost as if he too knew of her transgression. Of Caroline there was no sign.

The return train journey, mercifully, was not as crowded nor as long, and this time she managed to get a seat in First Class. She sat in a compartment full of women who eyed her with a mixture of disapproval and envy, but she was used to that, for that was how most women looked at Juniper. She was too beautiful, too elegant, too blatantly rich for them to warm to her. Wherever she went she knew she was regarded as a threat.

She read, she slept, she avoided thinking. There were certain moments, Juniper had decided, when too much thinking could be a dangerous thing. This was one of them.

It was late evening by the time Juniper let herself into her London house.

'Polly, you around?' she called out, putting down her case, and flicking through the pile of mail on the hall table.

Polly's head appeared over the banisters. 'Juniper! I didn't expect you for days. Is everything all right?' There was a tension in her friend's stance that worried her.

'No, it isn't. I need a drink.' Juniper began to mount the staircase wearily.

'What's the matter?' Polly asked anxiously, seeing Juniper's strained face. 'Is Harry all right?'

'He's fine.' Juniper dropped her fur coat on the floor and made straight for the drawing room and the drinks table. Polly picked up the coat, folded it neatly on a chair and followed Juniper into the room. 'I think I may have made a monumental mistake,' Juniper said, as she poured herself a large brandy. 'Do you want one?'

'No thanks, I've got some Ovaltine.' Polly picked up the cup she had put down when she had heard Juniper's key in the lock. A skin had formed on the milky drink and with a look of distaste she carefully removed it with the side of the teaspoon. 'What's happened?'

Juniper stood in the centre of the hearthrug, nursing her balloon of brandy. 'I slept with Leigh.' She looked at Polly almost defiantly.

'Oh Juniper, no. What on earth made you do that?' She was aghast. Quickly replacing her cup and saucer on the coffee table, she crossed to the drinks tray and poured herself a brandy.

'I don't know. Odd ideas of revenge and I was lonely . . . It seemed right at the time, but then it always does, doesn't it?'

'Does Caroline know?'

'Yes. Leigh, the fool, told her. What is it about men, Polly, that makes them rush to confess? He could at least have had the decency to wait until I'd left. It's so stupid and causes such unpleasantness.'

'The guilt of an honourable man,' Polly said quietly, remembering her own pain over five years ago when, by letter, Jonathan had confessed his infidelity to her.

'I like Caroline, too,' Juniper said sulkily.

'Then you should have thought of that before you leapt into bed with her husband, whatever the reason,' Polly said sharply. 'I don't understand this at all. You're not a vengeful person.'

'No, I'm not, am I?' Juniper said, cheering up considerably.

There were times when Polly longed to shake Juniper, she was the most frustrating person. She so often acted without thinking the consequences through. She was like a child and as one forgave a child so one tended to forgive Juniper.

'I'm a disaster, aren't I?' Juniper said as she drank her very large brandy.

'You are,' Polly agreed and suddenly wondered if Juniper knew how people reacted to her misdeeds. Did she rely on their reactions being indulgent?

'What shall I do, Polly?'

'There's not a lot you can do, is there? It's too late. You can only write to Caroline, and hope and pray she can find it in herself to forgive you.'

'I could send a telegram,' Juniper said brightly.

'No, Juniper, that wouldn't do. It'll have to be a letter.'

Juniper said nothing, but poured herself another brandy. 'And you're drinking too much, too,' Polly added.

'God, you sound just like my grandmother.' Juniper rolled her eyes in mock exasperation. She had been stupid, she thought, she should not have told Polly. She would never understand. Polly would never seek revenge whatever happened, she was too good for such tactics. And it had been silly even to mention loneliness as an excuse. Polly was lonely, she knew that, yet she would never be unfaithful to her Andrew, would never cheat on a friend. There was no point in wanting to be like Polly, she never could be. But then, she thought, as she topped up her drink, looking slyly at Polly and smiling to herself, she didn't think she wanted to be like her.

'The grandmothers telephoned last night. They had heard about the raids and were worrying about us. They're wondering when we're going to visit,' Polly said, attempting to change the subject. She felt embarrassed and wished Juniper had not confided in her. There were things she would prefer not to know; such knowledge could put her in an invidious position. 'We really ought to go and see them: we've got plenty of petrol coupons.'

'What a good idea.' Juniper was beaming now. In Cornwall she could put all uncomfortable memories of Leigh and Caroline right out of her mind. 'Let's go for a whole month. There's nothing to keep us here, is there? No one seems to want you.' She was teasing Polly.

Polly smiled. 'That's true, no one's queuing up for me. Anything to get out of London and these dreadful air raids. I think I'll ask your grandmother if she'll take Hursty for me. He's terrified here and it's too dangerous.' Hursty, her cat, was Polly's most precious possession.

'Has it been bad?'

'The last two nights have been hell. I didn't know it was possible to be so afraid and not die of heart failure.'

'You do look exhausted,' Juniper said, finally noticing.

'It's not surprising. I don't think I've had more than two uninterrupted hours' sleep for the last four nights.'

'Did you go to the shelter around the corner?'

'No, I couldn't leave Hursty. I've put two armchairs under the basement stairs. Everyone says that's as safe a place as any. We can sleep there tonight: the Germans are sure to be back. I don't think they'll give up until there's no London left.'

'No thanks. I'm staying up. I don't want to miss the excitement. I might even go up on the roof and watch.'

'Oh, Juniper,' Polly laughed. 'I can promise you one thing, it's far from exciting. Well, if you get scared you'll know where I am.'

'Me? Scared? I'm not going to let a few bombs scare me,' Juniper boasted.

Less than an hour later the air raid alert sounded. Polly collected Hursty and raced for the little nest she had made under the basement stairs. She had a large torch with spare batteries, a thermos flask of tea, a clock, some knitting, the latest Agatha Christie and two extra blankets. With Hursty cowering on her lap, Polly pulled the blanket close up to her ears and attempted to sleep.

'Polly?' Ten minutes later she heard Juniper whisper from the direction of the stairs. 'Polly, there's no electricity.'

'I'm over here. The electricity usually goes off.' Polly clicked on her torch.

'Is there room for me? You were right, it's bloody terrifying up there.' Juniper dived under the stairs and into the spare armchair. She snuggled under the blanket. 'Tell me when it's all over.'

5

The great granite house at the head of the steep valley was surrounded on three sides by towering cliffs which appeared to be holding it safe. For six hundred years a house had stood in this position and had grown with the changing fortunes of its owners, from cottage to farm to manor, until it became as it was now, a mansion. There had been no increase in its size for nearly four hundred years for, gripped by the cliffs, there was nowhere further for it to expand. And so it had escaped the changing fashions in buildings to which many Elizabethan houses had fallen victim. If a Tregowan from that time could return to his home, he would find it exactly as he had left it – the same building, the same furniture, the portrait he had proudly had painted of himself in oils still on the wall where he had placed it.

A small river ran through the luxuriant valley where the plants appeared to have run riot, but a keen gardener would have been aware what careful and thoughtful planning was required to achieve this wild appearance. In spring the valley was a blaze of purple, pink and white from the giant rhododendrons, followed quickly by the cerise, cream and gold of azaleas which in the balmy Cornish air grew into tall bushes. Summer filled the valley with clematis, roses and the giant mop-headed hydrangeas that were a feature of Gwenfer. Now in September, the red and purple droplets of the fuchsias and the last of the Michaelmas daisies were creating a last defiant burst of colour before winter came and blanketed the garden with mist for a few short weeks.

From its position the house surveyed its enemy, the sea. For countless millennia the great restless ocean had pounded and lashed at the entrance to the valley, wearing down the rocks, grinding them into sand, relentlessly pursuing its goal – the swamping of the land. There were days when it hurled itself with violent venom at the cliffs, its spray bursting far up the valley, and there were times when the water lapped gently and innocently at the rocks. But no one who lived here was fooled by this apparent placidity for the sea could change with barely any warning from a deceptively calm azure blue to a dark maelstrom of vicious strength, aided by its friend the wind which howled up the valley to attack the house with brutal, noisy ferocity.

Having searched the house and garden Alice hurried down the valley and finally found her friend Gertie on the beach. She smiled as she watched Gertie fussing about with spade and sacks, for all the world like an overgrown child making sandcastles. There had been a time, when Basil, Gertie's husband, was alive, when she had worn only clothes of a style dating from before the Great War. There had been two reasons for this strange manner of dressing, Basil's disapproval of modern dress and Gertie's total disregard for fashion and resentment at time wasted on it. But since her husband's death, the clothes of that other era had been stored away in trunks at her house, Mendbury, and she now affected a more modern style, if still somewhat bizarre. Today she was wearing an old pair of corduroy trousers which, although not tied up with string, looked as if they should be. The trouser legs were stuffed into an ancient pair of wellington boots. Her ample bosom was covered by a large misshapen navy woollen which Alice, with some alarm, had watched Gertie knit during recent evenings. On her head she wore a bright yellow sou'wester with the mistaken idea that it would keep her hair out of her eyes. But Gertie's hair had always had a life of its own and try as she might with pins, clips, tiaras, hats and now finally this sou'wester to tame it, the hair always won, appearing triumphantly beneath the brim in exuberant thick curls, grey now instead of the once luxuriant titian. Anyone looking less like a member of one of England's noblest families it was difficult to imagine.

'Gertie, what on earth are you doing?' Alice's voice bubbled with laughter.

Gertie paused in her task of filling the sack with sand, standing up straight without a hint of the arthritis that was beginning to plague Alice. 'Filling sandbags. Zac, put this one with the others,' she ordered the young man who was helping her.

'What on earth for?'

'Defences, of course. When I went to London last month all the buildings were sandbagged. I can't imagine why we haven't done it here. The ARP warden should have instructed us to do so, most lax of him.'

'But I don't think we're at risk of being bombed here, Gertie,' Alice said, smiling.

'Oh no? And what happened at Falmouth in July? Bombs. Think of the dreadful news of bombing this past week. We should be prepared for anything.'

'But there are no docks, no army camps here. There's nothing for them to bomb,' Alice argued reasonably. 'I think the wretched blackout is likely to kill more people than the bombs.'

'Planes have been known to stray off course. They are hardly going to carry their bombs back with them over that.' Gertie waved her arm in the direction of the ocean. 'They would drop them, no doubt on us,' she added sagely, nodding her head, which made the recalcitrant curls bob frantically. 'And what if we were invaded from the sea?' She pointed dramatically towards the looming bulk of the Brisons rocks. The early autumn sun was glinting on the water, its rays sparking the ocean with golden light, making it seem as though the great rocks were floating serenely by.

'If the Germans want to invade, they're hardly likely to choose the most inaccessible part of the coast, are they? There are rafts of submerged rocks out there that would rip a boat to pieces. This place is impregnable from the sea, no doubt the reason why my ancestors had the sense to build here in the first place.'

'I don't have your supreme confidence, I fear. Those perfidious Boches are capable of sneaking in anywhere. And forewarned is forearmed. Don't you agree, Zac?' she demanded of the large, fresh-faced young Cornishman.

'Yes, M'Lady,' he said. It was inevitable that he would not disagree, for Zac, in company with most of the population, was in awe and not a little afraid of the indomitable Lady Gertrude Frobisher.

Gertie stomped across the beach and picked up two buckets which she also began to fill. 'Anti-incendiary devices,' she explained to Alice before she could ask. 'In my hotel in London we had them on every floor.'

'I see,' Alice said, knowing from long experience that it was simpler not to argue with Gertie.

They had been friends for fifty years. Through separation during the long years when Alice had lived in America, through the birth of children and grandchildren, the death of Basil, Gertie's patient loving husband and Lincoln, Alice's first husband, a ruthless chameleon of a man; through everything that changed, the one thing that had never varied was their love and respect for each other.

Many would have found Gertie a difficult friend, for she was opinionated and fearless in stating those opinions even when she knew they would not find favour. But long ago Alice had reached the uncomfortable conclusion that Gertie was invariably right, no matter how much one tried to prove the opposite. And equally long ago she had learnt to listen to her friend. Gertie was bossy, there was no denying the fact, certainly she would never dream of doing so herself. But it was a bossiness based on good judgement and helpfulness, not that of a bully. Gertie plodded up and down the beach. When she decided to do something – as now – there was little point in trying to stop her.

Alice was always happy to have Gertie to stay, but even more so now. A month previously, her second husband, Phillip, who at the beginning of the war had offered his talents as an artist to help in any capacity, had been called to London to advise on camouflage. He had been moved to a large requisitioned house in Wiltshire, so she no longer had to fear his being bombed, but it still did not stop her worrying. And nothing, not even his frequent telephone calls, stopped her missing him. Having found such companionship, contentment and love so late in her life, it seemed doubly sad to be separated.

When Alice had heard that Gertie's estate in Berkshire had been requisitioned she had immediately invited her to stay 'for the duration'. There were distinct advantages, apart from her company, to having her here. With her she had brought her excellent cook and a maid, who were both too old for war service and grateful to remain in Gertie's employ. Together with Flo, Alice's maid of long standing, and Flo's husband, Cyril, the gardener-cum-handyman, they made up the household staff.

Alice waited for Gertie to finish and crossed to the large rock at the mouth of the cove, Ia's Rock, named after the other friend in her life. A friend of childhood, confidante of unfulfilled dreams, who had died long ago.

She looked out over the water. It was deceptively still. Across the cove was Oswald's Point. Ia's Rock, Oswald's Point – so, she supposed, maps were made. In time, no doubt, they would thus be marked.

It was over sixty years since Oswald, her brother, had been swept into the sea from those rocks and drowned. All that time had passed, but she had never forgotten him. She often wondered what their relationship would have been and what difference it might have made to her own life if she had had a brother to whom she could turn for support and advice. When she was dead no one would know how these rocks had come by their names.

'You're looking very morose. What are you thinking?' Gertie demanded, leaning on her spade.

'About Ia and Oswald and whether . . .'

'Don't. Thinking about the dead is a most unhealthy occupation.' Gertie placed her foot on her spade and returned to her digging.

'Yes, Gertie,' Alice murmured like an obedient child, changing her position on the rock, her back to her memories, and looking up the steep valley to the other great love of her life, her house, Gwenfer.

All her life Gwenfer had been a place of security. Here in this valley everything in life slotted into perspective in a way that it never did anywhere else. Faced by the restless magnitude of the Atlantic Ocean, the great swathe of sky, the solidity of the granite from which the house appeared to have grown like a beautiful living thing, problems, difficulties, people, one's own self importance were reduced to insignificant proportions.

The house was Alice's most beautiful possession. It stood four-square against the wind and sea, a haven for the Tregowans of Gwenfer.

She was sure that her granddaughter Juniper felt the same way about it. When troubled, Gwenfer was where she came. This was what was concerning her now, why was Juniper suddenly coming? What had gone wrong this time?

The last of the sandbags filled, Zac was instructed to collect his wheelbarrow and take them to the front of the house. Gertie, her task complete, turned her attention to Alice.

'Now, why were you looking for me? What is it?'

'How did you know I had something to say?' Alice was amused.

'Because you had an expectant look on your face as if you were bursting to tell me something.'

'And you carried on with your sandbags rather than find out?'

'I might have wanted to stop what I was doing and that would never do,' was the crisp reply.

'Polly and Juniper telephoned, they are driving down today, staying overnight at Hurstwood. Polly wants to check all is well there.'

'Excellent idea. That woman she's left in charge of Hurstwood looks an unreliable sort to me.'

'The Red Cross telephoned from Plymouth . . .'

'Yes?' Gertie stepped forward eagerly, forgetting her self-imposed discipline.

'It's bad news, I'm afraid. They thank you for your offer, but it seems they don't have a position for you. They're writing to you, of course.'

'I've never heard such insufferable rudeness. And why are my services not required, might I ask?' She glared at Alice as if the decision not to put Gertie in charge of this area was entirely Alice's responsibility.

'It would have been tiring for you, so much travelling to do for a start,' Alice said trying to lessen the disappointment.

'Zac could have driven me.'

'And all those speeches to write . . .'

'I love making speeches.'

This last was so true that it was not worth arguing about.

'It's because I'm not Cornish. I've always thought this a particularly insular county.' Again she glared at Alice as if the xenophobia of the Cornish was also her doing. This was most certainly an argument Alice had no wish to pursue, based as it was on a large element of truth.

'I'm sure you can help in the village in a less exalted position, giving first-aid lectures and demonstrations to the women,' she said diplomatically, though she doubted whether Mrs Trengwith would be happy to give up her position to someone from 'up country'. Nor could she imagine Gertie happy in a subsidiary role. 'And I shall need your help here,' she finally added.

'Filling sandbags? Do you really think I find that fulfilling?'

'No. Helping me with evacuees.'

'But they've left, scuttled back to London a fortnight after they arrived, ungrateful, snivelling brats. And the mothers!' Gertie threw up her hands at the memory of the ten evacuees plus three mothers who had arrived in the first month of the war. They had cried, wet beds and moaned non-stop at the lack of shops and cinemas until, much to everyone's relief, they had decamped en masse back to London when the expected bombs did not fall.

'Now the bombing has started in earnest, we're getting a new intake. They arrive next week. And quite honestly, Gertie, if you're not feeling your age, I am. I find the thought of having to look after half a dozen or so children daunting in the extreme.'

'Rats, Alice! You always did give up too easily. Well come on, there's no point standing about. We have work to do, my friend.'

Gertie trudged up the valley in her oversized boots and, quietly satisfied, Alice trailed behind her.

6

Gertie and Alice were not particularly pleased with their granddaughters. The two girls had written and telephoned, but both grandmothers felt that they should have visited them sooner. They were both more worried than hurt.

Gertie wished to set her mind at rest that Polly's ill-fated marriage to Michel had not damaged her irreparably. That apart, she needed to talk to Polly about the death of Richard – Gertie's son and Polly's father. When he died, no one could have been kinder or more supportive than Alice, but where grief was concerned,

Gertie felt strongly that it was a private matter, not to be inflicted on others. Her feelings could only be discussed fully with one of her own blood.

Alice's worries were more complex, but, with Juniper involved, this was inevitable. She was concerned about the effect Juniper's divorce had had on her and what possible explanation there could be for her virtually giving away her son. As so often, Alice feared for Juniper's future. She needed desperately to reassure herself that some measure of stability was an obtainable goal for her granddaughter.

Given these problems, the welcome for Juniper and Polly was so warm and both grandmothers so excited, that the young women felt ashamed that they had delayed their visit. Both regretted not coming sooner to bask in the love and sense of security the older women lavished upon them.

In private, though, both Alice and Gertie confirmed they had been right to worry. Polly was too thin, and there was a tenseness about her and a sad guarded look in her eyes, neither of which had been there before. Gertie determined, no matter how long it took, to find out the cause. She knew about Polly's dead husband Michel's disgusting sexual proclivities, but felt that Polly should have recovered by now.

Juniper was an even greater worry. She too was tense, but with the tenseness of a tightly wound spring that might at any moment uncoil, damaging to anyone standing too close. Alice was certain that after a few days her granddaughter would become calmer, she always had in the past. But, as she watched closely, it seemed that this time the magic of Gwenfer was not going to work. Each day Juniper became more restless, and Alice felt that she was avoiding all of them, including Polly.

Polly was equally perplexed by Juniper. When she thought of the closeness of their friendship in France, she could not understand this distance between them. She knew she frequently irritated Juniper and was at a loss to know why. She was the same, she was sure she was, and yet too often she saw Juniper's normally sweet-featured face flicker with boredom and annoyance at something she had said or done.

The Polly of the past would have fretted and worried over Juniper's attitude, but she was distracted by more serious worries now. There was not a day when her stomach did not crawl with fear for Andrew. She still refused to believe that he was dead. They had been so close, surely she would know. But then she had to face the prospect that he had been captured and no one knew how the Germans were treating their prisoners of war. She wished she believed in God, then she could have prayed for him and maybe found solace for herself.

Even though she was far from London she kept up her bombardment of requests for work through her contacts, augmented now by those of her grandmother. Gertie took Polly's inability to find work as a personal challenge and spent many hours writing explosive missives to government ministers and civil servants who had enjoyed her hospitality at Mendbury before the war when she and Basil had entertained lavishly. The sight of her distinctive handwriting made many a heart sink when the morning post arrived in Whitehall.

As a result of the fresh air of Gwenfer and the good and regular food, Polly began to put on weight and her colour improved. She had dreaded telling her grandmother about Andrew and their time together in Paris, fearing her censure of adultery. But, once again, Polly was in for a surprise where her grandmother was concerned.

'I'm so glad you found someone who could make you happy after your dreadful experiences with that revolting Frenchman,' was her gratifying response. 'Slater? Not related to the Slaters of Northumberland by any chance?'

'He must be, his parents live near Alnwick.'

'Ah, most suitable.' Gertie glowed with approval.

'Rowena Slater was a debutante with me and her husband served in the same regiment as your grandfather. Much better all round,' she said to no one in particular as she fitted a blackout blind in the room to be used as a dormitory for some of the evacuees. 'Now we must set about finding out where the poor boy is.'

'But how? The Red Cross have tried for me. The army has been very unhelpful. It's not as if I'm his wife. We weren't even engaged.'

'Then I shall find out for you. You don't think I'm going to allow those damned Huns to stand in the way of your happiness? Leave it to me.'

Polly felt a great blanket of reassurance enfold her. She should have told her grandmother right from the start. She should have guessed how practical she would be, how supportive to one of her own. Or was she one of her own? At that thought she shuddered.

'You're not getting a chill, are you, Polly?'

'No. I just thought . . .' She looked at Gertie, wondering how much she knew. Would she be as protective if she realized Polly was not her granddaughter? She had to speak, she had to know. 'Juniper told me that Richard wasn't my father. That her father, Marshall Boscar, had had an affair with my mother, that I was the result . . . that Richard was flying to France to tell me . . .' she blurted out.

Gertie threw down the blind she was holding with a gesture of exasperation.

'The problem with young Juniper is that she is an interfering busybody. I know all about this silly tale and I didn't believe it for one minute. You're Richard's daughter.'

'That's what I think.'

'Then that's the truth. Don't give that ridiculous rumour another thought. Spiteful gossip caused by . . .' Gertie paused. By Francine, her loathsome daughter-in-law, she would like to have said, but, feeling that that would be unfair to the girl, stopped herself. 'I shan't think of it again,' she said instead. 'You have a lot to forget, young woman, to remove that sad expression from your eyes.'

Polly found that by sharing her fears for Andrew with Gertie they were automatically halved. Gertie had contacts in the Red Cross and at the Swiss Embassy, she would find out all she could.

'You've a lot of letters to write because of me.'

'What are grandmothers for, but to try to solve wretched problems?'

'I love you, Grandmama.'

'You know, Polly, I love you too,' and she hooted with happiness, the loud ear-splitting sound that always made Polly collapse with laughter too.

Gertie and Alice, with a reluctant Polly, spent many hours debating what could be wrong with Juniper, but even if they had taken the bull by the horns and asked her what the problem was, she would not have been able to help them, for she did not know herself. She felt lost and inexplicably bored, which was a new and uncomfortable experience. It was not just a mental problem. Not only was the world suddenly devoid of books interesting enough to read and the countryside suddenly dull, but she could not get physically comfortable. It was as if her skin was crawling with tension.

Several times Polly tried to find out the cause.

'Was it seeing Harry?' she asked one day, as they walked on the beach at the head of the cove.

'Seeing Harry, what do you mean?'

'Made you depressed.'

'Me? Depressed? What nonsense,' Juniper had laughed, but it sounded hollow to Polly.

'Well, you must miss him.'

'Not a jot. I told you I'd make a dreadful mother,' and Juniper swooped on a shell that had caught her eye.

Another day, on horses borrowed from a neighbouring farmer, they paused on the cliff in the cool autumn sunshine to admire the sea, which that day was becoming restless.

'There'll be a storm tonight,' Juniper said in the knowledgeable way that those who live by the sea speak of the weather to those who don't.

'Do you miss Hal?' Polly ventured.

'You do ask some strange questions. Why on earth should I miss him, of all people? Good riddance . . . Race you back to the gate.' She spurred her horse and beat Polly with ease to the large wrought-iron gate of Gwenfer.

Whenever Polly probed too deeply, Juniper seemed to shy away from her and become even more distant.

Juniper herself preferred not to dwell too deeply on what ailed her for fear of what she might find. She knew some of the causes. She knew that in the past she had made that common error of mistaking sexual excitement and gratification for love, only to find at the end of an affair that she was even more alone than at the beginning. If she thought about her son, it made her sad, but it was soon shaken off, especially after a drink or two. The commonest thought she had was a silly one. She wished she had never had to grow up, that she could have stayed the well-loved, secure child she had once been. On her darkest days she sometimes thought that it might have been better if she had drowned along with her grandfather Lincoln.

Gwenfer had proved a disappointment. Always before the house had calmed her and restored her happiness. She loved it like a living being but this time even the house seemed to be rejecting her.

'Perhaps you should join Polly in trying to find war work?' Alice suggested one morning.

'Me? What on earth could I do that would be of use to anyone?'

'There must be lots of things.' Alice knew her voice sounded relentlessly bright even before she saw Juniper's exasperated expression. 'You can drive – drivers must be needed.'

'We both missed out on that, we got to England too late, all the posts had been filled. London is full of women wanting to do their bit, they don't need me too.'

'You can always stay here and help Gertie and me,' Alice said optimistically, even though she knew that such a thing was highly unlikely in Juniper's present mood.

Alice hoped the arrival of the evacuees would distract Juniper since everyone was going to have to help. A large staff was a thing of the past. Although Alice had been thrilled when Gertie's maid and cook arrived, she was now having second thoughts. They were both willing but getting feeble, and Alice feared it was only a matter of time before they became a liability. They had Zac only because he had failed his medical, though looking at him, strong and robust, it was a mystery why. However, his responsibilities lay with the farm animals. There were Flo and Cyril, but both were in their sixties and should have been thinking about retirement.

Alice's plan had been that they would all work together preparing the rooms, making beds, recovering and mending old toys. It didn't work out that way. Polly helped enthusiastically, but Juniper frequently found it necessary to take long solitary walks.

'Did Juniper get on well with Harry when she saw him?' Alice asked Polly as she stuffed the umpteenth pillow into a slip.

Polly busied herself with the blankets. These conversations were becoming trying. They had covered this ground so many times and she felt they were getting nowhere. She was afraid, too, that she might be letting Juniper down by confiding in Alice.

'It was all fine,' she lied and hoped Alice would drop the subject.

'I do wish she had brought the child here instead of packing him off to Scotland to Hal's family. It's too risky in the circumstances,' Alice said, avoiding the word 'divorce'.

'Hal and his brother don't speak to each other. She wouldn't have let them have Harry if they were the best of friends, I can assure you,' Polly said brightly.

'They're still related by blood. If there were to be trouble in the future I can tell you now where Leigh's loyalty would lie – with his brother.'

'Don't worry, Mrs Whitaker. It's the war that's upsetting Juniper, it's upsetting everyone,' Polly said, hiding behind the modern excuse of blaming the war for everything, but wanting to remove the worried look from Alice's lovely face.

'I was wondering, Mrs Whitaker, if I might leave my cat with you. He's so frightened in London.'

'Of course, my dear, of course you may . . .' Alice said vaguely, her thoughts on other issues.

Zac George inched the farm cart, drawn by the old shire horse, gingerly down the steep drive of Gwenfer which snaked down the cliff and had given many a visitor an attack of vertigo. In the cart sat four tired and despondent-looking children. Each child had a small battered suitcase, the ubiquitous gas mask case and a large luggage label tied to his or her collar.

Alice, Gertie and Polly waited on the steps to welcome them. At the sight of the weary faces, the slumped, defeated shoulders, all three women stepped forward involuntarily, their hands held out in welcome.

'The poor little things, they look totally exhausted,' Alice exclaimed.

'No mothers, thank goodness. That's a decided improvement,' Gertie muttered with feeling, the memory of the evacuee mothers of a year ago still fresh in her mind. 'And only four of them, that's a relief.'

'They're probably alive with lice,' said Juniper off handedly when she finally appeared, curiosity having got the better of her.

There were two brothers, Robin and Fred, who looked as if they were seven and eight, but turned out to be seriously undernourished nine- and eleven-year-olds. May, their sister, was a competent twelve-year-old. But the child whom Alice felt immediately drawn to was the smallest, huddled at the front of the cart as if loath to dismount. She was small and could be barely four years old. She had huge grey eyes which studied the women with a serious expression that no child of her age should have had. But what made Alice clutch her throat and nervously finger the pearls at her neck was her hair, cut short and almost white –

'Ia,' she found herself saying out loud.

'What?' Gertie barked. 'What are you talking about?'

'That child, she reminds me of Ia. You remember, the little girl from the mining village who became my friend.'

'Remember? How could I ever forget. For the fifty years I've known you, you haven't stopped talking about her.'

'Haven't I?' Alice laughed.

'You live too much in the past, Alice. I've told you before, it's dangerous. Now come along, you three, I'll find you some nice hot soup.'

Gertie began efficiently to usher the three older children and their bags towards the house.

The small girl still clung to the side of the cart as if for comfort.

'Come, my dear,' Alice held out her hand. 'Come with me and we'll find you a nice bed.'

Gingerly the little girl moved along the cart. Alice lifted her down.

'And what's your name?'

The little girl stared at her seriously but said nothing.

'She don't talk, that one,' May volunteered. 'She ain't said a word all the way here. But she's called Annie.'

'Then come, Annie. Welcome to your new home.' And holding the child's hand, which gave her the strangest feeling of solace, Alice led the child into the large house, and the door closed behind them on the night and the wind that was beginning to whip in from the sea.

All four children wet their beds that night. Flo was puffed up with angry indignation, loudly declaring that bottoms should be slapped. Alice and Gertie were appalled at such a suggestion.

'They're unsettled,' said Gertie.

'It's nerves,' added Alice.

'My mother always smacked me. Dirty little tykes.' Flo was not impressed by reason.

'Now, Flo, you won't lay a finger on them. We've no idea what these children have seen or suffered. Lady Gertrude was in London and experienced the bombing – it was terrifying.'

'If I was afraid, can you imagine how frightful it must have been for a child, Flo?' Gertie arched her brows questioningly and wondered what the world was coming to when she had to explain herself to a servant.

'Who's to do that there washing then? That's what I'd like to know.' Flo stood in front of them, hands on hips, her jaw jutting forward aggressively.

'Really, Flo. You will, of course,' Gertie said in her best no-nonsense voice and shook her head with disbelief. This was even worse, it was horrifying how things had changed in such a short time and to such an extent, that a servant should speak to her mistress in such a way.

'At least we have plenty of sheets, Flo,' Alice said in a placatory way. If Flo decided now to take things easier they would be in a mess.

Flo fell silent and appeared about to embark on a sulk, her way of dealing with life when things were not going right, but she suddenly swung round.

'You know they're alive?' she said almost triumphantly.

'We expected as much. I can see to it, Flo. You need not worry.'

'*You'm*, Mrs Whitaker?' Flo asked with disbelief, a

little put out that she was unable to make a small drama out of the lice.

'Yes, me, Flo. Who helped Queenie with Ia's hair when she first came here, and you and Sal, the housemaid, made such a fuss and were far too grand to help?' Alice laughed as much at the memory as the shocked expression on Flo's face.

'But, Mrs Whitaker . . .'

'This is wartime, Flo, and we all have to do things differently. Now, if you wouldn't mind washing the sheets? There's a nice wind today and it will dry them in no time.'

'Yes, of course, Mrs Whitaker,' Flo replied respectfully.

An hour later Alice had the four children lined up in the old schoolroom on the top floor, freshly bathed and wrapped in large towels, and began efficiently to clean the children's hair.

Gertie found Alice with Robin's head over a news-paper, calmly combing through his hair with a fine-toothed comb.

'Isn't it amazing how much one learns in life without realizing it?' Gertie beamed with approval. 'The billeting officer for the evacuees is downstairs and I don't like her.'

'Oh dear, why not?'

'She's bossy.'

'Ah!' said Alice smiling to herself. 'She's going to have to wait until I've finished with Annie here.' Gently she lifted the little girl on to the table, concerned to feel how thin the child was. She'd have to feed her up. Plenty of milk and eggs, she'd watch her diet closely.

'Don't get too fond, Alice, will you?' Gertie said quietly.

'What do you mean?' Alice asked, looking up from the fine blonde hair.

'She might not stay. You'll get hurt.'

Alice looked at Gertie over Annie's head. 'There are some things you can't help, Gertie,' she said softly.

Gertie bustled out to do battle with the unsuspecting

billeting officer. The hair treatment finished, Alice found a large box of toys and books for the children to sort through and, telling them to stay where they were until she returned, she went to join Gertie.

'It's a paltry sum. You can't feed a child adequately on that,' she heard Gertie say as she entered her parlour.

The billeting officer was Mrs Audrey Penrose from Penzance, who was not bossy at all, but a kind and highly efficient woman who had dedicated her life to helping others. And, as a Penrose, she was surely related to Queenie Penrose, the nursemaid who had been like a mother to Alice. The name of Penrose was always a recommendation with Alice. She really could wish that Gertie did not always make such snap decisions about people.

'That's the allowance.'

'Less than two pounds, Alice, that's what you're going to have from the government to feed and clothe those poor scraps.'

'Hello, Mrs Penrose. You must be very busy.' She smiled at the woman, whose face showed noticeable relief at seeing Alice.

'Sadly, yes. There are so many children. It's tragic. Most have never been in the countryside before and it's proving strange and rather frightening for them.'

'I heard of a little boy who had never seen a cow,' Alice said.

'That's common. They think milk comes in bottles, you know. We've had some who . . .' Mrs Penrose coughed delicately, 'who were not aware what the sanitary arrangements were for.'

'Good gracious!' Gertie was appalled. 'When this war is over, whichever government we have must do something about the slums in London. It's still Dickensian in some parts – a disgrace.'

'What concerns me is what will the effect be on the children? Here they live in comfort and in some cases undreamt-of luxury. Are we to expect them to return to the slums and then settle contentedly?' Alice asked anxiously.

'Revolution, that's what this war could lead to and about time too,' Gertie said excitedly, as she always did when discussing radical politics. Alice often thought that Gertie had been born into the wrong class, she would have been an ideal leader for the oppressed. She noticed Mrs Penrose fingering her collar rather nervously, her features twisted with a worried expression at such novel opinions.

'I don't need money for our evacuees, Mrs Penrose. Perhaps you could give it to others who need it more,' Alice said, turning the conversation back to the matter in hand.

'I don't think I can, Mrs Whitaker. There's no system to redistribute the money, you see.'

'It's a ludicrous sum,' Gertie interrupted.

'It's more than most of these children's mothers have ever had to feed them,' Mrs Penrose said sharply, more courageous now with Alice in the room.

'It would appear that finding the food, if this rationing gets worse, will be more of a problem than the money,' Alice said worriedly.

'We've got bed wetters.' Gertie glowered at Mrs Penrose who immediately began to apologise as if she had been responsible.

'It doesn't matter, Mrs Penrose,' Alice intervened. 'It will stop once they've settled. Tell me, do you know anything about little Annie Budd?'

'Ah tragic. There was a direct hit on her house. The whole family wiped out and her father's in the army – God knows where. Annie was discovered under the stairs, her mother's body over her. She must have shielded the child.'

'No wonder her eyes are so sad, then.'

'Is she speaking yet?'

'No, Mrs Penrose, but she will,' Alice said, with a confidence she was far from feeling. Annie was proving more difficult than she had at first feared.

'Perhaps we should get the doctor to see her?'

'Not yet, Mrs Penrose. Too many strange people might make matters worse. I'm sure she'll speak when she wants to.' Alice realized she was sounding defensive. 'Would you care for some tea?' she said quickly, as if to make amends.

The wet beds, much to Flo's loudly proclaimed annoyance, continued for a week and then overnight the problem stopped. The older children had settled well. They were with their friends from school and their own teachers, so there was a degree of continuity to their lives.

But Annie was a different matter. She rarely spoke and would sit in a chair, clutching an old doll which had belonged to Alice, staring into space. Alice and Polly took turns reading to her and she would listen politely, but never comment. When they talked to her and tried to bring her out of herself, it was as if a shutter were pulled down over her eyes and she retreated further into herself. Once or twice they had tried to take her for a walk, but she had screamed with terror. The moor frightened her and the sea reduced her to a trembling wreck, so they decided to allow her to remain in the house for the time being until they could persuade her outside.

Although she screamed she would never cry. Alice was convinced that she had not cried once since she had been found in the ruins of her home. She was sure that if only the child could cry she would come back to them.

'She needs professional help, Alice,' Gertie said one evening, when yet again they were discussing the problem of Annie.

'She needs love.'

'It's all too dangerous it seems to me.'

'I think Lady Gertie's right, Grandmother. You spend far too much time with that child.'

'What on earth do you mean, Juniper? How on earth could I be spending too much time with her? She needs all the attention we can give her.'

'But not to the neglect of everyone else,' Juniper said

sharply, so sharply that both Gertie and Alice looked up with surprise and then at each other questioningly.

At weekends the older children had to be entertained. May was no problem, as she liked to cook. Her weekends were spent baking in the huge Gwenfer kitchen and learning all she could from Gertie's cook. May and her brothers had apparently lived in a small tenement with their mother and three other children. Their alcoholic father had long since disappeared. May was used to cooking for her brothers, but never in her life had she had such a well-equipped kitchen nor the range of ingredients that were available at Gwenfer.

Polly kept the boys content. She taught them to ride and they took turns on the old coach horse, long since retired, who lived in the stables. She also took them on visits to the farm, where they helped with the milking and feeding of the animals. She played cricket and football with them. She organized picnics and helped them to make small gardens of their own, dug ready for bulb planting in the autumn.

Because of the petrol-rationing, Alice had had Zac renovate the old governess cart which had been mouldering in the stables since she was a girl and a pony was purchased. Alice was delighted with the resurrection of the pretty yellow cart. At last she did not have so often to suffer Gertie's driving, which was haphazard at the best of times. Like a modern Boadicea Gertie felt that everything else on the road should give way to her, and, to save petrol, she had adopted the rather alarming habit of freewheeling. But as soon as Gertie put the car in neutral she seemed to forget she had a brake.

Gertie also fell upon the governess cart with hoots of joy.

'I've never enjoyed the motor car, you know, Alice. Never trusted them, not like a good horse,' she confided.

'Me neither,' Alice replied with feeling.

Juniper was still being difficult. She refused to help Polly with the boys and since she had never been known to enter the kitchen, helping the cook and May was out of the question. As for Annie, she completely ignored the child. If she came into a room, invariably Juniper would get up and walk out.

One Saturday, Polly had taken May and Flo shopping in Penzance; no one knew where Juniper was. Gertie was writing letters and the boys were in the old schoolroom playing with what remained of an old and battered train set. It was a glorious October day. The sun was shining, the air full of the sweet smell of autumn decay. The sea at the end of the cove was as blue as the sky so that it was impossible to see where one ended and the other began.

'I'm going to go and sit on my favourite rock and watch the sea. Would you like to come, Annie?' Alice asked the girl, who was sitting huddled in a wing chair in the parlour, as always clutching the doll to her.

Silently she slipped to the floor and to Alice's surprise took her hand. In the hall she buttoned Annie into her coat and hat. Hand in hand they made their way to the cove.

Alice's pleasure in the day was shattered as they reached the beach. Out on the promontory, Oswald's Point, were the two boys, laughing and joking as they waggled sticks tied to long strings into the sea. Alice's hand shot to her mouth – of all the places in the cove, that was the most dangerous. Around those rocks the sea whirled and eddied, currents sucked to right and left. She had forbidden any of the children to come down here unattended.

'Robin, Fred,' she called, but they could not hear as a wave larger than the others hit the rock. The two boys danced with glee as the water lapped at them. Alice clutched Annie's hand tighter. They would never hear. She quickly crossed to Ia's Rock and lifted Annie on to it.

'Sit there and don't move, there's a good girl,' she said, trying to keep all hint of panic out of her voice.

Alice ran across the beach, on to the rocks, and along the spine of the promontory.

'Robin, Fred, come here,' she shouted. The two boys turned just as a still larger wave lashed the rock and effortlessly lifted Fred into the sea. Robin began to scream. Alice ran faster.

'Go, get help,' she ordered the boy. Kicking off her shoes, she leapt into the dangerous, sea and struck out to where she had last seen Fred's head before he sank into the water. She dived, her hands outstretched, desperately searching. She touched him and grabbed at the choking, pawing child.

On the surface again she shouted at him to keep calm, but he was fighting her. She could feel the undertow take hold of her legs. Clutching the boy under the arms, with almost superhuman effort, she kicked with all her strength towards the shore away from the searching tentacles of the currents.

The beach seemed a mile away as she laboriously swam back, the boy, still fighting and exhausting her. As she felt her strength diminishing, the cold numbing her limbs, she knew they would not make it. Then strong hands grabbed at her and Zac was pulling them both ashore, as a horrified Juniper and Polly raced on to the sand, where Alice collapsed, blue with exhaustion, fighting for breath.

'Alice, no!' The cry was so full of pain it curdled the blood of those who heard it. 'Alice, don't leave me,' and towards her across the sand hurtled Annie, her face streaked with tears. She flung herself at the woman and clutched her for dear life. 'Don't die, please don't die,' she sobbed.

Alice held the child tight, her own tears mingling with Annie's.

'There, my darling. You must not be upset. I'll never leave you,' and through her soaked clothes she could feel the thin, heaving body of the sad little girl.

Alice looked up. Polly's face was creased with anxiety. Juniper had a strange twisted expression that she could not understand.

'I've decided, Grandmama, I'm returning to London –
tonight,' she said coldly, before turning on her heel and
walking back up the valley.

8

The journey to London through the night was spent
mainly in silence. Juniper was driving far too fast given
the inadequate lighting allowed by the blackout. Polly
stoically hung on to the leather strap and, at the sharper
bends, closed her eyes.

Juniper appeared to be angry, although apart from her
uncommon silence it was difficult to tell. In all the time
she had known Juniper, Polly had never seen her angry,
nor once lose her temper.

What the problem was, Polly was as much in the dark
as Gertie and Alice had been. The excited, fun-to-be-with
Juniper of their adventurous trips through France was
someone she now wondered if she had imagined or
dreamed. The simplest thing would have been to ask
Juniper what was the matter, except that Polly had always
been aware that she knew only one part of Juniper. It was
as if Juniper lived her life in different compartments; you
might be invited into one but not necessarily another.

There were advantages to this attitude for Juniper
herself never pried into anyone else's life. You told her
what you wanted her to know and she never asked for
more information, no matter how curious she might be.
There had been times when Polly was grateful for this
and now she could only respect Juniper's desire for
privacy.

What concerned Polly most was knowing that Juniper
was deeply unhappy. Hal had damaged her severely, she
now realized. In France Juniper had laughed and joked
about her husband and his male lover, but she had
obviously been using humour as a shield.

'Why don't you go back to America?' To her surprise,

Polly found herself speaking her thoughts. In the dark she looked guiltily at Juniper. 'It is your home, after all.'

'I don't feel it is. Don't forget I left when I was thirteen. Gwenfer was my home . . .' Juniper lapsed into silence again. Polly would have liked to ask her why she spoke in the past tense, but thought better of it. 'Strange, isn't it? I've lived in England fewer years than in the country where I was born and yet I don't regard America as home. I don't want to go there.' Although Juniper spoke out loud, it was as if she were talking to herself.

'Not strange really. The years you've lived in England have been important to you.'

'Important?' Juniper snorted. 'What's been important about them? A failed marriage, a child who doesn't know me, let alone like me.'

'Poor Juniper.' Polly tentatively put her hand out and touched her friend's arm. Juniper changed gear abruptly, so that Polly's hand slipped back on to her lap. The engine complained at the unnecessary change. Then they drove on in silence again.

Juniper's house in Belgravia was large. A tall, solid house built by Cubitt overlooking a square. A home that before this war would have had an army of servants tucked below stairs in the basement. But now, because of war work, they were reduced to one maid and a cook. The cook's predilection for the bottle made meals rather a hit-and-miss affair. Polly would have sacked her for incompetence, but Juniper with typical contrariness found her antics amusing and seemed not to notice the frequently singed and unpunctual meals and, increasingly, their non-appearance. When this happened she would merely laugh and suggest they go out to a restaurant.

Juniper had rented the house part furnished, but she was not the most careful of people and glass rings began to appear on good furniture, drinks were spilt on the carpets. And the house was too large for the one maid to care for properly.

65

The expense of everything was a constant worry to Polly. Even without a full complement of staff, the upkeep of the house must be horrific. It worried her that, despite her grandmother's efforts, she was still, after a year, without work and, with scant funds of her own, could contribute little. She had rented out the home farm at Hurstwood but all the income, and most of the other money she had went to maintain the house. She lived in hope that someone would rent it for the duration of the war, but she was still waiting. The small allowance she gave herself was not a problem. When living in Paris on her own she had become accustomed to managing on little, but she minded not paying her way with Juniper. Not that Juniper would take money when she offered it.

'Don't be silly, Polly, I've masses,' she would say airily.

'But I must pay my way.'

'What for? Money's for spending, isn't it? When I haven't got any, then I'll come to you.' She laughed at such an unlikely notion.

To justify her keep, Polly helped. She assisted the maid, she cooked when the cook was under the table, she did the shopping, queuing for hours for food, something that Juniper would never have had the patience to do, and generally made herself useful.

'You know, Polly, you don't have enough money,' Juniper said one day as they ate a late breakfast – Juniper's breakfasts were always late.

'I'm fully aware of that fact,' Polly said, smiling over her toast. 'The problem is Hurstwood, the house is expensive to maintain and it gobbles up every penny I have. But when I find work . . .'

'I shall give you an allowance.'

'You'll do no such thing.' Polly sat upright with concern.

'It's not fair. We are sisters, after all, and I have so much and you so little.'

'Juniper, no. I don't want your money, I've sufficient. It's kind enough that you allow me to live here. It would be a struggle if I didn't.'

'Please let me. I want to. Don't spoil things.'

'No, I'm sorry . . .' Polly looked down at her plate. She could not bring herself to say what she was really thinking, that she did not want to be Juniper's sister. She said nothing because she did not want to hurt her friend.

'You don't think you are my sister, do you?' Juniper said in a mournful voice.

Polly forced herself to look Juniper straight in the eye. 'Juniper, I don't know. When you told me in Paris, it was a shock and one I couldn't really take in on top of my father dying. But when I think about it now when I think of him . . .'

'You don't want to be my sister.'

'It's not that. It's just that I can't believe I am.'

'Why don't you ask your mother?'

'My mother.' Polly laughed. 'I should think my mother has forgotten herself what the truth is.'

'But don't you understand, Polly? I want you to be my sister more than anything else in the world. I need you to be,' and she grabbed Polly by the hand so tightly that it made Polly wince.

'I'm your loving friend. I think that's preferable!'

'You see,' Juniper jumped up and pushed her chair back dramatically. 'What's wrong with me?'

'Nothing's wrong with you, Juniper. I love you, I couldn't love you any more if you were my sister.'

'You promise?'

'I promise.'

But it was a subject that Polly was aware continued to fester away between them. There were times when she thought it might be simpler to agree that she was this passionately longed-for sister. But she could never bring herself to say it for it would have meant denying her father, and that Polly could never do.

The garden was excavated and an Anderson shelter erected. Juniper furnished it in style with Chippendale table and chairs, a small bookcase, rose tinted oil lamps, chintz covering the metal walls, on the floor a Persian rug. They slept there one night – the next day it rained and a foot of water filled the shelter. Polly removed the Chippendale and hung the rug on the balcony to dry, and they went back to the space under the basement stairs.

From this time Juniper's social life became increasingly frenetic. From the moment she awoke she searched out company and it seemed to Polly that every minute of Juniper's day had to be filled with chatter and activity, as if she were afraid of solitude.

When she had been married to Hal Copton they had entertained on a large scale, but these were not the people she now chose to see. Juniper was building a different group of friends, not one of whom had anything to do with her earlier life. Polly wondered if she was trying to obliterate that past, but if that were the case, why was she herself allowed to remain?

Juniper went to bed at dawn and was not seen again until mid-afternoon. Once dressed she would be out of the house as quickly as possible, visiting, shopping. She returned to dress for the evening, for dinner, the theatre, a dance or a night club – whichever that night's escort was taking her to. There were days when Polly felt she saw only Juniper's back as she tripped down the steps before another taxi door slammed and whisked her away.

Juniper was never without a romantic interest. Men were in constant attendance, but none of them lasted. Polly longed for Juniper to find someone she cared about. She might appear to be happy but it was a forced gaiety and Polly was beginning to worry seriously.

Polly was getting used to being on her own. Still unable to find official work, she had volunteered to help at a canteen for servicemen in the West End. The place was always crowded and noisy, so on the days she worked there she was quite content to have the house to herself in the evenings. Then she could listen to music of her choice, her favourite programmes on the wireless, read in peace, write letters and dream about Andrew. She wrote frequently to her grandmother and regularly to Jonathan, who was stationed somewhere in the Middle East – for friendship's sake.

Polly's only other regular outing was to her mother. She visited once a month on a Sunday, but there was no pleasure in it for either of them. After each trip, Polly wondered why she bothered, her mother's voice, whining, moaning, nagging, still ringing in her ears. She went out of a sense of duty, which she wished she did not possess.

Juniper always invited Polly on her forays into London night life, but Polly had a good reason not to go. Even though her grandmother had failed to find her work, she had had more success in the search for Andrew. From her Swiss friends, Gertie had discovered that he was a prisoner of war.

Each evening Polly would write him a letter, posting it via the Swiss Red Cross. She had yet to receive a reply. But now she had real hope again, hope for a future and so there was no question of any other man being attractive to Polly.

'You ought to come; it's not healthy mooning about here. God knows when you'll see Andrew. You must have some fun,' Juniper said one evening as she made a last check of her appearance in the mirror. 'And you worry too much about this house. Let it get in a muddle, I don't mind.'

'But I do. Don't worry about me. I'm perfectly happy. I couldn't enjoy myself knowing where Andrew is, could I? It would make me feel so guilty. And in any case, I quite like looking after the house.'

'Ah well, that's different, isn't it?' Juniper gave one of her dazzling smiles, then the doorbell rang, Juniper scooped up her bag and cape. 'See you later. Watch out for bombs and don't wait up,' she called, as she did every evening.

They were no longer alone in the house. One spring night in 1941, Juniper returned from a night club just as a raid was about to start with two young men in tow, who claimed to be artists and conscientious objectors. They came for the weekend but six months later they were still in residence. These two were followed by a steady stream of 'guests' who stayed a day or two before leaving. It was like living in a hotel, Polly thought, as yet again she helped the maid to change the sheets.

'I think I'd best tell you, madam, I'm leaving,' Stella said one day as she straightened a cover.

'Oh no, Stella. Why?' Polly asked anxiously.

'I'm sick to death of this place, if you must know, madam. Apart from you no one keeps regular hours. All the comings and goings – it's all too much for one body.'

'I'm sorry, Stella, I'll help more.'

'No, madam, it won't do. I'm off to the munitions factory. I can get four times what I get here and maybe more appreciation.'

'I can't say I blame you,' Polly said calmly, to Stella's astonishment. 'You go, and good luck to you.' And she found herself wishing that she could leave as easily.

Then one day that summer, they were joined by a countess of middle European origins and middle years, who Juniper had befriended in a club. To Polly she was not a welcome addition for Sophia von Michelberg was arrogant and imperious. She had a maid, Martha, with a swarthy complexion and a sullen mien, who spoke no English and made no attempt to learn any and who hated the cook on sight. Polly hoped that her arrival would at least mean help with the chores, but nothing was further from Martha's thoughts. She worked for the countess and no one else.

The very same day that the cook and Martha had a most spectacular row, Polly at last found work as a clerk in the Ministry of Information, in the department that published advice for the hard-pressed housewife. It did not fill Polly with elation, but it was an official job, and one for which, much to her amusement, she had been made to sign the Official Secrets Act.

Polly returned from her interview bursting with the

news that after all this time she was finally going to be doing something useful. She found the house in uproar and the cook gone.

'Of course you can't take the job, Polly. I've never heard of such selfishness. We need you here.' Sophia was at her most authoritative. 'It's not as if you've been called up.'

'I want to help. I've felt so useless this past year.'

'Bah! Giving advice to peasants, what's the use of that?' the countess said with a sneer.

'Weeks ago I drew up a rota of work which depends on everyone in the house helping,' Polly said with studied patience. 'If everyone does their bit, I'm sure we can muddle through.' She stood in front of the fireplace in which a meagre fire smoked balefully. Seaton and Giles, the 'artists', were lying indolently in chairs on either side of it.

'I don't mind cooking,' Juniper said brightly. 'It might be fun; and if not, one can eat out. I don't mind paying.'

'Juniper!' Polly said with exasperation. 'You can't keep paying for everyone.' She glared at the other occupants of the room, who blithely ignored her.

'Polly, taking this job is out of the question,' Sophia said regally.

'Oh no, Sophia darling. She must. She's been waiting ages for this opportunity, haven't you Polly? We'll manage,' Juniper said, as if bravely taking on the whole management of the war rather than a little cooking and housework.

'It's not much of a job, but it might lead to other things.'

'Of course it might, Polly. No, we won't hear of you not taking it.'

Polly thanked her but at the same time found herself feeling inexplicably guilty.

One bitterly cold night, just before Juniper and Polly's second Christmas in London, they were joined by two young women. Juniper had found Maureen and Pam in the street, after a particularly heavy raid, pushing a pram loaded with all they possessed, rescued from their bombed out home. Of course she could take them in, she said. Of course they must stay for as long as they liked. Of course the fact that they had no money was irrelevant.

Maureen and Pam were pleasant. They tried to help, if a little ineffectively, because, like Juniper, they were both night owls. Their clothes were flashy, their language earthy, their make-up heavy. Polly supposed they were what her grandmother would call 'common', but she liked them and forgave their over-sleeping and the racket they made, for the help they gave.

When Polly eventually realized what was happening in the house, she felt embarrassed by her naïvety.

'Juniper, have you noticed that Maureen and Pam seem to have rather a lot of male visitors?'

'So?' Juniper smiled up at her from the manicure she was attempting to give herself. Her own manicurist and hairdresser had been killed in a direct hit the week before.

'You know what I mean,' Polly said, feeling uncomfortably hot around the collar.

'I'm afraid I don't, Polly, what are you trying to say?'

'I think they might be prostitutes.'

'Oh, no doubt about it,' Juniper held up her hands to admire her handiwork. 'Do you like this red?' She flashed her painted nails at Polly.

'But Juniper, it could get you into a lot of trouble. You could be accused of running a brothel. You can go to prison for that.'

Juniper laughed. 'Oh Polly, you sound so prim at times. They were homeless, I came to their rescue. As to their profession – I doubt if the authorities care that much, with everything else that's happening. In any case, they're only amateurs and are providing a much-needed service.'

'What on earth would Alice say?'

'I don't give a damn what my grandmother would think, or say. I don't stand in judgement.' She smiled as she turned away, leaving Polly feeling very much in the wrong.

About this time the parties began. Juniper had often given parties in the past, but these were different. They would start late, usually about midnight when Juniper became bored with whatever club she was in. She was quite likely to invite who ever was there home with her, often with the band.

The party would rage through the night into the morning. They were loud relentless parties; sirens would wail followed by the drone of the bombers, then the bombs would fall, the house shake, the lights flicker and fade, but they simply lit candles and carried on, oblivious to the mayhem in the world outside.

Soon complete strangers were ringing the doorbell asking if this was where Juniper's party was being held, for she and her hospitality were becoming famous in wartime London. There were complaints from the neighbours but, as Juniper always sweetly explained, what was the difference between the noise the Germans made and the noise of her parties? And, she would add, blinding the complainants with her brilliant smile, it was to help the poor fighting men relax and who could object to that?

It was certainly true that every armed forces' uniform was to be seen most nights, accompanied by a variety of languages and accents spoken – American, Canadian, Free French, Polish, Scandinavian. Everyone searched out Juniper's house during their precious leave.

Sleep was becoming a problem for Polly. She stuffed cotton wool in her ears, she put her pillow over her head, but it made no difference. She knew that eventually she would be forced to move out, but she lingered, mainly because she did not want to hurt Juniper. But she also knew she should not leave her for fear of what Juniper might do next. She was drinking too much and Polly rarely saw her eat.

Eventually she managed to catch Juniper in her room, for once alone. Tentatively she suggested that, since

Juniper looked so tired, a couple of parties a week were enough for anyone.

'You can be such a boring old maid, Polly. Why don't you just relax and enjoy yourself?'

'The expense must be prohibitive.'

'Do you ever hear me complain?'

'Well, no.'

'So the money doesn't matter. Gee, Polly, what have I always said to you – money's for spending.'

'I have to get more sleep if I'm to do any job properly.' Having started this conversation Polly felt bound to press on.

'Well, this is my war work and I see no reason for stopping. Move your room to the top of the house, it'll be quieter there,' was Juniper's advice.

Six months into this regime, with another winter approaching, Juniper stopped the trips to the night-clubs and restaurants. At weekends, when Polly was at home all day, she realized that the parties never ended. People grabbed some sleep and by early afternoon the drinking and the music had started again.

Polly had long ago moved her room to the attics, and her bedroom and the kitchen were the only places in the whole house where daylight was ever seen. In the other rooms the shutters and curtains were firmly closed. It was as if Juniper were building a cocoon for herself. If she shut the world out – that world now so ugly and frightening – then she could ignore everything that was happening.

Food and drink might be in short supply elsewhere but not at Juniper's. There was a regular supply of food parcels from America but these were insufficient to feed the crowds, so she had built up a string of connections with men who only called at night, who spoke out of the corner of their mouths while their eyes flickered restlessly and who acquired for the household everything they needed.

Often when Polly met strangers on the stairs it was she who felt the odd one out. She sensed that she and Juniper were drifting apart and she began to wonder if they would ever find each other again.

9

By the spring of 1943, the only times Juniper ventured out of the house were to visit her dressmaker or the large department stores. Not for her the annoying restriction of insufficient clothing coupons: the sinister men who visited under cover of darkness saw to that. The only time she rose early was when her son was brought to London, about every three months, for a long weekend. Then Juniper would rush out of the house to meet him and his nanny, taking him for treats, buying him presents, lavishing money and attention upon him. For someone who claimed she did not care about her son, she seemed to Polly to be remarkably happy to see him. During the nights the boy was in London there would still be parties, but at least Juniper went to bed before dawn. Her other excursions were for long exhausting conferences with her lawyers over the custody of Harry.

With increasing anxiety, Polly watched Juniper's complexion lose its bloom and take on the dull, greyish look of one who rarely sees the sun. Her face was puffy from too much drink and she was losing weight. She talked non-stop and was always restlessly moving about. When she laughed it was as if she could not stop, the slightest thing could bring on these attacks of laughter. But on the days when she had been with her lawyers she returned looking worse than ever, drawn and still greyer, then she would drink twice as much and her laughter was shrill and ugly. Polly felt she was watching the Juniper she loved disappear and was at a loss to know what to do.

'Aren't things going well?' Polly asked solicitously one evening when she returned from work just as Juniper's taxi arrived at the door.

'Fine. There are no problems,' Juniper said lightly as she unlocked the door for both of them. Once inside, she kicked off her shoes and slipped out of her coat, which she dumped unceremoniously on a chair. She peered at herself in the hallway mirror. 'God, the light in this hall is awful. I look yellow. Get brighter bulbs, Polly.'

'I can't. They've only got these dim ones in the shops.'

'I'll ask Sid to get in more powerful ones next time he calls. Drink?' she asked Polly over her shoulder as she ran up the stairs. She entered the drawing room and crossed to the ever-loaded drinks trolley.

'Juniper, do you think it's right to use spivs like Sid? It's not fair on other people,' Polly said, following her into the room.

'What on earth do you mean? If I didn't buy from Sid and co. someone else would, so why not us?'

'But if no one bought from them they'd go out of business, then there wouldn't be any black market, would there?'

'Polly, you are so naïve at times. In war people like that always surface, ever ready to supply people who can afford them. The world isn't the pretty place you seem to imagine.'

'But it's so unpatriotic.'

'Dear Polly, there are times when you can sound intolerably priggish. Do you realize that we never have a conversation these days? All I get from you is lectures and nagging.' Juniper spoke sharply and as she poured her drink she swayed slightly.

'Juniper, are you all right?'

'I will be once you shut up,' Juniper said savagely. Polly was rigid with shock. But then Juniper turned to face her with a tired smile that immediately aroused Polly's sympathy.

'I'm sorry, Juniper. You must be exhausted. You never look well when you've been with the lawyers.'

'Oh Polly, they're so boring, droning on and on. Always lecturing me too.' She slumped into a chair, her feet curled up under her and, in the dim light of the table lamp, looked like a girl again.

'It's probably for your own good. Quite honestly, Juniper, I'm worried sick. The way this house is run – all the parties and drink and the hangers-on . . .'

'They're my friends,' Juniper said spiritedly.

'No, they're not, Juniper, they're using you, and worse than that, they're giving you a bad reputation.'

'Oh gee, not you as well. Aren't the lawyers enough?' Juniper rolled her eyes heavenward exaggeratedly.

'We're not *nagging*. We're concerned about you and what the Coptons could make of all this in court . . .'

'You're jealous, Polly. It's your one big failing, it always has been. You'd rather that none of my friends was here, so you could have me all to yourself.'

Polly was speechless. She looked down at her friend with blank surprise.

'It's true, isn't it?' Juniper beamed up at her.

'No, it's not.' Polly said flatly. 'I loathe these people but it's because they're no good, not because I'm jealous.'

Juniper studied her pretty pink nails with apparent intensity and said nothing.

'I'm worried about the outcome of your court case, that's all.'

'I told you, there's no need for anyone to worry. I've got the money to fight that old crone, my mother-in-law. Look how long we've managed to keep this stupid case off the boil – two and a half years – my money has bought me that time. Money can always win for you, Polly.'

'Not always, Juniper.' Polly sighed with exasperation. 'Don't you see you're risking your son's future?'

'If your own life had been an unmitigated success, Polly, you might be in a position to lecture me, but in the circumstances, well, you're hardly the one to talk . . .'

Polly was hurt, deeply hurt. She turned on her heel and silently left the room. She went straight to her attic where she wrote to Alice pouring out her worries. Reading the letter over, her fears and complaints sounded spiteful and small-minded, and she tore it up and threw the scraps in her wastebin.

That scene was the nearest the two of them had come to arguing. They would never have a full-scale row, for Juniper took care never to row with anyone. Even when she was angry, she always spoke sweetly and reasonably, with a smile – which was infuriatingly frustrating for anyone on the receiving end. A really good argument might have cleared the air. Instead Polly felt she would have to leave and find a room of her own somewhere. If she stayed, she feared they would end as enemies. She had tried to help but was not strong enough to deal with Juniper. She ought to tell Alice, but her sense of loyalty was too strong. The worry was pulling her down, it was time she began to think of herself.

The next morning she began to look for other accommodation but it was to be more difficult than she had imagined.

In the following week the two women hardly spoke to each other. Polly was still smarting from what she saw as Juniper's unjustified attack. Juniper, on the other hand, was blissfully unaware that Polly was avoiding her. Polly had not told her about her decision to leave. Their hours did not coincide: when Polly left for work, Juniper was still in bed. When Polly returned, Juniper was invariably getting ready for the evening. Since Polly rarely joined the parties, her absence was not unusual. As a result, although Polly knew that the custody hearing for Harry was imminent, she was not aware that it had taken place until she opened her bedroom door to an urgent rapping.

Standing on the landing was a distraught Juniper, her face streaked with tears. She flung herself into Polly's arms and began to sob.

'I lost.' Polly managed to make out the words from Juniper's rising hysteria.

'Oh, my God! Has Harry gone to live with Lady Copton?' She led Juniper by the arm into her room, dampened a flannel with cold water from her jug and somewhat ineffectually began to dab at Juniper's face.

'He's to stay in Scotland,' Juniper gulped between sobs.

'But I thought you said . . .'

'Lady Copton's going to move up there. She and Leigh have got custody together. Glory be, I need a drink. Have you got anything up here . . . ?' She looked wildly about Polly's neat attic bedroom.

'I'll get you one.' Polly, for once, felt the best thing for Juniper was a large brandy.

She was quickly back with two glasses and the bottle and poured herself a large measure too. Juniper downed hers in one and held out her glass for more while Polly sipped hers. In a rush, the sobs subsiding, Juniper poured out the afternoon's happenings.

'. . . and do you know, they've been having us watched for months. Detectives, strings of them. They had a list of all the people who come here, they knew about Maureen and Pam and the fact they're prostitutes. The noise. They'd talked to the neighbours – it was all there, it was so shaming,' and Juniper covered her face with her hands and shuddered.

'But I thought Lady Copton was poor. How could she afford detectives on that scale?'

'Hal, I presume.'

'But he's got no money either.'

'I gave him some. When he went to America I arranged with Charlie Macpherson, my lawyer, to let him have a large lump sum . . .'

'The cad. To use your money to fight you. That's unspeakable. Did you see Leigh?'

'Oh yes, I saw dear Leigh. He couldn't even look at me. Liked me in bed well enough . . .' The tears threatened to fall again. 'At least I had the satisfaction of seeing Caroline squirm, having to tell the judge about Leigh and me.'

'Won't you be allowed to see him?'

'The judge was so generous,' she laughed bitterly. 'I can

79

see him one afternoon a week and one weekend a month, by arrangement. But I have to go to Scotland to see him. He's only allowed to come to London with the permission of the court.'

'Well, that's not so bad. You'll see more of him than you do at the moment.'

'No I won't. I can only see him if Lady Copton or Caroline chaperones me. I'd rather not see him at all.' She shook her head defiantly.

'That's silly, Juniper. You'd be cutting off your nose to spite your face . . .' but she did not finish the sentence. Juniper looked at her, and Polly found herself looking away from the despair she saw.

'I don't understand, Polly. I didn't think I cared. You know I've always said I didn't love my son, couldn't love him. And then today when I saw him . . . when he rushed up to me, he did, you know, he was happy to see me, really glad.' She spoke as if she didn't believe it was so.

'He was there?'

'Yes. Outside with his nanny. And I suddenly wanted him, needed to hold him. I felt, too late, that perhaps I did love him after all.'

'I never doubted you did. You'd been through too much, Juniper, when you decided to let Leigh have him. You couldn't have been thinking straight after finding out about Hal. It was the worst time to make such an important decision. And think about it, you were still a child yourself. I think you've been hiding that love even from yourself. Perhaps, having been so hurt, you were afraid of loving your son.'

'Oh Polly, what have I done?'

There was no question of Polly leaving now; she did not dare for Juniper seemed bent on self-destruction. The drinking increased and Polly cursed the large cellar stocked with wine and spirits. Despite the shortages elsewhere, Juniper always had a supply of her own. Her food intake – little at the best of times – virtually ceased, and she made no secret any more of the fact that the little silver knife and straw she had were for the white powder she regularly acquired from a doctor of dubious ethics in Harley Street. Polly had never asked what it was, she was too frightened.

Polly planned to get time off work to travel to Gwenfer, explain her worries and predicament and to ask Alice to come back with her – surely Alice would be able to make Juniper see sense? But it was one thing to plan to take leave and another altogether to get it. Mrs Anstruther, the senior member in Polly's department, filled her and the other young women with terror. Leave was rarely given so it took Polly several days to work out a case for why she should be allowed time off. And it took several requests before she got an appointment with the self-important woman.

The evening before the meeting was due, she returned from work to find a letter from Andrew's father waiting for her. Polly's hands shook as she read the contents. A captain in the Guards had escaped with Andrew from the POW camp in March 1942. With the help of the French Resistance, the captain had made his way slowly back to England; his dangerous journey had taken a year. The moment he arrived he had visited the Slaters to tell them that a week after their escape he and Andrew in the dark had accidentally stumbled across a German patrol which opened fire on them. Andrew had been hit. Andrew was dead.

Polly slumped on to her bed. She felt cold and sick. The news she had dreaded in her worst nightmares had become reality. Andrew had been dead for over a year and she had not known. He had lain in a grave in some foreign land, unmourned. She should have known, she should have felt his fear, his pain, why had she not? She had nothing of his but her memories. When she left Paris with Juniper, she had had time to pack one small case and most of the mementos he had given her she had had to leave behind, except for a small silver locket and a photograph. Those she had lost when her case was stolen at Biarritz. She wished now that her cat was with her and not at Gwenfer. At least Hursty had known him, Andrew's hands had stroked his fur.

Alone, she buried her face in her pillow and for once the sound of the party was deafened by her own crying. The worry about Juniper receded. All she could think of was how she would survive without Andrew when she did not even want to.

She went to work the next day as usual and did her tasks like an automaton. Her red eyes and puffy face revealed her loss. There was nothing anyone could do or say to help, the death of a dear one was all too common these days. Solicitously the other staff made her tea and even Mrs Anstruther laced a cup with a large measure of whisky and asked her if she wanted to talk. Polly said no, in her grief she had forgotten her appointment with the woman.

The next day she made her own tea and Mrs Anstruther was back to shouting at her. She had missed her chance of asking for leave. For, later in the week, when she timorously asked for a few days off, to go to Gwenfer, to be with her grandmother and have time to grieve, the request was refused. Andrew was not her husband, her father, her brother, her son – he was not even her fiancé, she was told sharply. There was no compassionate leave for the love in one's life, it transpired.

Juniper was kind. She even avoided her rackety friends and spent a couple of evenings with Polly. At the kitchen table, a bottle of wine between them, she listened while Polly talked and reminisced endlessly and she comforted her when she cried.

But there was a war on – that hateful catch phrase that permeated everything they did these days. On the third evening Polly found herself alone in the kitchen and Juniper once more at one of her interminable parties.

The grief did not lessen, she did not expect it to. But

gradually she seemed better able to control it and make some semblance of getting on with her life. Her longing for Andrew was always with her – she never wanted it to go away, she clung to the longing for then it was as if she was still clinging to him.

When she walked to work and the weather was fine and the sun shining, and the bombs had not fallen the night before, then the thought that she would never again share such a day with Andrew was unbearable. She would walk along, silent tears pouring down her cheeks to the embarrassment of passers-by who looked away quickly from her grief as if fearing it was contagious. But Polly wasn't even aware of them.

While he was missing, she had followed the news avidly. Now she did not care. Whole armies could disappear, bombs could fall, she no longer cared and she no longer felt afraid.

10

For three months Polly lived in her own grey world. She was unaware how detached from other people's troubles she had become until one morning, on her way downstairs to go to work, she passed the door to Juniper's bedroom which, unusually at that early hour, was open. From inside Polly heard the unmistakable sound of retching. There was no answer to her tap, so she peered round the door gingerly, but the room was empty. She waited. Juniper appeared from the adjoining bathroom looking white-faced and exhausted.

'Juniper, what's wrong?'

'Too much goddamn brandy.' Juniper attempted to laugh and swayed on her feet. Polly caught hold of her and helped her to the bed.

'I'll call the doctor.'

'No, you won't.' Juniper weakly held up her hand. 'I hate doctors prodding me. It's a hangover, that's all. I'll be right as rain by this afternoon.' She started to cough and hauled herself up on the pillows the better to breathe, flopping back exhausted as the spasm subsided.

'You look and sound dreadful.'

'Thank you very much, dear Polly, that makes me feel just wonderful.' Juniper smiled feebly.

'Let me take you to Gwenfer. Damn Mrs Anstruther, I'll telephone in, say that I'm ill . . . we could be there by dinner.'

'No . . . I'm not going to Gwenfer.'

'But you're happiest there. Alice will look after you, make you better.'

'There's nothing wrong with me, I told you. But in any case, even if I were ill, she's far too busy for me, with precious Annie Budd to care for.'

Polly looked at Juniper with surprise. 'Oh, Juniper, no . . .'

'Oh, Polly, yes . . .' Juniper aped her. 'Every damn letter I get, it's Annie this and Annie that. Each telephone call, all she wants to talk about is that brat.' Juniper began to pleat and unpleat the sheet with short, jerky movements.

'Poor Annie,' Polly began to remonstrate but the expression of unmistakable pain on Juniper's face stopped her. This was not the time. Juniper was ill. 'Some tea?' she said instead.

'No thanks.' Juniper pulled a face at the thought of tea and suddenly began to shiver. Polly fetched a woollen wrap which she placed around her shoulders, ashamedly aware of how much thinner Juniper had become. She pulled the eiderdown up and tucked it firmly around her. 'Poor Juniper. You are in a pickle, aren't you?' she said lightly, to cover her genuine concern, then turned towards the door.

'Where are you going?' Juniper leant forward, her face creased with anxiety.

'I'm phoning Mrs Anstruther to tell her that you're ill and I'm not coming in.'

'Ah, that's good . . .' Juniper slumped back on to her pillows.

Polly was exasperated by the time she had to waste arguing with Mrs Anstruther before the woman reluctantly gave her the day off. Next she went to the kitchen to heat some milk and porridge. The first thing to do was to try to get Juniper to eat. Fifteen minutes had elapsed by the time she returned with a tray.

'You must eat . . .' she began, then the tray dropped to the floor with a clatter. In the centre of the room, collapsed in a heap, lay Juniper, unconscious, her breathing loud and stertorous. 'My God,' Polly exclaimed. Kneeling down, she patted Juniper's cheek. 'Juniper, wake up,' she begged. Juniper gave a small groan. She turned Juniper's head to one side, covered her with an eiderdown and then frantically began to search through the clutter on Juniper's desk for her address book. Once found she leafed rapidly through it, but her hands felt numb and clumsy, she kept losing her place and dropped it twice. 'Calm down,' she muttered to herself. Having checked the number, she dialled with shaking fingers.

'I don't care if he is with a patient. This is an emergency,' she said sharply into the mouthpiece.

'If you'll just tell me the problem, I'll . . .'

'Get me the doctor, now!' She was screaming at the receptionist. When Juniper's doctor came on the line she hardly took breath as, with panic rising in her voice, she gabbled a description of Juniper's condition, trying to answer the doctor's many questions. As she did, the wail of an air-raid siren began. 'Please, doctor, you've got to come here this instant. I'm afraid for her.'

'Young woman, with a raid on we shall waste precious time if I come. Do as I say, try to stay calm. You're not going to help Lady Copton by panicking . . .' The line went dead. Polly shook the instrument with frustrated fury.

She ran from the room and along the corridor banging on all the bedroom doors, shouting at the top of her voice.

No one appeared. She raced from Seaton's room and then to Giles's and back again, banging and kicking at the doors, yelling incoherently as she battered at them.

The countess appeared wrapped in a large silk shawl with a huge fur hat set slightly askew on her head.

'What is this appalling commotion?' she asked, pulling the shawl more closely around her.

'It's Juniper, she's collapsed. Can you go to her? I'm trying to wake the men to help me carry her downstairs.'

'Call a doctor,' the countess said, making no move towards Juniper's room.

'I have, he's meeting us at the hospital. Please go and sit with her.'

'What can I do? I'm not a nurse.'

'Oh, my God, don't you ever think about anyone other than yourself? You can sit with her, hold her hand, make sure she doesn't choke, can't you?' Polly was shouting with exasperation.

'Screaming like this isn't going to help anyone, Polly. Pull yourself together and behave with more dignity if that's possible.' At last Sophia moved towards Juniper's room. Polly stood in the corridor, taking a deep breath to try to control herself. She turned and rapped sharply on Giles's door.

'Giles, please open this door,' she said clearly. 'Juniper's ill. Get the car, we've got to get her to hospital,' she ordered.

'Can't you call a taxi?' A bleary-eyed Giles appeared, running his hands through his rumpled hair.

'My God, you're all unspeakable . . . after all she's done for you . . .' she began and then thought better of it. 'Please, Giles. She's going to die at this rate.'

Seaton's head appeared round his door.

'Where's the fire?' he grinned.

'This isn't a game. Please help me.' Polly was begging. Even Giles and Seaton became aware of the desperation in her voice. Giles flung a coat over his pyjamas and loped towards the stairs. 'We need a stretcher, Seaton.'

'There's a screen in my room,' Seaton said, practical for perhaps the first time in his life.

Carrying the finely painted canvas screen between them, Polly and Seaton went to Juniper's room to find Sophia ineffectually wandering around, rubbing her hands together as if she was washing them in invisible water. 'She's dying.' She swung around to face Polly. 'I sense it. I've always been sensitive to such matters,' she added dramatically.

'Stop talking such rubbish. She's going to be all right, I know she is,' Polly said sharply, sounding far more confident than she felt. She tore a blanket from the bed, folded it and placed it on top of the screen. Sophia followed her across the room with a pillow. 'No pillow,' Polly said briskly, 'we must keep her flat,' and she silently thanked God for her weeks in France helping to ferry the wounded.

'The car's outside, Miss Bossy Boots,' Giles said, entering the room. 'Bloody hell!' he exclaimed at the sight of Juniper, who was moaning and had begun to stir. As she did so a small trickle of blood appeared at the corner of her mouth.

'Quick. Gently now . . .' Polly instructed as, with difficulty, they lifted Juniper on to the screen.

From outside there was a huge explosion. The windows shattered, paintings fell from the walls. The two men stared at each other with terror and looked as if they were about to drop Juniper. 'It's only a bomb; come on, it's exploded, it can't hurt us now.' Polly held the door open wide and the two men gingerly manhandled the makeshift stretcher out into the corridor.

By this time Maureen and Pam had appeared, woken by the commotion, and were fluttering about with concern, trying to help with the stretcher as they slowly negotiated the staircase.

Outside, the car was covered in rubble, the windscreen shattered.

'You can't drive that, look, there's no windscreen,' said Giles, puffing from the unusual amount of exertion.

'That won't stop us. In any case, I'm not driving, you are,' Polly said as another wave of Heinkels droned overhead. Another stick of bombs fell, but they were streets away.

'Not bloody likely, not in this. Come on, Giles, it's not safe out here,' and to the women's astonishment the two men lowered Juniper to the ground and scuttled back up the steps into the house.

'Men!' Polly spat out the word.

'I hate the whole stinking lot of them, bloody useless when you most needs 'em. Call yourselves men?' Maureen shouted after them. 'Come on, Pam, give me a hand. Let's get her into the back of the car.'

The two girls were far stronger than they looked and quite deftly, given the circumstances, managed to settle Juniper on the back seat, covered her with a blanket and sat either side of her, like bookends, supporting her.

Juniper looked worse. Her pallor was ashen and a thin veil of sweat covered her face. Her eyes looked dazed as if gauze was covering them. Polly put the car in gear and, one hand on the horn, negotiated the fallen masonry with skill and sped up the road.

It was a nightmare drive to the hospital: bombs falling, streets blocked from collapsed houses, burst water mains, fires. Every possible catastrophe seemed to present itself. Polly was not panicking now but was expertly, and with commendable coolness, driving towards the hospital, a small private clinic in Devonshire Place. The doctor was already waiting with a porter, two nurses and a proper trolley. As the professionals took over, Polly stood on the pavement, ashen faced herself. Maureen put her arms around her.

'There, there, love. She's in good hands now. Let's go and get a cuppa, you've had a nasty shock.'

'Oh no, I must stay with Juniper.' Leaving the car with its doors wide open, and the two girls, she sped after the medical staff.

Polly's wait in the corridor seemed to last a lifetime.

She sat impotently watching as nurses rushed in and out of Juniper's room. The first doctor was followed by a second. A few minutes later a third came running. Their sense of urgency fuelled her terror.

A young nurse noticed her, and called one of the doctors who advised her to lie down. Polly refused. They gave her sweet tea which she did not want, but the nurse stood over her as if she were a child, until she had drunk it. Eventually Juniper's own doctor appeared.

'Are you Polly?'

'Yes, Polly Frobisher.'

'I thought so, Lady Copton keeps calling for you and someone called Hal. Does the name mean anything to you?'

'Can I see her?' Polly jumped to her feet, ignoring the question.

'Shortly. There are some questions you might be able to answer. Lady Copton drank, I presume, everyone does these days. But how much?'

'The odd brandy . . .' Polly began and then sense prevailed. Lying to protect her would be no help to Juniper. 'It's only a guess, you realize, but nearly a bottle of brandy a day and then there's the champagne. She is going to be all right, isn't she?'

'We're going to have to operate and I think you should call her next of kin to come.'

'Oh no!' Polly's hand shot to her mouth at the implication. She looked at the doctor, he had to know, she was not betraying Juniper, she was helping her. 'Doctor, there's something else. I'm certain she takes drugs too – not often but, well, I've seen some – a white powder,' she added lamely, wishing now that she had asked Juniper what the substance was.

'The silly girl,' he shook his head. 'Why do they do it?'

'Doctor Wilday.' A nurse's head poked round the door. 'Please come,' she called.

'Please wait here, Miss Frobisher.'

But Polly didn't, she rushed after the doctor. Juniper was as white as the sheet on which she lay. Polly crossed to the bed and took Juniper's hand.

'Is she a Roman Catholic?' Doctor Wilday asked Polly after a whispered conference with the other doctors.

'I don't know. I don't think so. She never said. Maybe she is. Why?' she said, her voice rising with her anxiety.

'We feel we should call a priest, just in case she's a Catholic.' The matron stepped forward and took hold of Polly's arm as if to support her. 'We think perhaps she should have the last rites,' Matron whispered.

'Bugger the last rites!' Everyone swung round. Somehow, God alone knew how, Juniper was smiling at them. 'You keep the priests away from me, Polly, you promise,' she croaked.

Both grandmothers travelled to London.

Annie had proved a problem, dissolving into paroxysms of tears at the idea of Alice leaving her. Alice had had to promise the sobbing child she would return safely. This she hated to do, fearing that, in such uncertain times and especially with Gertie sharing the driving, such a promise was tempting fate.

They were exhausted when they rang the doorbell of Juniper's house in the small hours of the morning. The door was immediately thrown open by Polly, as if she had been standing waiting on the other side.

'Both of you,' she spread her arms in welcome. 'Thank you for coming.'

'We thought, given the hour, it was best to come here first rather than go to the hospital,' Alice explained anxiously, fearing that they might be too late.

'She's safely through the operation. I telephoned again at midnight and she was sleeping peacefully.'

'Thank God,' Alice and Gertie said in unison. On the floor above, a door opened and there was momentarily the sound of music and laughter.

'We'll be best off in the kitchen, it's warmer there,' Polly said, not explaining the noise. 'You must need some tea or something.'

'The "something" sounds preferable to tea,' Gertie said accompanied by her familiar hoot.

In the kitchen, Polly found them port, biscuits and cheese.

'Now, Polly. What happened?'

Polly explained about Juniper's collapse and the race to the hospital. But she did not mention the drinking or the drugs.

'An ulcer, you say?' Alice looked at her enquiringly.

'Yes, it perforated and she bled a lot.'

'Good gracious, who ever heard of a young gal of twenty-four with an ulcer?' Gertie shook her head with disbelief.

'Tell me, Polly, has Juniper been drinking excessively?' Alice asked. Polly looked away embarrassed. 'I know you don't want to tell me, that it would make you feel disloyal. But I must know.'

'Yes, Mrs Whitaker. Rather a lot, I'm afraid.'

Gertie and Alice looked knowingly at each other across the kitchen table.

'Just as she did over that sad miscarriage business,' Gertie said to Alice.

'And this time I suppose it was because of Harry?' Alice probed gently.

'She was deeply upset by it all, yes,' Polly replied.

'If only she had let me help. If only she would listen to others. But Juniper always knows best. I would have fought the Coptons myself, had I known what the outcome was going to be.'

'And have yourself declared unfit as well? A pretty kettle of fish that would have been.' Gertie wrestled with the large fox fur around her neck, the clasp of which had somehow got entangled in her hair. 'You mark my words, Alice. That Copton creature – her father was in trade you know, blood will always out – that woman is capable of anything, she would have dug up all the unfortunate things in your past, Alice, I can assure you of that.'

'It seems so wrong to fight over a child. Divorce is sad enough . . . The boy doesn't even know me.' Alice sipped thoughtfully at her port, her expression bleak; her whole life had been scarred by incomplete relationships with those close to her by birth. She suddenly felt totally exhausted and she wanted to be alone. 'If you could show me my room, Polly? I think I'd like to try to get a little sleep.'

'I'm afraid you're in the attics, in the servants' old quarters.'

'The attics?' Gertie sounded astonished.

'It's quieter there.'

'Unless the bombs fall,' Gertie said with another hoot. 'That port's made me feel quite alert. If you don't mind I think I could do with something a little more substantial to eat. I'll be up in a short time, Alice.'

'I'll cook you something, Grandmama.'

'No, no, I can manage. I'm very capable these days, you know – the cook left, her feet . . .' she said in vague explanation.

Polly returned from showing Alice to her room to find Gertie busily scrambling eggs.

'We brought these from Gwenfer, and some rations. Alice and I don't wish to be a burden.'

Polly cleared a space at the end of the table, pushing her leather writing case to one side, putting on top a pile of official buff enveloped letters, bound with a red ribbon.

'Am I to hope such a large pile of correspondence indicates a new interest in your young life?' Gertie asked a shade archly as she placed a plate of eggs in front of Polly.

'These? Oh, no. They're from Jonathan Middlebank. I keep in touch, he likes getting letters from home.'

'You're a kind forgiving girl, Polly.'

'It works both ways. I like getting letters too, even heavily censored ones.'

'I see,' Gertie said, smiling knowingly. 'Now tell me everything – no secrets, Polly.'

Polly, who had not eaten all day, suddenly realized she was ravenous. She quickly took a mouthful of food. 'I'm so glad you're here, Grandmama. Juniper's been behaving strangely for some time. She rarely goes out. She totally ignores the raids. She pulled the blinds down a good year ago and hasn't opened them since.'

'Hasn't she tried to get work?'

'No. She does nothing.'

'No wonder she's been drinking so much. Always a sad creature, Juniper. All that money, but somewhat lacking in inner resources, I've always felt. But where on earth is Juniper getting such quantities of alcohol from? No one else can.'

'She bought masses when we first arrived from people selling up their cellars. And one thing I'm learning in this war, Grandmother, is that if you're rich you can get anything.'

'So unfair. Doubtless the silly girl paid inflated prices, just to ruin her health.'

'There's something else. I don't know whether to tell Mrs Whitaker or not. When we all thought she was dying she called for Hal.'

'Good Lord.' Gertie's knife clattered on to her plate. 'That would never do, most unsuitable,' she said, as if speaking to herself. She leant across and patted Polly's hand. 'Best say nothing to anyone, my dear.'

The kitchen clock struck three.

'Bed, Grandmama? You must be so tired.'

'A little. Perhaps it would be a good idea.'

With what she realized was somewhat impolite haste, Polly ushered Gertie out of the kitchen and, carrying her bags, led the way up the stairs. She sped up to the first floor, past the drawing room, hoping Gertie would not notice any noise, and up a further flight and then another to the attic floor. Her grandmother settled, Polly flung herself on to her own bed fully clothed and was almost immediately asleep.

11

The three women were at the hospital by ten the next morning. Alice and Gertie were horrified by Juniper's appearance. Polly had warned them that she had lost a lot of weight, but had not prepared them sufficiently for how much. Polly, on the other hand, was relieved to see her friend looking so much better.

'Juniper, you're the only person I know who could have a tube sticking out of her nose and still look beautiful,' Polly said happily.

Juniper smiled and patted the sticking plaster on her cheek which was keeping the tube in place. 'I'm going to make it the latest fashion accessory.' She smiled, although it was a pale imitation of her usual one.

'They didn't tell me you were having to have blood.' Alice looked anxiously at the bottle hanging above Juniper's bed and seemed mesmerized by the thick drops that dripped with the regularity of a pulse down another tube and into Juniper's arm.

'I feel like a vampire,' Juniper said, chuckling hoarsely.

'Oh, my poor darling,' a tear escaped from Alice's eye and she hurriedly brushed it away, but not quickly enough.

'Don't cry, Grandmama,' Juniper said. 'I've been incredibly stupid, but I've also been incredibly lucky. I'll be fine.'

'As soon as the doctor says you can move, you're coming home with me,' Alice said, sitting gently on the side of the bed. 'I'm going to make you better, put some weight on you.'

'I'd like that,' Juniper laid her head contentedly on the pillow. 'Christmas at Gwenfer, that would be wonderful.'

Anxious not to tire her, they left after half an hour. Alice asked to see the doctor, but afterwards almost wished she hadn't. He assured them that Juniper would recover but . . . It was the 'but' that filled Alice with fear. Unless her granddaughter changed her lifestyle dramatically the doctor could not rule out a recurrence. The next time she could die, he warned.

'But why does she live this way?' Alice asked later as they sat in a restaurant waiting to be served, her fingers nervously tearing at a bread roll on her plate.

'I should have been sterner with her,' Polly said lamely.

'Don't blame yourself, Polly. My granddaughter has always done exactly what she wants – all her life.' Alice was now rolling the bread into small pellets on the linen tablecloth.

'Polly, you must tell us everything,' Gertie said, with the certainty of one who knows she will be obeyed.

'What else could there be?' Alice enquired.

'There are other noxious substances which could be damaging her, Alice,' Gertie explained.

Polly looked anxiously across the restaurant, willing the waiter to serve them and stop her grandmother's questions.

'Right, loves, what you want?'

They all looked up at the young, rather scruffy waiter. Gertie glared at him.

'I'd like the pâté and a lightly grilled lamb chop, please,' Alice said politely.

'One or the other, love.' The waiter tapped his pencil impatiently against his pad.

'We're only allowed one course, Mrs Whitaker, unless you want oysters or caviare – they're not covered by rationing.'

'Oh, I see. Then the chop will do beautifully.'

'For me too,' Gertie added.

'And me,' Polly followed suit.

'Drink, loves?'

'No thank you. And I should be obliged if you would

refrain from presuming that I'm your love, young man,' Gertie said sternly. 'And why isn't he in the army, I wonder?' she added, suspiciously, and glared angrily at his retreating back. 'Um, flat feet – look,' and the others craned their necks to see the flat-footed waiter plod towards the kitchen.

'I suppose they have to take who they can in wartime,' Alice said, with her usual reasonableness.

'Then they might teach them not to call the clientele "love" – it's offensive.'

'I don't know, I think I rather like it.'

'Alice!' Gertie exclaimed with exasperation. Polly looked from one to the other with amusement, relaxed now, thinking the moment of danger was over. 'I'm talking about drugs, Polly,' Gertie said, suddenly turning to face her. 'A friend of mine became tragically addicted to belladonna,' she said earnestly.

'Oh, I don't know anything about belladonna,' Polly could say truthfully, vaguely remembering Victorian heroines in books using it. 'Her friends don't help,' she added and, deftly sidetracking her grandmother, she launched into an angry explanation about those 'guests' who for months now had been a constant source of irritation to her.

Later Polly took the two women to the cinema to take their minds off the worry for a couple of hours. The film was *Mrs Miniver* which Polly liked so much that she had seen it three times. Alice loved it but Gertie found it bourgeois and trite.

'Far better to read a good book,' she was saying as Polly opened the front door for them. A burst of loud laughter sounded above them. 'And what is that, pray?' she asked, sweeping towards the staircase without removing her hat and coat. Alice followed quickly and Polly trailed anxiously behind them.

Gertie flung open the double doors of the drawing room. There were about twenty people in the smoke laden room. From the gramophone the music, *You'll never know* . . . was blaring into the room. The party was small by Juniper's standards. News of her illness was now widespread and those who cared about her had stayed away. The countess leapt agilely to her feet and swept towards them, hands outstretched.

'You must be Juniper's beloved grandmother,' she gushed, taking Gertie's hands in both of hers and pumping them energetically.

'I'm Gertrude Frobisher. This is Mrs Whitaker,' Gertie said, extricating her hands with an expression of distaste.

'My dear Mrs Whitaker, I am Juniper's friend, Sophia von Michelberg.' Sophia, almost pushing Gertie to one side, grabbed Alice by the hand and pulled her towards her. 'Dear Juniper has told me so much about you. Come, talk to me, tell me how the dear child is.' Alice was pulled reluctantly across the room and shepherded to a sofa. The countess sank down beside her, still holding her hand. Sophia had the ability to create an immediate intimacy with whoever she was speaking to. Invariably these were people whom she felt were important to her, the rich or those with contacts. She would lean close to her subject, speaking with a whispered intensity which immediately made that person appear to be in league with her, and against all others in the room.

'Poor Mrs Whitaker, everything must be such a worry for you. I've tried, how I've tried.' She momentarily let go of Alice's hand and clasped her own together as if in prayer. 'I've spent hours with that poor child, trying to show her the error of her ways. And now . . .' Dramatically she took Alice's hand again, 'I've failed you and dear, sweet Juniper.'

'You must not blame yourself,' Alice said rather stiffly.

'Oh, but I do. I do.' Sophia moved even closer. 'I've tried to be a mother to her.' The soft, accented words hissed out.

Across the room Gertie watched the tableau on the sofa and snorted loudly.

'I've seen that type before,' she said, turning to Polly.

'Middle European, poor as a church mouse, undoubtedly titled, has been assiduously worming her way into Juniper's confidence.'

'Good gracious, how did you know all that?'

'Life, dear Polly. One grows antennae,' and Gertie moved regally towards Alice. Taking up a position at the side of the sofa, her arms folded, feet firmly planted, Gertie stared impassively down like the guardian of a Pharaoh's tomb.

'I haven't been able to sleep with concern,' Sophia continued, rewarding Gertie with an irritated glance.

'And no doubt the noise has kept you awake.'

'Noise? I'm afraid I don't understand, Mrs Whitaker.'

'This noise,' and Alice stood up, shrugging off Sophia's soft pink hand. She walked to the gramophone and lifted the needle. As the music stopped, the couples dancing slid to a halt and looked expectantly around them. Sophia jumped up looking agitated.

Alice clapped her hands for silence. 'With Juniper lying ill in hospital, I feel this is no time for a party. I think I should tell you that there will be no more parties, so you had better look elsewhere for your entertainment.' One by one the partygoers sheepishly left the room, saying nothing until they were safely out of the door where they erupted into audibly disgruntled comments.

Only Maureen and Pam, Seaton and Giles and Sophia remained. Alice swung round to face them.

'As for you people, how could you live here and see what was happening to my granddaughter and not help her?'

'But I told you, Mrs Whitaker, I did all I could, she wouldn't listen,' Sophia whined.

'Quite honestly, I don't believe you. Polly was the only one of you who did anything, the only one of you with any decency.' Alice ignored the objections being raised. 'I want you all to vacate these premises, first thing,' Alice ordered. Polly was astonished; this was Alice in a temper, something she had thought never to see. But being Alice, it wasn't a shouting, raging temper, but a dignified, controlled anger.

'I'll be destitute.'

'I doubt it, Countess. I'm sure you've managed to feather your nest quite adequately at my granddaughter's expense. And no doubt,' she turned to the young men, 'you are quite capable of wheedling your way into the confidence of some other naïve person.'

'This isn't your house – you've no right to speak to us in this way,' Giles tried to bluster.

'I have every right. I have the protection of my granddaughter to consider. If you're not out of this house by noon tomorrow, I shall call the police. I'm sure they will be most interested to find out who has been supplying this household with drugs. Now, if you don't mind, I'd rather you went to your rooms.'

'That statement is slanderous,' Sophia swung round. Her mouth was twitching, her eyebrows fluttering, her hair loosened. Her beads clicked, her bangles jangled, her stole slipped from her shoulders scattering feathers as she twirled and her taffeta skirt swished. Everything about her was in agitated motion.

'Not when it's the truth,' Alice said with a deceptive calmness that silenced the countess.

'Well, we've had a good run for our money,' Maureen said shrugging her shoulders, and she joined the others who were leaving the room chattering indignantly.

Alice crossed to the drinks table and poured herself a large brandy while Polly clapped enthusiastically

'Wonderful, Mrs Whitaker. You were marvellous.'

Alice's shoulders slumped and she sat down heavily on the nearest chair.

'I don't feel very marvellous.'

'Did you know about the drugs, Polly?' Gertie asked angrily.

'Yes. I did.' Polly hung her head in shame.

'Did we not explain that we have to know everything if Juniper is to be helped? Don't you see, Polly?'

'Yes, Grandmama. I'm sorry.' Polly felt herself blushing that her stupid loyalty had been found out. 'But how did you know about the drugs, Mrs Whitaker? Who told you?' she asked avoiding her grandmother's stern gaze.

Alice looked up at Polly with a sad expression. 'It was their eyes. When I met the countess and those young men, I knew immediately. My daughter Grace, Juniper's mother . . .' but she couldn't finish the sentence, could not, even after all these years, admit out loud that her own daughter had been an addict. She shuddered at the prospect of history repeating itself.

Chapter Two

1

Gwenfer was a house which the evergreen garlands of Christmas suited well. The great hall with its hammer beam roof, plain white walls and the large granite fireplace, with the banners and arms of the Tregowans as its only decoration, lost its austere beauty when Christmas came. Long looped fronds of holly and ivy were swathed around the walls. A twelve-foot pine tree decorated with cream candles, tinsel, and balls of gold and silver stood in one corner and giant bowls full of painted pine cones were placed down the centre of the refectory table. The hall looked like a mature and graceful woman decked in jewels for a ball.

Alice stepped back from adjusting the last ribbon of tinsel on the tree and smiled at the eager faces of the evacuees. 'What do you think?'

'It's lovely, Mrs Whitaker. I've seen trees like that in Oxford Street, but we never had nothing like that at home,' May explained solemnly.

'It doesn't look like a tree any more, it's a magic tree now.' Annie's eyes were wide with wonder as she slipped her hand into Alice's. In the first years of the war Gertie and Alice had not decorated the house, it seemed the wrong thing to do when people were dying not only in Europe but in the houses and cities of England. But they both felt that the war might go on for ever and the children had never had Christmas decorations, so this fourth Christmas together they relented for the sake of the evacuees.

Gertie bustled in from the small parlour where for the last hour or two she had been engrossed in wrapping presents, using a roll of old wallpaper she had found at the back of a cupboard. It had been difficult finding suitable presents for the children. Toys were scarce in the shops and so they had cajoled Zac into making wooden boats for the boys. Alice had embroidered a pyjama sachet for May, made from an old blouse she never wore, and Gertie had made her a frilly petticoat using a nightdress from Edwardian times which was heavy with lace. They both knew May would never before have possessed such a luxurious garment.

The greatest disappointment was Annie's present. For months, in a window of a toy shop in Penzance there had been a large teddy bear with a blue satin bow. Annie had been fascinated by the bear but when Alice tried to buy it the shop owner had told her it was not for sale. Alice was furious when, a few weeks before Christmas, they found the bear had been sold, for an inflated price. She was angry that the shop keeper, knowing her interest, had not contacted her. But she was even more angry at the assumption that she would not have wanted to spend so much on Annie, an evacuee. There were some who showed a marked prejudice towards the evacuees, an attitude neither she nor Gertie understood. But Alice's fury was nothing compared with Annie's uncontrollable grief the day she found the bear was no longer there.

Both Alice and Gertie had tried everywhere to find another one but with no success. There was nothing for it but to try and make one. Alice took out a rarely worn nutria-fur coat and from it attempted to make a cuddly toy bear. The result looked more like a buffalo than a teddy, so Gertie made Annie a cloth doll as well, with clothes that could be taken off, in case she was disappointed.

Alice herself was as excited as the children as Christmas approached. On Christmas Eve, Phillip was returning for two precious weeks. The day before Juniper telephoned to say that Polly had managed to obtain a week's leave and that she had been discharged from the hospital. They would arrive by train also on Christmas Eve. It would be the first time since the war began that they would all be together.

For weeks Alice and Gertie had been hoarding food, saving their coupons for as many luxuries as they could find. They had three large chickens which they had been fattening up and, though Alice dreaded the day they would be killed, she steeled her heart, for this Christmas was going to be a memorable one for all of them.

Phillip arrived in the late morning by road and Alice was horrified by his appearance. He had lost a considerable amount of weight since he was last home and looked beaten with exhaustion. He was nearly seventy, and should not be working the long hours he told them about, Alice thought.

'But Phillip, there must be thousands of artists who could advise them on their wretched camouflage. Why you?' Alice asked, fussing about him as he sat in the wing chair in front of the parlour fire.

'The young are fighting, even the middle-aged are now, there's only the old duffers like myself left.' He smiled down at her as she knelt in front of the fire and put his hand out to touch her, marvelling that it was possible to love someone so much.

'It's not fair, Phillip. You didn't look this tired when you were last home three months ago. I don't think you should go back.' Alice sat back on her haunches and looked up at him, her beautiful face marred with anxiety.

'We'll see,' he said gently, a sad expression on his face which worried her even more. 'For the time being, if you've got some soup or something, I'm rather hungry,' he said apologetically.

'My darling, I'm sorry. I was so busy worrying about you that I forgot you must be starving. Eat here in the warmth – the dining room is still freezing cold even though I've had a fire in there for two days. Don't move,' she ordered as she got to her feet and left the room, happy to be doing something for him.

'How's she managing with the evacuees? Not doing too much, I hope?' he asked Gertie, who had been sitting silently on the window seat. Gertie crossed the room and stood looking down at him.

'What's wrong, Phillip? You can't fool me. You're ill.'

'I've got cancer,' he said simply.

'How long?'

'Six months, a year if I'm lucky.'

'No operation?'

'No.'

'I see,' Gertie said, squaring her shoulders as she faced this information.

'I don't want Alice to know. She'll worry. It wouldn't be fair.'

'It would be less fair not to tell her.'

'I don't want her distressed.'

'She will be more so if you keep this dreadful secret. Alice has weathered many problems in her life, she would want to share this one with you.'

'I don't know,' Phillip said doubtfully.

'Well I do. But not now. Let her enjoy Christmas, she's looked forward to it so much. Tell her afterwards.'

'How's Juniper?' Phillip asked, leaning forward and poking the fire in a desultory way.

'Alice thinks she's fine – the operation was a complete success and she feels Juniper has learnt her lesson and will not return to her former wild ways. I have my doubts. She's unstable, Phillip. Until she has stability in her life, I fear the worst.'

'Poor Alice. She doesn't deserve all these problems. There's no justice in life, Gertie.'

'Sadly, no. But if anyone can overcome such injustice, it's Alice.'

'Juniper hates me, did you know, Gertie?'

'I wouldn't say "hates", that's far too strong a word. She's jealous of you. She wants Alice all to herself – not to live with, you understand, but always to be there at her beck and call when and if she wants her. A very selfish young woman, but then, when you think of her upbringing . . .' Gertie spoke briskly. Her sharp ears had caught the clink of cutlery, and she put her finger to her lips and crossed quickly to the door. Alice brought in a tray with soup, freshly baked bread and most of her personal butter ration for Phillip.

Polly and Juniper's taxi from Penzance drew up in time for tea. Juniper looked radiant. She had put on weight; no alcohol and rest in the hospital had brought back her good looks, and she was bursting with energy.

'Oh, it's so wonderful to be back. Home!' She threw her arms up in the air and twirled around with happiness.

'We would have been here earlier, but Juniper insisted on going shopping,' Polly said, laughing from behind a large pile of boxes she had carried in from the taxi, helped by the driver. She laid them on the refectory table, kissed everyone hello and went back to the car for the rest of the parcels.

Gertie looked suspiciously at the large turkey, the ham and an enormous box of chocolates.

'Not black-market, I trust?' she said, her back stiff with disapproval.

'No, Lady Gertie, those were presents to me, I promise you. I have friends in the American army. It's wonderful what they can get hold of and I get lots of parcels from America. Oh Grandmama, the tree looks beautiful, it's going to be the most marvellous Christmas. Come on, Polly, we've got to wrap these presents in secret. Oh, isn't it all thrilling?' She turned towards the staircase where Annie was sitting on one of the treads solemnly watching the grown-ups in the hall.

'Little Annie. And how are you?' Juniper smiled at the child who looked as if she were not sure how to react, so she put her thumb in her mouth instead. 'You wait until you see what Father Christmas has got for you. Come on, Polly, do!' and Juniper was racing up the stairs, two at a time, as if she had never been ill in her life.

*

The carol singers had been, they had feasted on mince pies and mulled wine, the children were in bed, the candles on the Christmas tree were glowing and the only other light was from the log fire and the two oil lamps which Alice had brought into the great hall. It had been a perfect evening. They were sitting contentedly, knowing they should go to bed, but all of them too comfortable and relaxed to make the effort.

'If only Harry were here, it would all be perfect, wouldn't it?' Alice said dreamily.

Her words created a complete silence. Alice looked up and immediately realized her error. Juniper's expression had changed as if a shutter had been pulled down across her face.

'Juniper, I'm so sorry. I didn't think . . . I shouldn't have said . . .' Alice said feeling guilty and flustered.

'I don't know what you mean, Grandmama. You talk as if he's dead, for goodness sake. I wouldn't want him here.' Juniper laughed harshly and shook her head as if in defiance. 'Let's go to church, to Midnight Mass.' She jumped to her feet. 'Come on, you're all going to sleep.'

'You should be going to bed, Juniper, not leaping up the cliff to church,' Alice said, relieved at the change of subject and stretching comfortably in her chair.

'Oh, do come on, all of you,' Juniper cajoled.

'Not me, Juniper, it's too cold out there for my old bones.' Gertie moved closer to the fire.

'Grandmama, come with me, do.' Juniper held out her hand and looked appealingly at Alice.

'I never go to church, Juniper, you know I don't and I don't think it's right just to use it for glamorous, sentimental times like Christmas,' Alice said reasonably.

'Phillip?' asked Juniper and Polly noticed that she was tapping her foot almost imperceptibly. Polly felt herself holding her breath.

'No, thank you, Juniper. I'm far too content here,' and he leant over and gently stroked Alice's hair. She turned and smiled at him, her love for him plain for all to see.

'Well, there's only you left, Polly.' Juniper swung round to face her, her eyes shining dangerously.

'I don't think so,' Polly replied, sensing that Juniper was about to make problems.

'Oh gee, you always do what everyone else wants, never what I want,' Juniper said, her usually low voice rising with irritation.

'Juniper, that's not kind to Polly,' Alice admonished.

'It's all right, Mrs Whitaker. Juniper's tired, that's all.'

'I'm not tired. I want to go to church and I don't want to go on my own. You're being selfish, Polly.'

Phillip sighed and looked deep into the fire as if searching for a solution. Nothing had changed, he feared. Alice's hand searched for her pearls which she twisted. Gertie frowned and Polly stood up.

'I'm sorry if you think I'm being selfish. I don't want to go. There's no point in my going.'

'Don't be such a bore, it's only a ceremony.'

'It isn't. It's worshipping a God I can't believe in – not a God who would allow the horror that's going on in the world. Not a God who kills young men before they've even begun to live . . .' Polly said with feeling.

'Polly, oh I'm sorry. Forgive me.' Juniper rushed to Polly and flung her arms about her. 'Typical of me, I didn't think, what a selfish fool I am.' She turned to face the others. 'I apologize, everyone. I'm over-excited, that's my problem – getting out of that dreadful prison of a hospital.' She was laughing now. 'Hot chocolate, that's what this reformed Juniper needs. Anyone else want some?' She smiled at them and everyone relaxed again into the comfort of their chairs.

2

Goods were scarce but for the rich, such as Juniper, gifts were easier to find.

All morning the children had been prodding and

poking the large pile of gaudily wrapped parcels set out under the tree. It was with the utmost difficulty that Alice had persuaded them to go to their rooms to wash and change for luncheon.

They usually ate all together in the stillroom, which was small and easy to heat, but for today Alice had opened up the dining room. The evacuees looked about them with awe at the unfamiliar large panelled room, the sideboard groaning with silver, the long table set with the best silver and crystal. Mealtimes were usually noisy affairs, but the children, overwhelmed by the grand room, sat silent and ate with a forced politeness that amused Alice and at which Gertie nodded her approval as everyone tucked into the unaccustomedly large and rich meal.

Alice had been worried about serving drinks over Christmas, feeling it might be safer for Juniper if they had none. But, as Gertie had pointed out, Juniper could not expect to spend the rest of her life attending dinners and lunches where no alcohol was served. After all, the doctors had not banned her from drinking completely – moderation, they had advised. After the meal Alice wondered why she had worried. Juniper had only had a couple of glasses of watered wine. She had declined brandy afterwards but instead accepted half a small glass of port. Alice allowed herself to relax.

The present-opening was a riot of paper, screaming children and exclamations of pleasure at the gifts, especially the magnificent ones from Juniper. Juniper sorted out the presents, using the children as postmen. When Annie was given Alice's gift, she tore impatiently at the wrapping.

'A bear!' she squealed.

'You've got a good imagination.' Phillip chuckled at the sight of the strange animal with a large blue satin bow around its thick neck, but Annie was already burrowed into Alice's arms thanking her.

Ten minutes later she was opening the large box which

was Juniper's present to her. Inside was the finest teddy bear any of them had ever seen, dressed in a splendid red waistcoat.

'Thank you very much, Juniper,' Annie said politely. 'He's lovely,' she went on, clutching Alice's animal to her and leaving the immaculate teddy in its box.

'Well, you obviously prefer my grandmother's gift to mine,' Juniper said, with a stiff smile. Phillip thought it petulance, but Polly knew it was from hurt.

'Alice made him,' Annie explained simply, clutching the bear to her tightly.

'I think a little girl like you should call my grandmother Mrs Whitaker, don't you?' Juniper was still smiling, but her words were icy.

Annie, looking perplexed, turned towards Alice.

'Of course you can call me Alice, Annie.' Then turning to Juniper, 'It was the name she called me the first time she spoke.'

'Well, I think it's wrong and disrespectful.' Juniper was pale with suppressed anger. The others began to shift uncomfortably. Annie stood, thumb in mouth, looking from one to the other. Alice picked her up and placed her on her lap, stroking her fine blonde hair.

'I have all the respect I need, Juniper. You're not to worry.' Alice smiled sweetly at her granddaughter. In the background Phillip looked at Gertie, exasperation on his face, and poured himself another drink.

After several games of charades, hunt the thimble and snap, the exhausted children were led away to bed by Flo. Alice went to tuck them in and kiss them goodnight as she did every night. One by one she attended to them, smoothing the sheets, listening patiently to what they had to say until it was Annie's turn. Annie flung her arms round Alice's neck and kissed her.

'I love you, Mrs Wh-it-a-ker,' she stammered.

'I love you too. But I told you, call me Alice. I like it.'

'Miss Juniper will be angry with me.'

'No, she won't. Look at the lovely present she gave you.

She loves you too.' Alice bent down and picked up the bear Juniper had given the child which had slipped on to the floor. She tucked it in beside Annie. 'There, a bear either side, you look like Goldilocks,' she said, laughing. 'Goodnight, my sweetheart,' and she moved gracefully across the room and switched out the light.

As the door closed Annie threw Juniper's bear back on to the floor and cuddled up close to Alice's.

Alice loathed to play bridge, so Polly went in search of Juniper to make up a four. She tapped gently on Juniper's door.

'Who is it?' she heard Juniper call.

'Me,' she replied, pushing the door open. Juniper moved quickly to hide something behind her back, but not fast enough. It was a bottle of brandy. 'Juniper, no!' Polly said, her voice full of the disappointment she felt.

'You shouldn't barge into people's rooms like that,' Juniper said, on the defensive.

'I didn't. You called out.'

'I didn't say "Come in" did I? It's your own fault, if you had waited *politely* you needn't have found out.'

'Oh, Juniper, you don't understand anything, do you? I'm glad I've found out.'

'So that you can begin to nag me again, I suppose. Happy days!' Juniper pulled a face.

'Why is it when anyone disagrees with you, it's nagging? Can't you see that people don't want you to be ill again, or kill yourself?'

'Who'd care?'

It was the sulky tone of Juniper's voice, reminding her of a spoilt child, which annoyed Polly. 'Oh, for goodness' sake, Juniper, stop talking like that and feeling sorry for yourself. You sound like a child who always has to be the centre of attention,' she said with sharp irritation.

Juniper sat down with a bump on the dressing stool, a shocked expression on her face.

'You've never spoken to me like that before.'

'Maybe it's a pity I haven't. Perhaps I should have spoken my mind sooner.'

'You haven't finished then?' Juniper said, yawning ostentatiously. This only increased Polly's anger.

'No, I haven't. Your grandmother has worked hard to give these poor children a wonderful Christmas. Then you try to undo it all just because you're jealous. It's undignified of you and, quite honestly, it's also pathetic.'

'But . . .'

'The grandmothers have looked forward to this Christmas and I'm not going to stand back and allow your selfishness to ruin everything. That's all. I've said my piece.' Polly stood in the middle of the room, her heart thumping, shocked herself at the way she had spoken.

There was a long silence. Juniper sat still, staring at her reflection in the mirror. 'Finished?'

'Well, yes.'

'I'm glad that's all then.' Juniper began to laugh. 'You go pink when you're angry, did you know?' She swung round on the dressing stool. 'Am I really so awful?'

'Sometimes, yes,' Polly said stoically. She'd gone so far now, there was no point in pretending.

'You're not alone. I don't like myself much either.'

'I didn't say I disliked you, Juniper. I love you and that's why I thought it time I spoke out. Is this the only bottle?'

Juniper said nothing.

'Oh Juniper, you're impossible. Where did you get it? You didn't buy it in London.'

'The cellar, of course. My grandfather, Lincoln, laid down a good cellar. My sainted step-grandfather hardly drinks. It seemed a shame, all those lovely bottles going to waste.'

'Drinking won't solve anything and will break your grandmother's heart.'

Juniper held the bottle of brandy out to her. 'Take it, then. I won't touch another drop. Throw it away.'

Polly took the bottle.

'Why, Juniper? Why do you want to destroy yourself all the time?'

Juniper shrugged her shoulders. 'I don't know, Polly. But you're right, you're always right.' She was smiling now, she could afford to. Hidden in her wardrobe were another two bottles. She jumped up. 'I tell you what, I'll be absolutely sweet to dear little Annie and then you'll all love me again, won't you?' She put her arm round Polly. 'You're such a good friend to me, aren't you?'

Polly had been standing taut with anxiety, but, lulled by Juniper's promises, she allowed her body to slump with relief.

Juniper kept her word. Each day over the Christmas period she searched Annie out. She suggested outings, she lavished presents on her, she offered to read to her, but each time Annie backed away and said nothing, just stood and stared.

'You see, the ungrateful kid doesn't want to be friends with me,' Juniper said with exasperation, when Annie had silently refused a walk, but five minutes later rushed excitedly off to find her coat when Polly suggested one.

'I think she's frightened of you.'

'But I'm sweetness itself to her.'

'Maybe she senses you don't really mean it. Children are like animals, they can sense things, read our minds.'

'Gee, Polly, what tosh you talk. Well, I'm getting bored with the whole silly game. If the brat doesn't want to know me, that's fine by me.' And Juniper went in search of a book to read while Polly and Annie set out on their walk.

It was New Year's Eve. Polly felt a mixture of happiness and sadness. It would be 1944 – a year Andrew would never see, and yet she would be glad to see the back of 1943, the saddest year of her life.

'Why are you sad, Miss Polly?' Annie looked up at her curiously as they made their way down the valley towards the sea.

'I loved a man, a soldier, who was killed and I can't get rid of the sadness.'

'My mum died and I felt all empty inside me.'

'Yes I know that feeling,' Polly squeezed her hand.

'But Alice made me better. She loves me, perhaps you'll find someone to love you too.' Annie skipped along. 'Then you'll be happy again.'

'That would be nice, but I don't think I'll ever forget Andrew.'

Annie stopped in her tracks. 'Oh, you mustn't. He wouldn't like that. My mum's in heaven and she's looking down on me, Alice told me. She'd cry if I forgot her.'

'You're right, Annie.'

They had reached the beach and were sitting on the large rock that overlooked the bay and the valley. Annie was amusing herself, flicking over some shells she had left on the rock the last time she had been here.

'You're nice,' she grinned at Polly. 'But Miss Juniper, she's sad too.'

'Why do you say that?' Polly asked with keen interest.

'Because she thinks no one loves her and they do. She's silly.' She piled the shells into her handkerchief. 'Can we go up the cliff? In winter you can walk right up the side. Come on . . .' Annie held out her hand towards Polly and ducking under the branches of the huge rhododendrons they climbed to the top of the cliff.

Two days after the New Year, Alice and Gertie stood on the steps of Gwenfer waving Polly and Juniper goodbye. Polly had to leave because of her work, but Alice had harboured a faint hope that Juniper would stay longer. It was a forlorn hope for she was aware that Juniper was quickly becoming bored with the quiet of the countryside. She feared that, once back in London, Juniper would revert to her frenetic ways. At least she could console herself that Juniper's drinking was now under control. She had received a scare, serious enough to have brought her sharply to her senses. The women turned back into the house congratulating each other that Christmas had been a success.

Phillip's two weeks' leave slid into three. Alice did not say anything for she was afraid that she might push him into returning to work. His war work was voluntary, so he could come and go as he wished. It was his highly developed sense of duty which had kept him away from her for so long.

With all the children back at school and the grand-daughters away, much as she missed them Alice looked forward to settling back into her old routine. Christmas was highly disruptive, she thought.

Having set up the easels and paints in the room she and Phillip had set aside as a studio, she was surprised when he said he did not feel like painting. She could not remember this ever happening before. She started to paint herself, but unexpectedly found she did not enjoy it, again a new experience. So she packed away the paraphernalia and took out some sewing instead.

Phillip's lack of appetite began to alarm her. Despite the rationing, she contrived to cook him his favourite dishes, going without herself if necessary, only to see him push the plate away, the food half eaten.

They had always enjoyed brisk walks together, but now she found they were taking gentle strolls and short ones at that.

'Gertie, I'm worried there's something wrong with Phillip. What do you think?' she asked one day. They were in the kitchen where Gertie, with much misgiving, was attempting to make a carrot cake which Lord Woolton had assured the nation was delicious.

Gertie looked up from her task. 'He's quieter, but he's tired. We're all tired, Alice. Look at us. I'd always been waited on hand and foot, why, I didn't know one end of a kitchen range from the other. Now we cook and clean, you're doing the ironing and, quite honestly, Alice, I'll be glad when this damnable war is over and I can go back to being indolent.'

'You, indolent? That's a joke, Gertie. You were always busy at one thing or another.'

'Admittedly, but not menial tasks. How our poor servants survived the boredom I shall never know.'

'That's if it'll be possible to have servants after the war. What girl who's been in the forces or in a factory is going to want to return to the drudgery of service?'

'True. But no doubt if one is willing to pay, one will find staff. I fear it'll be a very mercenary world in the future, don't you?' And Gertie congratulated herself on the neat way she had diverted Alice from the subject of Phillip's health.

Gertie had spoken to Phillip several times about telling Alice and each time he had promised 'tomorrow'. Obviously nothing had been said. Gertie admired his consideration and his courage in bearing his illness alone, but all the same she felt he was wrong. Another week passed and it was a week in which Alice's worry grew until she could contain herself no longer.

'Phillip, are you unwell?' she asked him one morning just after breakfast.

'Why do you ask?' He looked up with a pretence of surprise.

'You haven't eaten your egg.'

'Oh Alice, you are sweet, just because I don't eat an egg,' and he laughed as he folded his napkin. But he did not look at her as he said it.

'There have been a lot of eggs, and other things, you haven't touched. And you're tired and you don't paint any more.'

'Has Gertie been talking? Typical of her . . .'

'What do you mean? Does Gertie know something I don't?' Her heart was thumping. It must be serious if he had confided in Gertie rather than her – he was shielding her. 'Tell me, Phillip, I have a right to know,' she said quietly and with dignity.

He looked at her for some moments before he spoke, moments that he knew were to be the last of her happiness. He had loved her the instant he set eyes on her and that love had never diminished, only grown. He had planned and wanted to be with her, to care for her and guard her for the rest of her life and now it was not to be. A little bit of him died that morning as he told her and as he had to watch the pain in her beautiful kind grey eyes.

Late that afternoon Alice went where she had always gone when in distress and in need of solace. She went to Ia's rock, and sat hunched there, in the late-January drizzle, her gaze turned to the ocean. She waited for the sea to calm her and give her strength, as it had always done in the past, but this time she waited in vain.

Gertie found her there an hour later. She put the mackintosh she had brought with her round Alice's shoulders and sat silently beside her friend, waiting for her to speak.

'It's so unfair, Gertie. All those years of loneliness and dissatisfaction I had with Lincoln, but I'm only allowed these six short years with Phillip.'

'But wonderful, loving years.'

'It doesn't help.'

'I know, I know,' Gertie patted her hand ineffectually and longed for words of wisdom, but they did not come. 'Would you prefer it if I left? I can go and stay at Hurstwood, Polly won't mind, or with my son Charles.'

'Gertie, don't even think of it. Please don't leave me.'

'I thought you'd rather be alone with Phillip until . . .' and Gertie shook her head, finding there were certain words that even she, forthright as she was, was incapable of saying.

'No. I shall need you, Gertie, and your strength. I hadn't expected this and I don't know if I have the courage to face it.'

'Rats, Alice. You're the bravest woman I know,' and, although not normally a demonstrative person, Gertie scooped Alice into her arms and held her tight, letting her cry and rocking her as if she were a child instead of a grown woman.

'You always used to say "rats" a lot, do you remember?' Alice smiled through her tears. 'Such a silly word.'

'From a silly person,' Gertie said gruffly, close to tears herself.

'Oh no, my dear friend, never silly.' She looked out across the grey, chilly sea, as chill as a tomb she thought, and shuddered. 'There'll be no sunset to watch tonight. When the sun slips into the sea, people say that if you're lucky and you watch carefully, you might see a beautiful green flash.'

'Have you seen it?'

'Never. Yet all my life I've watched for it. When Juniper was a child she said perhaps you only saw it when you were about to die.' And she shuddered again.

'Children say strange things, don't they? All nonsense,' Gertie said in her normal brisk manner; then she got to her feet and held out her hand for Alice. 'One of Juniper's wonderful martinis is what you need, my dear.'

3

Juniper and Polly had been back in London for a month, during which Juniper had lived very quietly. She rose at a sensible time and went to bed at a reasonable hour. She read a lot, wrote many letters, walked in the park, and ate whatever food was put in front of her. She did not appear to be drinking and saw nobody from the days before her illness. It was a state of affairs that should have made Polly happy and relaxed, but this behaviour was so unlike Juniper that Polly became worried that it was an act. Why, or for whom, she did not understand, so she waited apprehensively, expecting any day the old, wild, uncontrollable Juniper to reappear.

Polly had received a letter from Alice, telling her of Phillip's serious illness and leaving it to her discretion whether to tell Juniper or not; she wanted nothing to disturb Juniper's equilibrium. Polly had telephoned

Gwenfer the following Sunday when Juniper was out on one of her long walks. She was worried that Juniper might return before she had had time to make her call; trunk calls were becoming harder, sometimes the connection could take hours. Luckily, within an hour and a half she was talking to Alice.

'I felt I should talk to you, Mrs Whitaker, it's too important to discuss in a letter.'

'How is she, Polly?'

'She seems very relaxed, not at all like her former self.' Polly stood in the hall facing the front door so that she could change the subject the moment she heard Juniper's key in the door.

'Then don't tell her, Polly. There will be time enough,' Alice replied gently.

'Are you all right, Mrs Whitaker? Is there anything I can do?'

'I'm very sad, Polly, my husband is a remarkable man. But you are helping me enormously, at least I know that you'll look after Juniper for me. That's one worry less.'

Polly replaced the receiver and stood deep in thought. Was it right not to tell Juniper? They were treating her like a child and was that fair? How would Polly feel in such circumstances? Once Juniper found out they had been keeping Phillip's illness from her, was that not just the sort of situation that might annoy her sufficiently to make her drink and behave stupidly again? But then, knowing about Phillip was just as likely to make her behave the same way. It was an impossible dilemma. Whatever action they took Juniper was at risk.

Polly climbed the stairs to the drawing room. She shut the double doors that bisected the long room, knowing that Juniper would fling them open again as soon as she returned. She liked large spacious rooms, she kept explaining to Polly, small rooms made her claustrophobic. But large spaces had to be heated. With fuel supplies critical, heating half the room was a problem, let alone the full length. She crossed to the meagre fire and put a

few precious lumps of coal on it, remembering the roaring
fires at Gwenfer during Christmas. At least in the country
there was plenty of wood available. She looked out of the
window at the square. A fine drizzle had begun to fall and
what she could see of the sky above the rooftops was
leaden coloured with heavier rain to come. It was cold;
even the trees, bare of their leaves, seemed to huddle
against the damp chill. The beginning of any year, those
first two months when almost everything in nature was
still dormant, were enough to depress anyone. Polly
shivered and pulled her cardigan closer to her. A lone
figure was hurrying towards the house; it was Juniper. She
looked up at the window, waved to Polly and smiled.
Immediately the February gloom of the square lifted;
Juniper's smile could change anything.

Polly met her in the hall as she was taking off her
soaking coat and shaking the damp from her blonde hair
which was curly these days from a permanent wave. Polly
had preferred it when it was long and straight.

'There are snowdrops in the park and you can just
begin to see the crocuses. Isn't nature wonderful?' Juniper
said, allowing her coat to slip to the floor as she always
did. Polly bent down and picked it up, as she always did.

'It's beastly chill though.' Polly shivered in the hall and
wondered if it was the cold that ailed her, or the
conversation with Alice.

'Did you light the fire?'

Polly nodded.

'Good. I want to curl up with a book and some music.
How about some tea?' She swung round to face Polly.
'Gracious me, you look so full of doom, what's the
matter?'

'Juniper. I don't know whether to tell you or not . . .'
she began.

'If it's bad news, better not. I don't want to hear.'
Juniper flicked her hair with her fingers. 'I don't think this
perm really suits me, do you?'

'It's gone a bit frizzy in the damp.'

'I wish I'd never had it done now.' She turned towards the stairs. 'You make the tea. I'll check the fire and put some music on; I'll pull the curtains and we'll be like two contented old spinsters,' she said laughing and ran up the stairs.

There was a good fire burning by the time Polly returned with the tea tray. What she would have given for a Dundee cake or even a Victoria sponge. Instead they were going to have to make do with the last of the digestive biscuits.

'What's this news, then?' Juniper stood in front of the fire.

'I thought you didn't want to know,' Polly replied, placing the tray on a small table.

'Best to get it over with.'

'It's Phillip. He's very ill. I'm sorry, Juniper, but I'm afraid he's dying,' Polly said, watching her friend closely for any sign of hysteria.

Juniper reached up to the mantelpiece and took down a box of matches.

'My lighter's broken. There's not a hope of getting it mended. I love that lighter,' she said, striking a match for her cigarette.

Polly poured the tea but, watching Juniper with an eagle eye, spilled half in the saucer. 'Oh drat, look what I've done,' she fretted.

'You needn't watch me like a night nurse. I'm not going to start screaming and shouting, if that's what you think. I never liked him much, if you must know.'

'But Juniper, your poor grandmother.'

'Yes. I'm sorry for her.'

'Don't you think you should go to her, help her?'

'Me? Help anyone?' She chuckled. 'Oh come on, Polly. What use would I be? No, my grandmother will cope, she always does. Are these the only biscuits? So boring . . . when this war is over I shall live on cream cakes,' she announced.

'And get disgustingly fat.'

'Probably. And breed dogs, bulldogs, I think.' She laughed gaily. 'What do you want to hear? Glenn Miller or Beethoven?'

Polly did not mention Phillip again.

In her own life Polly was far from happy. Her longing for Andrew continued unabated. Her need for him and sadness at his death were like a great block of stone inside her which she felt destined to carry for the rest of her life. She knew other girls whose man had been killed and who, a few weeks later, were out on the town with a new love on their arm, laughing as if nothing had happened. She did not know how they did it, she certainly did not wish to emulate them, but at the same time the fear that she would never know happiness again depressed her. She wanted to be happy, but it appeared fate had decided against it.

Nor did it help that her work was repetitive and boring, and she had begun to question its value. Did housewives take any notice of the endless homilies on 'make-do-and-mend' which her office churned out by the cartload? And if possible she disliked Mrs Anstruther even more than before.

One bleak late February morning, when she had retyped *Washing-up Without Soap* three times to reach Mrs Anstruther's pernickety standards, she was summoned to see Gwendoline Rickmansworth, their new boss, who had joined barely a month previously. Polly felt puzzled and apprehensive as she put the cover over her typewriter. She chose to ignore one of her colleagues, who with obvious relish informed her she was 'for the chop'. But by the time she was standing outside Mrs Rickmansworth's office, she had whipped herself into a fine state of nervousness.

The office was a surprise after the regimented tidiness of the main office: it was chaos. Files were strewn on the floor, charts covered the flock-papered walls, clothes lay in piles everywhere and the top of Mrs Rickmansworth's desk was completely obliterated by paperwork.

'Come in my dear.' Mrs Rickmansworth, a surprisingly young and attractive woman, had stood up and was holding out a hand in welcome. 'Sit down. Coffee?'

Polly had expected an old dragon, but this woman was no older than her mid thirties. She was smartly dressed in a suit which, from knowledge of past, if not present, fashion Polly knew had cost a small fortune. Her blonde hair was styled in a becoming roll and her make-up was bright and perfect.

'Thank you,' Polly said, surprised at the invitation.

The woman crossed to the door, stuck her head out and called breezily, 'Philippa, two coffees and biscuits, chop chop.' She crossed back to the desk, shoved the papers to one side and offered Polly a cigarette, which she declined, then lit one for herself. 'Excuse the mess.' She waved at the piles of clothes. 'I'm collecting jumble for the WVS.'

'I see,' Polly said, politely amazed she was being apologized to.

'Do you enjoy working in Mrs Anstruther's department?' she went on, after the secretary had brought in their coffee.

'Well . . .' Polly began, wondering if this were some inter-departmental trap. What the hell she thought. 'Not if I'm honest, Mrs Rickmansworth. It's rather repetitive.'

'Splendid. Do you drive?'

'Yes. Not that I've been able to do much recently.'

'You'll soon relearn. I'm in need of a secretary who can drive. Would you be interested?'

'Gosh, yes, I'd be thrilled. But I should confess, although my typing is fine, my shorthand isn't very good.'

'We'll muddle through. I shall just have to dictate slowly.' Mrs Rickmansworth beamed at her and Polly could not believe this was happening. She couldn't remember Mrs Anstruther smiling at her once. 'How's your grandmother?' Mrs Rickmansworth asked as she helped herself to a biscuit.

'You know her?'

'Gracious, yes. My great-aunt, Augusta Portley, was a

debutante with her. Wonderful woman. I knew you were here. For a month I've been meaning to see you, but you know how frantic this place is. Your grandmother said you were happy, otherwise I'd have had you out of Anstruther's talons the moment I arrived. And your mother?'

'You know her too?' Polly asked, astonished. She had never thought to meet anyone who knew both such sworn enemies.

'Not well. I shared a cruise in the south of France with her, ten or eleven years ago. Gracious, how time flies, it must have been eleven; I was on my honeymoon, actually. It was on Marshall Boscar's yacht.'

'Good God. I live with his daughter.'

'We English are a very clubbable lot, aren't we?' Gwendoline chortled. 'Right, to business. Where are we? Wednesday. I've got to go to Wales tonight. There's little point in your starting today, so take the rest of the week off. Report here at eight on Monday, then you can sort me out, I'm in such a fearful muddle.'

'Thank you. Until Monday then,' Polly said, flustered, as she picked up her bag and made for the door before anything could change.

It was foggy outside. Since the bombing the fogs that plagued London in winter were even worse. She supposed it was the dust and debris constantly in the air which made the fogs denser and eerier.

She had only walked a hundred yards, though shuffled would have been a better description. Normal walking was impossible in the swirling grey, yellow mist. Once it had been easier moving from railing to railing, but they had long ago been torn down to be turned into guns. She thought she should turn left at the next road, but landmarks and even street names were obliterated by the fog. There was no point in cutting across the park, she would risk becoming completely lost. With one hand touching the wall she inched round the corner. A man hurrying in the opposite direction cannoned into her.

'I'm so sorry. Are you hurt?' came a familiar voice.

'Jonathan. It's Jonathan Middlebank, isn't it?' Her voice was full of pleasure.

'Why, yes.' He peered down at her from his tall height. 'Good Lord, it's Polly. Polly, how extraordinary.' And in the fog, unseen by prying eyes, he picked her up in his arms, kissed her firmly on the cheek and twirled around with excitement. 'I was just coming to find you. I popped in to see Juniper, she said you had a lunch break about now. Care to join me?'

'I'd love to,' she said rather breathlessly, aware that her heart was thudding as she felt the wool of his army greatcoat against her cheek.

4

'What about the Savoy?' Jonathan looked down at her.

Polly laughed. 'Are you rich these days?'

'No, poor as ever,' he said grinning back.

'There's a good British Restaurant just round the corner. I often go there.'

'Dear Polly, still as practical as ever. I'm not that poor. I'd like to celebrate the start of my leave in a slightly grander style.'

'But not the Savoy – I wouldn't dream of it. I know a good fish restaurant and it's still got a reasonable cellar.'

'Let's hope this meal doesn't get spoilt by a bomb, like the last time.'

At the restaurant, they ordered their food and Jonathan sat back with a contented expression.

'Isn't this nice?'

'Very,' she said and tried to look at him closely without it being apparent. He had fought in the Spanish Civil War and had seen action in North Africa and yet, apart from a few extra lines on his face, he looked as untroubled as he had all those years ago when they had first met at Hurstwood, she still in the schoolroom and in awe of this, to her, sophisticated student.

'What are you thinking?' he asked.

'That you look the same . . . that war hasn't changed you.'

'You've changed though – you look sadder.'

'Do I? I don't think so.' She looked away, not wanting her sadness to spoil this meal for him.

'But you look like Polly again. You look just how you did when I first came to Hurstwood on visits. Not the smart sophisticated lady I knew in Paris, but a far more beautiful one.'

She found herself blushing at his compliments. She had never forgotten his attractive voice. Voices were important to her, she could never love a man with an ugly voice. She sat up straight in her chair, startled at thinking such thoughts.

'I never liked being that mannequin Michel created,' she said, realising she was flustered.

'Why did you let him?'

'It seemed easier. It gave him great pleasure to remake the little English girl he'd married into a chic French-woman. The trouble was that it was only skin deep.'

'I heard he was dead. I don't know quite what to say. I can't say I'm sorry, that would be too hypo-critical.'

'Don't worry. I feel nothing any more. It's almost as if I had never married Michel. I don't even think about him these days. I don't blame him for anything. He was as he was, to him his behaviour was normal. And he could be very kind and was generous to a fault.'

'You amaze me, Polly. You can always find it in yourself to forgive, can't you?'

She looked away. Was he wanting to hear her say that she forgave him and Juniper? If so, why? She did not want to be reminded of it. That was the past. She did not want anything to spoil this meal, this reunion. She wanted to be happy, in fact was happy. She leant back in her chair savouring that thought. She had not felt like this for so long, not since she last saw Andrew.

'How's your boyfriend? Andrew Slater, isn't it?' he asked, as if reading her mind.

'You knew about Andrew?' she said, surprised.

'Yes. Someone, I can't remember who – Juniper I suppose – told me you'd met a good bloke. I was happy for you . . .' he paused, 'even if I was jealous of him.'

Polly felt herself blush again. 'He was killed,' she said simply, and quickly despised herself. She was blushing at his compliment and to cover that confusion she had spoken of Andrew's death – that was unforgivable.

Jonathan moved his hand quickly across the table and took hold of hers. She made no move to remove her own.

'Polly, I'm so sorry. You didn't mention him in any of your letters.'

'There had been such confusion over his whereabouts. I didn't think that was the sort of news to write to a soldier in danger. It wasn't as if you knew him.'

'When did it happen?'

'Escaping from a POW camp. I didn't know for over a year – that was the hardest part, I think. Before that he'd been reported missing in action. That was bad enough, but at least I had hope. Hope is amazing, the way it keeps you going. When it dies you seem to lose everything.' She looked sad, and he feared she might cry, but she didn't. These days Polly could talk about Andrew and the tears were no longer shed outwardly.

'Is there anyone else?' he asked, looking casually around the restaurant as if the question were of little importance.

'No, I haven't wanted to find anyone. No one could take Andrew's place,' she said quietly.

'Of course . . . just being nosy.' He looked down at the table, an ashamed expression on his face.

'Juniper and I are like a couple of old spinsters with our books and cocoa.'

'It's difficult to imagine Juniper behaving like that,' he said, laughing.

'But not me?' She forced herself to smile to cover the flash of resentment she had felt.

'Neither of you, that goes without saying. But how is Juniper? I just dashed in to her house to find out where your office was. She looked well . . .' Again Polly was aware that he was trying to sound nonchalant. Despite herself, she felt a surge of disappointment at his obvious interest in Juniper.

'I'm surprised you didn't want to take her to lunch,' she said a shade sharply.

'No, it was you I wanted to see,' he replied, apparently unaware of, or perhaps ignoring, the tone of her voice. 'Honestly.' All this time he had been holding her hand; when he let it go she was sorry.

'She's been desperately ill, but she's better now and living very quietly, thank goodness. She was quite a responsibility for some time.' She could laugh at the memory now. 'Would you like to come back with me? I'm sure she'd love to see more of you before you go back,' she said. He looked up sharply to see if there was irony in her expression, but could see none.

'I'd like that,' he said, as their food arrived. And they settled down to eat and talk of books and other things.

'Are you still writing?'

'Yes, it's difficult to find the time but I scribble whenever I can. I've finished the second draft of my book . . .'

'That's wonderful . . .'

On the walk to the house Polly felt happy, almost elated, and she had not expected ever to feel this way again. She found she was more than pleased to have met Jonathan, and she realized it was more than the pleasure of meeting an old friend after such a lapse of time. She sensed he felt the same. Since Andrew's death she had given no man a second look, but Jonathan was different, with him she thought she might feel comfortable. She had known Jonathan long before she had met Andrew – it would be less of a betrayal in a way. First, however, she had to see Jonathan and Juniper together. She had to find out whether there was still a spark of interest between them. She could not take the risk of the two of them hurting her again.

'You're very quiet,' he said, as he loped along beside her in the fog which was becoming denser towards evening as householders lit their fires and added to the pall of smoke. Only the sick or imprudent lit their fires in the morning. Most people saved the meagre fuel rations for the evenings.

'I hate to breathe in too much of this foul fog,' she said as an excuse, 'but we're here now.'

She led the way up the stone steps to the pillared front porch. She let them in and called out for Juniper.

'You're early,' Juniper called back from the library. They entered the downstairs room, which they rarely used, and to her annoyance Polly saw a fire glowing in the grate. Juniper was rapidly folding some papers on the big partners' desk, almost guiltily.

'You've caught me out. I didn't expect you until six. Sorry about the fire, I was freezing.' She smiled apologetically. 'Jonathan!' Her face lit up with pleasure. 'I hoped you'd be back.' She moved gracefully across the room towards him, her arms outstretched in welcome, and kissed him lightly on the cheek. Each movement, each fleeting expression was watched closely by Polly, who felt like a prison warder. 'Polly must be thrilled you've turned up out of the blue. She's been so lonely, poor sweet. Just boring old me as company.'

'You look so well, Juniper. Polly tells me you've been unwell. I'm sorry.'

'Entirely my own fault, Jonathan,' she said airily. 'But this is a reunion. It calls for champagne, don't you think, Polly?' Polly did not have time to reply. 'Jonathan, be a pet. I'm terrified of the beastly cellar, it's so dark and creepy.' She smiled up at him.

Polly poked the coal viciously. Juniper had never been afraid of the cellar before – in the past she had often made several trips down there in an evening. It was all for Jonathan's benefit, Polly thought. She dug into the coal again with even more violence.

'What a surprise!' Juniper beamed at her. 'But why are you back so early?'

'Did I catch you out, writing your memoirs?' Polly said rather tetchily and to her astonishment saw that Juniper was blushing. 'Am I right?'

'Not my memoirs but . . . just recently . . . when I'm on my own . . . I've been trying to write.'

'That's marvellous. May I see?'

'Gracious no. No one can *see* it, not yet. Don't breathe a word to Jonathan will you, I mean, he's a professional.'

'I'm glad you've found something to amuse you,' Polly said stiffly.

Jonathan reappeared carrying two bottles of champagne. 'Will the Dom Perignon '19 do? I brought up two to be on the safe side.' He grinned at Polly. To most people Jonathan was a pleasant-faced but rather undistinguished fellow, slim, with a good posture, but definitely not handsome. To Polly, his face was one of the most attractive she had ever seen.

'You still haven't explained why you're home so early,' Juniper said, after they had toasted Jonathan's return.

'I've been given a new job – as secretary-driver to our overall boss, Mrs Rickmansworth. And guess what? She knows my mother and grandmother and she knew your father, Juniper.' But Juniper seemed to be totally uninterested in this information. 'She gave me the rest of the week off. I start on Monday,' she continued.

'Wonderful! Then you can spend every minute of my leave with me,' Jonathan blurted out. He beamed at her.

'Isn't this all lovely.' Juniper clapped her hands with pleasure. 'I shall telephone Gaston's and book a table – my treat, I insist.'

'Please, Juniper, that's not necessary,' Polly said

quickly to cover her disappointment. She had wanted to spend the evening alone with Jonathan now he had declared it was her he wanted to be with.

'It's very kind of you, Juniper, but I'd rather planned to take Polly out myself,' Jonathan said, looking embarrassed and fearful that he sounded ungrateful.

'Of course you did. I'm not coming. You'll want to be alone. It's so sweet seeing you both together again. Two of my favourite people in the whole world.' Juniper put one arm around Polly, the other around Jonathan and hugged them excitedly.

They stood in the swirling fog outside the restaurant.

'I don't think we should go here. Juniper already does far too much for me,' Polly said, looking up at the small, discreet restaurant which, if one were rich and a regular customer, would serve virtually anything one wanted – at a price.

'I hear it's one of the best in London. She might feel insulted if we reject her offer.'

'She won't mind. And I think it's abusing Juniper's hospitality,' Polly persisted.

'Very well. Where do you suggest then?' Jonathan slipped her arm in his. Polly hoped it was her imagination that he sounded reluctant about not going into Gaston's.

When they returned, long past midnight, it was to find Juniper drunk.

5

Polly said nothing to Juniper the following morning. This was not out of kindness, but rather that she didn't want anything to spoil her own happiness. For that night, after they had returned from the restaurant, after they had helped Juniper to bed, wordlessly Polly had taken Jonathan's hand and had led him up the stairs to her attic room. In another age, another time, she would have allowed him to court her, would have waited for them to marry. But in this moment in the history of the world there was not time, happiness had to be grabbed and clasped to one in case it slipped tragically away. The bombing had now decreased, but there were still raids, and everyone in London was at risk. Jonathan did not know where his next posting would be and whether death waited there for him. It was the first night in a long time that Polly did not think of Andrew as she fell asleep, marvelling at how happy she felt.

The remaining days of Jonathan's leave sped past in a haze of excitement, of rediscovering each other and making love at any hour of the day or night. The novel that Jonathan had gone to Spain to write all those years ago, before the world had descended into madness, was finished. He wanted Polly to read it.

Polly felt nervous as she picked up the manuscript. She wanted it to be perfect. Jonathan had gone out for a walk, unable to sit and watch as she read. She had read the first draft in Paris and had thought it good. She was not prepared for this final version.

Polly sat on her bed and was transported back in time to the days of her youth in London. It was about her and Jonathan, and yet it wasn't. He had described the time, the places to perfection. But although she knew it was her, it did not seem to be really her. She did not like this heroine and hoped that wasn't how Jonathan saw her. There was a shallowness to the characters. The novel was well-written and constructed, but it was as if it were written by someone with no heart, about people who lacked depth.

His face, rather pale, appeared around the door.

'So, what do you think?' he asked nervously.

'It's a very clever book,' she said. 'I enjoyed it.' She spoke the truth, she felt unable to criticize it in too much depth and by now was wondering if she had expected too much of the book. 'I'm not saying that because I love you, but because it is.'

'Do you mean what you say? That you love me?'

She laughed. 'I don't make a habit of going to bed with men I don't love.'

'Polly, thank God! I was afraid the past would get in the way and stop you loving me. My darling Polly, marry me.'

'Yes please, Jonathan. I'd like to very much,' Polly replied simply, with no need to think about her answer.

Polly had cooked a special dinner. She had managed to get a good piece of salmon and the meal – vegetable soup, then the fish followed by an apple pie – was a feast. Polly and Juniper normally only had one course. She would have liked to dine alone with Jonathan to celebrate their engagement, but felt it was unkind to exclude Juniper. Tomorrow was his last night, they could celebrate then.

Over the meal Jonathan had a surprise for her. He explained that while Polly had been reading his manuscript he had felt so nervous that he had walked over to his regimental headquarters.

'It's most odd. I've been pulled out of active service,' he announced.

'Thank God,' Polly exclaimed.

'That's lovely,' added Juniper.

'I'm to learn Russian, of all things.'

'Russian?' Polly and Juniper said in mystified unison.

'What on earth for?' Juniper asked.

'It seems someone told them my French and Spanish are reasonable . . .'

'You're fluent in both,' Polly interrupted proudly. 'And what about Arabic? You're good at that too.' She sounded like a mother listing the accomplishments of her child.

'Let him finish, Polly. We all know he's brilliant,' Juniper said, laughing.

'I'm to go on an intensive course for a year. It's all very hush-hush.'

'Where?'

'I can't tell you, Polly, it's *that* secret, but I can give you the number of a pub where you can contact me in an emergency. The pub's in Cambridge.' Jonathan imparted this information as if releasing the date of the invasion of Europe. 'I'd appreciate it if neither of you told anyone.'

Juniper shrieked with laughter. 'Oh Jonathan, you are divine. I do love men so, don't you, Polly? They do enjoy all this cloak-and-dagger business, don't they?'

Jonathan looked embarrassed.

'But why Russian?' Polly asked, feeling sorry for his discomfort but at the same time agreeing with Juniper. It did all seem unnecessarily secret.

'There are those who think that when we've finished with the Germans we shall have to go on and take a swipe at the Russians.'

'But they're our allies,' Polly said, puzzled.

'While the Germans are unbeaten, but what then? Will Russia want to take over where the Germans left off? They could quite easily become the enemy.'

'Jonathan, what a dreadful idea. There'd be no end of war, it could go on for years. I don't want to think about such a thing.' Polly, feeling suddenly chill, moved closer to the fire.

'At least I shall be able to see more of you, that's the wonderful part.' He leaned forward in his chair and took Polly's hand.

'When do you go?'

'Day after tomorrow for a month, then I get three days' leave. That's when we ought to get married. Then you could move closer to wherever it is I shall be. My weekends will be free, it'll be paradise.'

'Can I move too?' Juniper said, smiling at them both. Polly and Jonathan looked at each other in dismay, then looked away shamefaced.

'Of course you must. We couldn't possibly leave you alone here.' Polly spoke as warmly as she could, but her heart sank at the prospect.

'Don't be silly, Polly. I was only joking.'
But Polly was not so sure.

Towards the end of Jonathan's first month on the language course, Polly telephoned the number he had given her to say she had to travel to Cornwall and would miss his three-day leave. She had, during various calls, made friends with the landlady.

'Perhaps you could ask him if he'll marry me on his next leave?' she joked lamely, bravely covering the bitter disappointment she was feeling.

'You poor love. What a blow. You've had bad news?' The landlady's voice was warm with concern.

'The husband of a close friend has died and I feel I must accompany her granddaughter to Cornwall for the funeral.'

'What a good friend you are. Captain Middlebank's a lucky young man, I hope he knows it. I'll have to tell him to make sure.'

'Thank you, Mrs Greenstone. I'm the lucky one.'
She replaced the receiver.

'And what makes you think this granddaughter's going to the funeral?' Juniper's voice made Polly jump with surprise.

'I thought you were still in bed.' Polly swung round to find Juniper standing hand on hip, cigarette in hand, effortlessly elegant as always, but to Polly's disapproval dressed in a red dress, a black cashmere cardigan slung over her shoulders.

'Of course you must go to the funeral.'

'There's no "must" about it. I'm not going, and I'm sure there's no need for you to trek all the way down there either.'

'But I want to go. We *should* go. Alice might need us.'

'She's got your grandmother with her. There's nothing we can do.' Juniper turned towards the library, as if the conversation were over. She was spending a couple of hours each day toiling at her writing. Polly followed her.

'You're going and that's that. You can't fool me, Juniper. You're frightened to go.'

'I hate funerals.'

'Everybody hates funerals – it's never easy. But this is one you can't run away from.'

'We never got on, Phillip and I.'

'Your relationship with Phillip is irrelevant. It's Alice you should be thinking of. She'll need you, don't you see?'

'Do I really have to go?' Juniper smiled appealingly.

'You know the answer to that. And get changed, that dress is most unsuitable. You've got an hour, we can catch the 10.50 from Paddington if we hurry.'

'Gee, Polly, why are you always so bossy? And why are you always so goddamn right?' Juniper spoke without resentment in her voice.

'I must be taking after my grandmother,' Polly called over her shoulder as she left the room.

'She isn't your grandmother,' Juniper said, but Polly had left the room. 'Oh damn,' she said to herself, 'why do I always have to do what other people want?' She dutifully went upstairs to change, all the while hoping that something, a direct hit on Paddington, anything might happen to prevent their going.

Polly was getting agitated. Juniper had taken too long over getting ready and packing. Now their taxi cab was caught in a traffic jam at Marble Arch and progress was at a snail's pace. Polly looked at her watch for the umpteenth time, drumming her fingers on the watch face.

'Calm down, Polly, do. I've never missed a train in my life.'

'There's always a first time for everything.' She leant over and slid back the glass partition. 'You don't know of any short cuts do you, driver? We'll miss our train.'

'Sorry, miss. It's up ahead – an accident, I think.'

Polly let down her window to peer out and thus did not notice the car that drew level with them on the other side. She did not see the young boy, about six years old, looking into their taxi, excitedly pointing them out to the woman who sat beside him. She was unaware of him pounding on the window with his small fists, shouting 'Mama', attempting to be heard over the noise of the traffic, the blaring of impatient horns. She was oblivious of the expression on Juniper's face, a face turned ashen as the blood drained from it. Juniper turned her head away from the child and looked steadfastly ahead of her, searching with shaking fingers for her cigarette case and matches.

The taxi lurched forward.

Polly flopped back into her seat.

'Thank goodness for that. We might just make it,' she said, looking again at her wristwatch. 'What do you think?' She turned to Juniper. 'Are you all right? You look dreadful, as if you'd seen a ghost.'

'I'm fine, just fine. It's the fumes.' Juniper smiled pallidly at her. 'Don't fuss.'

A limousine slid alongside; for a split second Polly saw the occupants. She looked again, not sure if it was Caroline Copton and Harry. She opened her mouth as if to speak and then thought better of it. Juniper hated to hear her son mentioned. After all, it probably wasn't him.

Polly was out of the taxi almost before it had stopped. She called for a porter as she paid the taxi driver. Juniper still sat in the back of the cab.

'Come on, do. What is the matter with you?' She felt as if she was about to snap with irritation. The porter rapidly weaved his way through the crowds towards the train. Polly followed, not looking to right or left. She hated stations these days. For every happy reunion there always seemed to be a dozen sad farewells. That depressed her and always made her think of Andrew.

The cases in the train, the porter tipped, she turned round to find Juniper was not with her. Asking a fellow traveller to save their seats she raced back through the corridor.

Juniper was standing on the platform looking wan and lost.

'Juniper, we're leaving,' Polly called as the train doors were slammed shut. The guard began to unfurl his green flag. 'Juniper, please,' she shouted over the racket on the bustling platform.

'I can't. Don't ask me why. Please, leave me alone.' Juniper looked up at her and Polly was horrified at the despair she saw in her friend's eyes.

'But Juniper . . .' The train began slowly to move. 'I'll phone . . .' she called as the train picked up speed. She hung from the window and watched as Juniper turned, a small slim figure that was soon lost in the hurrying crowds.

6

Juniper scurried along the platform, head down, as if afraid the train might stop and Polly leap off to reclaim her. She looked wildly about her, not certain what to do or where to go, for she felt confused and deeply upset.

Wherever she looked on the crowded concourse all she seemed to see were couples: couples kissing and clinging to each other, couples crying in each other's arms, hands held longingly as the time came for them to part. She stood stock still and felt immeasurably alone. A door to her left opened and she heard a loud burst of raucous laughter. She weaved her way through the throng, pushed the heavy door open and closed it quickly.

The refreshment room was crowded, a thick pall of cigarette smoke polluted the air. The filthy floor was littered with kit bags and cases which made reaching the counter an obstacle course. Several soldiers and sailors were slumped on the tables asleep, their heads resting on the debris of someone else's meal. To the noise of laughter and conversation was added the rattle and clatter of crockery and cutlery apparently being hurled about.

Juniper joined the queue that inched slowly towards the counter where one buxom, bad-tempered-looking woman was pouring tea from an enormous teapot which she moved rhythmically up and down the lines of cups so that more tea slopped on to the counter than into the cups. Her assistant, a quarter of her size, with an even more unpleasant scowl, was responsible for the clattering of crockery as she hurled large baskets of dirty dishes through a wide hatch where disembodied hands appeared to grab them.

Slowly the queue moved forward and it was Juniper's turn.

'A large brandy, please,' she ordered.

'A what?' The large woman boomed back.

'A large brandy,' Juniper repeated, with just a trace of a smile.

'Where you been? Don't you know there's a war on?' The woman leaned forward belligerently.

'Yes, I am aware of that,' Juniper said sweetly. 'It doesn't alter the fact that I'd like a large brandy.'

'I'd go back up west if I were you, love. There ain't no brandy here. Whatever next? What she think this is, the Ritz?' the woman consulted the rest of the queue, her surly expression finally breaking into a somewhat wintry smile. The queue muttered and Juniper blushed.

'I'm sorry. Then tea, no milk . . .'

'It comes with milk.'

It was Juniper's turn to say 'what?'

'You heard.' A large, thick cup, chipped on the side was pushed towards her, the pale milky liquid slopping over the sides. 'You pay along there.'

'Sugar?'

'There.' A fat stubby finger pointed at the bowl of sugar. 'One spoon only, mind.'

'Could I have a spoon, please?'

'Good God, girl. You still in nappies?' With an irritated gesture the large woman shoved a teaspoon, attached to the counter by a long piece of string, across to Juniper.

Blushing even more deeply, she stirred her tea, turning her face away with embarrassment from the grinning faces in the queue. Gingerly she picked up the overflowing cup and moved carefully towards a table which was suddenly free.

'Cor, her type shouldn't be allowed out on her own,' she heard the burly woman complain to her attentive queue.

Juniper sat at a table and felt even more miserable. The woman was right. She was useless. She never went anywhere on her own. In the past she had always had friends about her and recently she had never gone anywhere without Polly, only for a walk in the park. She really had no idea how people were living, how this war affected ordinary people. She had been living in an ivory tower. She was no use to anyone. If she disappeared off the face of the earth, her presence wouldn't even be missed. Polly was helpful, useful, unselfish – she would be missed by hundreds, whereas for Juniper only Alice would grieve. Maybe, having let her down once again by not going to Phillip's funeral, even Alice would sigh with relief if she were no more.

She moodily sipped the tea and grimaced at the over-milked, stewed taste of it. She would have to phone Alice and try to explain that seeing Harry had brought on this crisis of uncertainty. She was not sure whether she had failed to get on the train because she was too upset, or whether somewhere in her mind there was an idea that if she stayed in London she might see the child after all, might pluck up the courage to demand the right to a visit.

She arched her back wearily. Would that be fair? Would not her return into the child's life upset him? But then, he had been banging on the window of the car to attract her attention. He had looked so excited. But was it at seeing her, or the memory of the presents she had showered on him in the past?

Her money, that was all she had. Her money and the

way she spent it, was the only good thing about her. She was generous, at least that could be said about her.

'You're looking dreadfully down in the dumps.'

Juniper looked up angrily, not wishing to be distracted, to find Jonathan looming above her. He was frowning, but a small anxious smile flitted uncertainly across his face as he sensed he was not welcome.

'Jonathan, how lovely to see you. Sit down.' Juniper smiled at him, quickly covering her initial irritation. She moved some dirty plates to one side, giving him room to put down his plate of sandwiches, an apple and a cup of tea. 'This place is filthy. I'd no idea such places existed.'

'Well, you wouldn't, would you? I must admit you're the last person I'd expect to find in a station buffet.' He grinned at her as he picked up his sandwich and took a bite. 'Ugh, spam! When this war's over I'm going to shoot every tin of spam I see.'

'What are you doing here?'

'I got away from Cambridge early. I got a garbled message from Polly's office that she was off to Cornwall. You weren't at the house so I rushed here – in time to see the train pulling out of the station. Did you miss it? Where is she?'

'No. She's on it. I changed my mind. I wanted a brandy quickly and came here.'

'Ah, I can help you there. Hold on.' He dug into the pocket of his greatcoat and brought out a silver hip-flask. 'This'll pep your tea up,' and he moved to pour the brandy into her cup. Quick as lightning, Juniper grabbed the flask from his hand.

'Gee, don't waste good brandy in that muck,' she exclaimed. Putting the flask to her lips she took a large swig. 'Ah, that's better,' she sighed, sitting back in the chair and letting the brandy flow through her. She lit a cigarette and inhaled deeply. 'I feel human again,' she said, chuckling at him.

'So why aren't you on the train as well?'

'I didn't want to go. I hate funerals.'

'My message didn't say anything about a funeral. My God, who's dead?' he asked anxiously.

'My grandmother's husband.'

'Oh Juniper. You should have gone . . .' His voice was full of disapproval.

'I know, I know . . .' She shook her head. 'I couldn't face it. You know what I'm like.'

'Do you think you and I are destined to sit for ever in restaurants and debate whether or not you should go to funerals?' He smiled kindly at her. 'Do you remember in Paris, before the war, we had a conversation just like this about your father? You didn't want to go to his funeral either.'

'He was my father. Phillip isn't.'

'But he *is* your grandmother's husband. And what about your grandmother? She'll need you.'

'He didn't like me. I think I irritated him and he thought I was spoilt. I don't think he would care if I was there or not.'

'You don't go to a funeral just for the dead, you go for the living also.'

'Don't lecture me, Jonathan, I've had enough.'

'Sorry.'

'It's all right. You spend so much time with Polly that you're turning into a nag just like her,' she said and smiled. But there was an edge to her voice as she spoke.

'Polly isn't a nag. She cares about you. Maybe you're not even aware how much. She loves you and worries about you,' he said defensively.

'I was being horrid. I apologize. Polly's my best, my only friend. Just trust me, Jonathan. I didn't want to go, and that's all there is to be said about it.'

'Okay, okay . . .' Jonathan held up his hands, palms facing her as if warding off her annoyance. He began on his apple, carefully peeling it, turning the fruit in his long sensitive fingers. 'It's such a bore missing her. Two of our instructors are ill – one with pneumonia, the other with measles, of all things. I've got a whole week's leave, can you imagine, and no girl to spend it with.'

'You could catch the next train,' she looked at him slyly.

'I can't intrude on your family at such a time.'

'You're welcome to come back to my place, but there's just me there, so it might be boring for you.' She raised an eyebrow and looked at him quizzically.

'I don't know.' Jonathan looked down at the table. He could just imagine Polly's feelings if she found he was staying alone in the house with Juniper.

'I could always invite some other people to stay. It would be more fun for you.' She took another drink from his flask. 'And they could act as chaperones, if you like,' and she chuckled her low husky laugh.

He looked at her sheepishly with the uncomfortable expression of one who feels his mind has just been read.

'Thanks, Juniper, that would be fun,' he found himself saying, against his better judgement.

'Great. Let's get out of this dreary dump. Let's find some excitement!' She stood up quickly, pushing her chair back. 'Come on, I'll race you to the taxi rank,' and she laughed, all depression completely gone.

7

Alice had faced all the problems of her life with courage. Prepared, as she had been over the months of his illness, for Phillip's death, she faced its reality four-square and did not waver. Did not waver until, standing at the end of the platform at Penzance, she saw only Polly walking towards her, a shamefaced Polly who seemed to be dawdling along the long length of platform as if loath to reach her.

Tears which she had only allowed herself in private now filled her eyes, even though she stood amongst a small knot of people who were waving, shouting and jumping with excitement as they greeted loved ones from the train.

'I'm sorry, Mrs Whitaker,' Polly said despondently.

'Why didn't she come?'

'I don't know. When we got to the train she just refused to get on.'

'I see,' Alice said, even though she didn't, and for the first time since Phillip's death she realized how totally alone she now was in the world. It would have been nice if Juniper cared, but she could not, nor should she expect to, rely upon her for support. She was young, she had her own life to lead. As if aware of her tears for the first time, she rapidly wiped them away with the tips of her gloved fingers, braced her shoulders and held her head high. Insisting on carrying one of Polly's bags, she led the way across the wind-whipped station yard to her car.

They drove back to Gwenfer in silence. Polly was not embarrassed by it for she realized that Alice was controlling her grief and coming to terms with something Polly could only guess at. They arrived in time for supper with the evacuees, supervised by her grandmother in the kitchen. Gertie's greeting, in the circumstances, was restrained.

'Where's Juniper?' she asked immediately.

'She didn't come, Gertie. Polly doesn't know why,' Alice explained as she removed her hat and coat which she hung carefully on the back of the door to dry. 'Your coat, Polly. The rest of the house is so damp in this weather . . .'

'Why?' Gertie's authoritative voice barked at Polly.

'I really don't know, Grandmama.'

'That child is thoughtless and irresponsible,' Gertie said, as she ladled out mashed potatoes and corned beef for Polly and Alice.

'Not now, Gertie, please,' Alice said wearily and pushed her plate away from her.

'You must eat, Alice.'

'I know, Gertie. But not at the moment.'

143

Gertie looked at her friend, decided she had had enough for one night and kept silent for once.

'What a good girl, Annie. You've eaten everything up.' Alice stroked Annie's hair.

'Lady Gertie made me a house,' Annie explained. 'It tasted lovely.'

'A house?' Alice looked up questioningly at Gertie.

'Just a silly notion – out of the potatoes,' Gertie looked embarrassed.

'And the doors and windows were corned beef and the smoke from the chimney was brown sauce. It looked lovely, Alice. It's the only way to eat corned beef.'

'Thank you, Gertie.' Alice smiled at last. Annie was a finicky eater and Alice had tried all manner of ways to get her to eat. Normally Gertie subscribed to the 'if you won't eat your lunch, you'll have it again for tea' school of discipline and Alice was surprised but grateful that she had given in.

'Mr Phillip's gone to heaven, Miss Polly,' Annie said.

'Shut yer mouth, Annie,' May intervened.

'Language, May, language.' Gertie rapped the table.

'I know, Annie. It's sad, isn't it?' Polly answered.

'Oh, I don't know. They say heaven is lovely. Mind you, he'll be happier when he's got Alice with him.' Annie wiped up the last of the brown sauce with a crust of bread and looked up shyly at Alice. Polly looked anxiously at Alice, but she was smiling affectionately at the child.

'Well I'm not going yet, Annie. I want to stay with you,' she said with a smile.

'Good. I hoped you'd say that.'

'Can we get down please, Lady Gertrude?' Fred asked.

'You may, once you have learnt to say may we and not can we – when will you learn?' Gertie tutted. 'And once you've removed your plates. One hour play and then bed. No nonsense, you understand,' Gertie said seriously. But the children grinned, fully aware now of the twinkle in her eye.

The three older children clattered from the table,

stacking their dishes on to the draining board, and then stood in a silent row.

'Now what?' said Gertie. To Polly's surprise she realized that the children were giggling and that she was witnessing a ritual. 'Oh, very well. May, the bar. Fred, the razor.' May and Fred ran over to the dresser to return with a Mars bar and a razor blade. Polly watched, astonished, as with the delicacy of a surgeon Gertie cut four paper-thin slices of the chocolate. 'Their treat,' she explained to Polly. 'We can make the bar last a whole week this way.' Polly felt ashamed that she had not brought some of the chocolates that were always arriving in Juniper's parcels from America. She had mentioned several times that they should share the parcels with the grandmothers, but Juniper was sometimes evasive about them and when she did agree, simply forgot to send them on. The children noisily left the kitchen. Annie slipped from her chair and tried to climb on to Alice's lap.

'Not now, Annie; Alice is tired . . .'

'I don't mind, Gertie.'

'Yes, you do. Annie, out – go and play.' Gertie pointed sternly towards the door and Annie walked with agonizing slowness towards it, trailing her now much-patched teddy bear behind her.

'I don't want her upset,' Alice said, as the door was slammed behind the small figure.

'You've got to think of yourself, my dear. And in any case you're spoiling that child stupidly.'

'You can't spoil a child.'

'Can't you?' Gertie raised a cynical eyebrow and the other two women knew she was thinking of Juniper.

Fred's head appeared round the door. 'Phone for Polly.'

'Telephone call for Miss Polly,' Gertie said resignedly.

'Sorry,' Fred grinned, not in the least put out.

Polly raced to the telephone in the draughty hall. The line was impossible and she could barely hear Jonathan, but at least he had got her message. She wondered why he had bothered to go to London when she was in Cornwall.

When she returned to the kitchen it was to find her grandmother doing the washing-up alone. Alice had retired to bed early.

'Why are you doing that? Where's the staff?' Polly said, shocked at seeing her grandmother swathed in a large pinafore, washing up, of all things. She quickly picked up a teacloth to dry up.

'Would you believe Flo has a mother?' she laughed.

'Flo? But she's so old.'

'Well, her mother is alive – she is getting on for a hundred but it doesn't look as if she'll reach it now. She's got pneumonia and it's unlikely she'll last the week. Flo's gone to nurse her.'

'But your maid and the cook? At Christmas I presumed they were on holiday.'

'They left ages ago.'

'You should have told me.'

'And have you worrying? No point in that. We allowed the cook to say it was her feet, but in fact Alice and I had decided she was too profligate with the rations. And somehow it seemed wrong, Polly, to have a cook in times like these – unpatriotic.'

'Hardly. She was unlikely to find work in a munitions factory.'

'No. I got her a job with a minister in the government. Apparently she can crack eggs to her heart's content there.' Gertie sniffed her disapproval. 'As to my maid, she lasted six months. Then her nerves got her – or so she claimed. I think she was bored.' She swished the water from the basin around the sink and scrubbed it quickly with a wire brush.

'Do you see your mother?' she asked suddenly.

'Not often. I used to visit her every month, but I don't any longer. It seemed a waste of time; we have so little in common.'

'I should think not,' said Gertie indignantly. Busily she crossed the kitchen to hang the damp teacloth on the rail of the kitchen range. She disappeared for a moment and returned with a large broom with which she proceeded to sweep the floor.

'Let me do that, Grandmama,' Polly exclaimed.

'Nonsense. It takes a minute only. We're very organized.'

'You should get the children to help.'

'We do, but Saturday is their night off. We have a rota.'

'But why give them all the same night off?'

'It's more fun for them,' Gertie said in an indulgent voice. She crossed to the dresser which stretched the length of one wall. From the cupboard she took a bottle. 'Port? Our vice. Every night Alice and I have a small indulgence.' She hooted loudly. 'You'll join me?' She offered the bottle and Polly nodded eagerly. 'Is Juniper drinking again?'

'No, she's been very good recently. I think her illness frightened her into sanity.'

'Umph.' Gertie's whole posture was of one filled with cynicism. 'Didn't want to come to a funeral, I suppose? So thoughtless.'

Polly sat silent.

'I know you are fond of Juniper, Polly, you've proved that frequently in the past. But do you think she's the right friend for you?'

'I don't understand, Grandmother.'

'She puts upon you, Polly. It's not fair. She takes advantage of your good nature. That sort always does.' Gertie sat down at the pine table and took Polly's hand in hers. 'You're a sweet girl and too unselfish for your own good.'

'It's not like that, Grandmother, it really isn't. Juniper's been a good friend to me. She's made mistakes in the past, but they're mistakes I'm sure she now regrets. She's so generous to me; it would be quite difficult in London without her and the secure base she gives me.'

'I know all that. But her generosity is a different matter from most people's. It doesn't mean any sacrifice on her part, after all. I've often wondered if she isn't using her money to purchase friendship.'

'Oh, I don't think so. Maybe in the past, but not now. She leads a very quiet life these days.'

'With you waiting on her hand and foot, no doubt.'

Polly laughed. 'Well, she's pretty useless, you know. She needs a nanny.'

'Does she? I can't believe that Alice who, after all, had a big say in her upbringing would have allowed her to grow up useless. Then there was that sensible Tommy woman she had for a companion. I can't believe either of them failed to make sure that Juniper could cook and sew and run a house.'

'I don't think they could have done. She can't boil an egg,' Polly said. 'She'd starve beside a fully stocked refrigerator.'

'Um.' Gertie began to study her rings intently. Sounds like laziness to me, she thought.

'In any case I think with someone like Juniper there's not a lot one can do. I do get annoyed with her – and angry sometimes. She's untidy and inconsiderate, and so unpunctual. I've lost count of the hours I've wasted waiting for her at various times. But as soon as I've decided I'm going to say something to her, the door opens and in she comes, full of charm and joy – and I find I can't say anything. I'd hate to hurt her, Grand-mother . . . I feel she suffers enough pain.'

'Um, that smile. Used abundantly, isn't it?' Gertie said, with marked scepticism. Then seeing Polly's dejected expression, she took her hand and patted it. 'You're a dear child, Polly. I only hope Juniper is aware of what a gem of a friend she has in you.'

'I was upset when she wouldn't come. I did try to persuade her, but she looked terrified at the prospect. It wasn't normal.'

'There are people who run away from illness and death, I know. But this is different, this is her family. I'm so angry for dear Alice's sake. She needed that young woman here. She's devastated with grief. I hear her at night . . . I know what she's going through. But our upbringing taught us to grieve in private and to carry on, and Alice will.'

'At least she's got Annie. She's obviously very fond of the child. She really is a little character, isn't she?'

'It's a mistake. What happens when the child goes back to her father? It'll break Alice's heart all over again. She talks of having her to visit, paying for her education, even adoption if her father should be killed. I tell her it's unfair on Annie, but she won't listen. Once the child is back in her own environment, it would be too cruel to take her out of the slums into this life and then send her back again. It would be too unsettling for her. And what would Juniper have to say to that, I wonder.'

'But it's already too late. Annie's here – she's already living in a beautiful house surrounded by lovely things, all of which she's going to have to leave. The upset has already occurred.'

'She's only eight. There's time for her to forget.'

'But will she? Isn't it the Jesuits who say "Give me the child and I'll show you the man" or something like that?'

'Maybe,' said Gertie, sounding unconvinced. She began carefully to straighten a pile of tissue paper she had in front of her. She cut it neatly into squares and threaded a piece of string through the stack of paper. 'Toilet paper,' she said in explanation. 'There are some things I shall never forgive the Hun.'

The few tears at the station were the only ones Polly was to see Alice shed. Her grandmother had been right: all through the days before the funeral, the sad ceremony itself and the reception afterwards, Alice behaved with dignity and control.

Watching her, Polly wondered whether she would be able to behave in such a manner if anything happened to Jonathan. But, she reminded herself, when she heard that Andrew was dead, her heart had felt broken and still she went to work, still she had carried on. Maybe she too could call herself a daughter of a granite land as Alice did. Cornwall was not the only land of granite, there was Dartmoor too. It was a comforting thought to cling to in these uncertain times.

Even so, she doubted whether she and Juniper had the strength of character of the two grandmothers. Their adjustments to these difficult days was remarkable. Who would ever have thought that both of them would cook and clean and do all the domestic chores?

Both amazed her. She discovered that the household hints she had laboured over in the office, and had so often suspected to be a complete waste of time, were followed with almost religious devotion at Gwenfer.

There was not a hedgerow safe from Alice, Gertie and the evacuees. Rosehips had been collected for their valuable syrup. Foxgloves, nettles, hawthorn leaves, marigold flowers and shepherd's purse were all picked in season for sending to Culpepper's, the pharmaceutical firm, for processing for the valuable drugs they contained. Rose haws were munched by the pigs by the bucketful. Elderflowers, blackberries, rhubarb, apples, parsnips and even carrots joined the rosehips at the jam-making centre in the village organised by the WVS.

Gertie, after her initial disappointment over the Red Cross's lack of interest, had found her métier. She had contacted her old friend, Lady Reading, founder of the WVS, and volunteered her services for Gwenfer, as yet without its own group, and was in her element organizing the local women, resplendent in her smart dark-green uniform and beetroot-red jumper. No empty jam jar escaped her eagle eye, nor unused blanket. She drew up a rota of drivers to ferry the elderly to hospital appointments. She sorted out problems with the numerous evacuees in the area. She taught her women how to cook on field cookers, in dustbins, in hay boxes. Gwenfer was well prepared for any eventuality, even the still feared invasion.

Every other day at Gwenfer a beachcombing party went out searching for driftwood. Their cove had been deemed too small and unapproachable for mines and barbed wire to be necessary. The woods were scoured for fallen branches and twigs. The evacuees often complained, but Alice and Gertie enjoyed themselves enormously.

Walking about Gwenfer at night was a dangerous occupation since both women had taken heed of Polly's department's advice to remove light bulbs where not necessary and replace all others with dimmer ones. The fact that Gwenfer had its own generator did not alter the requirement since fuel was so scarce that each watt of electricity saved was an achievement.

Each bath now sported a black plimsoll line in gloss paint at five inches' depth. Polly doubted if anyone in the house dared to cheat, even behind the privacy of a locked door. She certainly did not.

They had the leaflet recommending a mixture of salt and vinegar to clean brass. They had cut up old felt hats and made slippers for the children. And both women spent every rare spare moment knitting, often from old jumpers washed and unravelled, the wool carefully wound into hanks to stretch it. Alice's efforts were successful; Gertie's alarmingly misshapen.

Rationing was scrupulously observed, and Polly was certain that both women gave more than their fair share of the household's allowance of food to the evacuees. Certainly all their clothing coupons went on the children. As Alice explained, neither minded what they looked like, so their large wardrobes of clothes, hats and shoes from pre-war days would hopefully see them through to the end of the war.

Polly decided she would insist that Juniper send some of her American parcels here, where they were really needed. She and Juniper lacked little and, although Juniper claimed it was all thanks to her parcels, Polly was not convinced. She feared that when she was at work Juniper was still doing shady deals with the spivs.

Polly did not have to hurry back to London. First she received a telegram from Gwendoline Rickmansworth saying she had to rush off for a family funeral of her own, then a second telegram arrived from Jonathan with the disappointing news that he would not be able to get away for the weekend, so she decided to stay until the following Wednesday.

She was glad to have the break. It was wonderful to have Hursty to sleep with her again and it was good to be able to help the two older women; their work seemed endless, though neither complained. And it wasn't until she was at Gwenfer that she realized how tired she was. It was suddenly an effort to get up and she had to force herself to help; all she wanted to do was sleep. It was understandable however; five years of war, five years of endless worry, had taken their toll. The sleepless nights, the unaccustomed hard work, the sheer difficulty of getting from A to B in the everlasting blackout, the endless queues for everything, the lack of proper holidays, added to concern, then grief, for Andrew, all had contributed. Polly was not alone, the whole nation was becoming exhausted.

Juniper sounded cheerful when Polly called to check that she was all right. She insisted that Polly should stay as long as she liked, she was fine, 'being good' she said. The Germans had launched a new blitz, but compared with 1940 it was nothing and Polly was not to worry. Juniper sounded so happy that Polly wondered if, perhaps, she had met someone else at long last. She did hope so, there was nothing she longed for more than for Juniper to find a good man who would take care of her. Polly felt she had been so lucky, first Andrew and then Jonathan – she chose to forget Michel – that it did not seem fair that Juniper always seemed to have such bad luck.

Once or twice she had tried to talk to Alice about Juniper, but each time it was as if a veil was dropped over Alice's fine features. She was still too hurt to discuss her granddaughter. She mentioned her only once. She was standing on the platform at Penzance station looking up at Polly hanging out of the open carriage window.

'Tell Juniper I love her,' was all she said as the train began to move and she lifted her hand to wave.

It was strange, she had only been away for twelve days and yet when she returned everything looked different. The houses appeared smaller than she remembered them, she supposed it was in contrast to the wide sky and seascape of Gwenfer. After the cleanness of Cornwall, the streets were so dirty and dull, and the air felt thick to breathe and laden with dust and dirt.

There was a note for her from Juniper saying she had gone to the country for a short break and would be back on Friday. Polly smiled to herself; she had been right, Juniper had found someone.

The first thing Polly decided to do was to visit the shops she normally frequented, to let them know she was back. Being a regular customer was the only way to be sure of obtaining any treats available. She received a touching welcome. These days, when people were not seen again they could so easily be dead.

She was rewarded with an apple from the greengrocer, a lamb chop for her supper from the butcher and a whole pint of shrimps from the fishmonger. She would have a feast tonight. She slipped into Boots lending library where she was greeted like an old friend and was lucky enough to get the latest Angela Thirkell, although she was sure there must be a waiting list for it. Living in London was just like living in a village, she decided, if one was loyal and shopped only in one's own district.

It was a pleasant evening. Since Juniper's illness, this must be the only time she had had the house all to herself and she luxuriated in the sense of isolation. At about eight she called Jonathan, to be told he was not in the pub and had not been seen all week. This worried her, she hoped he wasn't ill. She left a message that she was back in London, then ate her supper by the fire, curled up with the Thirkell. All that was lacking was Jonathan in the chair opposite and Hursty purring on her lap.

The next morning she overslept and wondered why she felt so guilty about it. Did it matter if she stayed in bed all day? She tried, but quickly felt uncomfortable. Polly was not the sort to lie idle. She was soon up, dusting and polishing and looking forward to Juniper's return.

Juniper arrived by taxi in the late afternoon in her usual flurry. Polly was surprised by the taxi, she would have expected Juniper to drive to the country since they hardly used their petrol ration in the city. Perhaps she had gone too far to drive.

'My, you look well,' Juniper said, as she kissed Polly welcome.

'You do too. You obviously needed your little holiday.'

'You can say that again,' Juniper laughed, kicking off her shoes and slipping her coat from her shoulders. Polly went to pick them up and then, remembering her grandmother's words, left them where they were.

'You didn't drive, then?'

'Yes. I crashed the car.'

'Oh, Juniper, no. Are you hurt?'

'No, but the car's sorry for itself.'

'Was anyone with you?'

'What do you mean?' Juniper said quickly.

'Any passenger who was hurt?'

'No, I was all on my own.' Juniper looked away.

'Where did it happen?'

'In the country.'

'Where?'

'Lordy, I don't know – it was all grass and trees.'

'Well, it would be, wouldn't it?' Polly smiled.

'Gee, you're full of questions, aren't you?'

'Am I? Sorry, I was just curious. Can the car be mended?'

'Yes. I'm to pick it up next week. From,' she paused for a fraction of a second, 'from near Oxford. I'm collecting it on Monday. I thought I'd take the opportunity of going away for a couple of days again.'

'You've met someone?' Polly clapped her hands with excitement. 'Oh, I'm so pleased, that's wonderful news.'

'No, it's not. It's not serious. He's . . . he's engaged . . . It's just a little adventure before he settles down.'

'Juniper, no!'

'Don't lecture me – I've just arrived. How was it? Am I forever in the doghouse?' She smiled at Polly.

'Alice says to tell you she loves you. That's all.'

'Glory be. Why can't she be angry with me? That just makes me feel even more guilty.' Juniper sighed and curled up on the chair. 'I should have gone. What was it like?'

'Yes, you should have. It was a beautiful ceremony – so simple and dignified. The weather was perfect.'

'What a crass statement, Polly. How can the weather be perfect for a funeral, for goodness sake? Does it matter one way or the other?'

'You know what I mean. What else is there to say? You asked,' Polly almost snapped.

'Was Alice crying her eyes out?'

Polly turned to face Juniper, shocked by the light tone of her voice. 'No, she wasn't. She's too dignified to make a scene. But she was devastated by Phillip's death. My grandmother often heard her crying at night.' Polly spoke crossly. Juniper shrugged her shoulders as if totally uninterested. 'At least she's got little Annie to comfort her,' Polly said, suddenly leaping to her feet. 'I'll start dinner,' and she left the room quickly, shocked at the satisfaction she had felt in saying that. But if she could not physically shake Juniper for her insensitivity, perhaps she could shock her out of her cold complacency.

*

Jonathan arrived on Saturday, his left arm in a sling and with a limp.

'A stupid accident, nothing serious,' he reassured a worried Polly, not quite meeting her eye.

'I *knew* there was something wrong when the people at The Green Man said they hadn't seen you all week. Why on earth didn't you let me know?'

'I didn't want to worry you, my precious.'

'But I was already worried. How did it happen?'

'I told you, an accident,' he replied, as she helped him out of his greatcoat.

'Yes, but what sort of accident?' she persisted.

'I was in a car and it got wrapped round a tree.' He was already halfway up the stairs and spoke over his shoulder.

'Gracious, you and Juniper make a fine pair,' Polly said lightly, as she followed him up.

'What do you mean?' His voice was casual, but he turned to face her.

'She's had an accident with her motor too, but she's not hurt. My poor darling, are you in pain?'

'No, no – throbs a little that's all. Is Juniper here?' he asked, rather nonchalantly, he felt.

'Yes, she's waiting in the drawing room.' Polly opened the door for him. 'Look at my poor wounded soldier,' she announced gaily.

Juniper, who was standing in front of the fireplace staring vacantly into the mirror, swung round.

'Poor dear Jonathan. You are in the wars. What happened?' She crossed towards him and kissed him lightly on the cheek.

'I hear you've had a crash too, Juniper,' he said cautiously.

'Yes, near Oxford. Too stupid of me.'

'How odd, with my accident near Cambridge.' He laughed loudly.

'A drink?' Juniper asked him, frowning slightly as if warning him about his laugh.

'A bit early for me, thanks,' he said, glancing at his watch.

'How dull. I never find it's too early.' She crossed to the drinks tray and began to pour herself a gin and tonic. 'No point in offering you anything, Polly, I suppose?'

'No thanks,' Polly said, and it was her turn to frown as she watched Juniper lift the glass to her lips.

It was a pleasant weekend despite the fact they could not go to an art exhibition Polly had wanted to share with Jonathan. And the theatre was out too – his ankle was, she felt, giving him far more pain than he would acknowledge. Instead they spent the weekend reading and listening to records, and Jonathan managed to do some writing; at least it was his left hand which was damaged, not his right.

At night they slept close in each other's arms. They had tried to make love, but Jonathan was in too much pain. Polly did not mind in the least, in fact she rather liked it. Just lying quietly together made her feel almost as if they were married. When an air-raid alert sounded they merely pulled the eiderdown over their heads and held each other even tighter. By the time Jonathan had to leave, Polly felt that it had been the happiest weekend they had spent together.

It was a rush that Monday morning. Juniper, never at her best too early in the day, was rushing about looking for 'important' items she had lost – a particular silk scarf, a pair of earrings, her cheque book. She was sharing a taxi with Jonathan.

'We might as well,' she had said the night before; 'I'll drop Jonathan at Liverpool Street and then go on to Paddington.'

'Would you, Juniper? That is kind. I've got to be at work at eight. I daren't be late on my first day back,' Polly had said with gratitude.

She waved the two travellers on their way and by seven-thirty was on her own way to work. She carried her gas-mask case as she always did in London, but now there was no gas mask in it, only her sandwiches, a small thermos of tea, her driving licence and identity card and a lipstick. She wondered what she would do when the war was over and women returned to using handbags; the square, box-shaped gas-mask case was wonderfully handy.

She arrived at her office on time, only to find Gwendoline Rickmansworth already there.

'I'm not late, am I?' She held her watch to her ear to check whether it was still ticking.

'No, my dear. Don't flap. I stayed the night – I often do. I've a little truckle bed I put up. I hope you have no plans this week?'

'No, nothing, only at the . . .' but she did not finish in time to say she had definite plans for the weekend.

'Good. I should have telephoned you, but this came up late on Friday and I've only just had confirmation. We're off to the north, you and I – Birmingham, York and Edinburgh. You'd better go home and pack for at least ten days and meet me here at eleven.'

'Oh, I see,' Polly said, her voice dropping with disappointment.

'Messes up your plans?'

'No.' She shook her head. 'Nothing I can't sort out,' she said, as lightly as she could muster.

Back at the house she packed her case. She left a note for Juniper and luckily got straight through to The Green Man and left a message for Jonathan. She was back at the office by eleven, checked out the large Humber motor car supplied by the Ministry of Information with a full tank of petrol, a supply of petrol coupons and an ominously large can of engine oil. By noon, she and Mrs Rickmansworth had cleared the city and were bowling up the Great North Road.

By noon Juniper was safely ensconced in The Green Man. She had a light lunch with several glasses of wine and then set out to explore Cambridge, a city she did not know.

Jonathan was free of his classes by six and found Juniper already in the bar.

'Cambridge is divine,' she announced. 'I think I might move here.'

'That would be wonderful,' Jonathan said, beginning to wonder if it would be possible to continue with Juniper as his mistress if he and Polly were living here too.

'It's so leafy and the colleges are delicious, Jonathan, it's the only word for them. And there are so many young men about – a divorced woman's paradise,' she chuckled.

'I'd have thought they'd be too young even for you,' Jonathan said shortly, finding he did not like Juniper to talk of other men in this way.

'But think, when the war's over – and it won't be long now – all those weary heroes will be pouring into the university.' She smiled at him over the top of her glass and he couldn't make up his mind whether she was teasing him or not.

'Mr Middlebank, there's a message for you,' the landlady called to him from the other side of the bar.

'Yes? What?' Jonathan called back.

'I've written it down for you. Here . . .' She held up a small piece of paper, waved it in the air and smiled coyly at him.

'Excuse me.' Jonathan stood up and crossed to the bar. 'Thanks, Glad.' He took the slip of paper and looked at it, but it was blank. He looked at her questioningly. The woman leant conspiratorially towards him.

'It was that nice girl, Polly,' she whispered. 'She's had to go north for ten days or so. I thought as I should be discreet in the circumstances.' She nodded towards Juniper.

'Thanks, Glad, that's really thoughtful of you.'

'You're a right one, aren't you?' She slapped his hand playfully. 'That poor little Polly, you shouldn't have her on like this, she sounds so nice on the telephone – I really feel sorry for her.'

'Yes, Glad.' Jonathan felt himself blushing and shuffled

his feet with embarrassment. 'Things aren't what they seem.'

'Oh, aren't they? Pull the other one, Mr Middlebank.' She roared with laughter and Jonathan returned to Juniper wearing a hangdog expression. She looked up.

'Bad news?' she asked and, as she did so, realized how many times she had asked that question in recent years.

'It was Polly.' Jonathan slumped down beside her.

'Oh Lord, she isn't on her way here, is she?' Juniper looked alarmed.

'No, she's gone north for ten days.'

'How wonderful!' She clapped her hands together. 'Ten whole days together – it couldn't be better.'

Jonathan took a sip of his warm beer. 'Don't you feel guilty?' he asked.

'No. Why should I?' She clicked open her handbag removing her cigarette case.

'She is your best friend after all. We've done this once before and look what happened – she married that French bastard.'

'She won't do anything like that again. She's wiser now. But why should she find out? I shan't tell her. I only told her last time because I knew you would confess and I wanted to get in before you.' She laughed gaily. Jonathan looked nervously into his tankard. 'You would have confessed, wouldn't you?' she asked, leaning towards him.

'Yes. Probably.'

'There you are then. So don't even think of confessing, will you?'

'But it's not that simple, Juniper.'

'Isn't it? What's complicated about it? We like each other, we like being together. We both love Polly and would never do anything to hurt her.'

'Good God, Juniper, how can you say that?' He laughed ironically. 'Of course we're hurting her.'

'Don't be silly. How can she be hurt if she doesn't

know? I've not taken you away from her – I was as good as gold last weekend. I kept out of your way, didn't I?'

'Yes,' he agreed grudgingly, and looked at her with puzzlement. It had been agony for him in bed with Polly, knowing Juniper was in bed, alone, on the floor below. He was glad he had exaggerated his aches and pains so that Polly had quite happily accepted that he could not make love to her. There were limits after all. 'I lied to her about the weekend before that to make sure she would stay in Cornwall.'

'That was your decision, Jonathan, not mine. I didn't ask you to lie. I didn't even know you had until you told me,' she said firmly.

'God, Juniper, I'm in such a muddle. I don't know what to do.' He placed his glass carefully back on the table and took one of her cigarettes, unusual for him for he normally smoked a pipe. 'I love you, Juniper, but I love Polly too. God, what a mess.'

Juniper sat up straight, her large hazel eyes widening with alarm. She ground out her barely smoked cigarette with deliberation. 'Don't talk like that, Jonathan, ever. This was just fun, just an adventure. Don't love me. I don't want you to. I don't love you and never will.'

'Juniper, don't say that.'

'I mean it, Jonathan. I can't love anyone – don't you realize?' she said more seriously.

'But how could you . . . I mean, doesn't it mean . . . I don't understand . . .'

'I like going to bed with you. I don't like sleeping alone – I get lonely. But there's nothing more. You make love to me because you want to, not because I *want* you to.'

'I don't believe what I'm hearing.' Jonathan pulled his left hand through his hair in despair.

'Well, I'm sorry if you don't like hearing it, but it's the truth. That's why I don't feel guilty about Polly – I'm not taking anything from her.'

'God, Juniper, what sort of woman are you? You're made of stone.' He looked at her with horror.

'Jonathan Middlebank . . .' a voice from the bar called. A group of RAF officers were leaning against the bar. One of them left the group and approached them.

'Hullo, Dominic,' Jonathan said, glowering with displeasure at the young man for interrupting them.

'Aren't you going to introduce me?' Dominic was grinning at Jonathan's obvious discomfort.

Jonathan reluctantly made the introductions. His anger increased as he saw Juniper's face light up with interest and noticed the laughter in her eyes as she shook Dominic's hand in greeting.

Chapter Three

1

The prisoner stood in the middle of the exercise yard, the threadbare stuff of his prison uniform useless as insulation against the cold. He willed himself not to shiver as the easterly wind whipped about him. He had found, from past experience, that if he concentrated on each set of muscles, tautening and relaxing them in turn, he could generate a modicum of bodily heat that kept the teeth-chattering and the shivering at bay. To shiver smacked of failure, he would not give the bastards the pleasure of seeing him flinch.

He looked into the distance as if seeing beyond the rows of prison barracks, past the guards, the machine guns in the turrets, the dogs, the wired fence. He ignored the row of prisoners standing beside him naked, shaking with cold and fear – at least he had his clothes, inadequate though they were. His captors' only concession to his state as a soldier he presumed. And he wasn't afraid; he had long ago come to terms with fear and had found the strength to reject it.

He was a man of thirty who looked more like fifty, his once muscular body emaciated and his blond hair grey now, not that he knew for it was years since he had seen his reflection in a mirror. But his blue eyes in the sunken, ruined face blazed with hatred.

The day was dark, ice underfoot. He allowed himself a glance at the sky. It took all his control not to sway with despair as he saw the fat yellow clouds, obese with snow, congregating above him. If it snowed he would shiver, he knew it. And these poor sods beside him would die.

He had twice before endured this punishment. Once in

the boiling heat of summer, plagued by flies and the stench of the place, the second time in pouring rain, but this time their greatest enemy, the cold, might beat him.

He was surprised to be here at all. The last time he had tried to escape they had told him that next time he would be executed: shot, garrotted or gassed – they would decide at the time. But then when the time had come and his latest pathetic bid for freedom had been discovered, they had not murdered him immediately, but had stuck him out here in the icy wind of the exercise yard.

They called it execution, he called it murder. Maybe they knew better than he did, maybe they were fully aware he would not be able to last the fourteen hours that he calculated were left of the twenty-four of his sentence.

The first snowflakes fell. He watched them scudding in the wind, whirling first one way and then the other, a source of horror here but in another time, another place, a beautiful sight. He shook his head and blinked the flakes from his eyelashes.

Another place, another time. '*Liz*,' he said the word softly and then repeated it again, speaking into the wind, amusing himself with the fantasy that it might scoop up her name and carry it through the forest, across the mountains, and over the Channel, and that somehow she would know he was thinking of her.

The wind strengthened, the snow increased as if in competition, great swirling drifts. Across the open space he heard shouting, through the snow he saw the gate open, a lorry begin to enter and then grind to a halt, blocking the gateway. He heard the guards shouting instructions to the driver, heard the impotent wail of the engine, the screeching of the wheels. He turned his head away without interest.

Liz. He returned to her. They could starve him, abuse him, take away his dignity, demoralise him into a husk, but there was nothing they could do about his mind and the memories stored inside it. It was thinking of Liz, and their happiness during the short time they had shared, which had seen him through the past four years. She had been in his mind when he was captured. During his first months of imprisonment, when he had been in solitary confinement, her presence was so strong it was almost as if she were in the cell with him. When his gaolers had finally decided he knew nothing, that he was what he had said, a soldier in the wrong place at the wrong time, and he was let out into a POW camp, it felt as if she were with him. There had been moments of fear that she might have forgotten him and found someone else. But then her letters had come, two of them, and he knew she loved him. That knowledge gave him the strength and determination to escape, to get back to her.

Each time he had tried he had been recaptured. Once he was wounded and he was always punished, but he could not stop: it was as if escaping had become his reason for living. He had been moved from one POW camp to another, each one harder to get out of than the previous one – it never stopped him. But then when he had been recaptured again nine months ago, it was not the friendly faces of fellow officers that awaited him, but the shuffling, almost dead, apathetic inmates of this concentration camp in the depths of Poland and the accusations from his captors that he was a spy and the interrogation had started all over again.

Here, his most precious possession had been taken from him – Liz's letters. Losing them had laid him lower than at any other time. His depression cocooned him from the suffering around him, the agony, the dying. His depression saved him from giving up in those early days as so many did. He came through it with anger and hatred his motivation. Hatred at the bastards who'd stolen his letters and so the planning to escape had begun again – twice from this camp so far. Two failures, but the next time . . . The thought of that next time kept him going.

He grabbed at his memories, that was the way to survive. He was in Paris now in her tiny flat which always reminded him of a boat. He was sprawled on one of the large cushions, a drink in hand, surrounded by warmth – wonderful warmth from the aged cast-iron stove in the corner. He was laughing across at dark-haired, long-legged, beautiful Liz sitting curled up on another cushion, her cat draped on her lap.

He rocked suddenly as the wind increased in intensity. Liz was slipping away from him, he lifted his hands as if trying to hold on to her memory. She had gone.

He looked about him and saw nothing. He was in a white cloud. There were no buildings, no horizon, no ground, no sky. He thought for a second he was dead and then he realized he was in the centre of a blizzard, standing in a total white-out.

He stepped forward and paused. No one shouted. He took two more steps waiting for the click of a rifle bolt. There was nothing. He walked quietly, quickly. He walked in a straight line. He walked like an automaton.

He held his back straight. He was ready for the bullet, centre back, that's where it would hit. In a strange way he looked forward to it, almost longed for it – that's what having no fear gave one. And he longed for peace, he was tired of fighting – fighting to survive in order to continue to hate.

He was walking now head high, striding with pride. He wouldn't die a cur – not him.

The bullet didn't strike. He did not crash forward in the snow. Suddenly the dense white lifted like a thick sheet being peeled from his eyes. All around him were trees. He was in the forest, the concentration camp three hundred yards behind him.

2

'I think the worst thing about this damn war is that one is never really warm,' Gwendoline Rickmansworth complained, rearranging the meagre lumps of coal with brass tongs, but with little improvement. She sat down again in an armchair so large that her slight form looked lost in it.

They were sitting in the lounge of a hotel in Edinburgh. It had been a strange trip, Polly thought, and a salutary one too. Living in London, she had soon become as insular as everyone else there, in the belief that nothing of any importance happened outside its limits. She had read with horror of the many Baedeker raids, but thought nothing could be as bad as London. She was therefore shocked to the core to see the devastation of Coventry and now entered a cathedral city in fear of what she might find.

Gwendoline had not explained the reason for the trip, but as its purpose began to sink in – from snippets of information gleaned from the letters Gwendoline wrote, and the report they were compiling – Polly hardly dared believe it could be true: Gwendoline seemed to be involved with post-war plans. It was no longer as far-fetched as it would have been the previous year, before the Allied landings in Italy. As the Allies moved inexorably up its spine Italy had finally surrendered.

Staying overnight in Liverpool, they heard that Ireland was virtually blockaded. This could mean only one thing: the government was preventing invasion plans reaching Dublin. Everywhere they travelled, troop movements were more apparent, all going eastwards. It looked as if the longed-for invasion of Europe was going to happen. Hope was tangible – the end of the war was in sight. Some optimists said next month, others six months and there were those who thought it would not be until the following year. Whenever it came, the very thought that an end to the killing was in sight and victory a possibility seemed to give everyone added determination to carry on, even with the irksome rationing and restrictions. Polly, like so many young women, began to allow herself to plan her future with Jonathan.

Their tray of tea arrived, with sardine sandwiches and cakes with synthetic cream. Polly poured.

'Did you get through on the telephone?' Gwendoline asked, waving both sandwiches and cake away and sweetening her tea with saccharin from a pretty jewelled pill box.

'I couldn't get through to Jonathan. That's three days now the lines have been jammed. And there's no answer from my friend Juniper . . . I do hope she's all right.'

'I shouldn't worry about Juniper. If she's anything like her father she's a survivor.' Gwendoline laughed, and changed her mind about the cake.

'Did you know him well?'

'Not very well. Not as most women knew him,' she said with a chuckle. 'I was on his yacht just that one time. Not a happy voyage . . .' Gwendoline stopped in mid-sentence, flustered. She had completely forgotten that Polly's mother was the unspeakable Francine who had also been on the same voyage, busily seducing Juniper's father. 'They were all a little too sophisticated for the blushing young bride that I was.' She patted her lips with her napkin to cover her confusion. 'I was wondering, Polly, if you would mind if we prolonged the trip by a couple of days. I think we should go to Newcastle.'

'Of course,' Polly said, hiding her disappointment. She wanted to get back to London by the weekend to see Jonathan.

'You could send Jonathan a telegram.'

'Yes. I'll do that.' She smiled brightly.

'I'll confess. I don't have to go to Newcastle, but my family are from Northumberland. I'd like to see my mother and also to visit a very dear friend. She's lost her only son and is very low. Her family are very worried about her. Her husband suggested that perhaps a visit from me might cheer her up a little, and I think I should try.'

'How do people ever recover from losing a child?'

'God knows. It was worse, in a way, for them; they'd been through so much. First he was missing, then they heard he was safe in a POW camp, then the next news was that he was dead.'

'I can sympathise. Exactly the same happened with the man I was planning to marry.' Polly's expression saddened as she talked of Andrew. 'He was from Northumberland too. Perhaps you know the family? Slater – Andrew Slater.'

'Good Heavens.' For the second time that afternoon the normally poised Gwendoline seemed at a loss for words. 'I don't believe it,' she continued. 'His mother is the friend I want to visit. I didn't know he was engaged. His mother never told me. I'm so sorry, my dear.'

'We weren't engaged – not officially. We didn't have time for that. We met in Paris, you see, just before the Fall. But we had decided, oh yes. As soon as we got back to England . . .' Her voice trailed off, she felt sad again.

'Then you must come and meet his family. Tell them how he was in Paris. Perhaps you'll be able to help her.'

'I'd like to do that. He spoke about them often and he was very fond of his mother in particular.'

'But you've met someone else? This Jonathan.'

'I've known him since I was a child. We keep putting off the day, though; things keep cropping up.'

'You shouldn't delay too long – not with a war on.'

The visit to the Slater home was not the success that they had both hoped. Polly's heart went out to Agnes Slater the moment she met her. She had the lost look of a child. She was thin to the point of emaciation, which was accentuated when she stood beside her large husband, Ferdie. He was bluff and cheerful and appeared to have come to terms with his grief.

Andrew's room had been left exactly as it was the day he had gone to war. The sheets he had slept in had been left on the bed, his pyjamas neatly folded on the cover. The book he had been reading lay open at the page he had reached. The flowers in the vase were long since dead.

Polly noticed some hair in the brushes on the dressing table and shivered. It was the room of a young boy – not the man she had known. School photographs hung on the wall, his cricket bat stood in the corner. They had been followed into the room by an old springer spaniel who whined as he lifted his snout in the air and sniffed the lingering smell of his dead master.

The room was a shrine and it took every ounce of Polly's self control to stand there and force herself to listen to Andrew's mother talking incessantly about her son.

Initially Agnes had welcomed Polly, but during the evening her attitude began to change as she realized that Polly had survived the loss of Andrew, that she looked well, appeared happy and had found someone else to replace the irreplaceable. By the morning, when it was time for them to leave, Agnes Slater's resentment of Polly was bitterly apparent.

'I'm sorry about that, Polly. It wasn't a good idea after all,' Gwendoline apologized.

'No. I'm glad I went. But that woman needs help – professional help. She should be recovering by now.'

'I know, but her family won't hear of it. I spoke to Ferdie last night. Very hot under the collar he got, accused me of saying Agnes is mad.'

'How sad and how silly. She's not mad, she's in despair.'

It was Tuesday, and April, before they were home in London. Of Juniper there was no sign. Once Polly had put on the kettle and checked her mail, she booked a call to Jonathan.

'Darling, I'm so sorry. Did you come to London expecting me to be here? I've been trying to get you for days but the telephones have been impossible.' The words tumbled out of her with excitement at being in touch with him at last. She needed to see him now to dispel the ghost of Andrew that the trip had suddenly recalled.

'No, I didn't travel up. When you didn't answer the

phone, I realized you were still away and then I got your telegram. They're moving us out.'

'Oh no. Where?'

'I don't know. I think the push is coming, don't you?'

'But you were safe there,' she wailed.

'I'll be all right, Polly. Don't worry. I think they're having to use everyone they can find. I'll be back here in a week or two.' His voice sounded flat.

'I've had a letter from my grandmother. She says that no visitors are allowed within ten miles of the coast – you have to get a permit to visit. I'd wanted to go down for a few days.'

'Bad luck,' Jonathan said. 'It's the same from the Wash down to Land's End,' he added, but he spoke as if totally uninterested.

'Jonathan, are you all right? You don't sound very happy.'

'I'm fine,' he replied, but she did not believe him.

'Juniper's not here,' she said, for something else to say.

'She's gone to Oxfordshire.'

'You've seen her?' Polly was aware of strain in her voice.

'Yes.'

'When, where?' Her heart was thumping.

'Oh, she turned up here.'

Polly had to lean against the wall. She realized she might be overreacting. Juniper had given no sign that she was still interested in Jonathan, but Polly long ago, had realized, that with Juniper one could never be sure about anything.

'What on earth for?' She congratulated herself on how level her voice sounded.

'God knows. Bored, I suppose, with you away. She's in love.'

Polly clutched the receiver of the phone so tightly that her knuckles gleamed white against the black instrument. 'Who with?'

'RAF chappie – Dominic Hastings. She met him here in the bar when he was home on leave. Love at first sight and all that guff. She's gone to Oxfordshire with him. He's a bit of a bore, if you ask me.'

'Oh . . . oh I'm so happy . . . Juniper needs to be in love.' She virtually sighed into the telephone. 'You don't sound very pleased about it,' she added with a laugh.

'Don't I?' Jonathan said shortly.

'I want to see you, Jonathan – desperately.'

'Me too.'

'When?'

'It's difficult.'

'Why?'

'I told you, they're shipping us out.'

'You'll telephone? Send a telegram. I'll be happy to go anywhere, just for an hour . . .'

'Fine.'

There was a rattling and clicking and the telephone went dead. Polly shook it with frustration, of all the times to be cut off. Reluctantly she replaced the receiver, suddenly feeling weary, went down the stairs to the basement and her tea.

She sat a long time in the kitchen staring into space as she sipped the tea. Jonathan had sounded so odd, almost petulant. He had not seemed too keen to see her, not as keen as she was. She needed to see him. Standing in Andrew's room had been a shock, it had opened the door on a thousand memories that were best forgotten.

3

Juniper sat on the small settle beside the log fire, feeling content as she waited for Dominic to return from the bar with her drink. They would have lunch and then she knew they would spend the afternoon making love, only appearing for dinner. Then the long night would stretch before them. But this afternoon bed must wait for a while.

She smiled to herself. Juniper was sure she was in love and was satiated with lovemaking.

A shout from the bar area made her look up. It looked as if a scuffle were breaking out, but it was only a young officer being bumped for his birthday. Up and down they threw him, roaring their approval. Higher he went until his nose almost brushed the meerschaum coloured ceiling. Juniper jumped to her feet with concern. They would hurt him. She stepped forward as if to stop them and then sat down again. There was no point, they would never hear her, let alone listen. When the boys got together and in this mood, there was no stopping them. Twenty-one bumps and the young man was dropped flat on his back on the red carpet. A pint of beer was poured over him followed by a bellowed *'For He's A Jolly Good Fellow'* which slid effortlessly into *'Roll Out the Barrel'*. Louder still they sang. Someone had been killed, she thought sadly, looking into the flames of the fire. They were always noisiest when one of their comrades had failed to return. The songs were sung more enthusiastically, as if by singing as loudly as possible they could blot out the memories of the night before, could erase the absence among them.

She could see Dominic battling his way through the press of uniforms towards her. She felt like pinching herself each day for she still could not believe she had found him.

It was three weeks since they had met. Even as Jonathan had been introducing them, something astonishing had happened. That impossible-to-describe moment. That mystical moment, spiritual, chemical, whatever it was, had happened. Juniper had fallen instantly in love.

In the past the men in her life had been noticeable for their elegant, showy looks. Dominic was different. He was tall and heavily built, with a strong chest and powerful shoulders. His hair swept back in a dark brown mane through which he often ran his fingers. His eyes too were brown and surmounted by thick eyebrows which gave him a serious expression. He smiled rarely so that, when he did, Juniper found its impact, and the change it made in his strong pensive face, electrifying.

He had emphatic views on every subject under the sun. He was clever and had no time for fools. This made Juniper feel complimented and important. At thirty he was older than most of the others in his group. Although he was somewhat detached from them, rarely joining in the heavy drinking sessions or the endless games of pool and darts, nonetheless the younger officers looked up to him and consulted him about their problems. There was a strength of character, a steadfastness, about him that Juniper was convinced she had spent all her life searching for.

He was a historian and before the war had taught in a state school. Brought up in a comfortable middle-class background, he had been shocked by the lives of some of his pupils. He had decided that, when the war was over, he would go back to university to study law and then hopefully to stand for parliament. He had an acute sense of social responsibility. Juniper, who possessed no social conscience whatsoever, had a lot of catching up to do. Overnight she became a dedicated socialist.

In the weeks since she had first met Dominic, Juniper had occupied herself with reading. He knew so much and she so little. He enjoyed teaching her and had compiled a lengthy reading list of books on political ideas and theory. The self-imposed discipline was hard for someone whose reading until now had been restricted to fiction, but she doggedly persevered. She wanted him to be proud of her, she wanted to be his intellectual companion – she knew she could never be his equal.

All this was because, unknown to Dominic, Juniper had made a decision. She was going to marry him. This time she would be the perfect wife.

The men in Dominic's circle were puzzled that someone as beautiful and apparently light-hearted as Juniper should be so infatuated with him; they were such opposites. Had

Polly met him she would have been able to explain to them. Dominic was a challenge to her. Juniper loved a challenge.

In these weeks Juniper had also had to learn to live with fear. She would kiss him goodbye as he left for duty, not knowing whether he would return. She would lie awake at night listening to the squadrons flying overhead, flying out to bomb the Germans into submission, wondering whether his plane was among them. As dawn broke she would lie sweating with terror listening to the returning planes, frightened that he had not got through.

But when he arrived, the happiness! Being so close to death every day of their lives, it was as if every feeling was heightened. Every minute had to be cherished. Every kiss, every caress took on a deeper significance. He only wanted to be with her, and his concentration on her and what she was thinking was at times so intense, it was heady. He swamped her with his attention and wrapped her totally in his world, his beliefs. It was as if he had taken her over completely and she gloried in it. At other times, there was a preoccupied air about him, a detachment, as if he were unaware of her presence. It was as if he were two people and this duality fascinated her.

And then there were their nights. What nights! It was as if having taken possession of her mind, he wanted equal control of her body. He enslaved her physically. And Juniper was certain she had never been happier.

This morning he had arrived with a forty-eight-hour pass. Two days of bliss stretched ahead of them and she had the most wonderful surprise for him.

'They get worse,' he nodded to the roaring, already drunk young men behind him.

'Who didn't come back?' she asked.

He frowned as if reluctant to answer. 'Pete Bradford.'

'But he was only eighteen!' she exclaimed.

'What are we going to do then?' he said abruptly. She cursed herself for her clumsiness in breaking the unwritten rule that no one should ask who had 'bought it'.

'I've a wonderful surprise for you.' She smiled up at him.

'What?'

'You must wait. We'll have lunch first, shall we?'

Somehow, Mrs Clemence, the landlady of The White Hart, always managed to have the best food available for 'her boys' whom she fussed over like a mother hen. How she managed was a mystery, but there was always a choice, always a roast and, more importantly, the beer never seemed to run out. Most of the young men here were not even based close by at RAF Benson but miles away, but it was here they chose to take their leave. Dominic was one of them.

They set off for Juniper's surprise well fed. Dominic walked towards his car, a battered MG held together by hope and prayer.

'No, there's no need for a car. Come.' She held out her hand to him.

They walked down the High Street hand in hand. Dominic was strangely quiet. They cut up a lane into the beech woods. Even in April there was a deep carpet of golden leaves on the ground that crunched and crackled as they walked. As their feet crushed the leaves the wonderful rich earthy smell of rotting vegetation rose in the air. The sun snaked through the rustling trees, the birds nested noisily, a rabbit shot across the path in front of them. Dominic stopped dead.

'God, what a wonderful day.' He flung his hands into the air and breathed deeply. 'It's almost too perfect,' and he bowed his head and stood silent and still.

Juniper waited for him to continue. He said nothing. 'Dom, are you all right?' she said quietly, gently touching his sleeve. As she did so she realized he was shaking. 'My darling, what's the matter?'

'Oh God, Juniper. I'm so afraid . . .' His voice was hollow with fear as he tried to control himself. 'I'm so tired of pretending I'm not afraid. I'm scared . . . scared to death I'm going to die.' He looked at her and she felt herself recoil at the stark terror she saw in his eyes. He looked away from her as if ashamed.

'Dom, darling,' she whispered and, putting her hand up to touch his face, found it wet with tears. 'My precious. Cry, let yourself cry . . . you won't die, I won't let you die.' And she put her arms about him and held him close to her and comforted him as best she could, for she could only guess at his fear. They stood a long time in the woodland holding each other, two young people who should have had everything to look forward to. Instead they clung to each other with the future too frightening even to think about.

In spite of Dominic's unhappiness, Juniper felt a glorious sense of elation. It was her he had turned to, she was the person he had allowed to witness this moment of vulnerability. He needed her. For the first time in her life she felt that she was needed for herself. She experienced a confidence in this relationship she had never felt in any other. She was aware of her tears, but they were tears of happiness.

'I'm sorry, Juniper,' he said eventually. 'That was pretty dumb of me.'

'You don't have to apologize to me, Dom. I'm honoured that you confided in me.'

'I'm being moved, you see, and on top of young Pete not coming back, and we lost three other crew . . .'

'You don't have to explain.'

'But I've survived all those bloody bombing raids. I was hoping to become an instructor – nice and safe. I should have, it was my turn. Now the fear will start again.' He smashed one fist into the other with pent up frustration.

'What on earth do you mean?' She was patting the tears from her cheeks with her small handkerchief.

'I've been posted to Benson . . .'

'But that's wonderful, it's just up the road. It makes everything even better.' She clapped her hands together with excitement, her mood changing in the instant.

'Come with me, quickly.' She ran ahead dodging between the trees, calling him to follow her.

They entered a clearing in which there stood a thatched cottage set in a garden wild with spring flowers. Creeper covered the red brick walls, tumbling across windows, arching over the doorway as if nature had thrown a green blanket as protection over the building.

'Climbing roses, honeysuckle, clematis . . . Imagine, Dom, what it will be like in summer. Come.' She took his hand in hers and led the way around the back where a cobbled yard with whitewashed walls faced south. 'I shall plant tubs of flowers here, put benches around, and we'll drink champagne and make love on long warm nights.'

'You've rented it?' He was smiling, the outburst in the woods momentarily forgotten.

'Better than that. I've bought it.' She grinned up at him.

'But it must have cost a fortune, property around here is dreadfully expensive.' He looked worried.

'I had some money. I wanted to have a base outside London. I'd planned to move,' she added quickly.

'Beautiful, and a woman of property too. Aren't I lucky? Let's see inside.'

She unlocked the door and paused in the doorway. She smiled at him and he; reading her mind, swept her into his arms and carried her over the threshold, kissing her as he did so, before gently setting her down on the oak planked floor.

The front door opened straight into the sitting room – a large room made from knocking three smaller ones into one. It was beamed in dark oak. The sun shining through the lattice work on the window cast diamond patterns of sunlight on the floor. Stairs led direct from the room and a door at the end led into a small kitchen. He peered up the large chimney of the inglenook.

'Does it work?' He pointed to the grate.

'The estate agent says it does.'

'Bet it smokes.'

'What do you think?'

'It's perfect. It's what every Englishman dreams of owning. How many bedrooms?'

'Two. A big one and a tiny one.'

'Good. No room for guests. We need furniture. I've got some savings.'

'No, no. It's all right. It's taken care of.'

'But how can you afford . . . ?'

'I have furniture in London that my grandmother gave me,' she lied. 'I thought I'd go there next week and arrange to have it moved here. There's no need for you to use your savings. I've even got a bed . . .' But she did not finish the sentence as he swept her off her feet.

'Who needs a bed?' he laughed. Laying her gently down on the dusty floor he began to make love to her.

That evening over dinner they planned their house, her only regret that there were still two days before it was finally hers.

'But at least, now you are stationed at Benson, you can live at the cottage. What luck!'

He looked away; he could not tell her what Benson meant. In any case he would not want to cause her further worry. He was to be taught extreme low flying, skilled flying, for secret sorties over Germany. But it was training which carried a high crash risk. Many pilots did not make it and deep within him was a growing conviction that he would be one of them.

4

'You've bought *another* house? Juniper, you're mad. You've got the one in Hampstead, the lease on this, one in France, God knows how many in America . . .' Polly looked across the kitchen table at Juniper, her soup spoon arrested between plate and mouth.

'Only one, and the apartment in New York.' Juniper grinned at Polly.

'But couldn't you have rented it?'

'Yes. But I wanted to own it. It really is the sweetest little cottage you've ever seen, Polly.'

'You don't exactly strike me as the cottage type, Juniper,' Polly said ironically.

'Oh, I shall be. It's perfect. Easy to manage and I'm going to cook. You needn't laugh. I did learn, you know, once. My grandmother and my companion, Tommy, taught me; now it will come in useful.'

'It sounds idyllic.' Polly smiled at her, thinking it was as well the house was small and easy to manage. 'So, tell me all about *him*.'

'Dominic? He's wonderful. I really am in love – it's been nearly a month. Me! Imagine!' She laughed. 'He needs me, Polly,' she went on, suddenly serious. 'That's the secret. And he knows nothing about me – the money and everything – so it's *me* he loves.'

'What about when he finds out? Maybe you should be honest with him. Finding out you're a millionairess could be a nasty shock.'

'You make it sound like a disease. No, I know what I'm doing. The beastly stuff always gets in the way in a relationship. I can't risk upsetting him – it's all so perfect. And Polly, when he makes love to me I feel I'm in heaven. You know it usually leaves me cold, so I can't lose him, can I?'

'I've never quite understood that particular problem, Juniper. Good heavens, there was Hal, and then that Frenchman and now Dominic. Three men in your life who make you happy in bed – sounds quite a lot to me, more than most women ever have.' Polly's smile took the sting out of her words.

Juniper threw a roll at Polly across the kitchen table. 'You're always so prosaic. I don't know why you're my best friend,' she said laughing. 'Do you mind if I take some pieces of furniture that are mine to the cottage?'

'Why on earth should I mind? You'll be giving up the lease on this house, surely?'

'Oh, no. I can't.'

'Why not?'

'Where would you go, and Jonathan?'

'My dear Juniper, I'll find somewhere else, of course.'

'I insist you stay. I shall go on paying the rent, so you might just as well.'

'Juniper, you are sweet. But don't you see? I couldn't afford to live here. The bills are too much on my salary.'

'I'll pay those too.'

'Oh no, you won't. You go, I go. It's as simple as that.'

'I've paid everything for the next three months. Stay that long then.'

'Very well. But I promise you, in one room.' Polly smiled indulgently at her too-generous friend. She was pleased for her, but worried too. Juniper was always falling in and out of love; would this time be any different?

Polly offered Juniper more soup, but she was too happy to be hungry. 'What are you going to do about the house in Hampstead? It seems such a waste, no one there but the housekeeper and the dogs – the world's most expensive kennels.'

'I've thought about it and I don't think this is a good time to sell. If everyone's right and the war will soon be over, property values are sure to rise.'

'Good gracious. Juniper being businesslike? I don't believe it.'

'It's not just that. I don't like the idea of making old Mrs Green homeless – her husband is missing, you know.'

'Is Mrs Green the woman who has been looking after the house for you?'

'Yes. I think I should wait until the war is finished or at least until she knows where her husband is.'

'I think you're the kindest person I know.'

'And how's the famous-to-be Jonathan?' Juniper said quickly. Praise of her generosity always flustered her.

'He's being moved. It's this invasion business. I haven't seen him. He seems a bit odd on the telephone.'

'Odd?' Juniper helped herself to another roll so that Polly could not see her anxious expression.

'He seems distant – as if he's making excuses not to see me.'

'Oh hardly, he's probably preoccupied.'

'No. It's something else.'

'Perhaps he's started a new novel. Aren't writers supposed to go into themselves when they do?'

'I can't see how he would find the time to write.'

Juniper, her head tilted to one side, looked closely at Polly as if deciding what to say next. 'Do you think he's right for you, Polly? He seems so, well, wrapped up in himself. Not very romantic, you know what I mean.'

'He's English. I've had enough of romantic foreigners. Don't forget I married one. I love him, I always have, since I was a little girl. It's as if we were destined for each other.'

'Now that *is* romantic. You know, this jam is absolutely delicious, may I have more?'

Polly handed the pot of jam to her. 'Take it, my grandmother made it.'

'Aren't the grannies wonderful the way they've adapted so well to their different circumstances?'

'Um . . .' Polly said vaguely. 'What did you really mean just now about Jonathan?'

'I just told you.'

'Please explain more.' Polly looked across at her with a worried expression.

Juniper pushed her plate to one side and began to light a cigarette. She regretted her comment now, but she loved Polly and she had to say something. 'If you must know, I don't think he's good enough for you.' There, she had said it, and to her surprise she found she felt a lot better for it. She had experienced the odd twinge of guilt over their behaviour but, having warned Polly, she had done her duty. And what she said was true. He wasn't good enough. He'd been unfaithful and if he could do that once he could do it again. She was looking after Polly, really.

'You do say some funny things, Juniper. Not good

enough? Gracious, Jonathan's superior to me in every way – intelligence, principles, courage. I'm amazed he wants to marry me – if he still does.'

'Of course he does, you're imagining things. And if he hurts you I'll personally kill him.'

'What a wonderful friend you are, Juniper. The best.'

It took far more trips than Juniper had anticipated to collect everything. The furniture was no problem; she arranged with the butcher's brother, who had a lorry, to take her things. He did a regular run to Oxfordshire for his brother, but she did not ask him what he went for; in these times it was always better not to know. But then there were food stores and wine to take, and although she did not mind entrusting the Sheraton and Hepplewhite chairs and the Constable and Turner paintings to the rather shady-looking young man, she transported her precious store of food and alcohol herself.

'Your grandmother must be wealthy if she throws out stuff like this,' Dominic said, admiring a particularly fine Chippendale desk.

'What? This old junk? Don't be silly,' Juniper said hurriedly, wondering if she had made a mistake and should instead have bought cheap secondhand stuff. It had been the difficulty of getting hold of any which had made her decide to bring the antiques. Cheap furniture was at a premium because of the number of bombed-out houses.

'I think it all looks wonderful. You must have been working like a Trojan. Come here,' he ordered, and independent Juniper did as he commanded and melted into his arms.

'I've got a huge fillet steak for you,' she said as they broke away.

'How on earth did you get that?'

'The man from London. His brother's a butcher.'

'I've no doubt it cost the earth. You're impossible. But I love you.' He ruffled her hair.

'Do you, Dominic? Really love me?'

'I've never met anyone like you in my life.'

She looked at him, willing him to say the words she was desperate to hear. But he did not ask her to marry him and she had decided, this time, she would be proposed to properly; unlike Hal, when she had done the proposing.

'Can we sort the wine tonight – before dinner?' she asked, turning away and fussing with a pile of magazines so that he could not see the disappointment on her face.

'Sure. Let me get out of uniform first,' and he was racing up the stairs. The moment was lost.

'This wine is fantastic. And look at the crates of champagne! Where on earth did you get all this from? There's a king's ransom down here.'

'My grandmother doesn't drink much.' She bent down and in the dim light of the wine cellar he could not see the grin on her face.

Juniper could not remember a time in her life when she had been happier. Because of the proximity to RAF Benson, Dominic was with her whenever he was not on duty. Many nights, when he was flying, she slept alone, tossing and turning with fear that he might not return. But in the morning there he was and they would fall into the bed she had just left. And there were a good many nights when he was with her, safe in her arms, and she often felt like weeping with happiness. Juniper never talked to him about his flying or the danger he faced, nor about her fear for him. When he was with her, she wanted to make him relax, to forget all that. She succeeded beyond her wildest dreams.

5

When Jonathan arrived the following weekend and put his arms about her, lifting her into the air in a giant hug, and Polly felt his lips on hers, she could not imagine what had made her worry so about him.

She settled him at the kitchen table and fussed about making him tea and sandwiches, lacing the tea with the remains of a bottle of whisky and sacrificing her own sugar since she knew how sweet toothed he was.

'Don't you use the drawing room any more?' he asked.

'Would you prefer to?' She jumped up, anxious to please since she felt so guilty at her disloyal thoughts.

'No. It's fine here – I've always liked kitchens. Sit down, relax.' He smiled at her over the rim of his cup.

'Since Juniper left I've kept to the kitchen and my bedroom to save money. I've moved down from the attic to the second floor. Now the parties are definitely over, there's no need to sleep up there.'

'I shall miss it. I liked the idea of us high up above the city, away from the herd.'

'We could move back up, if that's what you'd like?' She was on her feet again.

'What's the matter with you, Polly? You're like a nervous cat.' He patted her chair, coaxing her to sit down again.

'Where's Juniper living?' he asked, in what Polly interpreted with relief as the tone of someone merely making polite conversation.

'You don't want to hear about Juniper.' She was smiling now, glad that he didn't.

'Yes I do. I'm always interested in the flutterings of the "Golden Butterfly".'

'She's bought a cottage near Henley. I gather it's perfect – beamed and thatched, in a wood. She moved masses of furniture from here.'

'Is she alone?'

'No, she's madly in love. Someone called Dominic – but you know him.'

'Not well. He lives in Cambridge with his widowed mother, or rather he did.' He snorted ironically. 'I wouldn't have thought he and Juniper would last, he's a socialist. His father was a socialist MP.'

'Oh, I see,' said Polly noncommittally, thinking that

this would be another reason for Juniper not to tell him of her background. No doubt she was already engrossed in becoming a socialist, but how long did Juniper's enthusiasms survive? Meanwhile she would be enjoying this new game. But Polly could not help wondering how long such a subterfuge could last.

'Shall we go out tonight?'

'Sorry.' She jumped. 'What did you say? I was miles away.'

'What's wrong, Polly? Something's up.'

Polly found she could not look him straight in the eye.

'Darling, you look almost sheepish, as if you've done something wrong.' He leant across the table and took her hand in his. 'What is it?'

She paused and, still unable to look at him, studied their two entwined hands instead. She took a deep breath. 'I doubted you, Jonathan. I thought you were lying to me, making excuses not to see me, that perhaps you had met someone else. I'm sorry. It was unforgivable.'

'Sweet Polly.' He squeezed her hand and it was his turn to study their hands in embarrassment.

'And there you were working so hard, then being moved back to your unit. And all the time I was being stupid and selfish. Forgive me, Jonathan.' At last she looked up at him but he had turned away from her.

'There's nothing to forgive, Polly, darling,' he said gruffly, removing his hand and looking away from her.

Polly felt suddenly chill. 'There isn't anything, is there?' she asked, in a voice that was little more than a whisper.

'Silly goose. Of course not,' he said, after an almost imperceptible pause. He pulled her to him.

Smelling his familiar smell, a sweet honey-like aroma of tobacco, she burrowed her face into his neck and berated herself for being so stupid.

Silently, Jonathan released her, took her hand in his and pulled her towards the door.

'We've been apart too long, you and I. Which is your bedroom?' he asked, as he led her to the stairs.

They did not go out, but instead ate sausages and mash in bed.

'I think we should get married, Polly. We keep putting off the day for one thing or another. I'm not talking about next month or next year. I think we should marry now, don't you?'

'Because of the invasion of Europe?'

'Well. Something like that hanging over your head makes you think carefully about your life.'

'Oh my God, Jonathan. You think you're not coming back?' She got up on her knees, one of the sausages rolling off her plate on to the coverlet. He laughed as he attempted to prong it with his fork, chasing the sausage about the bed.

'It's a bit furry,' he apologised, as he put the sausage back on her plate.

'Tell me,' she said urgently, for she was not laughing. 'I've heard about people having premonitions – a girl at work did. She couldn't stay home, she felt she had to go to the cinema. When she got back the whole house had been flattened by a bomb.' She pushed her plate of food away from her.

Jonathan began to laugh a loud, happy laugh. 'My darling Polly, I just want to marry you. I've wanted to for long enough, from before I went to Spain in '36, remember?' He was laughing.

'But everyone says the war will end soon.'

'I think they're wrong. It'll take another twelve months at least.'

'Do you know when you're leaving England?'

'No, and if I did I couldn't tell you, could I?'

'No, you couldn't,' she said flatly.

'You don't exactly make a chap feel wanted.'

'What makes you say that?'

'You haven't given me an answer.'

'Oh darling. I'm sorry. You know the answer. It's yes, oh yes, let's get married as soon as possible.'

*

'Mother, this is Jonathan Middlebank.'

'I know you, don't I?' Francine stood back, one foot at an elegant angle to the other, and studied his face carefully with complimentary attention.

'I visited Hurstwood several times in the past. My uncle is Vicar of Tunhill.'

'Of course. I never, never forget a handsome man.' Her laugh was low and suggestive. 'And to what do I owe this honour, Polly? You can hardly call yourself a regular visitor, can you?' She was smiling, but Polly could hear the sharpness in her voice even though Jonathan appeared unaware. 'Polly neglects her poor mother, Jonathan. What do you think about that?' Francine turned all her attention upon him before twirling on her heel and, appearing to float across the room, sank into a chair in one liquid motion, the folds of her soft cream silk dress falling gracefully about her.

'Well . . .' Jonathan coughed and looked from Polly to her mother. She had no doubt her mother's charm would soon begin to work on him.

'It's difficult when people don't see enough of each other. Polly and I know that, don't we, darling?' he said eventually, with inspired diplomacy. He searched for Polly's hand and held it tight as if holding on to reality in the presence of the ocean of charm, beauty and manipulation which was Francine.

'If a bomb squashed this apartment block flat, she wouldn't come running, would you, Polly?'

'Oh, I'm sure . . .' Jonathan floundered. Polly stood silent.

'And you never come to see me on the stage, do you, Polly darling?'

'I said only the other day that we should come. Didn't I, Polly?' Jonathan blustered. Polly stood silent.

'But Polly hates what I do, don't you, Polly? Too low brow for her. Polly's an intellectual, don't you know, Jonathan?'

'She's very well read,' Jonathan said with greater confidence; Polly stood silent.

'Come and sit here next to me, Jonathan,' Francine went on, indicating the seat close beside her and not giving him time to answer. Reluctantly, Jonathan relinquished Polly's hand and crossed the room. 'It's a good thing you're so tall with Polly being such a beanpole.'

Polly started to shuffle her feet, feeling suddenly like the gauche teenager she had once been. She walked into the centre of the room.

'Jonathan and I are getting married,' she said firmly.

'Good Lord,' Francine shrieked with laughter. 'Are you sure, Jonathan?' She leant across to take Jonathan's hand. Jonathan leapt to his feet, pulling away his hand as if she had burnt him.

'I've no money you know, Jonathan,' Francine went on. 'I can't help Polly in any way. You'll have to support her yourself.'

'Lady Frobisher, I love Polly. It will be a privilege to support her. We came out of courtesy, not to ask for money.'

'I'm sure you did, Jonathan.' Francine was smiling again, the small, Madonna-like smile she used when attempting to appear innocent. 'And when is the wedding?'

'In a fortnight. I can wangle a seventy-two-hour pass.'

'Where?'

'Caxton Hall.'

'I shan't come, of course.'

'But Lady Frobisher . . .'

'No. Don't even ask me to. It would ruin your day.'

'But . . .'

Francine raised her hand. 'It would be impossible. There would be so many photographers and fans there to see me. I can't ruin darling Polly's wedding day, now can I?' She beamed at Jonathan who slid back on to a chair feeling bemused. A fuming Polly was sent to fetch champagne.

With only two weeks to prepare for the wedding, even though it was to be very simple, Polly was in a dither. She missed Juniper dreadfully and realized how much she depended on her advice where matters of style were concerned. Polly was quite happy to arrange the food and flowers, but what she was to wear stumped her completely. Obviously, as this was a second marriage, she had no intention of turning up in virginal white, but should she choose cream? Or blue? And what would everyone say if she wore what she really liked, a black suit which she had had since the first years of the war, bought for her by Juniper in Lisbon? She knew it suited her, made her look elegant and, in a strange way, made her feel lucky. But then, since it was May, would it be too heavy? Would it look out of place? Juniper would know.

Polly flopped down on a chair, rested her head in her hands and longed for Juniper to contact her. She had written immediately, but three days later still had not had a reply. If only she could telephone her, but Juniper had no telephone. She wondered how Juniper managed without one; it was hard to imagine.

She pulled her writing pad towards her and studied the lists which she had been making. At least she could tick off the cake. That morning she had been lucky and able to reserve the baker's cardboard wedding cake. With so many rushed weddings and no ingredients available for a real cake his false one, used as a window display before the war, was always in demand. Since she was living alone most of the time, she would be able to hoard sufficient butter and eggs to make a wedding sponge. The restriction of only forty guests per reception was no problem either, if they managed fifteen she'd be surprised.

Polly put the pen down. She had been back in England for four years and yet had so few friends. Of the fifteen, eleven would be Jonathan's pals. She herself had only

Juniper and Gwendoline, her grandmother and her mother; and if Francine came she very much doubted if her grandmother would come, so that left her with three guests.

She looked at the list mournfully. Why? Why had she not made more friends? She knew the reason: Juniper. Knowing her was a responsibility, a full-time occupation. Juniper was demanding and possessive – not that she realized it. And, although Juniper had plenty of friends, they were not, on the whole, Polly's kind of people.

After the war, married to Jonathan and living at Hurstwood, she would have to start building new friendships. It was a daunting prospect, for Polly was shy and found making friends the hardest thing on earth. Still, even at Hurstwood, Juniper would no doubt whirl in on frequent visits, adding excitement to their quiet routine. She was lucky to have her really.

She picked up her pen and returned to the lists. Sandwiches – they would be a problem. She would have to consult her grandmother. She knew that Gertie and Alice listened without fail every morning, to Mabel Constanduros on the radio. No doubt they would have a thousand sandwich tips, like the delicious 'banana' sandwiches she had had on her last visit. Gertie had glowed with pride as she confided that the bananas were cooked mashed parsnips with a drop or two of banana essence. Maybe one of Juniper's parcels from America would arrive in time with tins of ham, sardines and tongue; but no parcels had arrived since Juniper had moved.

What else had she to arrange? She'd booked the hotel at Windsor for their far too short honeymoon. She would wait to hear from Juniper about what to wear before she went shopping and perhaps wasted her precious coupons on something unsuitable. And then . . . she was interrupted by the ringing of the doorbell. She half stood, then sat down again. She was not expecting anyone or anything at this time of the evening. Best to ignore it. But the bell persisted. Eventually she stood up again and reluctantly went upstairs towards the front door.

She put the chain across the door before she opened it and peered out nervously. There was a tall, gaunt man standing on the step.

'Yes?' she asked tentatively.

'Liz?'

'I beg your pardon,' she said politely. 'I'm afraid you must have made a mistake. There's no one of that name here,' she added, momentarily saddened at the memory of how once she had been called by that very name.

'You don't recognize me?'

'I'm sorry, no. Should I?'

'I'm Andrew. Andrew Slater.'

'You're dead,' she said indignantly. If this was meant to be a joke it was far from funny.

'I'm afraid not. I'm very much alive,' he said with a laugh.

It was Andrew's distinctive laugh – deep and rich, bubbling with joy, and with a sudden snorting catch which always made her laugh in response. As it rang out Polly felt suddenly dizzy and had to lean on the door frame for support.

'Oh, Liz . . .'

That was Andrew's name for her. He had refused to call her Polly, he alone in the world called her Liz. She had never expected to be called Liz again by anyone.

'Andrew . . .' The word escaped as softly as a breath, as if saying it out loud would break a spell. 'Andrew,' she repeated, dazed.

Then, suddenly aware that she was whispering at him through the few inches the chain on the door allowed, she hurriedly apologized as she fumbled to open it. 'Excuse me, I've got to shut the door first to get this thing off. I'm so sorry, such a silly thing,' she apologized.

'A very necessary precaution.' He smiled at her, and her senses suddenly raced at the once familiar smile.

'I suppose so.' The door open at last, she stood with her

arms awkwardly at her side, unsure what to say. Then, to her amazement and horror, the strangest thought flickered into her mind, she remembered that beside her bed stood a framed photograph of Jonathan. What on earth made her think of that? Why should it matter? she thought with a jolt, and her right hand shot up to cover her mouth as if to suppress such a notion.

'May I come in?' Andrew asked politely. 'Or am I to stand here all night?'

'Andrew, forgive me.' She opened the door wide. 'I . . . I . . .'

'I'm a bit of a shock, aren't I?' He placed his bag on the floor. 'Sorry.'

She was staring at him, unable to stop. It was Andrew and yet it wasn't. This man was so thin, his hair was grey where Andrew's had been blond. Andrew was, her mind raced, he was only thirty – this man looked years older. His eyes were blue, but a hard, cold blue, not the gentle eyes she had spent hours looking into. And yet the smile, the laugh, the voice . . .

'It really is me, Liz. I know it's hard for you to take in.' They were both standing in the hall and in the light they could see each other clearly. 'I know I look different, but you – you look exactly the same.' He put up his hand to stroke her face with an expression of wonderment, but Polly stepped back quickly to avoid his touch. 'Don't be frightened, please.'

'I'm not frightened,' she said staunchly, but it wasn't true. She was afraid – afraid of the tumult inside her, the joy which was beginning to overtake rapidly the shock.

'Are you married?' he asked anxiously.

'No . . . I . . .' she began.

'Thank God for that – I was so afraid you might . . .' He lifted her left hand, looked at it, and bringing it to his mouth kissed the third finger. 'Not even engaged. How marvellous!'

'You'd like a drink? Some tea?' she asked prosaically,

unable to explain that she was engaged, the ring waiting until Jonathan could afford to buy one.

'You always were so wonderfully practical, Liz. Remember when I used to get away from the front in France? I'd arrive at your flat and there was always a drink waiting. You never asked questions – always let me relax first.' He suddenly moved towards her, then his arms were about her and he was hugging her to him with such desperation that she could not fight him, made no effort to get away. 'You don't know how often I've dreamt of this moment, my love.' He buried his face in her silky hair. 'I even managed to dream of the scent of your hair, hay and roses, that's the smell. Oh, my darling . . .'

They stood silent, holding each other close and Polly could not speak, could not break the spell.

7

'You must tell me everything.' Polly looked anxiously across the table at Andrew. They were in the kitchen, a bottle of Juniper's malt whisky between them and a hurriedly prepared stew – more vegetable than meat – bubbling on the stove.

'I don't know where to begin.'

'We were told at first you were missing, and later that you were a prisoner. Oh, the relief at that news – I was so happy. And then Captain Wishart turned up and told us that you had been shot dead, escaping.'

'Poor old Wishart. He'd have thought that. I remember going down like a ton of bricks, but the bullet only grazed me.'

'I was so unhappy, I wanted to die too. I felt I should have known that you were dead.'

'But you couldn't have,' he said triumphantly, 'because I was alive.'

'But why weren't we told? Why weren't you on the lists?'

'No doubt they intended I should die. I decided other-wise.'

'Who's "they"? The German army?'

'No. Not the army. There was nothing wrong with them, they treated us reasonably well. And most of the guards in the POW camp were fine. There was the odd bastard, but that's to be expected. No, I'm talking of where they sent me . . .'

'Where?'

'Don't ask my darling. Don't make me tell you,' and he looked at her with such anguish in his eyes that she couldn't ask further.

'How did you know where to find me?'

'I got two letters from you, from this address. I just hoped you were still here.'

'Does your mother know you're alive? I met her. She's not well, Andrew. She's grieving for you dreadfully.'

'Poor Mum. I'll phone, but not yet. Let me enjoy being alone with you a while longer.'

'I don't think you should telephone – it was enough of a shock for me, finding you on the doorstep. A telephone call out of the blue would be just as bad and probably too much for her to deal with. Perhaps we should send a telegram first to a family friend who could prepare them?'

'Whatever you think best, Liz.'

'Better still, I work with a friend of your mother's, Gwendoline Rickmansworth. We could tell her; she could pave the way. She's so capable she'll know what to do for the best.'

'Fine. But not now.'

'No, Okay. As you wish.' She stood up and stirred the stew. 'How did you get here?'

'I got fed up one day, walked out of the camp and carried on walking.' He grinned up at her and, in the dim light from the two candles she had lit in celebration, he looked young again, like a naughty little boy.

'And just walked?'

'I had some wonderful luck. I got picked up by some

friendly Poles who looked after me and then sent me on to another group of friendly coves – right across Europe, into Portugal, and hey ho, here I am.' He took a long swig of the whisky and she noticed he avoided looking straight at her.

He could not look at her because he could not tell anyone the full story, least of all her, could not speak of the fear of those weeks as he inched his way across occupied Europe – the gut twisting terror of being recaptured. He could not yet speak of the courage of the people who had helped him, souls far braver than he would ever be. Remembering them made him want to weep tears of gratitude. No, he could not tell any of that – not yet.

'You're so thin.'

'There's not much to eat where I've been.' He was grinning again, but with a jolt she realized his eyes weren't smiling.

'Then we'll have to feed you up somehow.'

'Has it been bad?'

'No, not really. I've been lucky too. Juniper gets endless parcels from America, so we get quite a few luxuries. The bombing was awful back in '41, but after that it wasn't too bad, until the beginning of this year when they seemed to be throwing everything at us again. But it's stopped now and everyone thinks the war will end soon. We've been expecting the invasion of France each month this year. It can't be long now.'

She concentrated on her stew again, which needed no help from her as it bubbled away. Here she was talking about bombs and food, when she should be telling him about Jonathan, the fact that she was getting married next week. But how to tell him so that she let him down lightly? Far better to tell him now, right at the beginning, before his hopes were raised too high. The metal spoon scraped rhythmically around the side of the saucepan. She could not tell him, not yet. Scrape, scrape. She could not tell him, because she did not want to. She shook her head

– that was silly. She loved Jonathan, she had always loved him, they were destined to marry. She turned from the stove.

'Andrew . . .' she began, and then she saw how defeated he looked as he sat huddled at the table, slumped over his whisky.

'Yes?' He looked up.

'How hungry are you?'

'Starving.'

'Then let's go out. There's a little restaurant around the corner, near Victoria, it's good. This stew will take forever.'

It was a difficult meal. It was easy to see from the start that Andrew was ill at ease. He jumped at every noise and kept looking furtively over his shoulder.

'It's all right. You're safe here,' she said gently, putting her hand over his. He grasped hers in return so tightly that she had to fight with herself not to cry out with pain.

'Be patient with me, Liz, please. It's been so long . . .'

'I understand, my darling. I'll look after you. No one's going to hurt you now,' and she leant over and brushed his cheek with a kiss. He put his hand up and touched where her lips had been, as if in a daze.

Their food arrived: a meat pie, which he began to eat noisily, bolting it down, as if afraid that it might disappear.

'Andrew. Slowly. No one is going to take it away from you. Promise.' She smiled at him as she began to realize what privation this man had suffered.

'Sorry. Force of habit,' and he was grinning his little-boy smile at her. Polly's heart went out to him, longing to protect him, to make everything better again.

By the time they got back to the house Andrew was obviously exhausted. He confessed he had not slept for forty-eight hours, so desperate had he been to get to her. Polly led him upstairs. She paused on the landing, opened the large linen cupboard and handed him a towel.

'The bathroom's that way. There's hot water for a bath. You, for this one time, can have as much water as you want. Then when you're finished, my room is this one.' She pointed to the door.

'I'll be quick.'

While he was in the bathroom Polly slipped into her room and quickly removed Jonathan's photograph from the bedside table. From the wardrobe she took his jacket and trousers, from the chest of drawers the shirts and underwear he always kept there. She bundled the whole lot up, stole along the landing to Juniper's room and left them there.

Polly stopped herself from exclaiming at Andrew's skeletal figure half-wrapped in the towel. His ribs looked as if they were about to burst through the paper-thin flesh.

'Liz, I . . . it's difficult.' He stood awkwardly, looking everywhere but at her.

'I know, Andrew. You need to sleep. Don't worry,' she said, hoping she did not sound too relieved. She led him to her bed, and helped him in and gently, as gently as if he were a baby, she covered him up. She leant over to kiss him goodnight. He burrowed his head in her pillow.

'It smells of you.'

'Good. That's why I put you here. Now sleep as long as you want.' She turned out the light and tiptoed from the room, certain he was asleep before the door was closed.

It was a very confused Polly who returned to the kitchen and, unusually for her, poured herself a large malt whisky which she gulped at greedily. What was she doing? It was not fair to put him in her room – he might misunderstand. She longed to help him, was so happy to see him, to be with him, but then had she not been relieved when he began clumsily to explain he was too exhausted to make love to her?

She stood up purposefully. She needed to talk to Jonathan. He would tell her what to do, how to handle the situation. She sat down again – she was going mad. Since Jonathan had rejoined his unit, she had no number to call. She did not even know where he was, even if she was pretty sure it was in Kent.

Gwendoline! That was whom she should call. Luckily, since they had become such good friends on their trip north, not only did Polly have her telephone number, but she had visited her in her home in Eaton Square.

'Gwendoline? It's Polly.'

'My dear, what's the matter? Your voice sounds odd.'

'It's Andrew. He's not dead, he's here.'

'Andrew? Andrew Slater?'

'Yes.'

'Good God . . .' Polly heard a clatter as if the telephone receiver had been dropped. 'Sorry, I had to sit down, quickly. How is he?'

'Under enormous strain and he looks dreadful – starved. He won't talk about it, but I think he's been in a concentration camp. He's only been on the run for two months and nobody could get so thin in that time.'

'How are you?'

'Me? I'm fine,' Polly said, puzzled. 'I've just put him to bed, he was so exhausted he hadn't . . .'

'You haven't answered my question. I meant how have you reacted to him? What about Jonathan?'

'I don't know, Gwendoline. I'm so confused.' To her horror Polly found she was crying.

'I'm coming over. Got any alcohol?'

'Plenty.'

'Good. It sounds as if you need it.'

Gwendoline hung up immediately. Polly sat in the hall waiting for Gwendoline who arrived in a flurry fifteen minutes later. She did not waste time with words, but bundled Polly into her arms and held her close.

'Come, we've a lot to talk about.'

'Do you mind the kitchen?'

'Is there anywhere else?' Gwendoline laughed. 'Has he telephoned home?' was her first question once they were settled with glasses of malt.

'No. I didn't think it was a good idea.'

'Good. I'll travel up tomorrow and break the news gently – well, as gently as one can break news like that. Do you want me to take him with me? Get him away from you?'

'Gwendoline, I don't know. I don't know what I want. I want him here, I want to help him, make him better. And then I think I wish he was miles away. Everything was turning out so neatly and now I don't know . . .'

'How did you feel when you saw him?'

'After the shock? After I realized it was him? I was happy. Deliriously happy. I love him, Gwendoline. But I love Jonathan too.'

'Oh dear God, this bloody war.' Gwendoline studied her tumbler of Scotch. 'You need time to think,' she said suddenly. 'I'll telephone Andrew's father, tip him off. I'll motor up with Andrew tomorrow for a couple of days – give you time, without either of them, to make up your mind.'

'How do I do that? How do I choose?'

'I'm sorry, Polly, my dear. No one can help you with this. It's going to be hard. You can't have them both, you're going to have to decide on your own.'

8

Andrew did not want to go to Northumberland. He looked bewildered as he appealed to Polly to let him stay with her. Her instinct was to agree; he obviously needed time to come to terms with his freedom and to forget what he had suffered.

'Perhaps for just a few days.' Polly looked at Gwendoline, her eyes beseeching the older woman to agree with her.

'He should see his mother,' Gwendoline replied firmly, placing her small attaché case on the floor and buttoning her coat, making it obvious she and Andrew were not staying.

'I want to see my mother but I want to be with Liz more.'

Polly's heart sank at his words. She had slept barely two hours and, during the long night, wrapped in a rug in an armchair beside the sleeping Andrew, she had tried to analyse how she felt. She wondered whether her reaction to him was pity rather than love. She thought of Jonathan preparing to go to France and fight, the fear he must be feeling, and realized that he needed her too. By morning she had decided to give Andrew all the help she could and to go ahead with her marriage to Jonathan.

Plans made in the quiet of the night are one thing, reality another. Once Andrew was awake, his need for her touched her deeply. Now she stood in the middle of the kitchen looking from Andrew to Gwendoline and back again and realized she was even more confused than she had been the previous night.

'Andrew, my dear, you must think about Polly, or Liz, as you call her.' Gwendoline looked at him kindly. 'Your arrival has been a shock to her. You must give her time to come to terms with your return from the dead. Do you understand?'

'Yes, of course I understand,' Andrew said shortly. 'I'm only asking for a few days.'

'And I'm telling you it's best to separate, to give Polly time to come to terms with what's happened. And what about your duty to your poor parents?' Gwendoline spoke in the businesslike, no-nonsense voice that so reminded Polly of her grandmother.

'Your mother is a sad person, Andrew. She needs help and you are the only person who can give it. I'll be here when you get back.'

'You promise?'

Polly paused before she replied. It wasn't fair to raise his hopes and yet . . . and he had to see his mother, it was essential he did. 'Yes, of course; I promise.'

'There, see, Andrew. It's all for the best. Now, the car's outside. I've telephoned your father and told him we're coming for two days. I can't afford to be away any longer.'

'Nor me. I'll see you on Saturday, Liz.'

'I'll look forward to that.' She smiled, still finding it difficult to get used to his pet name for her.

When Andrew left the room to get his bag, Gwendoline put her arm round Polly's shoulders.

'Take the week off. They'll think you're with me anyway. Good luck. I don't envy you.'

'I've made up my mind about what I should do. It's how to do it which is bothering me now.'

Polly waved them off and turned back into the house. She made herself some tea and sat so long silently staring into space that it was cold when she eventually came to drink it. She needed Juniper. She stood up, leaving the cup, and the dirty breakfast dishes, and ran upstairs, packed an overnight bag and let herself out on to the street, the large door echoing in the empty house as she slammed it shut.

On the Green Line bus she sat staring out of the window, unaware of the people and traffic passing by, oblivious of the lovely weather. It was not until the bus pulled into Reading that she came to with a start and for the first time wondered what she was to do if Juniper was not at home. She asked directions and caught another bus to the village of Nettlebed.

The black oak door of The White Hart creaked as she gingerly pushed it open. The lunchtime session was in full swing and she felt as if she were walking into a wall of noise. She looked about her, searching for Juniper. This was exactly the sort of public house that Juniper would love, with its huge fireplace, the low oak beams and the copper pans glinting on the walls. She could almost hear her exclaim: 'Polly, it's quaint, divine, really olde worlde!' She felt almost surprised when the familiar husky voice did not call out her name.

Polly was given directions to Juniper's cottage by the pleasant-faced landlady. She was glad to leave, finding herself blushing at the interest shown in her by the young men in air force uniforms crowded around the bar.

The lane led off the road, through the rustling leaves of beech trees. It was a walk which normally would have given her enormous pleasure. When the lane ended in an overgrown path, which opened out into a clearing, and she saw the rose-red brick cottage with its blond thatch and the garden a riot of early summer flowers, she understood why Juniper had had to buy it. If she had seen the house first, hidden away in the woods almost like a secret, she too would have wanted to own it.

The knocker in the shape of a smiling lion on the ancient door was burnished so brightly that the sun was reflected in it. Polly had to wait only a moment before the door was flung wide open and there was Juniper.

'Polly, my darling, what a splendid surprise! Spiffing,' she exclaimed, holding her arms out wide in welcome.

'Juniper, you look wonderful.' It was true, she had never seen Juniper looking so well. She had put on a little weight, which suited her, and there was a bloom about her which only a woman in love achieves.

'If I'd known you were coming, I'd have tarted myself up a bit,' she said, patting the scarf – Hermès, Polly was amused to see – tied around her head in a turban. In a plain white shirt, navy-blue slacks, and with no shoes on her feet and a face clean of make-up, she looked about sixteen.

'I decided in such a rush,' Polly explained, allowing Juniper to help her out of her linen jacket.

'I'm in a mess. You'll have to excuse it, I've no help in the house . . . well, you know me.' She chuckled, waving her arm about the low-ceilinged room. It was so tidy that Polly had to bite her tongue to stop herself saying how amazed she was. Two large sofas were set either side of the inglenook fireplace, their cushions, in beautifully tapestried covers, lined up as if they had been positioned with the aid of a ruler. A large oak chest stood between the sofas with books neatly piled, a bowl of spring flowers beautifully arranged and a silver cigarette box so highly polished that the room was reflected in it in miniature.

'It's lovely. So cosy too,' Polly said.

'You should see it in the evening when it's chill and we light the fire – it's bliss. We're like Darby and Joan with our books and music.'

'You're happy?'

'Happy? Some days I think I must have died and gone to heaven. You know, Polly, I always thought the best one could expect from life would be odd flashes of happiness, of perfection. And yet I'm in a state of delirious bliss from morning to night.' Juniper beamed at her.

'I'm so happy for you.'

'Coffee with cake? I made it myself.'

'Can I help?'

'No. I've always got coffee on the go, just like back home in the States. And the cake only needs putting on a plate. Sit down, make yourself at home.'

The sofas were as comfortable as they looked. Polly sank back on to one of the cushions. Just being here she felt better already. Juniper would help her to see what she should do, what she should say. There was a Juniper that most people did not know, one who could be so sensible and logical that it still sometimes surprised even Polly.

Juniper came back carrying a heavy silver tray for which Polly made room on the low oak chest. She waited for Juniper to pour the coffee and serve the cake. Serious conversation was out of the question until Polly had raved over how good the cake was, which, to her astonishment, it was.

'Now, why are you here? You're not the curious kind,' Juniper said, unpinning her turban and shaking her blonde hair free. She must be growing it, Polly thought, and marvelled how, in the midst of this personal drama, she could still admire furniture, flowers, cake, and register the length of her friend's hair.

'Andrew Slater isn't dead. He's been in prison, and escaped and turned up at the house last night.'

'Good God!'

'It was a shock,' Polly said, finding herself smiling at the inadequacy of the remark.

'And now you're in a turmoil. In love with both Andrew and Jonathan, and not sure which to choose and how to tell the other one without causing too much pain.'

Polly slumped back on the cushions. 'Yes. That's it in a nutshell. I've got until Saturday to make up my mind. I just don't know what to do.'

'I think you do. Deep down you've already decided,' Juniper said matter-of-factly, leaning over and helping herself to another slice of cake. 'This really is amazingly good, isn't it?' She beamed with pride.

'Have I decided?'

'Oh yes. Andrew, undoubtedly.'

'How do you know?'

'Because you're a sweet, unselfish girl and you think you can help him. Because you were madly in love with him when you were in Paris and it never came to a natural end – it was left hanging, in the air, unresolved. Death can't kill love, only people destroy their love for each other.'

'But what about Jonathan?'

'Ah, the "famous-to be" Jonathan. You love him, I'm sure you do. But do you love him as you loved Andrew when you were together? Have you really forgotten what happened with him and me all that time ago?'

'I forgave him ages ago, both of you, you know I did.'

'I didn't say "forgiven," I said "forgotten". I think when you've given someone your love and they shatter it – no matter how – it can never be put back together again whole. It's like a broken piece of china; you can always see the faults no matter how skilfully it's been mended.'

'No, it's not like that with us. I never gave it a thought.' Polly patted her mouth with her napkin so that she had an excuse to look down. If Juniper saw her eyes, might she read her mind, guess how panic stricken she had been only a few weeks ago when she thought Jonathan and Juniper might have been together?

'Sure?' Juniper raised an eyebrow.

Polly preferred to ignore the question. 'I love them both, that's the problem. But Andrew needs me. It's in his eyes. He's almost like a lost child.'

'He's probably seen hell. Living with someone who's experienced what he has could be another sort of hell. You can't marry someone just because you're sorry for him, you know.'

'I'm not just sorry for him. When I saw him, when I realized it was really him, I felt like I used to. When I visited his mother – I haven't seen you to tell you about that – I felt then as if he were with me, I couldn't get him out of my mind.'

'My poor sweet Polly. I wish I could help.'

'You have, really. I know only I can decide.'

'If you ask me – and even if you don't – I'll still tell you,' Juniper said, with a chuckle. 'As far as I remember, Andrew's the nicer bloke. I've always said you're too good for Jonathan.'

'What have you got against him? You said that the other day.' Polly leant forward guardedly. The cosiness, her joy in seeing Juniper, was suddenly fading.

'I wouldn't trust him if I were you.'

'You're a fine one to talk.' Polly was surprised to find she felt sharply irritated by Juniper's certainty, by what was almost smugness. Odd, she thought, after all this time. Although she had never learnt the details of who had seduced whom all those years ago, she doubted if it had been Jonathan who had been the seducer, he probably would not have known how.

'You're always going to blame me for that little incident, aren't you?'

'That "little incident", as you put it, led if you remember to Jonathan's going to fight in the Spanish Civil War and to my marrying that sadist Michel.'

'Good gracious, did I do all that?' Juniper looked amused.

'Yes, you did. By just doing what you wanted you could have ruined my life.'

'But I didn't, did I?' Juniper slowly began to light a cigarette, reminding Polly of her mother and fuelling her irritation further. She had not realized Juniper was going to be a source of such annoyance. She was compounding her confusion, not helping to solve it.

'What has got into you, Polly? It's not my fault that Andrew's turned up from the grave just as you're set to marry someone else, is it? It's a pity, in a way, that I've met Dominic. Maybe I could have helped you out by taking the reject!' Juniper kicked her legs up in the air and flopped back on the cushions, she was laughing so much.

'I don't think that's very funny.'

'No, I suppose you wouldn't. But I do,' and she started to bubble with laughter again.

'And you're wrong. I've made up my mind. But it's Jonathan, I've decided. I'll just have to let Andrew down as lightly as possible.' As she spoke she felt almost as if she were trying to spite Juniper and could not understand why she wanted to.

'Then I wish you luck, my friend. Rather you than me,' and she curled her elegant legs up beneath her.

'There you go again, being horrible about Jonathan. Why?'

'Ask him.'

'What does that mean?'

'What it says. Ask him why I'd rather you didn't marry him.'

'You're jealous.'

'Oh Polly, don't be silly. Of course I'm not jealous. I'm in love. I want you to be as happy as I am. I want you to know the security, the peace I've found. And you won't find that with Jonathan, I promise you.'

'What are you trying to say, Juniper?'

'I've just told you. You're my friend, I love you, I want the best for you.'

Polly, despite the warm day, suddenly felt icy cold. 'You did it again, didn't you? You and Jonathan behind my back. You bitch . . .' The word was spat out venomously.

'I'm not saying any more.'

'You don't need to. You whore. Why don't you charge for it? Why can't you be honest? God, no man's safe with you around. Does Dominic know?' She was standing now, looming above Juniper who, still curled up on the sofa, looked even smaller than usual.

'You leave Dominic out of this. You can't hurt me there – he knows everything about my past.' Well almost, she thought to herself and touched the oak chest for reassurance.

'Except that you're filthy rich. He wouldn't like that, would he – it would get in the way of his political principles, wouldn't it?'

'Oh Polly. Why are we arguing? Why are you saying these awful things to me? Just listen to yourself. Please, I'm your friend, I want you to be happy.'

'A strange way you have of showing it.'

'Don't you understand? I've done you a favour. How else would you know what he's like? What a bastard he truly is?'

'You're unbelievable, Juniper. You never do anything wrong, do you? You always twist everything round. Well, I'm finished with you. I never want to speak to you or see you again as long as I live.'

'But Polly . . .'

'There's no "buts" . . .' Her eyes blinded with tears, Polly was picking up her handbag, fumbling her arms into the sleeves of her jacket.'

'I was only helping you to make the right choice.'

'Helping? Helping?' Polly's voice was ugly. 'I hate you. You'll never know how much.' And she crossed the room and slammed out of the door.

'Polly, darling . . . I only wanted to help . . .' Juniper's voice trailed after her as she flung herself amongst her jewel-coloured cushions and punched one with frustration.

9

The door of the cottage opened.

'Polly?' Juniper looked up eagerly.

'Was she that mad woman who just cannoned into me?' It was Dominic. Juniper leapt up and rushed towards him.

'Hold me, Dom. Hold me tight.' She flung herself into his arms.

'Precious, what on earth's happened? Shush. Tell me.' Gently he led her back to the sofa. Once seated he took his large white handkerchief and mopped at the tears tumbling down her face. 'I didn't think I'd ever see you cry.'

'I don't cry. I've got dust in my eyes,' Juniper said, taking the handkerchief and blowing lustily into the clean linen.

'Do you want to tell me about it?' He took her hand and gently stroked it.

'It was all so silly. I was only trying to help her and then she flew at me, called me horrible names and flounced out, saying she never wants to see me again.' Her large hazel eyes were awash with tears again.

'She probably didn't mean it. She'll come back.'

'But I don't think she will. You don't know Polly, she never gets angry. She's the sweetest woman on earth. I can't imagine not having Polly to turn to.'

'Then what did you say to upset her so?' Dominic asked patiently.

'She's in love with two men. She's supposed to marry Jonathan next week and then Andrew, whom she was engaged to and whom she thought was dead, turned up out of the blue.'

'God, poor girl.'

'She couldn't make up her mind what to do, so all I did was to give her a little push, so to speak.'

'Oh yes, and what was that?' Dominic was smiling at her, a rather indulgent smile. It reminded her of her grandfather, which immediately made her feel safe and secure.

'Well . . . it was ages and ages ago, you realize . . .' She looked at him with wide-eyed innocence. 'I had a little fling with Jonathan, so I hinted, only hinted, at what had happened.'

'And when this "little fling" happened, he was alone?'

'No, he was with Polly. It just sort of happened. You know . . .' she trailed off lamely.

'Juniper! You idiot! You know no one likes to hear that sort of thing. Of course, she was bound to lash out at you.'

'I didn't know she was going to fly off the handle like that though, did I? I thought we'd talk about it sensibly, analyse it.' She pouted and he could not resist leaning over to kiss the tip of her nose.

'You're not angry with me over Jonathan?'

'No, why should I be? That was in the past. It's what we do in the present that matters. You know me – I don't like talk about the future,' and he leant over and touched the oak chest for luck. 'In fact, you've probably done her a favour. He's got quite a reputation you know, though he doesn't look the type at all, does he?'

'Jonathan?' she sat up with astonishment.

'Oh yes. I know of two girls when he was in Cambridge. There might have been more for all I know.'

'What girls?' she said, then aware that she sounded indignant, 'I mean, who were they?' she added quickly and less forcefully.

'There was one who worked in Heffers and another in The Whim – one selling books, the other buns,' he smiled.

'When was this?'

'Just recently. I'd only met him a week before I met you. It was the Heffers girl then.'

'The bastard!' she exclaimed and hoped Dominic thought her anger was for Polly. But she meant it. How dare he treat her so despicably. Juniper did not like anyone to cheat on her. 'Well, I really did do her a favour then, didn't I?' She brightened up. 'Do you want some of my delicious cake?'

If Polly had not been really aware of the scenery on her way to Juniper's, she was even less so on the journey back. She kept running over the scene with Juniper again and again – like a film with one sequence constantly repeated. She was astonished, when the bus stopped, to find herself in central London.

She walked back to the house like an automaton. She let herself in, went straight to her room and began to pack, haphazardly, angrily throwing her clothes into a case. A banging at the front door stopped her. She peered out of the window to see a bicycle propped up against the stone portico. 'A telegram from Andrew,' she thought, as she raced down the stairs, but instead it was one from Jonathan saying that he would be arriving at six and had a twenty-four-hour pass.

'Good.' She screwed up the buff-coloured form and hurled it into a corner of the hall. She looked at her watch. 'Even better.' She had only half an hour to wait. She put the door on the latch.

In the drawing room she poured herself a drink which she sipped rhythmically as she stood at the window and waited.

'Polly darling, it's me,' Jonathan called out as he raced up the stairs. 'You shouldn't leave the door on the latch like that, anyone could . . .' he said, as he entered the room, stopping when he saw the expression on Polly's face. 'What's the matter, my darling? What's happened?' He crossed the room rapidly and put out his hand to take hers. She stepped back, recoiling from his touch.

'Don't you call me "darling".' She stepped back a further pace.

'Polly.' As he moved towards her she retreated, stepping to one side so that a heavy chair now stood between them. 'Polly, why are you behaving in this way?'

'You know.'

'I don't know. I arrive, happy to see you, planning to make the final plans for next week. Good God, woman, it took me days of wheedling to get this pass – the balloon's going to go up soon.' He spoke with exasperation.

'Then you've a short memory, haven't you?' She paused. 'I've just got back from seeing Juniper,' she went on, deliberately slowly.

'Oh.' Jonathan stood feeling foolish, his mouth hanging slackly open.

'Is that all you've got to say?'

'What did she say?' he asked cautiously.

'You know damn well,' she retorted. In fact, on the journey back, as she had gone over the scene, she realized that Juniper had not said anything specific. But she had not needed to, the implication had been enough.

Jonathan sat down heavily on a chair. 'We agreed not to say anything.'

'She's obviously not reliable then, is she? I've certainly found that out, twice now.'

'God, Polly, I can't tell you how sorry I am. It doesn't mean anything. It just sort of happened, we got drunk . . .'

'Just as you did the first time. Remember? That was the excuse then. Maybe you should both give up drinking, it obviously has an unfortunate effect on your morals.'

'I realize how hurt you must feel, Polly. All I can do is beg your forgiveness.'

'You can't possibly know how I feel, how could you? I haven't cheated on you, so you wouldn't know. Twice now I've trusted you and what a fool I've been. That's how I feel, Jonathan – foolish and relieved. Relieved I found out about you before it was too late.'

212

'Polly, no! You can't mean this. I love you. All our plans . . .'

'Gone down the drain – that's where they've all gone.'

'What about Juniper? It took two of us to deceive you,' he said, with more spirit now.

'I never want to see her again, ever.'

'But she's your sister.'

'She is *not* my sister. That's her stupid idea, I've never believed it. I never wanted to be her sister, now I'm bloody glad I'm not.'

'She's convinced you are.'

'I don't give a damn how convinced she is. As far as I'm concerned the two of you deserve each other. As I don't wish to see her, neither do I wish to see you. That box over there contains all the presents you've ever given me and I should be obliged if you would remove them – and yourself – now.' Polly crossed the room quickly and opened the double doors wide. 'Now.' She pointed dramatically out into the upper hall.

'Polly, we've got to talk.'

'There is nothing further to say, Jonathan. Goodbye.' And with that, and head held high, Polly left the room and slowly climbed the stairs to her room. She shut the door and leant against it, her heart thudding. Then she put one ear to the door to listen. She stayed in that position until she heard Jonathan's footsteps on the stairs and the slam of the front door. She slumped against the highly polished mahogany and no longer knew what she thought.

'What on earth makes you think you can stay here?' Francine looked at her daughter with barely concealed annoyance.

'I don't know many people in London.'

'Your precious grandmother owns that mausoleum of a house.'

'It belongs to her eldest son but in any case, it's been requisitioned.'

'Then her friend – Alice Wakefield, or Whitaker, whatever her name is – hasn't she got a house in London she isn't using, now she's stuck in Cornwall?'

'I don't like to ask her.'

'But you don't mind asking me, I see. You drool over that Alice creature, spend all your spare time at her place, you never visit me and then expect me to take you and your fiancé in. Well, I can't.'

'You've room, Mother, and it will only be for a couple of days until I can find a room or small flat.'

'I shall decide whether I have room or not – not you. And in any case it wouldn't be proper, you and your young man sharing a room. I have my reputation to consider.'

'Oh, Mother,' Polly said with exasperation at the fatuous excuse.

'But you haven't told me why you've fallen out with your precious friend, have you?'

Polly stood silently by the table in the middle of Francine's bedroom, fingering the red roses on the large azure bowl which stood there. Her mother must be in-between shows, she thought inconsequentially, otherwise the bowl would be in her dressing room at the theatre. She would never go on stage without touching it first.

'Stop playing with that bowl, you'll damage it.' Francine snapped. 'Why can't your precious Jonathan put you up in an hotel for a few days?'

'I'm not with Jonathan. We're no longer engaged.'

'Really? How interesting, what's happened?' Francine sat bolt upright, her eyes alight with curiosity. 'Now, let me see. You've finished with Jonathan and you're not speaking to your best friend Juniper, so what conclusion can one reach?' She laughed gaily. 'Good gracious, is dear Juniper up to her old tricks? Have you caught her out with your young man? Oh, how funny!'

'I don't think it's at all funny.'

'So I'm right?' Francine leaned forward eagerly. 'Now

perhaps you'll listen to your mother about that unspeakable baggage.'

'I'd rather not discuss it further.'

'Yes, I'm sure. I expect you feel a real fool – serves you right, if you ask me.'

'Well, I'm not asking you, as it happens, Mother.'

'So, who's the new young man then, the one you want to bring here?'

'His name is Andrew Slater.'

'You mean you've tumbled out of one bed into another? That's a silly thing to do. Rebounds are notoriously dangerous.'

'I'm not on the rebound, Mother. Andrew and I were engaged when I was in Paris.'

'Don't talk such tosh, Polly. How could you have been engaged if you were still married to that dear little Frenchman?'

'It was unofficial.'

'Very unofficial, it sounds to me.' She studied her nails and, imagining an imperfection, swooped on the clutter on her dressing table until she found an emery board. 'Never use a steel nail file, Polly. It splits the nails.' She began to work on the offending nail. 'What I don't understand is why you're so poor. Your father left you Hurstwood and his investments – I got bugger all.'

'I need every penny of income to keep Hurstwood going. I'd hoped that some government department or a school might have been interested in taking it over for the war, but it's too small.'

'Well, sell the damned place then.'

'I couldn't do that. I love Hurstwood. My father adored it.' Polly stood rigid with shock at such a sacrilegious idea.

'Then you'll have to stay poor, won't you? Now, if you don't mind, I have to change for dinner. You'll have to go,' and Francine waved her hand in dismissal. She was being taken out to dinner by a particularly handsome American major and had no intention of allowing any of her admirers to meet her grown-up daughter. They might, by a process of mental arithmetic, work out an approximation of her age, and she did not stick to her beauty ritual in order to be found out that easily.

The evening post had arrived by the time Polly returned to the house. There was a letter from Juniper, and a note from Jonathan had been dropped through the letter box. She tore both up without reading either.

In the kitchen she made herself some cocoa. She had been stupid even to think that her mother would allow her to stay there. It showed the extent of her panic that she had approached the woman at all. She could see her mother's point of view. Why should she expect Francine to take her in just because she was her mother? You had to like someone to put yourself out to that extent. She smiled to herself, she would undoubtedly have got in the way of her mother's social life.

She had overreacted. Why shouldn't she stay here until she got something else sorted out? After all, she wasn't in the wrong. Or was she? Hadn't everything happened too conveniently? Had she not got what she wanted in the end – Andrew? To her shame she realized she hadn't even mentioned his return to Jonathan.

Ah well, she thought, it was too late for that now. She still had a future to look forward to, and with a man who really needed her. To be needed, she repeated the word aloud – the most precious thing of all in a relationship – need. She smiled to herself as she switched off the light and made for her half-packed room.

10

'He's far from well, Polly. You do realize what you're taking on?' Gwendoline asked her, as Polly made them tea. Andrew was upstairs unpacking his case.

'I love him,' Polly replied simply, as if love was the solution to everything.

'What about Jonathan?'

'That's finished.'

'Did you tell him about Andrew?'

'No, I found out something unpleasant about him and gave him the push. It was all very neat in the end.' Polly laughed, but the cynicism did not suit her.

'You're not on the rebound?' Gwendoline asked anxiously.

'No,' Polly said firmly. 'If Andrew wants to marry me still, and needs me, that's all that matters.'

'He talks of nothing else. Luckily his mother made no mention of your involvement with Jonathan. She was too euphoric over Andrew's return. It might be more difficult than you imagine, though. He's a bundle of nerves and has the most fearful nightmares.'

'It's hardly surprising, is it?'

'These are serious, Polly. Sufficiently bad to be described as a medical condition.'

'Then I'll find him a good doctor.'

'And his stomach is all to pot. He can't keep food down, and he's so thin.'

'Then I shall experiment until we find the right diet to suit him,' Polly said patiently.

'His parents wanted him to stay, but he was adamant about returning to you.'

'That's nice.' Polly smiled to herself. 'I do have one problem, though, Gwendoline. I've got to get out of this place. You don't know of any accommodation, as cheap as possible, do you?'

'You know how difficult it is finding somewhere to live. I've never understood why this barn of a house is always empty. I'd have expected at least ten people to be billeted here.'

'When the officials came round it was full of Juniper's friends. When they left she never told anyone. It must have been overlooked, I suppose.'

'Why do you have to move?'

'I'd rather not say.'

'Fair enough. But Andrew needs peace and quiet. In fact, I don't think London is a good idea at all, especially if the bombing begins again. It's quiet at the moment, but . . . Haven't you got a place in Devon?'

'Yes, but there's no one there, only an old housekeeper and the gardener. They're both too old to look after Andrew.'

'No, I meant for both of you to go there.'

'But my job with you?'

'Leave it to me, I'll explain. I think his need is greater . . . Andrew? Feel better for your bath?'

'Yes thank you, Gwendoline, and better for being back with Liz.' He crossed the room and shyly took Polly's hand in his.

'Well, I must away, my poor long-suffering husband will be wondering where the hell I've got to. Now don't worry, Polly. Go to Devon as quickly as possible. I'll sort officialdom out,' and in a flurry of scarves, her large handbag weighing down one shoulder, Gwendoline left after kissing both young people enthusiastically. 'Be happy,' she called to them as they stood on the top step and waved her goodbye.

'Would you like to go to Hurstwood, Andrew?'

'Very much. I'm not good at loud noises, I'm afraid.'

'I understand.'

'They make me shake.'

'Yes, of course.'

'And, Liz, it sounds daft, but I cry a lot – usually about nothing in particular.'

'That makes two of us, then.' She smiled at him.

'You are going to marry me still, aren't you?'

'Yes. You don't think I'm going to let you escape from me a second time?' She laughed up at him. 'I love you, Andrew, you see. I never stopped.' It was one honest thing she'd learned from Juniper; people not death destroy love.

A week in the peace of the Devon countryside had begun

to work wonders, Polly felt. Already Andrew looked fitter. They had discovered that if they stuck to soup, chicken and poached fish, his damaged digestive system could manage. The weather was unbelievably fine and each day they took a long walk across the moors. The exercise rebuilt his body, the scenery helped salve his soul. Sometimes when the larks were singing high in the blue sky their song seemed to them a celebration of their own happiness with each other.

Polly's previous wedding had been in a register office. Her husband had been a Roman Catholic, but Polly had refused to convert to his faith and having no faith of her own, she had stuck by her principles and had insisted on a civil ceremony. This time it was to be different. This time she was not eighteen, she was a mature woman of nearly twenty-six and in the intervening years she had learnt how to compromise on principles. She knew what happiness she would be giving her grandmother if she married in church.

There was one sticky moment at the vicarage where they had gone to arrange the ceremony. Old Julius Middlebank stumbled towards them in welcome, rheumy eyes peering at them from behind spectacles which could have done with a good polish.

'Polly, my dear – such a happy duty you ask of me. And Jonathan too.' He grasped Andrew's hand.

'This is Andrew Slater, Mr Middlebank. I explained to you.' Polly would have preferred to say this to him quietly but instead, because of his defective hearing, she had to shout.

'Andrew? But where's Jonathan?'

'He's with the army, Mr Middlebank.'

'But I always thought . . . Oh dear . . .' He flapped his hands in the air with irritation, incomprehension in his expression.

'I wrote to you,' Polly bellowed. 'I enclosed our baptism certificates, don't you remember?'

'Of course I remember. My sight and hearing might not

be as good as they were but I'm not senile, you know,' the old cleric said, affronted.

Polly looked abashed. He certainly was not senile, far from it. Despite his eighty odd years, his sermons were highly thought of and his knowledge of canon law was second to none. It was her fault, she obviously had not made things clear in her letter. Given the circumstances, it was not surprising.

'Who's Jonathan?' Andrew asked later, as they walked back from the vicarage to Hurstwood.

'Poor Mr Middlebank, he's confused,' Polly said quickly. 'Jonathan's his nephew. I used to have a school-room pash on him. In fact my father and the old boy used to joke about us getting married.' She felt intolerably guilty for implying the vicar was an old fool in his dotage.

'Ah, I see. For a nasty moment I thought I must have a serious rival.'

From their first day in Devon, Andrew had insisted on booking into The New Inn in Widecombe.

'I don't want you compromised. I know these country areas and the gossip there would be if I stayed alone with you at Hurstwood.'

'I don't give a fig about gossip. In any case they think I'm a lost cause anyway, going off and marrying a Frenchman.' She giggled, remembering the disapproval and gossip that it had caused.

'I care very much what people say about you. Until we're married I'll stay at the inn.'

'But we were virtually living together in Paris.'

'That was Paris, this is Devon. A million miles separate them where morality is concerned.'

Each evening, after dinner, he would give her a chaste kiss and walk back down the valley in the dark. She hated his staying in the village. Gwendoline had told her of the nightmares he was having. The idea of him waking in the night, alone and frightened, haunted her. So she telephoned her grandmother at Gwenfer and asked her to come as soon as possible to act as a chaperone.

'It's Andrew. He doesn't want my reputation compromised.'

'Andrew?' Gertie barked down the telephone. 'Who, pray, is Andrew?'

'Oh dear, I haven't explained to you, have I? I'm not marrying Jonathan but Andrew.'

'The sooner I come the better, it seems to me. It sounds as if you're in a dreadful pickle. At least he's a gentleman. Of course there's no question of his staying under the same roof with you unchaperoned. Whatever next?'

The whole business smacked of hypocrisy to Polly. She and Andrew spent every waking hour together alone. They had opportunities without number to misbehave. She thought of the many afternoons they had spent in bed together in her Paris flat. Not that anyone had any cause to worry here; Andrew was the perfect gentleman, in fact. Apart from the occasional kiss he had made no attempt to make love to her, much to Polly's disappointment, but she waited patiently for the two days until Gertie arrived and she could have Andrew safely under her roof.

Gertie Frobisher arrived with Hursty the cat in a flurry of activity as she always did. Even sitting still Gertie gave the impression of perpetual motion. She was gracious to Andrew and not for one second did she betray her confusion. She contained herself until after lunch when Polly suggested Andrew had a rest, for he still became easily exhausted.

'So he is the Andrew everyone thought was dead?' she was finally able to ask Polly as they walked in the gardens in the glorious sunshine. These gardens had been Polly's father's pride, but with only one old gardener left to tend them they were rapidly reverting to the wild, another casualty of war. 'How could such a cruel and crass mistake be made?'

'I don't know. He wasn't in a POW camp at the end. It was another sort of camp, so awful he can't bring himself to talk about it.'

'And you have had to choose between the two young men? My poor Polly.'

'It was an easy choice.'

'Then I'm glad for you.'

'It seems . . .' Polly stopped walking and gazed down over the lawn far into the valley below. The day was so still that the smoke from the chimneys rose vertically in the air. She stood silent for some time, wondering what to say. She was going to have to explain Juniper's absence somehow; it was probably better to tell the truth and get it over with. 'It appears that Jonathan had an affair with Juniper.'

Gertie stared at Polly, a look of horror on her face. 'Juniper? But she's your friend,' she said.

'Was my friend is nearer the truth. I found I couldn't forgive them, not this time.'

'*This time*?' Gertie was quick to grasp the significance of the words. Polly told her everything.

'The stupid, selfish child. I'd like to smack her,' Gertie said angrily then sighed. 'But what would be the point? She's such a sad creature, Juniper, she had an appalling childhood you know, despite dear Alice's attempts at creating normality – too much money. A fatal flaw of the nouveaux riches is to spoil their offspring, frequently with ruinous results. And she's so like her father, he was totally amoral. I've always thought that all that spoiling of her as a child would eventually come home to roost.'

'She's still very like a child.'

'Exactly. And, like a child, if she sees something she wants she just takes it. I'm certain you are the last person in the world she would really want to hurt,' Gertie said, attempting to salve Polly's pain while still inwardly fuming.

'I'm not too sure of that.'

'I am.'

'I doubt it. She'll have rationalized it in her mind; probably it's all my fault now, or Jonathan's. But even understanding her as well as I do, I can't forgive her. I could never trust her again, you see.'

'Nor should you. There's no question about it,' Gertie said briskly. 'But at the same time, one can't help but feel sorry for her, such a lost soul.'

'Well, I don't.'

'Of course you don't, but one day you will. And Andrew? You love him, you're not marrying him out of a sense of duty?'

'No. I love him.'

'Good. Well, that's all right then, isn't it? You really should do something about that montbretia, Polly, it's little better than a weed. It'll take over the whole garden if you don't watch out.'

Polly looked without interest at the offending plant; she quite liked them. 'Grandmother, there's just one thing. I don't want Alice to know. I don't want her worrying.'

'Neither do I, my dear.'

Both women suddenly shivered and turned back towards the house, complaining of a sudden breeze. But there was no breeze. They shivered from fear – fear of what the future might hold for someone like Juniper.

11

Polly had asked Alice if Annie and May could be brides-maids. She had really only wanted Annie, but felt she could not hurt May's feelings so had invited her too. She was surprised and secretly pleased to be told that May and her brothers had returned to London; now that the bombing seemed to be finally over, their mother wanted them home. 'So that poor May can skivvy, no doubt,' Gertie had sniffed in disapproval.

She had rejected Polly's favourite black suit as unsuitable for a wedding. 'This isn't a funeral, we shall have to go into Exeter and buy something. Alice recommends

Pinder and Tuckwell in the High Street or Marie Wilson in Market Street. You can have my coupons.'

At Marie Wilson's they found a pale yellow linen suit with white piping, which Gertie approved of, and in Colson's their luck held when a matching hat and handbag were tracked down. They relaxed over tea and toast in Colson's restaurant, feeling that self-congratulatory glow experienced by most women after a successful foray into the shops.

'Isn't everyone frightfully grand?' Gertie said, looking about the restaurant filled with expensively behatted women. 'You'd never think there was a war on, would you?'

'It's rather brave, don't you think?' answered Polly. 'This beautiful city is half in ruins and yet they haven't let it get them down. They're still in their glad rags as though cocking a snook at Hitler.'

'That's one way of looking at it, I suppose,' Gertie replied with a hint of disdain in her voice as she silently judged the women as lazy good-for-nothings.

Two weeks later Alice arrived with an over-excited Annie who was bubbling over with information about the pale yellow cotton dress sprigged with forget-me-nots, that Alice had made for her, the colour matched exactly from a thread of Polly's suit.

Throughout these preparations Andrew kept a detached male distance, but Polly sensed he was becoming depressed. It was hardly surprising, she reasoned with herself, his father had written wishing them both joy, but regretting that his wife was still too unwell for either of them to attend. His brother, whom Andrew had hoped to be his best man, could not get leave and now Gwendoline Rickmansworth had telephoned to say that, although she was moving heaven and earth, she very much doubted she could come. Polly had consoled Andrew by pointing out that she also had few guests, but he seemed to be reluctant to be cheered.

'I hope you're not having second thoughts,' she joked,

but it was a lame attempt. The thought had begun to take root in her mind that maybe she was rushing everything. Perhaps she should have let a few months pass to give him time to readjust to normal life again. She slipped quietly from the room where she had found him slumped in a chair with a book open on his lap, a book he was not reading. Instead, he was staring vacantly at the wall in front of him. She must be patient, she told herself. The Andrew who had returned to her was wounded – not in his body, but in his mind. Just because she could not see the damage did not mean that it did not exist. God alone knew what he saw when he sat blankly staring in that unnerving way. Only once had she asked, but his peremptory reply – 'I don't want to talk about it' – had made sure she did not ask again.

Gertie found to her distress that her relationship with Alice had altered. She did not want to blame Alice for what had happened between their granddaughters, but she found that this was the way her thoughts insisted on going, despite her efforts to think logically. If Alice had been stricter, Juniper would not have been so spoilt, not so likely to do whatever she wanted without thought of the consequences. She felt an anger with her friend that manifested itself in coolness. She knew that Alice was perplexed by her behaviour, but there was nothing she could do about it. She would have liked to talk to her, to discuss and analyse her feelings, but she could not. She had promised Polly that Alice would not be told about Juniper's behaviour with Jonathan.

Gertie was worried too about Andrew and even more about Polly.

'Do you think Polly is doing the right thing?' Alice asked her one day, thinking perhaps this was why Gertie seemed to be somewhat withdrawn from her.

'I think she sees it as her duty,' Gertie said.

'But "duty" isn't enough for a marriage in these times. Our generation often married out of familial duty, but look at the lifestyle – armies of servants, nannies, a busy social life. Andrew and Polly are going to live in this quiet backwater with little money, hard work ahead of them . . . you need love to survive a marriage in such circumstances.'

'I have the utmost faith in Polly to do the right thing – always,' Gertie said, evidently not wishing to continue the conversation.

Polly was married to the sound of church bells. Not only at Tunhill, but from Widecombe, from all the churches hidden in the folds of the wild moorland, the bells pealed out. They were not ringing for Polly, but for the successful Allied landings in France – D-Day had come.

Polly walked proudly down the aisle on the arm of an even prouder Gertie. When the vicar offered up prayers for the success of the fighting men overseas Polly added her own private one for Jonathan, who was now abroad. She was happy, on such a day she could not maintain any anger or bitterness towards him. But as soon as she had prayed she turned to Andrew, took his hand and squeezed it. As the ceremony proceeded she remembered her father and felt a sadness that he had not lived to see this day.

'I don't understand where Juniper has got to. So inconsiderate of her to be late on Polly's day,' Alice fretted as she and Gertie waited in the drawing room at Hurstwood for the bridal pair to appear for drinks before dinner. Since no one had told Alice that Juniper had not been invited her concern was natural. Gertie had suggested that she and Alice book into the Royal Clarence in Exeter in order to leave the young couple alone, but Polly would not hear of such a thing. She begged them to stay longer, but both women had insisted they leave in the morning.

'You don't think she has crashed, do you, Gertie? You know how fast she drives.'

Gertie said nothing, but sat, back straight, pretending to read an old copy of *Horse and Hound* which she had found in her son's study, where nothing of his had been touched.

'Gertie, what do you think? I'm worried sick.'

'She drives too well for that.' Gertie turned back to her magazine.

'It's unlike her, missing such an important day. She would know how much Polly wanted her to be here.'

Gertie glanced up from the magazine and gave Alice a look of obvious cynicism.

'Why are you giving me that look?' Alice was pacing up and down the room.

'What look?' Gertie said, all innocence.

'You know very well what look. A superior look.'

Gertie put the magazine down on a small table. 'I'm sorry if my look offends you,' she said, all dignity now.

'Your looks always mean something. Out with it.'

'I was remembering a certain funeral that Juniper just happened not to attend.'

'That's not fair, Gertie. You know it isn't. I understood how Juniper felt. She was obviously feeling too depressed to come . . .'

The snort that erupted from Gertie was impossible to ignore. Alice swung round to face her.

'Why are you being like this? What's the matter? You've been behaving oddly ever since I arrived.'

'I don't know what you're talking about.' Gertie picked up her magazine again.

'You're not reading that magazine, are you? Answer me, Gertie. Something's happened, hasn't it? Something's upset you.'

Gertie ignored the questions and flicked noisily through the magazine.

'For goodness sake, put that beastly thing down.' Alice crossed the room and snatched the copy from Gertie's hands.

'Well, really, Alice! What are you doing?'

'Trying to get you to speak to me, to tell me what you know.'

'I promised Polly I wouldn't.'

'You *must* tell me. I'm beside myself with worry. Anything could have happened.'

'I'll go so far as to tell you that they've fallen out.'

'Polly and Juniper? Oh, don't be silly, Gertie, they're as thick as thieves.'

'As you wish.'

'You mean it?'

'I'm not in the habit of saying things I don't mean, Alice,' Gertie said severely.

'No, of course you aren't. I'm sorry. What has made them fall out?'

'I'm not prepared to say.'

'You must.'

'I mustn't anything. It's not pleasant and it's not necessary to tell you. Polly is happy with Andrew and that's all there is to it.'

'Wonderful, so long as precious Polly is happy, that's fine. You don't give a thought to Juniper. After all she has done for Polly – fed her, put a roof over her head, lavished gifts and love on her.' Alice was angry now, an anger fuelled by fear for Juniper.

'All she has done for Polly?' Gertie roared, standing up. 'I'll tell you what she's done for Polly – stolen her fiancé, not once but twice. That's how much she cares for Polly.'

'You're lying.'

Gertie crossed her hands in front of her and faced Alice. 'You know one of your greatest weaknesses, Alice? You will never hear a word said against that wilful child.'

'Nor would you allow it of Polly.'

'There's nothing bad to be said about Polly, as you well know.'

'Oh no, there wouldn't be, would there? Not perfect, sweet Polly,' Alice said in a spiteful tone, which coming from her made it sound even more shocking.

They turned away from each other, both shaking with anger and both appalled by what was happening, but too far down this path of bitterness and recrimination to stop.

'So why did she marry him then? It must be lies. Polly wouldn't marry someone who had deceived her.'

'Not Andrew, for goodness' sake. Jonathan Middle-bank, that's who I'm referring to.'

'Jonathan?' Alice sat down hard on a chair, her hands at her neck agitating her pearls. 'I don't believe a word of this. Juniper can be wild . . . but Polly's her friend . . . I won't believe it . . . It's malicious gossip . . . You've been listening to filthy tittle-tattle, Gertie.'

Gertie seemed to increase in size as she glowered down at Alice.

'I do not listen to gossip, ever. This information pained me greatly. I can't say I'm surprised when you look at Juniper's background.'

'I beg your pardon?' Alice was on her feet again squaring up to Gertie. 'And what does that mean?'

'You allowed her grandfather and her father to ruin her as a child. You were weak, Alice, you stood back and let it happen. And of course even if she had been invited she wouldn't have come. Like you, she always runs away from difficult situations. Just as you ran away with Chas rather than face your father. And the way you ran away from America when you had some stupid notion that Lincoln, of all people, was a murderer . . .'

'He was. He confessed as much!' Alice raised her voice defensively.

'Did he? Lincoln? I doubt it. But you always overreact if your precious Juniper is criticised.'

'My God, you are a bully, Gertie. I can't imagine how I've put up with you all these years.'

'There's a simple solution to that, Alice. I shall remove my possessions from Gwenfer as soon as possible. I'm grateful for your hospitality in the past, but our position now would be untenable.' And Gertie, her head held high, turned towards the door. As she reached it, it opened and Andrew and Polly, holding hands and wreathed in smiles, entered the room. Polly's smile disappeared as she saw her grandmother's face.

'Grandmama, what's happened? Why are you crying?'

'Me, crying? Poppycock,' Gertie blurted out as she rushed from the room and up the stairs to the safety of her own bedroom.

'Mrs Whitaker, can you explain?' Polly asked, her face creased with anxiety.

'Your grandmother has been spreading evil gossip about my granddaughter. She's leaving Gwenfer and I must say I'm pleased she is. I never wish to speak to her again.' Alice stood white-faced in the centre of the room.

'About Juniper? My grandmother? But she would never do that.'

'Well, she has and I have to ask myself what might be the source of this poison . . . You've always been jealous of Juniper, haven't you – her money, her beauty? But I never expected you to go to these lengths! You're more like your mother than I thought, Polly.' Alice was shaking with rage.

'Mrs Whitaker, I don't understand what you're talking about.'

'Don't you?' Alice gave a short, cynical laugh.

'No, I'm sorry, I don't know.'

'Your precious Jonathan and Juniper, that's what she was talking about. I don't like it and, Polly, I won't have it. I shall be driving into Exeter to the Clarence. Perhaps you could make arrangements for your grandmother's luggage to be collected from Gwenfer. Goodnight, Andrew. Obviously none of this has anything to do with you.' And with that Alice swept from the room.

'What the hell was all that about?'

'I don't know,' Polly said. 'Honestly,' she added, and immediately regretted it for, the word somehow implied that she wasn't speaking the truth.

'Jonathan again. First the vicar, and now this. Haven't you something to explain to me, Liz?'

'I must see my grandmother, she'll be in a dreadful state. They've known each other for years.'

'Liz, sit down. I think you owe me an explanation.'
Andrew grabbed her arm as Polly made for the door.

Wretchedly, Polly sat down and haltingly began to tell
him the whole wretched story about Jonathan and
Juniper.

'And was that why you married me?' Andrew asked,
his voice strained with emotion.

'No, it wasn't. I know that's what everyone is going to
say, but it's not true. I'm being truthful with you when I
say that the minute I saw you again my mind began to
race, working out how to tell Jonathan I wasn't going to
marry him. You must believe that.' She looked up at him
anxiously. He studied her for what seemed a long time.
Polly realized she was holding her breath.

'Of course I believe you. If you must know, I think
you're better off without Juniper in your life.'

Polly flung her arms around him with relief. 'I'm so
glad you know – it's been on my conscience. It seemed so
wrong to begin our life together without being straight
with you.'

'I couldn't agree more – any more skeletons?' He
smiled at her and it was the first genuine smile she had
seen from him for days.

'No.'

'Good, then perhaps you had better go and see your
grandmother.'

Polly met Alice and Annie on the stairs.

'But why are we going? I like it here, I like Miss Polly,'
Annie was complaining as she bumped her small case
down the stairs.

'Mrs Whitaker, I wish you would stop. Let's talk about
it all.'

'I've nothing further to say,' Alice said shortly, man-
handling her large suitcase with difficulty.

'Let me help you with that.'

'I can manage on my own, thank you.'

'Miss Polly . . .' Annie was anxious now, sensing
Alice's anger, 'what's wrong?'

'I don't know, Annie,' Polly said, bending to kiss the child.

'Annie, come,' Alice ordered and, shocked at seeing her beloved Alice in a temper for the first time, a sobbing Annie followed disconsolately to the front door.

Polly banged and banged on the door of Gertie's room, but she would not let her in. Polly could hear her grandmother sobbing – an unheard-of event.

'Go away. Leave me alone,' was all she would say.

Polly returned to Andrew and to what was supposed to be their wedding dinner.

'Not much of a wedding feast, is it? Poor darling Liz.' He smiled at her from the other end of the table, the empty place settings for Alice and Gertie standing in mute reproach.

'It's perfect. I've got you, after all.' She smiled back bravely.

Finally, in bed together, with Andrew's arms about her, his lips on hers, Polly felt secure and safe. This was how it had been in Paris. This was how he always made her feel.

'I'm sorry, Liz,' Andrew was saying to her twenty minutes later. 'I don't know what's wrong.'

'It doesn't matter – we've had an exhausting day.' She kissed him gently, put her arms about him and cradled her head against his breast. 'There, there, let's sleep.'

In the dark she listened to the changing pattern of his breathing as he slipped into sleep. Polly lay wide-eyed, looking at the ceiling, an ache in her body and fear in her heart. And bitterness began to form; his knowing about Jonathan had caused this to happen, it was all Juniper's fault. In her distress all logic fled. In the long night hatred began to take root as she laid the blame for Andrew's impotence at Juniper's door.

12

From the Royal Clarence Hotel in Exeter Alice wrote to
Gertie. It was a curt note informing her that she would be
away from Gwenfer for a week, which would give Gertie
the opportunity to collect her luggage with the minimum
of embarrassment to everyone.

This note hurled Gertie into a dark depression. She had
allowed herself to believe, on seeing Alice's handwriting
on the envelope, that it would contain a note of apology
similar to the one she had already written herself. The
shock of its contents was, therefore, doubly wounding.

Polly now had two depressed people to contend with.
The smiles of his wedding day had disappeared, and
Andrew was once again staring into space and had
suggested to Polly that he should have his own room.
She resisted this suggestion vehemently. If they were to
solve this problem, separate beds were not the answer, she
told herself. But to him she said, 'No, my darling. I'm
happy just sleeping beside you. I've told you that you're
not to worry.'

But what to do about her grandmother was more
complex. Since she had never before seen her in this
state, she did not know the best way to deal with her.
Instinct told her it was best to leave her alone to come to
terms with what had happened. Meanwhile she reassured
Gertie, 'Nothing would make us happier than for you to
stay here with us for as long as you like.'

Two days later Alice left her car at St David's Station in
Exeter. She did not have enough petrol for her journey, so
she and Annie took the train. When they arrived in
Nettlebed, she booked a room at The White Hart and
made enquiries as to where Juniper lived. Then she set off
to find her.

'Grandmama, what a wonderful surprise. Come in,
do.' Juniper beamed with pleasure. 'And Annie too, how

sweet,' she said, but, as Annie noticed, the smile was switched off for her. 'Tea, coffee? A drink?' Juniper fussed about her grandmother, helping with her coat, her hat, her gloves. 'Don't you just adore my little cottage? Isn't it perfect? I have no toys for Annie. Would you like to draw? There's some paper . . .' As she searched in the dresser for paper Juniper kept up a barrage of talk. Alice must have been to Polly's wedding; her arrival here was ominous to say the least. All she could do was delay the inevitable interview and pray that Dominic did not arrive. Because of the invasion she never knew when he would appear.

'Juniper, sit down. I need to talk to you,' Alice ordered, and the severity of her tone made Juniper begin to feel distinctly nervous. She glanced towards Annie who was sitting on the sofa, legs stuck out awkwardly in front of her, hands demurely folded in her lap. There was a stillness about the child that made Juniper feel uneasy, as if Annie already knew everything whereas she herself didn't. Alice saw the glance and registered the flash of irritation.

'Annie, go and play outside for a minute, there's a good girl.' Dutifully Annie slipped from the sofa and made for the door. Her obedience annoyed Juniper, it wasn't natural.

'Is she always such a "Goody-two-shoes"?' she asked.

'She can be as naughty as the next child. She's tired,' Alice replied defensively and Juniper frowned, resenting Alice's attitude. 'I want to talk about Jonathan.'

'What about him?' Juniper said airily and flopped on to the sofa opposite her grandmother.

'I gather you've misbehaved with him.'

Juniper burst out laughing. 'What a quaint expression, Grandmama.'

'There's nothing quaint about such behaviour, nor the consequences.'

'What consequences?'

'You obviously broke Polly's heart and she rushed

234

straight into the arms of Andrew. And that young man is in no fit state to marry anyone.'

'I didn't make Polly do that – she wanted to marry Andrew. Jonathan was in the way.'

'So, this only happened after Andrew came back into Polly's life?' Alice asked, hopeful for a moment that things might not be as bad as she feared.

Juniper could feel herself blushing, not a slight blush but a deep red, a blush that could not be ignored and would contradict any lie she chose to tell.

'Well, no . . .' She looked down at her hands, and then took an inordinate interest in one nail in particular. 'Not exactly . . .' she added when her grandmother said nothing. Gingerly she looked up and smiled at the woman sitting opposite. But her enchanting smile failed to disarm Alice.

'I want the whole story, Juniper, and I'm not leaving until I hear it.'

'There's little to tell. Polly was away and I felt sorry for Jonathan and invited him to stay – and it just sort of happened.'

'Just the once?'

'No. We saw a lot of each other for several weeks.'

'Juniper, how could you?'

'What difference does it make? Once or a dozen times – the die was cast, wasn't it? It was done and that was all there was to it.'

'But she's your best friend.'

'Of course she is, Grandmama. But don't you see, I did her a favour. He obviously didn't love her enough, or it wouldn't have happened, would it?'

'I can't agree. He's a man, you're a woman. It was up to you, not him. We both know what men are capable of.'

'Oh really, Grandmama. I resent that and it's ridiculously old-fashioned. Okay, we shouldn't have done it, but he's as much to blame as I am. More so, in fact. He was engaged to her, I wasn't.' Juniper sat forward on the

235

sofa, her face animated now. 'I'm sick to death of the woman always getting the blame. And coming from you, I'm astonished. When you became pregnant with my mother, who suffered the most? Whom did society blame? You! You're the last person I'd expect to hear such claptrap from.'

'Juniper, really!'

'It's true, Grandmama, and you know it.'

'It doesn't alter the fact that you might have ruined your friend's life.'

'Gee, Grandmama, of course I haven't. Glory be, she'd been having an affair with Andrew for months in Paris. She's the best thing that could possibly happen to him. As for Jonathan, he's weak, he'll always stray.'

'If you knew that, why encourage him?'

'Because I wanted to,' Juniper said, annoyed at this interference in her life.

'Dear God, you're still a child, aren't you? I want, therefore I can have. Don't you yet realize that you can't go through life always having what you want and to hell with everyone else?'

'I don't see why not. I get lonely, I need people.'

'Aren't you ashamed of yourself?'

'Of course I'm ashamed. If you don't like me, if Polly hates me, what do you think I think about myself? I loathe me, but I can't help what I am.'

'Oh Juniper.' Alice crossed over to her and, sitting beside her, took Juniper's hand in hers. She had spoken with such deep feeling, Alice thought. 'My poor darling. Life was too easy for you, now it's too hard.'

'No, it isn't, not now. I'm in love, Grandmama, I really am this time. I'll never be like that again, I promise.'

'You've probably punished yourself far more than I can. You must have been so unhappy over this whole sorry affair.'

'Oh I was, Grandmama, I was,' and Juniper looked up at Alice, widening her large hazel eyes, pleading for forgiveness. Even if she had not felt any self-loathing it

236

seemed better to agree and then this horrible conversation would end, she thought.

Three days later, on a Monday morning, Alice took the train to London with Annie. They went straight to her small house in Chelsea which smelt stale and musty as it had been shut up for so long. Alice opened the windows and removed the dustsheets, Annie helped to make up two beds and they went to the shops to buy a few groceries.

Alice had not intended to come to London, but she had told Gertie she would be away a week. That week would be up the following day. She could have stayed at Nettlebed, but the resentful atmosphere Juniper had built between herself and Annie had begun to grate on Alice's nerves. Since there had been no raids for weeks it would be safe to take Annie to London, where they could spend a few days sightseeing. Annie had left London when she was four. Now eight years old, she was an intelligent child with an insatiable curiosity. It would have been fun to take her around the museums and art galleries, but most of England's treasures had been taken to the country for safekeeping. However, there were still the buildings. Alice need not hurry home, there was, after all, no one waiting for her at Gwenfer any more.

The next day they were up early and took the bus to Trafalgar Square to feed the pigeons. Annie looked up from the bag of stale bread which Alice had given her to feed the birds.

'Alice, you do love Lady Gertie, don't you?' she asked, as she shared the crumbs out carefully between the flock of birds crowding about her feet, landing on her head and her outstretched hand.

'Of course I do. But it doesn't alter the fact that I am very cross with her.'

'But you will make friends again, won't you?'

'I don't know, Annie.'

Annie's face creased with a frown. 'But she's your best

friend in the whole world. You must make it up. You must.'

Alice bent down and taking hold of Annie's hands looked at her seriously. 'Annie, listen. This is important. Yes, I'll always love Gertie, no one can ever take her place. But you see, I don't think I shall ever be able to forgive her.'

'Why?'

'She said bad things about Juniper. Juniper is my family. No one criticises her to me, no one. Do you understand?'

'Not even if Juniper's been bad?'

'Well, it depends on the spirit in which the criticism is given . . . but then . . .' Alice frowned. 'No, Annie, not even then,' she said, more sure of herself now. 'Loyalty to your family is the most important thing. At the end of the day they are all you have. You must protect them at all cost. No one, no matter how much you love them, can be allowed to hurt them and expect to get away with it,' she said with intensity, holding the child tight as she emphasized each word.

'You're hurting my arm,' Annie complained.

'I'm sorry.' Alice let go of her. Annie stood rubbing her wrist where Alice had held her too tightly.

'What if Gertie says she's sorry and won't ever do it again?'

'I might forgive, but I'll *never* forget.'

'That's sad.' Annie twirled around. 'Oh, look Alice, that poor one over there, he's not getting any crumbs,' and she raced off in pursuit of the pigeon which, frustratingly, fluttered away at her approach.

The crumbs all gone, they went to a concert in St Martin-in-the-Fields. During the recital Alice was aware of an occasional crumping noise, which seemed to be far away, but she noticed that most of the audience was restless and not concentrating on the music. She hoped the crump wasn't the sound of an air raid – she realized she did not even know what a bomb sounded like. How awful for Annie if she had inadvertently put her in danger. She put out her hand to hold the child's and smiled encouragingly at her.

As soon as the concert was over she walked firmly out of the church holding Annie's hand tightly.

'I think we'd better go home now,' she announced.

'But I want to see the Houses of Parliament and Westminster Abbey. You promised.' Annie jumped from one foot to the other. 'Please, Alice, please.'

'Oh, very well. You'll wear me out at this rate.' Alice smiled down at her, finding, just as she had when Juniper was little, how difficult it was to refuse a polite and smiling child anything.

It did not take long for Alice to realize that no one was strolling. Everyone walked quickly, purposefully. Suddenly there seemed to be fewer buses, fewer taxis. Halfway along Whitehall they heard a low rumbling noise, rather like a beaten-up motor car with holes in its exhaust. Above them, in the sky, flew a long, cigar-shaped object, flames pouring from the back. Abruptly its engine cut out. The people in the street disappeared into doorways, racing to take cover. Alice and Annie stood staring up at the ominous machine.

'Duck, you bloody fool!' a voice shouted, but Alice stood transfixed. A man shot out of the entrance to one of the ministries, pulled Alice and Annie into the doorway and pushed them to the ground. The explosion ripped down the street, deafening them. It was followed by a strange silence which was suddenly rent by the noise of shattering glass and falling masonry. People began to stand up, shook themselves and dusted each other down.

'What on earth was that?' Alice asked of no one in particular.

'God knows. Did you see there weren't no cockpit, no pilot,' a man said with shock and astonishment.

'But there was no warning,' Alice said, feeling aggrieved at the negligence of the authorities.

'That looked like a rocket. There won't be much

warning with them buggers, pardon my French. You'd best be off home with the little one,' the man suggested. 'Not from these parts?'

'No, we're up from Cornwall for a few days.'

'I'd get back there, and bloody quick, if I were you.'

'Yes, I think you're right.' Alice managed a wintry smile. 'Come along, Annie, we'll see if we can find a taxi.' She put her hand out to Annie who moved away from her, cowering in the office doorway. 'Come on, darling. We'll go home, we'll be safe there.' Annie began to shake. 'Dear heart, it's all right, the nasty bomb has gone now.'

'You'd best get that little one out of danger, looks as if she's in shock,' the friendly man said, glancing with concern at the white-faced Annie.

'But how?' Alice peered anxiously into the street. 'There's not a taxi in sight.'

'Where do you want to go?'

'Chelsea.'

'You'd be better off scuttling back to Cornwall, if you ask me. But I'll take you for a quid.'

'A pound?' Alice was horrified at the extortionate sum.

'That, or wait for a taxi,' the man replied, as if totally uninterested in her decision, 'I'd be going out of my way. But you'd better make your mind up.'

'Fine, a pound.'

'Come on then, we'd better run. My car's down on the Embankment.'

Unable to persuade Annie to run with them, Alice scooped her up in her arms and the child hid her face in Alice's shoulder.

As she closed the door of her small house behind her, Alice leant against it and sighed with relief. They were safe, she told Annie, who stood silent, staring, looking as she had done when she first arrived at Gwenfer. Even as she reassured the child, she realized that here in this city nowhere was safe.

That night Alice had Annie in bed with her. The girl

would not go to bed without her and it was unlikely she would have stayed alone in her room. Curled up with the little girl held secure in her arms, Alice was comforted by her presence. Annie was exhausted and though she fought it, within five minutes she was asleep.

Alice could not sleep. She felt her body rigid and aching with fear. She had drawn the curtains back for she felt, illogically she knew, that if she could see the flying bomb coming, then somehow they would escape it. She watched the sharp pencils of light of the search-lights crisscrossing the night sky and their presence was a slight comfort.

Alice heard its approach. The relentless spluttering of the engine, the misfiring – her body tensed for the silence that she now knew preceded its fall and detonation. But time and again the engine burst back into life and lurched on with its payload of death. The sound seemed to be travelling miles as if that whole area of the city had fallen into terrified silence at its approach. She could hear the flames now, snaking out at the back – it was very near. 'Dear God, please don't let it stop,' she muttered. But the engine did stop. The ensuing silence seemed to last an age and then across the window, across the bed, across Annie's sleeping face, a great shadow fell, the evil elongated shadow of the bomb as it slunk silently down her street. Alice hurled herself across Annie's body, aware of the child fighting her, pummelling her with her small fists and screaming that she didn't want to die. Alice prayed. She, who all her life had rejected any God or religion, prayed as hard as any devout Christian.

The explosion when it came rocked the house, shattered the window and covered them with shards of glass. 'Oh, thank you, thank you,' she kept repeating with relief, hugging Annie to her and knowing how wrong it was to feel such elation that the bomb had chosen to fall elsewhere, had destroyed another house, killed other people.

'There, you see, Annie. We're all right. I wouldn't let anything hurt you.'

'I thought we were going to die, Alice.'

'Tush, what a silly idea.' She smiled despite the beating of her terrified heart.

The next morning Paddington was in chaos as crowds thronged to the station, intent on escaping London and this new terror. Alice tried not to listen to the rumours, but found that she too was as morbidly fascinated as the next person to hear that Hitler had a thousand of these rockets, a hundred thousand, a million – the figures began to grow in proportion to the fear. That rumour was that these were small ones, that there were bigger ones to come. Alice pulled herself together, it wasn't helping Annie to listen to such talk, she thought, and she bustled the child away as her train was announced. She had to fight her way on to the train as everyone pushed and shoved as if the whole of London wanted to escape to Cornwall with them.

A soldier took pity on Alice and gave up his seat to her. She sat with a silent Annie on her lap as the train lurched slowly to safety.

13

Juniper was not sad to say goodbye to her grandmother. Although on the surface it would seem that Alice had forgiven her about Jonathan, Juniper was unsure. She had intercepted the odd thoughtful look aimed in her direction and Alice was frequently short with her, when she had once had all the patience in the world. For the duration of the visit Juniper had felt wary, expecting the subject of Polly and Jonathan to be raised again at any moment. This insecurity made her feel very edgy and tired.

She was also glad to see the back of Annie. It was true, and she did not mind who knew it, that she was jealous of the child. It was something she could not help. She resented the time the girl spent with her grandmother, resented the attention she received when once it had all been hers. She loathed the easy familiarity between the two of them, hated the knowledge that it was possible for her grandmother to love someone other than her. Still, she consoled herself, once this boring war was over, the child would return to her own home and that would be the end of it, whereas she would still be there, still loved by Alice. It gave her great satisfaction to think so and there had been odd moments when she longed to remind the child that this was what would happen.

She had been proud to show Dominic off to her grandmother, was pleased to see them get on so well, was thrilled to see her grandmother's approval. But their short times together were precious and she had, after the first meeting, resented sharing Dominic with Alice. She wanted him all to herself. She had confided, just as the car approached the station, that she and Dominic were getting married. Alice beamed with relief. Juniper had had to be vague about when they were to marry for the simple reason that Dominic had not yet asked her, but she was sure it was only a matter of time.

And then there was the subject of alcohol. With her grandmother in the house she had to watch what she drank, and when. On her return from the railway station Juniper immediately poured herself a large gin and tonic and drank it gleefully, feeling free again.

A week later Juniper found a maid. Servants were a rare commodity, but by paying well over the odds she had been lucky. The woman did not live in, but instead had a permanent room at The White Hart.

'But darling, can you afford one? I certainly can't,' Dominic said, when he found out.

'I'm not paying. My grandmother wanted me to have her. She was worried I was doing too much.' Juniper smiled up at him and was pleased to note how easily he accepted the lie. He had also complimented her fulsomely on the meal, but she did not tell him that she now had an arrangement with Mrs Clemence, the landlady of The White Hart, whereby whole meals were sent up to the cottage in plenty of time before Dominic appeared. For the truth was that the novelty of housework and cooking was wearing thin for Juniper, it had been a game, but it was one of which she had quickly tired. It was beyond her comprehension that some women spent their whole lives doing nothing else.

The army's advances across Europe were rapid and everyone – not just the optimists – now talked of the end of the war. It was time for plans. She would lie on the large sofa in the cottage, her head on Dominic's lap, and listen to his hopes for the future.

'I shall go to Oxford and read law. Then it's Westminster for me, I hope.'

'There's no hope about it. They'll be begging you to become a candidate.'

'It's not as easy as all that. You have to be selected first, I might have to apply to several constituencies before I'm accepted.'

'What rot you do talk, my darling. The first one you apply to will take you, I'm certain.' She smiled at him with pride.

Now when he was not with her she would daydream of life as the wife of an MP. She could imagine herself standing proudly at Dominic's side as he made his brilliant speeches. His promotion would be rapid; he would be a minister of state and she would be a dazzling hostess for his dinner parties and his political receptions. And when he was Prime Minister, as he surely would become, how she would enjoy that. And when he retired from office and was given his peerage she would be the Lady of a man who had earned his reward. It wouldn't be the same as with Hal, a Lord merely for something some long dead ancestor had done, or stolen. They were pleasant dreams she used to while away the hours until he returned.

Once or twice she had tried to write again, but when she read over what she had written in the past she tore it all up and threw it away. When Jonathan's book was finally published, she read the adulatory reviews, was astonished to hear how talented he was and decided that perhaps it would be better if she forgot about writing a novel and concentrated on poetry – it did not seem so much like hard work.

Dominic still did not know she was rich. It was a problem which after the war she was going to have to do something about. He had asked her to give a dinner party for him one evening, inviting some people whom she gathered were likely to be useful to him later in his career. She had listened horrified to their views on money and the ownership of property. When asked, she had agreed wholeheartedly that extreme wealth was an abomination, crossing her fingers under her napkin as she did so. She had had to cross her ankles as well when agreeing that all wealth should be distributed equally. She had run out of parts of her anatomy to cross by the time she nodded her head vigorously at the 'obscenity of inherited wealth'.

'You don't really think all those silly things, do you?' she had asked Dominic when their guests had gone and they were tidying up the glasses and ashtrays.

'But of course. It's not right that some should have so much when others have so little. They're not "silly" views at all, they're serious.'

'But what if your father had left you a small fortune? I bet you would think differently then.'

'He didn't, so the problem never arose. But I'm sure I would have felt exactly the same.'

'People can't help being left things, can they?'

'No, but there's nothing to stop them giving away what they do inherit. But it's not a problem that's likely to affect us, is it? Unless Alice leaves you a vast fortune.' He laughed. 'She won't, will she?'

'Her money comes from a trust, it isn't hers really.'

'Ah.' He looked relieved. His expression filled her with hope. He didn't want her to be left riches and that could only mean one thing: that in his plans for the future he was including her.

A lot of her time was preoccupied with the thought of what to do about her inheritance. Giving it all away was not a solution that appealed to her. She supposed she could give some, perhaps that would assuage his conscience. There was no need for him ever to know the full extent of her wealth; she did not know herself, so she could never explain it fully to him any more than she had to Hal. And there was always the hope that once he found out and enjoyed her money he would change his attitude. This really was a strange country; in America any man with political ambitions would thank his lucky stars for a rich wife willing to fund his campaigns. Perhaps she could get him to change political parties – that would be the best solution after all, but somehow she thought that might prove difficult, even for her. She still regarded his opinions as well meant but rather naïve; she had met enough socialist millionaires in her time to know that having money need not be a stumbling block in politics.

Certainly, when they were married she no longer wanted to pursue her dream of life in a cottage with him. It was fine for a short time, it had been fun, a novelty. But the lack of space was getting her down; used as she had been all her life to rooms of gigantic proportions, she did find the cottage claustrophobic.

He had proved he loved her in word and deed. This was what she had needed in her life, to have it demonstrated that she was worthy of love and was loved for herself alone. But that was done. Now she wanted to be rich again, with all the comfort that could give her. Not having money in wartime was hazardous, of course, but there was little to spend money on. In peacetime, not being rich was likely to prove boring in the extreme. But when to tell him and how?

As soon as the fighting was over they would move from here, and he would find out about her houses in London. Maybe she had better give them up, buy something smaller. She would wait until they were married before she told him.

But still he never mentioned marriage.

One evening in late July, they were sitting in the garden, with one of the last bottles of champagne – Juniper hoped the war would finish soon, her wine cellar was becoming dramatically depleted. It was a perfect end to a wonderful day. They had gone into the beech woods for a picnic. Now they were tired and relaxed.

'Where shall we live after the war?' she asked, stretching her hands up above her head.

'I shall be in Oxford, I hope. I don't know where you will be.'

It felt as if a bucket of ice cold water had been thrown over her. She dropped her arms, resting her hands in her lap. She sat staring at them, feeling an uncomfortable pricking behind her eyes and her throat constrict.

'I see,' she said eventually, in a tight little voice.

'You probably don't. I'm sorry, darling.'

'It's been fun. You don't want to spoil it, do you? I can understand that. You're probably right, nothing more boring than domesticity, is there?' She sounded brave; she felt she was dying.

'It's not that, Juniper.'

'Isn't it?'

'I love you.'

'Oh, yes.' She allowed a bitter, ironic laugh to escape her and regretted it – men did not like bitterness. 'So you keep telling me.' She forced a lightness back into her voice that she was far from feeling.

Dominic had risen from the seat opposite and come and sat beside her. He put his arm about her, but she looked away, afraid to look at him in case he should see the disappointment and pain in her eyes.

'I'd love to ask you to marry me, my darling. But it wouldn't be fair. It'll be ages before I can afford to marry you. I've got years at university and God knows how long it will be before I'm sufficiently established to be able to take a shot at politics, let alone marriage.'

Juniper sat silent. Was this the moment to tell him that

he need not worry about money ever again in his life? Should she take the risk? Perhaps not, perhaps it would be better to leave it a while longer yet. She needed to ease him into the idea of her wealth: it always changed people's attitude to her. But her heart was singing now. He wanted to marry her, that was the important thing. She would arrange it, she could be confident now. She knew she was important to him; she would make herself indispensable, that would decide it.

'I don't mind, my darling, that you have no money. I have some from my grandmother, as you know. I don't mind supporting you.' When she lied about her money, now there were times when she could almost believe it herself.

'That wouldn't be right. I want to support my wife myself.'

'Such an old-fashioned man, and I thought you were such a radical,' she said gaily.

'Some things shouldn't change.'

'Then I'll wait. I don't mind how long it takes. I'll be clinging on like a little limpet.'

He leant forward and kissed her. 'It doesn't seem right to expect a beautiful creature like you to wait.'

'That's for me to decide, isn't it? I'll move to Oxford, get a dear little cottage somewhere – something a teeny bit bigger than this,' she added hurriedly. 'Would you like that?' She smiled at him ingenuously.

'Oh, darling. What do you think?'

Juniper leant back on the cushion of her seat and was happy again. It was only a matter of time and they would be husband and wife.

The news of the doodlebug raids on London was serious; the destruction was bad. One day, alone in the cottage, Juniper decided to go to London: there were a few things left in the Belgravia house that she would not like to be destroyed.

She drove her car into the square and stopped. At some

time in the past few days the house had received a direct hit. She climbed out of her car and crossed to the pile of rubble. There was nothing to salvage, anything that had survived had long since been taken – she did not mind, in wartime it wasn't like stealing. She stood a moment looking up at the ruin, remembering the parties, remembering those serving men who had passed through its doors and had gone away to die. She had no memory of her collapse; just as well she supposed. She had not been happy here, and it had never really been her home, it had been a base, that was all. She found she felt nothing for the loss of the house and the few things remaining that had been hers. Ah well, she thought, smiling to herself, it wasn't her house, only rented and at least it helped the problem of what to tell Dominic. Now she only had to explain the empty house in Hampstead, and maybe she wouldn't even bother to do that. She crossed to her car, got in and without a backward glance, turned on the ignition and inched the car down the rubble-strewn road.

Her plans now in disarray she decided to motor to Mayfair. She would visit her dressmaker – she hadn't bought one new thing since she had met Dominic. It was time to treat herself. For the first time in the war she had a legitimate supply of coupons.

There were detours everywhere. She found herself being directed along Piccadilly and to the left. As she passed one site of rubble, the remains of what had been a block of flats, her eye was attracted to the pile of debris being swept up by a workman. She slammed on the brakes.

'Excuse me, does anyone own this?' she asked one of the workmen, pointing to the pile of rubbish.

'But it's broken, luv. Look, there's several bits. I don't know if it's all there.'

'It doesn't matter. I can have it mended.' She smiled back at the workman, who willingly began to help her sort out the pieces of china from the rest of the wreckage.

'The people in this building – are they all right?'

'Cor no, luv. A doodlebug got them. All dead, I reckon. Not many survive a direct hit like this. Why? You know someone who lived there?'

'Yes, vaguely. She owned this bowl.'

'Well, she won't be wanting it now, I reckon.'

'No. Thank you.' She smiled again as into her hands he gently placed the fragments of an azure bowl.

Part II

Chapter Four

1

The noise of the traffic streaming along Fifth Avenue was a muted rumble from thirty floors up. The people scurrying along the sidewalk so far below were ant-like. Hal Copton spent many hours by this particular window of the penthouse. It was his favourite place, where he liked to sit and think. So far above the rest of humanity he felt an agreeable superiority. It made him feel that anything he wanted to do was possible, that he was apart from everything, as if life as it was lived by most people had nothing to do with him, which, he supposed, was a fair statement. There was nothing about Hal's life which could be described as ordinary or commonplace.

Of the twenty rooms in the penthouse this was the one he liked best. It was a large room, on several artificial levels – the various platforms and flights of steps were his own creation. One wall consisted of glass sliding doors which opened on to an enormous terrace where he had created a garden that was the talk of Manhattan. Out on that terrace, sitting in the bower of trees, surrounded by herbaceous borders, with the gentle splashing of the fountain into the pool where giant carp swam lazily, it was easy to forget one was atop a building in the centre of New York. This spring he was planning to have a gazebo built, trailing with clematis and honeysuckle, just like the one he had enjoyed at home in England.

He sat in a chair of the softest white suede and looked at the room with his customary pleasure. As other men might spend hours gazing at a sculpture or a painting they owned, Hal gazed at the beautiful room he had designed. When he had first come here the whole apartment was an expensive jumble of antiques; there were huge oil paintings in ornate gilt frames and priceless crystal chandeliers in every room – even the lavatory, he had been amused to note. Then it had been the creation of his father-in-law, Marshall Boscar. Luckily for Hal, his then wife, Juniper, had taken such a violent dislike to her father that she had insisted on the whole place being gutted, as if she was obliterating him from her life.

It was then that Hal had discovered his true métier – interior design. Juniper had helped, but it was he who made the final decisions, he who had done most of the work. She, pregnant at the time, had been happy to leave most things to him. The rooms had been transformed from their antiqued clutter to a spanking modern apartment, sparse and beautiful. Upon his return to New York at the outbreak of war he had refined what they had begun. Each item of furniture was chosen for its line, so that it was not just the abstract paintings and sculptures that were pieces of art but each table and chair also. With his use of white and primary colours, of chrome and steel, of black lacquerwork, the flat had been breathtakingly avant-garde. Ten years later it still was, and the best possible advertisement for his business. As soon as clients saw these rooms they insisted that they had to have the same, expensive as such simplicity invariably was.

For a good five years now Hal Copton had been the designer to whom moneyed New Yorkers turned. Being an English peer had not been a disadvantage either – he was fully aware of the snob appeal of the English aristocracy. Nor was he in the least bashful about using his title at every possible opportunity.

His houseman entered and padded silently across the sixty feet of specially woven white and black carpet – a geometric pattern of Hal's own design. He approached his master who was sitting beside the narrow window which, like an arrow slit, stretched from floor to ceiling, giving him a bird's-eye view of the sidewalk far below.

'It's Mr Macpherson on the telephone, M'Lord.'

'Thank you, Romain.' Hal turned to pick up the instrument on the small table beside him. He had not answered when it rang; Hal never answered the telephone himself.

'Hal? I've got to see you urgently,' the gruff voice of the lawyer rasped down the line.

'It's not convenient.'

'Please, Hal. It's important.' Charlie was pleading with him, he realized.

'You sound somewhat desperate.'

'I am.'

'Very well. I can give you five minutes in-between appointments. See you in an hour then, at five to six?'

He replaced the receiver. He had no appointments, but it did one no good in this country to appear idle for even one minute of the day. People here did not respect anyone who was not perpetually busy, doing deals, making money. Hal had learnt a lot about America in the past years.

He stood up almost lazily, a tall man, a good four inches over six feet. His black hair was short and neatly oiled against his scalp so that it shone like the lacquer furniture he was so fond of. Above his full lips his moustache was perfectly trimmed. He was a handsome man, and he knew it.

'I'll change now, Romain, before Mr Macpherson arrives,' he informed his man.

By five to six he was back in the room, showered, scented and immaculately dressed in a black dinner jacket. Even when alone Hal always changed for dinner.

He turned as Romain let in his expected visitor.

'What the hell's the matter, Charlie, that you couldn't tell me over the telephone?'

'We might have been overheard.'

'You're paranoid, Charlie. Who's going to want to listen to our telephone conversations? Drink?'

'The largest bourbon in the house.'

As he poured the drink – just one, it was far too early

for Hal who never drank before seven – he looked across at his companion. Charlie looked in a bad way. His face was covered with a fine patina of sweat and his usually florid complexion had taken on a nasty yellowish tinge. He took the drink and downed it in one.

'Now, tell me,' Hal finally said, seating Charlie in a comfortable chair with yet another drink beside him.

'It's Juniper. Have you heard?'

'The last news I received was that she had remarried – one Dominic Hastings, a war hero,' he said with an almost imperceptible sneer. 'That was almost three years ago though, back in forty-six. Is she dead?'

'No, nothing like that. She's arriving here, that's the problem.'

'When?'

'This evening, that's the other problem.'

'You might have told me sooner, Charlie.' Hal crossed his long legs and tweaked at the razor-sharp crease of his trousers, the only indication that he was in the least put out by this news.

'I couldn't, I've only just found out myself. I received a telegram yesterday. I assumed she was coming by sea and that we had five to six days to plan our strategy. I was tied up all yesterday, otherwise I would have called you. But no, Juniper's flying, isn't she? Arrives nine tonight at Idlewild.' The words tumbled out rapidly from the mouth of the distraught man, leaving him breathless.

'She always hated the sea. It reminded her of her grandfather drowning, she once told me. Yes, she'd take advantage of flight,' Hal said calmly. 'Well, that doesn't leave you much time then, does it, Charlie?'

'Goddamn it, what do you mean leave *me? Us*, more like it.'

'That's where you're wrong, Charlie, my dear chap. Nothing can be traced back to me, as well you know.'

'How do you know that I didn't make a note of every cash transaction you and I made?'

'I doubt if you would ever have done anything quite so

256

incriminating, Charlie old boy. No, not your style. And if you did, then it's just your word against mine, isn't it? And I can tell you now which of us my dear ex-wife would trust the most.'

'Your lifestyle might take a bit of explaining,' Charlie said, a triumphant gleam in his eye.

'Not really. I've invested shrewdly, and you know what a thundering success my interior design company is. Such a busy beaver I've been – and all legitimate.' He laughed, but Charlie did not join in the laughter. 'My real-estate interests go from strength to strength. Thanks to your generosity to me, Charlie, I'm a rich man in my own right. I couldn't have done it without you, you know.' Hal chuckled at the irony.

'But you still have to explain how you got started, and that might prove difficult.'

'I've always been a gambler, Charlie, all my life – sometimes successful, sometimes not. Fortunes have come and gone through these hands.' He held up his long-fingered, elegant hands to make the point. 'My wife knows that better than anyone. The cards in America have been good to me, that's all I have to say, the only explanation required. But why the panic? You know Juniper. Is she likely to want to delve into the books? If she did, she hasn't the wit to see the discrepancies. No, she's never taken any interest, as you know. Just keep her supplied with money, that's all she requires. Of course, it might be a different story if she's bringing her new husband with her. There's always the risk that he might take an interest in his wife's fortune. Are you afraid he's going to do what I did, find you out for the crook you are?'

'It's not just the books any more, it's other things you don't know about.'

Hal leaned forward in his chair. 'My, my, are you telling me that you haven't always been straight with me? Cheating on your employer and cheating on me too, your old friend? That's not nice, Charlie.' He snorted, a short unpleasant laugh. 'What sort of things?'

'Some property – well, most of the old man's town, primarily.'

'Now, that was stupid.'

'When the sauce business got into difficulties and I sold it off, there seemed little point in my hanging on to the rest of the property.'

'Charlie, it would appear you have a slight problem in remembering that it wasn't a case of your hanging on to things. How could you when they weren't yours in the first place? I assume you sold them and declared less than half of what you got to Juniper?'

'She doesn't know anything about it. I never told her. I stopped bothering her with the details of the business years ago. Once she married and the trust was broken, I didn't have to explain my actions to the courts anymore, as you know. And she was always so uninterested.'

'You didn't tell her that her beloved grandfather's pickle and sauce business had been sold? She won't be happy about that. I think that was the one thing she would have had an opinion about. She worshipped that old bastard. I doubt if she would have allowed it to be sold.'

'It couldn't be helped, it had to go. There was nothing wrong in that. I had her power of attorney and it was my professional opinion that it was better sold.'

'Come, come, Charlie. That business was a little gold mine and you know it. It was never in difficulties. Wherever you go, any diner, any grocer's, any deli, what sauces and pickles do you see? Wakefields. It's still a thriving business. She could sue you over this, you realize, power of attorney or no. God, Charlie, weren't you creaming off enough? But you were greedy. You couldn't let a big one pass you by, could you? You're a bloody fool, Charlie.'

'I know,' Charlie said morosely into his drink. 'I don't need you to tell me.'

'What are your plans then? Stay and brazen it out? No, a bit uncomfortable for you, I imagine. Brazil then, or

Mexico? I suggest you scuttle off there damn quick. But what about Mrs Macpherson, such a tower of strength to New York society and charities? Will she enjoy that? Will she settle, I ask myself.' He smiled unpleasantly. 'Buenos Aires, that's where you should go. Your wife would be far happier there; they have a good opera house, just right for someone as cultured as her.'

'You bastard, Copton.'

'Yes, I'm a bastard, but then so are you, Charlie. And, it would seem, a far greedier bastard than I am.'

'What about this penthouse? She's not going to be too pleased to find that you of all people have been living in it for the past ten years.'

'The one thing you can never say about Juniper is that she's mean or vindictive. She won't mind I've been here, in fact, I'll bet you a hundred dollars she thanks me for looking after the place for her. Very fond of me, my little ex-wife is. Pity in a way she's remarried, we might have got back together again.'

'You're a louse, Hal. The worst thing that ever happened to that little lady was you entering her life.'

Hal laughed at the insult. 'You're a fine one to talk about "poor Juniper". Just think of the millions you've stolen from her.'

'But will you help me, Hal? Help me explain to her?'

'Are you mad? I shall do no such thing. Help you and I damn myself. And you mention me in relation to anything we've been up to and I warn you I shall shame you and your family, bring you so low that there won't be a country left on this planet that you can escape to. Get out, Macpherson, you're a pathetic greedy bum.' Hal looked at him with arrogant disdain, stood up and left the room to the frightened man.

It was a deeply thoughtful Charlie Macpherson who travelled home to his perfect wife and his immaculate mansion on the upper East Side. While his wife changed for dinner he told her he had some work to finish.

In his ornate study he sat at his desk, a desk that had

once belonged to Prince Albert, and he wrote a letter. He remained some time, apparently staring vacantly into space, but he was looking at his choicest possession, a Rembrandt self-portrait. If anyone had told him when he was a struggling student that he would one day own such a painting he would never have believed them.

He looked from the picture to a photograph standing on his desk – sepia-coloured in its silver frame. It had always stood there, a picture of himself taken in the first year of his employment by Lincoln Wakefield. Next to him stood Wakefield himself. He looked at the face of his employer – a hard face. He knew what Lincoln would have done to him if he were still alive. He would be a dead man. He had once had such pride in the trust the old man placed in him and now he had let him down beyond forgiveness. He seemed to be about to speak to the photograph, but instead he turned and unlocked a drawer and from the back withdrew a small brown bottle. He emptied the contents on to the desk; white pills cascaded over the fine leather. He collected them carefully and arranged them in neat rows, before pouring out a full tumbler of bourbon. He studied the lines of white tablets for a minute, then scooped half a dozen into his hand and with a swig of the drink he swallowed them and raised his glass to the photograph as if in salute. He continued until all the pills had gone. He sat, tears pouring down his cheeks, staring intently at the image of Lincoln Wakefield, the man whose faith in him had given him his start, enabled him to acquire everything he owned, which his granddaughter would surely now take away.

2

On the long flight via Newfoundland, Juniper had plenty of time to think. She wondered if she should have stormed out so dramatically. All husbands and wives had disagreements, but not all of them had the wherewithal to catch the first available aeroplane to America. A normal couple would have had to continue in the same house, at the same table, sharing the same bed perhaps. They would have had plenty of opportunity to come to terms with their differences, to discuss them, to make up.

Discuss them. That was a joke. One thing she had learnt in this marriage was that one did not discuss anything with Dominic, he did not allow it, did not give one a chance to say anything as he lectured one. That was really why she had finally walked out, frustrated one time too many by his hectoring and refusal to let her put her side.

Money, that was the problem. She leant forward in her seat, wiping the condensation from the small window shaped more like a porthole, and peered out to see whether the wings were covered with ice. But as soon as she cleared the window, rivulets of water reformed and she gave up trying. Money had always been her problem and she wondered if it would always be. This time she had been determined that it should not interfere with her relationship, but, insidiously as always money had reared its head and created problems.

She had kept her promise to herself and had not told Dominic of her great wealth until they were safely married. In 1946 she had finally got her wish at the Oxford Register Office. When she told him about the money she had made a joke about it. She could still remember that evening so well. She was lying on the bed in their honeymoon hotel in Brighton; they had just made love for the first time as man and wife. She was laughing up at him, at something he had said, and he was pouring them both champagne. She felt so relaxed, so happy, so confident, that she decided it was the right moment and still chuckling, she told him she had a dreadful confession to make. She was laughing but her heart was thudding dramatically.

'And what's that, that you're a bigamist?' he joked back.

'No, worse than that. I'm filthy rich.'

'I beg your pardon,' he said, carefully replacing the bottle of champagne in the ice bucket.

'I think you heard me, Dom,' she said quietly, aware, now that the words were out, that there could be no going back to the lies and the pretending.

'Why didn't you tell me before?'

'It's always difficult for me when I first meet someone. I don't know why, but the money always acts as a barrier to friendship. I wanted you to like me for myself alone, not my money.'

'That's a bloody insulting remark, Juniper,' he said angrily, as he slipped on his dressing gown.

'I didn't mean it to be, believe me. You don't know what it's like to be me, to have people making friends and knowing they're sucking up to me because I'm rich. It's hateful, it makes me feel demeaned.'

'Not nearly as much as I feel – that for one minute you could think I was a gold-digger. I can hardly believe I'm hearing this.'

Juniper scrambled up on the bed and knelt on the edge, her hand out to him, but he ignored it and turned away. He crossed to the window and stood staring down at the rain-swept front. She waited for him to say more, but finally could no longer bear the oppressive silence.

'It's happened to me before, don't you see? Hal, my previous husband, only married me for my money. He despised me, I finally realized, and it was too much for me.'

'You told me he was a homosexual and that was why you were divorced.' Dominic finally swung around from the window; he looked so angry that she almost wished he hadn't.

'That was the last straw. Before that he was always asking for money. I gave him a fortune. Can't you see how an experience like that could make me wary?'

'No, I don't see it at all. You didn't trust me, that's what this conversation shows me. That's one hell of a way to start a marriage.'

'It's more complicated than that. When I met you, I was cynical about people. Then I found I loved you, I would have confessed, but when I listened to how you and your friends all felt about wealth; I was frightened to tell you in case you would have nothing more to do with me.'

'The cottage? Did your grandmother help you buy it?'

'No, I bought it.'

'And all the furniture?'

'I bought that too.'

'The wine, the champagne, the maid? I assume your grandmother had nothing to do with any of it?'

'No. That was all my doing.'

'Then you lied to me, you've done nothing but lie since the day I met you. The house in Oxford, I suppose you bought that too, not rented it as you told me?'

'Yes,' she said miserably.

'How the hell am I to know when you're telling me the truth? How can I ever trust you about anything again?' He swung around and stormed into the bathroom, taking his clothes. Eventually he came out, dressed for the street, and made for the door of their suite without looking in her direction.

'Where are you going?' she asked.

'Out, to think.'

'I'm sorry,' she called again, as she heard the door slam, his footsteps march along the corridor. She listened to the clang of the lift gates and then the whining of the mechanism as it carried him down. Maybe he wouldn't come back.

For two miserable hours she sat huddled on the bed, cursing her misfortune, longing for his return.

When she heard his key in the lock her immediate reaction was to run into the bathroom and lock herself in so that she wouldn't have to listen to what he had to say. But instead, she hid her head under the pillow, afraid to see his face and the thunderous expression she expected. She felt the bed give as he sat on it, felt the pillow being lifted from her head, but she kept her eyes closed.

'How much?' she heard him ask.

'A lot.'

'A hundred thousand? Two?'

'Millions.' She ventured to open her eyes, but could not quite bring herself to look at him.

'Bloody hell! How many millions?'

'I don't know, I never asked,' she replied in the tiniest of voices.

To her astonishment he bellowed with laughter. 'Juniper, you're priceless. Who ever heard of someone not bothering to ask how much they are worth?'

'Past a certain sum there doesn't seem much point in knowing.' She ventured a smile.

'Do you know the source of this money?'

'My grandfather founded his fortune on a family pickle recipe – Wakefields – there's not a table in America doesn't have our sauces and pickles,' she said with pride, as she always did.

'Pickles.' He shook his head in disbelief.

'And then there's loads of real estate and a film studio – JP Films – you must have seen the trademark at the cinema. That's me, Juniper Productions,' she added, still proud after all these years that her grandfather had named the studio after her. 'And I don't know what else.'

'Oil?'

'I wouldn't know.' She shook her head.

'And there's just you?'

'My grandmother has an income for life, but that's all.'

'Who controls it?'

'Lawyers in America, one in particular – Charlie Macpherson, he knows everything – it's him you should talk to if you're interested.'

Dominic poured himself some of the champagne which was flat now and Juniper noticed that his hand was shaking, she hoped from surprise and not anger. She put out her hand and stroked his, gently.

'I understand how you feel, Dominic. I realize what an embarrassment this could be to you and your future plans. I've given the money a lot of thought ever since we met and I gathered where you stood on the subject of inherited wealth. I could ask Charlie to set up a charitable trust – educational, or something for poor children – here in England if you prefer. And I've often wondered if it would be possible to re-open the tin mines at Gwenfer, my grandmother's home. There's masses of ways we could get rid of it.'

'Get rid of it!' he exploded. 'Are you mad?'

'But . . .' she started.

'This will accelerate my political plans no end.' He stood up and began to pace the hotel room. 'I can apply immediately for a constituency – I've only got eighteen months before I finish my degree. I won't need to toil away at the Bar for years making enough to support my career. In fact, this could turn out to be wonderful news.'

'But you were so angry,' she said, puzzled.

'Because you hadn't told me before.'

'I rather enjoyed it, our little house in Oxford and pretending to watch the pennies.'

'But don't you see, now we can live wherever we want – a place in the country and a house in London, close to Westminster.'

'I assumed you would want to live very much as we do now, with a small house, car, that sort of thing,' she said vaguely.

'Certainly not. There's nothing wrong in your having money.'

'No,' she replied. But that evening was the beginning of what, over the next three years, was to be increasing disillusionment. She had admired her husband for his integrity, even though his principles were awkward for her. Now she found that, like everyone else, he stuck to those principles only for as long as they suited him. Just like Hal, despite a generous allowance, he always needed more money. And now, perhaps worst of all, he had been adopted by a constituency and was on the road to Westminster at the next general election to be held, at the latest, in 1950. And he had become pompous, insufferably pompous. She would sometimes look at her husband as he held forth on one of a dozen subjects that he could be guaranteed to drone on about and she began to wonder seriously what she was doing with him. The man she had fallen in love with was no longer in evidence. Now she wondered if he had ever existed. He had become middle-aged long before his time. Now their friends were chosen on one criterion only – would they be useful to Dominic's career?

Juniper had become bored with their life and the circles they moved in, bored with seeing the same people time and time again, bored with listening to the same conversations. There were never discussions or arguments, for everyone was in agreement – that death knell of a good evening's conversation.

Dominic had begun to tell her how to dress, how to behave, what make-up to wear, what food to serve, what books to read – intrusions on her personal freedom which she resented bitterly. She was lonely, for none of the other wives was as young as she and she had not found one whom she wished to make a friend.

She had walked out the previous day when Dominic told her there was no way they could take the holiday she had planned – a trip to America to see her estate at Dart Island. Juniper had been looking forward to this trip. It was years since she had been there; the last time was with Hal, before the war, in 1936. She longed to see the house again, for it had played a large part in her life. It was there she had lived with her grandparents and had been happy as a child. There were times now when she wondered whether she was ever destined to be happy again. Perhaps she had hoped to rediscover their old magic at Dart Island. Instead Dominic wanted to join a group of his friends and their wives at a farm in Wales to discuss their electoral strategy. Juniper had put her foot down and insisted on America. That was when he had called her a spoilt brat, and that was when she had walked out of the house with an overnight bag and had driven to Heathrow. Now she was approaching the land of her birth for the first time in over twelve years.

Juniper was entranced as the large aeroplane lumbered towards the lights of New York. She felt a quite illogical pride in what she saw – illogical since she rarely regarded herself as an American.

The stewardess came to tell her to fasten her seat belt ready for the descent. She hoped that Charlie Macpherson had booked her into a hotel. She did not want to go directly to her penthouse, there would be too many memories of Hal there for it to be a comfortable place to stay.

She was quickly through customs and looked about the crowded concourse for Charlie.

'Juniper, over here,' a familiar voice called.

She swung round and to her consternation found her heart pounding as she saw her handsome ex-husband, Hal Copton, waving to her.

'Hal, what a wonderful surprise,' she was astonished to hear herself say. She should hate this man, should spit at him, not smile.

'Darling, Juniper, you look wonderful, as always,' and Hal kissed her gently on the cheek.

3

'What a surprise to find you here,' Juniper said to Hal and realized how banal she sounded. She had often imagined what she would say to him when next they met – invariably cutting and sarcastic remarks, well-honed from hours of practice, usually composed in her bath, or late at night if she could not sleep. But all of them had deserted her at the shock of seeing him again.

'Charlie Macpherson told me you were due in, we could not have you arriving with no one to meet you, now could we?' He smiled his crooked, slightly sardonic smile. It was an attractive smile and she remembered how it had been one of the first things to draw her to him.

'I could have taken a cab. I'm not helpless,' she said, a little sharply, annoyed at herself for her unexpected response to him.

'No one said you were, Juniper.' He looked about for a porter and waved to the man to come and collect Juniper's case. 'Is this all? My goodness, you must have changed.'

'I intend to do some shopping while I'm here.'

'Ah, then you haven't changed.' He laughed, displaying his perfect white teeth. That was something else about him which had attracted her instantly, she thought. Englishmen in her experience frequently had dreadful neglected teeth, but not Hal.

He placed his arm under her elbow and Juniper found herself being guided by him through the crowds. She wondered why she was allowing it and shook off his arm with irritation. She should have told him where to go right from the start, not let him take control. It really showed the most appalling nerve on his part to come to meet her, to presume that she would be pleased to see him. As they reached the long sleek Cadillac, the chauffeur was standing with the door open for her, her case already stowed away in the trunk.

'Thank you very much, Hal.' She held her hand out to shake his, speaking formally, wanting him to take the hint and leave her alone.

'Don't I get a lift too?' He tilted his head to one side, all the time smiling, not letting go of her hand.

'Of course. If you want.' She wanted to sound brusque, but merely sounded flustered. She yanked her hand from his grasp, slipped quickly into the rear of the car and slid along the leather of the back seat, moving as far over to the other side as she could get. She placed her handbag on the seat beside her, a small patent-leather barrier between them.

The car purred into action and slid out into the traffic, the air-conditioning giving a welcome break from the oppressive humidity of the New York summer. Although she looked ahead she was sure he was looking at her and she found herself pulling her long full skirt even further down to cover her legs.

'I've arranged dinner for you at the apartment. That is, unless you want to go out? A lot of good restaurants have opened since you were last here, but another night perhaps?'

'I thought I'd rather go to a hotel,' she said primly, wishing he did not sound so relaxed and at ease.

'What on earth for? The penthouse is there. I've been looking forward to your seeing it, I've done a lot of work on it.'

'That's kind.'

'You don't want to disappoint me, do you?'

Juniper said nothing further, but turned her head to look out at the approaching city and found herself wondering why on earth she should find his voice so appealing after all the hateful things he had done to her.

'I've been living there, I hope you don't mind,' he said, when it appeared she was not going to reply.

'Why should I? I wasn't using it. Thank you for looking after it for me,' she said, without looking at him.

It was Hal's turn to look out at the traffic so that Juniper could not see his self-satisfied smile; that was a hundred dollars old Charlie owed him. 'When I said I had arranged dinner for you, I meant just you. I realize you hardly want me as your dinner companion. I've moved out most of my stuff, you needn't worry.'

'Oh, you shouldn't put yourself out for me. I don't mind your things being there,' she heard herself saying.

'So, you're happy to go to the penthouse?'

'Why, yes, I suppose so,' she said, after a pause. It seemed silly to make an issue about the hotel. And why, just because of him, should she pay for a hotel when she had a perfectly good home of her own to go to? 'I shall be interested to see what you've done to it,' she added politely.

'It's largely how we envisaged it when we were here together. I've simplified some things and embellished others.'

'Do you like living in New York?' She ventured to look at him.

'Immensely,' he replied. 'I think I should have been born an American.'

'You?' She chuckled. 'You're far too English. Why, you're the epitome of an English lord. Hal a Yankee . . . ?' She found herself laughing and was amazed at how civilized and polite they were being to each other, not at all how she had imagined,

The Cadillac slid to a halt. Hal was out of the door and holding it wide for her before the chauffeur could get around the vehicle. Juniper stood on the sidewalk, craning her neck to peer up at the skyscraper soaring above her. She supposed that, compared with other newer buildings, it was old-fashioned now, but she never wanted it to change. The building had been her father's concept; it was his memorial, she decided. It was good to be back. She crossed to the door beneath the dark-green scalloped canopy which stretched across the sidewalk.

'It's Delmar, isn't it?' She smiled at the large doorman, dressed in livery of the same colour as the canopy, 'Wakefield Towers' embroidered in gold on his cap, which he hurriedly doffed.

'Why, yes, Miss Juniper. I never expected you to remember me.' White teeth flashed in his black face and he found himself fumbling with the door which he normally opened smoothly several hundred times a day.

In the shining white marble hall she stopped abruptly as she noticed, hanging at the end of the hall and lit from above, a large portrait in oils of her grandfather. It was a good likeness.

'Hal, that painting wasn't there before. What a wonderful idea.' She swung round to him, smiling properly this time, the smile he had never forgotten. He thanked his lucky stars that he had had the foresight to have the picture hung there that morning. The porter dancing attendance, Hal led her across to the lifts. Taking a key from his pocket he opened one of the doors.

'This elevator is your own private one. It goes express to the penthouse. It means you don't have to travel with the peasantry.' He handed her the key.

'It's new, isn't it?'

'Charlie had the idea about four years ago,' he said easily; best to blame Charlie for all his own more expensive ideas. 'It was a service shaft,' he explained, as he pressed the button and the small green-leather-and-gold decorated lift ascended rapidly to the top of the building.

The lift door opened directly on to the hall of Juniper's penthouse, which was bare except for two modern abstract sculptures at either end, both standing in front of large sheets of mirror glass, so that the sculptures and hall were reflected again and again into infinity. Juniper paused on the threshold.

'Hal, it's stunning,' she said with genuine pleasure.

'You've seen nothing. Come on.' He led her into the main reception room.

'This is special.' She twirled around in the centre of the enormous room. 'Is that a garden?' She pointed to the wall of glass, beyond which lay the garden, illuminated for the night. 'Hal, you've been so clever.'

'I have, haven't I?' He gave a small bow, then rang the bell and a smart young butler entered, accompanied by a young maid. 'Lady Copton will want to see her room, Sally,' he ordered.

'But, Hal . . .' Juniper began to say and then thought she would leave it and explain later, when the servants were no were not present.

'Is dinner in an hour too soon for you, Juniper?'

'No, that's fine, thank you,' she said, as she followed

the maid. She was halfway to her room before she realized that she felt like a guest and not the owner of this place.

An hour later she returned bathed and changed but still slightly ill at ease. She took the glass of martini Hal offered her and, wandering across to the window, looked out at the brightly lit scene.

'Everything in England is so boringly grey and dull. I hadn't realized how much until I saw all of this.' She looked out at the skyscrapers, transformed by night into great glittering shafts of light stabbing the sky.

'Still?' He joined her at the window.

'Oh, the lights are on, but everything is so drab, even the people. I think we all expected things to change overnight and, when they didn't, everyone gave up. Everyone's so weary, there's no sense of excitement as there is here. It's almost as if no one has any energy any more.'

'You should have come sooner.'

'Yes, maybe I should. There was much to get away from,' she said thoughtfully, tracing a pattern on the glass with her finger. 'This martini is delicious. They never taste the same in England somehow, like tea in France,' she said, too brightly, as if she were turning away from thoughts she did not wish to face.

'Poor Juniper, has it been awful for you? If you want to tell me about everything, you can, you know. After all, who knows you better?'

'I thought we were talking about the war,' she said icily, surprised at his temerity.

'Of course. What did you think I meant?' he lied, resolving not to rush her on the subject of her husband. 'I meant the bombing and everything.'

'Oh, the war was rather fun, looking back. People were very friendly and we managed some good parties . . .' She looked at him. 'But you know that, Hal, don't you? From your mother's detective, no doubt paid for by you.' And suddenly there was steel in her voice.

'Not now, Juniper. Don't let's spoil your first night

back home. Time for acrimony later. What do you say?' One eyebrow was arched quizzically.

She looked away, staring into the distance as if coming to a decision. She must be thirty, he thought, yet she still had the wide-eyed innocent look of a child in her wonderful hazel eyes which were flecked with gold. Nothing about her had changed; always petite, she was still slim as a reed. Tonight she was dressed in grey with a scarlet silk stole draped elegantly over her shoulders – he remembered how she only ever wore black or grey with touches of red or white, never any colours. It had been her personal trademark, apparently it still was. Her fine blonde hair was styled in a shoulder length page-boy, style, the hair falling forward attractively, accentuating her fine cheek bones. Her skin was smooth, that of a much younger woman, and needed only the lightest of make-up. She had always been beautiful. Hal found himself wondering if she was not even more beautiful than before.

'Yes. You're probably right,' she said eventually. 'Anyway, you know me, I can't be bothered with arguments and boring things like that.' She spoke glibly but wondered if there would ever be a time when she would forget the pain this man had caused her.

Romain announced that dinner was served. Juniper was ecstatic about the dining room. The carpet was white, the walls black suede. The table was made of glass, with alternating chairs – one white leather, the next black. The china, the candles, the flowers, the bowl in which they stood, all echoed this contrasting use of the two colours and she had a white napkin, he a black.

Romain placed a perfect dish of hors d'oeuvres in front of them. 'I'll see to the wine, Romain,' Hal said. Silently the man left the room.

'I don't think I'll ever get used to his name,' she whispered.

'He's an actor really. I suppose he thinks it'll help him in his profession.'

Juniper felt her face stiffen. 'Of course, you like actors, don't you, Hal?' she said, not bothering to disguise the bitterness in her voice.

'Now, Juniper. That was a long time ago. Don't let any bitterness mar what could be a new friendship between us, please.' His dark eyes looked intensely at her. 'Please, Juniper,' he said in a low voice.

'This apartment should be featured in a magazine,' she said, glancing about the room to avoid looking at his disturbing eyes.

'It has been, often. I'm a designer now, Juniper, and very successful. I designed this furniture, everything.' He waved his hand to encompass the whole room and she smiled at the pride in his voice. 'One should have modern things in a modern world, that's my philosophy. The trouble with England – and what will remain its curse – is that it lives only in the past.'

'Don't you miss anything?' she asked.

'Nothing. The best decision I ever made was to come here and start again,' he said complacently. He stood up to pour the wine. She watched him as he fussed over her wine glass, rearranging it so that it was in perfect symmetry with the other glasses. They had been living in different worlds, she and he. Had he any conception of what his countrymen had suffered, what a luxury it was to be able to care about a perfectly aligned glass?

'Didn't you feel you should have stayed, fought with everyone else?'

It was a question she had to ask. Too many she knew had died; his answer would be critical if she and Hal were to regain any sort of friendship, if she were ever to feel comfortable with him.

'I couldn't fight.'

'Why not?' She looked puzzled.

'No one told you?' he asked, as he took his seat again.

'Told me what?'

'I failed the medical. Something wrong with my ticker. I had no idea. I couldn't stay in England and not do my bit. I couldn't have faced just being a pen-pusher, so I left.'

'Hal!' She knocked over her glass of wine and the delicate crystal shattered. She mopped ineffectually at the spilt wine with her napkin. 'Why wasn't I told? Are you all right?'

'I asked that you shouldn't be told. I didn't want any one to know. I'm fine, really. I probably won't make old bones, but . . .'

'Hal, I'm so sorry.' She touched his hand gently as he poured her a fresh glass of wine and refilled his own.

'Should you be drinking?' she asked anxiously.

'Probably not. But, if I can't eat and drink as I want then I'd rather not live.' The meal progressed. Each course perfectly cooked and served. They returned to the large salon.

'Hal, there's something you don't seem to know, either. I've remarried . . .'

Hal leant over and put his finger gently on her lips. 'I do know. I'd just rather not think about it. And I certainly don't want to know anything about your husband, not tonight, especially.'

Embarrassed, Juniper looked down at her drink, unsure what to say.

'How's "Goody-two-shoes", Polly?'

'I didn't know you didn't like Polly.'

'Did I say I didn't?' he countered.

'She lives in the depths of Devonshire, in idyllic wedded bliss with an Andrew Slater.'

'Don't you see her?' Hal asked, picking up the sharpness in Juniper's voice.

'No, she was cross with me.' Juniper looked up at him with widening eyes, which made her look even more innocent. 'I was bad,' she said with a chuckle. 'I slept with one of her fiancés – Jonathan, you met him. She was a bit annoyed.'

Hal laughed loudly. 'Yes, I see. Polly wouldn't understand.'

'And do you?'

'I think so. I think you were always like a little girl, taking what you wanted. I doubt if you've changed.'

'You make me sound horrible.'

'On the contrary. I think it's rather charming.'

'I should hate you, Hal,' she said, serious now.

'I suppose you should. But then you don't, do you? You always forgive in the end – even me. That's another of your admirable characteristics.'

'I felt humiliated, Hal. If you had been unfaithful to me with a woman I could have understood. I would have known what to do, how to fight her – but a man?'

'I suppose it's a bit late for apologies and explanations, but I would love to be forgiven by you. Robin was an aberration. Even then, things were not as they appeared, but would you ever believe me? I still don't know why I made him my friend. Quite ridiculous. I suppose I was bored and curious. I paid dearly for my curiosity.'

'We both did,' Juniper said, so softly that he had to lean forward to catch her words. He put out his hand and took hers.

'Why don't you see Harry?'

'It hurts too much. He's better as he is.'

'I heard about you and Leigh. Now that did make me laugh – my pompous brother.'

'He isn't, he's rather sweet,' she said defensively, and then burst out laughing.

Romain came in to announce a telephone call for Hal. He crossed the room to the instrument. 'Copton speaking . . .'

Juniper picked up a magazine and flicked idly through it. She heard a strangled noise of exclamation from Hal, and saw him go suddenly white and sway on his feet. He replaced the receiver, crossed to the decanter of brandy and poured himself a large measure.

'What is it, Hal?' she asked anxiously, jumping to her feet and crossing the room to stand beside him.

'I think you'd better sit down, Juniper.' He led her back

to the sofa. 'I'm afraid it's bad news. Charlie Macpherson has killed himself.'

'Charlie?' She was stunned. 'Why ever should he do that?'

Hal sat down beside her again. 'I think I know why, Juniper. This isn't nice, my sweet, but I'm pretty sure Charlie has been embezzling money from you on a very large scale.'

'Charlie? But he worked for my grandfather. Lincoln would never have employed a cheat.'

'He probably wasn't – then. It could only have started after you inherited the money outright. When it was a trust he had to report to the courts each year to account for his conduct of your affairs. And then, well, when I was no longer your husband and unable to keep an eye on things for you . . .' Hal shrugged his shoulders.

'How much?'

'As I say, these are just suspicions, I wouldn't know the exact figures. We shall have to look into everything. I'd begun to sniff around. He must have guessed I was on to him and, with you arriving tonight, he couldn't face you with the truth.'

'Hal, this is terrible,' she said in a small voice.

'I know, my darling, it's ghastly.' Hal had himself well under control by now. 'But I'll look after things, don't worry.'

Juniper was close to tears. She did not know if she had a marriage to return to, she was tired, she was confused by her reactions to Hal and now she felt somehow to blame for this latest development.

4

Juniper did not go shopping. She did not go out to lunch, the theatre or the opera as she had planned. Old friends she had meant to look up went uncalled. Each day, Hal and a team of accountants he had employed, toiled over the accounts and books of Wakefield Enterprises, triumphant at each discrepancy they found in the figures.

Juniper sat in the large salon and watched as they pored over the ledgers and papers strewn all over the floor and on every flat surface of the once-immaculate room. To one side Hal had erected a large blackboard and easel and as each stolen dollar was discovered it was added to the tally. Juniper huddled on the sofa, watching her enormous fortune diminish daily in size.

A week later, escorted by Hal, Juniper attended Charlie's funeral, a large, expensive affair, with a mass, in St Patrick's Cathedral. A representative of the President of the United States, a clutch of senators and congressmen and the Mayor of New York were amongst the congregation. A large contingent of film stars, directors, producers and movie moguls had flown in from the West Coast. The best of New York society sat with captains of industry, opera singers, entrepreneurs: Charlie had been a very popular man, famous for his generosity. Juniper heard them talk of this generosity, not only in his hospitality but in the way he had dipped time and again into his wallet for so many worthy causes. Without doubt he was greatly mourned. But Juniper, seated in the front pew, looked at the ornate oak coffin with an expression of anger and loathing that was alien to her normal character and out of place in these surroundings.

At the equally expensive wake in Charlie's opulent home she found it difficult to be polite to his wife, Pearl. Juniper had never known the woman well, but there were things about her, the way she could not quite bring herself to look Juniper straight in the eye, the clamminess of her palm, that convinced Juniper she had known what her husband was about, that she was fully aware that everything she now owned was really Juniper's.

Juniper's only satisfaction was when Pearl, with the skill of years of extracting funds for her favourite charities in the most subtle ways, engineered the conversation around to the funeral and hinted at the dreadful expense of it all. Realizing that Pearl expected her, as Charlie's boss, to pay for the crook's last rites, she looked at the woman with cold enmity, turned sharply on her heel and told Hal she wanted to go home.

On the night Charlie killed himself, it was Pearl who called Hal, hysterically telling him of the suicide and even reading over the telephone a letter Charlie had left. Now, it seemed that the letter no longer existed. With the greasing of a medical palm here and a judicial one there, Charlie's death had overnight become an overdose caused by carelessness, brought on by a particularly bad attack of influenza. Thus he had been laid to rest by a cardinal in hallowed ground.

'Do you want me to call in the police?' Hal had asked her as they were driving from the wake.

'There would be little point in that. As his wife bribed them to keep secret about his death, undoubtedly he bribed them in life. They wouldn't listen to me.'

'Don't you think your grandfather's name still counts for something?'

'He's been dead too long.'

'You'll probably get some of the money back.'

'Hal, I doubt if I'll see a cent of that money. He'll have squirrelled it away in numbered accounts in Switzerland. But I don't mind about the money so much. What enrages me is that that man cheated on the memory of my grandfather. No one does that to a Wakefield and gets away with it. If he hadn't killed himself, I'd have done it for him.'

'Quite,' said Hal, fingering his black tie nervously at the coldness of her voice and the hard, determined expression on her face.

'If I can do anything to harm Pearl then I shall. That's the only satisfaction left to me that I can see. They have children, I seem to remember.'

'Two sons. Both married.'

'Good,' she said, but explained no further. She stared out of the window of the limousine, but saw nothing of the passersby. They returned to the penthouse, the accountants and a cable from Dominic demanding her immediate return. It was the curt tone that annoyed her. She dictated a reply, but made no mention of her financial problems. Someone might read the cable. She did not want anyone to know what had happened to the once-proud name of Wakefield, neither was she ready for Dominic to know about it.

Every other day cables came from Dominic, always short and to the point. Not one of them said he was sorry, that he missed her, or that he loved her. Some days she replied and others she did not.

She cried only once. That was when they told her that her Grandfather's plant for the manufacture of sauces and chutneys – the cornerstone of all his wealth – had been sold. Worse still, along with the factory the town he had built for his workers and which bore his name had also gone out of her ownership.

'Could we not buy it all back?' she eventually asked, angry with herself for weeping in front of the accountants. Lincoln Wakefield would have despised such weakness. 'Offer them twenty per cent over their purchase price,' she ordered.

'It would mean selling other assets.' The senior accountant, Brian Williams, looked doubtful.

'I don't care about other things. That business is the one that counts. I shan't rest until it's all mine again.'

The accountants began their negotiations, but got nowhere with the new owners who were demanding fifty per cent over their purchase price. An impossibly high sum, Juniper was advised, too much, given the circumstances, for her to risk.

'At least it still carries your family name,' John Robinson, the youngest accountant, said comfortingly. 'Your grandfather won't be forgotten for many generations.'

'Ha. And how long before they want their own name on the brands?'

'No, they won't change it, ever,' Hal said confidently. 'That'd be like Heinz or Kellogg changing names: it wouldn't make business sense.'

'Are they allowed to use my family name?'

'Yes. I'm sorry. The name was sold with the product.'

'God, I wish that bastard was alive, how I would make him pay.' Juniper thumped the sofa with frustration. 'I let my grandfather down,' she added miserably.

'Of course you didn't, Juniper. Old Lincoln left your affairs in the hands of a crook. You weren't to know.'

As the sums on the blackboard increased to alarming proportions Hal had the decency to be glad he had not embezzled more himself; what he had helped himself to was quite modest in comparison. The team of accountants he had chosen was good; some days, too good. More than once Hal felt sick with fear as they nudged closer to a deal in which he had been involved, only to sigh with relief when the danger passed. It was a comforting thought that all his negotiations with Charlie had been in cash. Nothing was traceable back to him. All the same, using his concern for Pearl and her affairs as an excuse, he contrived to be alone in Charlie's study. He searched it diligently, just in case the fool had left incriminating evidence behind, but he found nothing.

'Is my grandmother's money safe?' Juniper asked, another day.

'Yes. Her money comes from a watertight trust. There was nothing he could do there, the courts would have noticed anything amiss,' John explained, smiling his gentle smile at her. Of all the accountants she liked John the most. The others seemed only intent on figures and money. John, it appeared, had grasped that it was the insult to her grandfather's name which bothered her most. He was more sensitive than his companions, had interests outside the world of money.

Another day she asked about JP Productions, the film studio that bore her name.

'We would be better off selling the whole enterprise as real estate,' said Brian.

'But what about the films? It was doing so well.'

'Nothing of note has been made since your grandfather's death. As far as we can make out, Charlie was using the place more as a club – starlets on tap for his buddies when he was out West. No doubt it made him feel big. If there was a proposed film treatment no one else would touch as too risky, or unmakeable, Charlie was willing to make it – probably for favours that he picked up then or later,' the senior accountant said with distaste.

During the whole of this traumatic period, Juniper could not have been more grateful to Hal. In the intervening years she had allowed bitterness to get in the way and had forgotten how considerate he could be. His anger on her behalf was very real. Of course, she realized that much of his concern must be for his son's inheritance, but at the same time she felt he was genuinely worried for her. He had no social life during the whole of this time, but spent every waking hour with Juniper and the accountants. They ate late at night – more snacks than formal meals. Each night he would kiss her on the cheek and they would go into their respective bedrooms. She began to find herself wishing he would join her.

Juniper began to feel that she had never been lonelier in her life; she also began to feel that she had never been lower. She had flown from London to give herself time to think about Dominic, their marriage, and the best way to handle their problems. She did not want another failure. She felt that mentally she could not afford the damage of another divorce, yet she dreaded returning to Dominic and the rigid routine of their life together. And her feelings about Hal were confusing her. Instead of thinking about Dominic, she let that set of problems sink to the back of her mind. But problems not faced, but hidden away, have an unfortunate habit of corroding from neglect. Her marriage, her re-awakening interest in Hal, were the backdrop to the urgent financial situation and the one problem worked on the other, driving her deeper into depression.

'Juniper, I think you should go away for a few days. You've been shut up in this apartment far too long, three weeks now,' Hal said at breakfast one morning.

'I don't feel like going anywhere, especially on my own.'

'Of course you don't, sweetie. Would you like me to come with you? I thought perhaps we could go to Dart Island; you should see what condition your estate's in. At least Charlie left you that. I know it won't be easy for you, but it's something that's got to be done.'

Juniper knew Hal was right. She needed to get away. It made sense to inspect Dart Island – even though too many memories lurked there for comfort. But anywhere else would lack the privacy of her own estate.

That privacy was becoming necessary. Rumours had already started to multiply that all was not well with Wakefield Enterprises. The telephones rang constantly and outside the apartment block the sidewalk was never without a crowd of reporters with photographers in tow, all hoping for a glimpse of Juniper or a word from her accountants.

They left for Dart Island at dead of night, when even the most persistent reporters were in bed. And they left by the service entrance. The car crossed the wooden bridge which linked the island with the mainland, just as dawn was about to break. Just before it reached the corner in the long drive where Juniper knew she would get the first glimpse of the house, she asked the chauffeur to stop the car.

She stepped on to the driveway, across the lawn of long grass, and stood under an enormous Canadian beech and waited. Like a ghost emerging from the night the great house slowly showed itself, as the pink and gold of the early morning sun swept across the lawn and up the steps, across the porticoed terrace, playing games with the shadows made by the stark pillars.

Once, when she had come here, she had been afraid of the shadows and a multitude of ghosts of her own imagining. She had felt her dead grandfather's presence. She had wanted to see him and yet had been terrified that she would. Now she leant against the comforting rough bark of the tree and once again she knew that he was here. She closed her eyes and remembered him.

Lincoln Wakefield was tall and strong, with the deep chest and muscular shoulders of a workman rather than a business man. His large head, in proportion with his body, was topped with a mane of white hair which he would toss sometimes from irritation and always when angry, but never at her. There were only smiles, hugs and kisses for Juniper. He had loved her above all others, had sacrificed his relationships with those he adored to safe-guard her. She thought she had stopped loving him; now, feeling him close, she knew that was impossible. He had loved her so deeply, so totally, that nothing could destroy it.

She spread her arms behind her around the trunk of the tree and she longed for him and the safety and security that he had always brought her. 'What shall I do?' she asked aloud of the wind and the rust-coloured leaves. She opened her eyes, her head on one side, and to Hal, watching from the car, it looked almost as if she were listening to something. Mystified, he watched her leave the shelter of the tree and with hurried steps cross the wide lawns, past the ornate Italianate fountain from which water no longer spurted, towards the sea.

He frowned with concern. The last time they had been here, soon after their marriage, she had behaved very strangely. Admittedly she had been pregnant and women in that condition might do strange things. Then she would not go anywhere near the sea; understandable, he had thought, since it was in the bay that her grandfather had drowned. But now, nonplussed, he watched her almost rushing to the water.

Hal ordered the chauffeur to continue along the driveway to the house. He sent the man in to find staff and to organise some breakfast for them, then he stood on the terrace, leaning against the stone balustrade, and watched Juniper, a small figure now, standing in the distance, close by the water, gazing out to the horizon.

He took a cigarette from his case, lit it and turned to look at the house – a monstrosity he had always thought. It was neither one thing nor the other. It had started as a pleasant enough colonial house of good size, but Lincoln had found it necessary to add to it. Roman pillars, pediments, a touch of Tudor, a little baroque and he had managed to ruin a perfectly adequate house. Hal could never understand Juniper's devotion to this monument to lack of style. Maybe now she would allow him to knock half of it down as he had suggested all those years ago.

Tired of standing, he sat on the wide sweep of steps, idly smoking and wishing she would hurry her communing with the gods or whatever it was she was doing, for he was starving. He jumped quickly to his feet when he saw her suddenly swing round and make her way hurriedly back to the house.

'Feel better?' he asked kindly. 'Nothing like a good belt of sea air.'

'Yes. I feel completely better. Call the chauffeur, Hal, I want to go back to New York.'

'But we've only just got here. You need to rest.'

'That's the last thing I need, Hal. I've decided to sell all of this.'

'Really?' he said, trying to keep the surprise out of his voice. 'Shall we go indoors? I've organized some breakfast.'

'No.' She clutched her handbag tightly to her and stepped back, a look of alarm on her face. 'I don't want to go in, I don't want to see any of it. I've seen enough.' She turned on her heel, ran down the steps and climbed into the back of the car leaving Hal to call the chauffeur who came on the run, his face bulging from hurriedly grabbed toast and bacon.

'Do you want to explain?' Hal asked, as the car rattled over the wooden slats of the old bridge. She had not looked back once.

'The solution is simple.' She smiled and it was the first time, he realized, he had seen her smile in the past weeks. 'If I sell all of this – these estates so close to New York are worth a fortune these days, every new millionaire wants one – then I can buy my grandfather's business back.'

'Are you sure that's what you want? I know the sauce and pickle concern is important to you, but the name still remains,' Hal said pleasantly enough, although the fact that Juniper's fortune had been based on a pickle recipe had always rather embarrassed him. He had never confided it to his friends back in England; they would have laughed him and Juniper to scorn. 'The price those crooks are asking is exorbitant.'

'It's what my grandfather would have done. What he would want me to do. He loved that business – it was the very core of the man. I've made up my mind.' She leant back on the car cushions, closed her eyes and pretended to sleep. She could not explain further, she could not expect anyone to understand. But she was certain. Back there by the sea her grandfather had come to her to advise her. She might say it was her decision; it wasn't, it was Lincoln who had decided what was to be done, that the home he had loved should be sold for the business he had loved even more.

5

The change in Juniper was dramatic as she began to take control of her own destiny. Instead of sitting on the sidelines and listening despondently to the comments of Hal and the accountants, she now insisted on everything being explained to her in detail. She evolved her own system of keeping track of money lost and money saved, a system she found much simpler and more precise than that proposed by her advisers. She took the chair at meetings and it was she who headed the new negotiating team to win back her grandfather's company. Juniper, who had never queried anything to do with money, whose only requirement was that it should continue to pour into her bank account so that she could, as rapidly as possible, send it out the other side, was becoming expert in the way her finances were invested. Hal would watch her with an amused expression and tell her how proud her grandfather would have been. Her ability to grasp financial detail could not be genetic since she had been Lincoln's step-granddaughter. He must ask her the full story some time. He'd heard that old Lincoln had rescued Alice Tregowan and her illegitimate daughter Grace from the gutter – penniless and abandoned in New York. A romantic tale but difficult to believe when one looked at regal, dignified Alice.

The cables from Dominic continued. Then he began to telephone. The static on the line was always bad and conversation was difficult, but static or not, there was no mistaking the tone of his voice as he bellowed down the phone.

'I have problems here, I can't leave,' she shouted back.

'I demand your immediate return, you're my wife.'

'Oh, boil your head,' she snapped and slammed the receiver on to the cradle.

'Am I to gather that was your beloved?' Hal looked up at her from the papers he had been studying and smiled mischievously.

'He's so bossy. You can't imagine how pompous he is.'

'Wasn't he pompous before you married him?'

'I suppose he must have been, but I didn't notice. He could be fun. I do remember we had fun – once. But now all he talks and thinks about is his future in politics. He's boring. I feel cheated.'

'Poor Juniper. You don't seem to be a very good selector of husbands.'

'Never marry a politician, Hal.'

'I don't think it's likely.' He looked amused at the idea. 'Mind you, I see the poor chap's problem – a beautiful young wife alone in New York, with so many predators around. Don't you think you should at least write and tell him the predicament you're in?'

'I can't. I don't want him to know.' This was the truth. Whereas Dominic had once despised money, he was now dependent upon it. If he thought she was now poor, would he lose interest in her completely? As she was unhappy in this marriage, she had to face the prospect that he was equally dissatisfied. Maybe he felt cheated too. She knew for someone with his ambitions she was the wrong wife and once he was elected things would get worse. She knew too what her future held – endless committee meetings with other wives, wives who were perfect and supportive, smiling through endless jumble sales and fêtes. She shuddered at the thought and was amazed that there could have been a time when she had found the prospect glamorous and exciting. She knew exactly what her problem was: she did not want him, but on the other hand was too afraid to face life without him. Frightened as always of being completely alone. Since there was no one else to turn to, that would be her inevitable fate.

But now there was Hal. She could not ignore the change in her feelings towards him. They had slipped back with such ease into a relationship that was far better than anything they had had when married. She had come prepared to hate him, not to find that he was her friend. Everything was threatening to become more complex. Once again she found herself physically attracted to him. In the past she would have thought nothing of taking the initiative and making advances to him, but no longer. She had suffered his rejection once too often.

Yet he was so solicitous now, always charming. She could hardly remember how moody he had been when they were married, how his depressions had frightened her, left her unsure how to deal with him. She faced the fact that now he was happy, and that with her he had not been. She even considered the possibility that it might have been she who had failed him, she who had paved the way for the marriage to founder. Looking at things this way was a new experience for Juniper, who had previously found she could always blame others for her misfortunes.

'What are you thinking?' He leant across and lit her cigarette.

'I was thinking how different you are. You were a difficult man to live with, you know . . .' She paused as if uncertain whether to go on. 'But now, you're an angel,' she said smiling gently.

'Thank you, but I don't deserve the compliment. I was a bastard. I didn't deserve you,' he replied, to her astonishment. 'It was not having anything of my own, no business, no money I could call mine. It rankled, soured me.'

'I was insensitive,' she replied, noticing with a thudding heart that he had moved closer to her along the sofa.

He put out his hand to her, began to speak and then the telephone rang and broke the spell. 'I'll answer.' She jumped up quickly. She rarely answered the telephone, fearful of reporters, snoopers and latterly her angry husband, but by answering it this time she was able to cover her confusion and her disappointment.

It was a woman's voice, a low husky voice that asked to speak to Hal. He took the receiver and, smiling half-apologetically, turned his back on Juniper, his hand cupped around the mouthpiece, and began to speak quietly and intensely. Juniper stood for a moment, feeling strangely let down. There seemed little point now in staying up, she thought, and left Hal still talking almost in a whisper into the telephone.

Curiosity about this woman, who now phoned almost daily, began to occupy Juniper's mind. Who was she and what was she to Hal?

'You don't need to curtail your social life for me,' she said one evening after a particularly long call.

'I wouldn't dream of leaving you alone.'

'I don't need a keeper. If you want to see your girlfriend, it's all right by me.' She spoke as lightly as she could.

'What girlfriend?'

'The woman who keeps telephoning you and never gives her name.'

'Who said she was a girlfriend?'

'She calls often enough,' she retorted.

'You'd like to meet her?'

'I didn't say that.'

'No, but that's what you're thinking,' and he was smiling again, that sardonic smile which always disarmed her.

Three days later Maddie Huntley was invited for drinks. As soon as she saw her, Juniper wished she had not agreed to the meeting. Maddie was very tall; all her life Juniper had loathed her own shortness, had been envious of tall women. She was dark haired, as Juniper longed to be. She had pale translucent skin, while Juniper's in summer was as warm as a gipsy's. And she had huge brown eyes and the long-limbed body of a model, Juniper noted, with envy. She was intelligent and she was amusing. Juniper sat and watched Maddie intently.

Later Hal invited Juniper to join Maddie and himself for dinner. Looking at Maddie's arm linked through Hal's in a proprietorial way, Juniper pleaded a headache.

After they had gone she poured herself an extra large drink. She stood looking at it for some time.

'No,' she said aloud to the empty room. 'That's what I always do, get drunk.' This time she would behave differently. She had work to do, work that required a clear head. She put the untouched glass back on the table and picked up some papers instead. Clutching them to her she walked purposefully towards her bedroom, firm in her resolve. But it did not stop her feeling extravagantly sorry for herself.

*

Despite Charlie's activities Juniper was still rich, richer by far than most people dream of being.

'It's all relative, isn't it?' she said pragmatically one day. 'Let's face it, I had far more than any one person deserved. I could never have spent it all no matter how hard I tried.' She chuckled. She was happier now than she had been for a long time. For the first time in her life she had a purpose – the saving of her family name. 'I've always thought too much money a bore.'

'I admire your courage, Juniper,' Hal said, with genuine admiration. If he had been in her shoes he would have been sick with anger at his losses. But courage was not involved. Juniper had always had money for whatever whim she chose. The idea of not having any was beyond her imagination.

Her pragmatism, however, did not make her give up on the task of buying back her grandfather's firm. After a month of tense negotiations it was hers again.

She and Hal and their retinue of accountants travelled to the small town of Wakefield to inspect the factory. They had managed to repurchase the houses in which the factory workers lived, but there was considerable property in the town that was no longer hers. When she saw the houses owned by other people, the shops in new ownership, she vowed then and there that she would not rest until everything was hers again.

Juniper's welcome from the workforce was worthy of royalty. She stood on the platform in the works canteen and told them what had happened, keeping nothing from them and pledging that no such thing would ever happen again, that their jobs, their homes, their futures were as secure as they had been in her grandfather's time. She found herself basking in their cheers.

Back in New York she at last did the shopping she had promised herself and looked up her old friends. She asked several of them if they knew Maddie, but no one could recollect meeting her. Once again she ventured out to restaurants and the theatre, always with Hal. Everyone was beginning to accept them as a couple again. No doubt they assumed they were lovers. She found herself hoping so. For the first time for years she started each day with excitement and optimism.

She and Hal were booked to fly to Paris. Until now she had not realized that Lincoln Wakefield had had businesses in Europe, but it transpired that his interests stretched like tentacles around the world. She must visit France and Germany. Now the war was over she wanted to investigate what was left of those enterprises and what her claims on them could be.

She had confidence in herself now, the confidence she had long needed to face the truth that her second marriage was over and to recognize that she wanted to work alone in Europe. She needed to prove herself to Hal.

The bags were packed. In the half hour before the car was due they sat in the salon having a last-minute drink.

'Hal, would you be insulted or hurt if I told you I wanted to go alone?'

He looked at her thoughtfully. 'Insulted, no. Curious, yes.'

'I want to prove to myself I can do these things without you there to hold my hand.'

'Fine. I think that's an excellent idea.'

'And I'm going to stop off in London to see my lawyer. I've decided to get a divorce.'

'Have you now? I can't say I'm sorry.' He smiled at her, a smile of such intimate intensity that it made her pulse race. 'But why bother yourself. Get the lawyers to write to him and tell him it's all over and you want a divorce. There'll be less unpleasantness that way.'

'I can't do that to him. I have to see him and explain.'

Hal sat silent, looking at her. 'Juniper, I don't want you to see him,' he said eventually.

'Why not?' Juniper felt breathless.

'Because I'm afraid if you see him you'll change your mind.'

'But . . . I don't understand . . .' she said, flustered.

'I haven't said anything before, Juniper. I know you came here to make decisions about your marriage and it wouldn't have been fair of me to complicate the issue further. But while you're away from me I want you to think about the possibility of us getting back together.'

'Oh, Hal,' she said quietly.

'It seemed an impossible dream. But these past weeks I'd begun to think perhaps it wasn't such a ludicrous idea. I've been so alone, Juniper.'

Juniper smiled enigmatically and said gently, 'Me too, Hal.'

'But don't say anything now, my darling,' he went on hurriedly, seeming embarrassed by his own outburst. 'You must go. You have a lot to think about, a lot to weigh up.'

'You'll come to the airport with me?'

'I hate goodbyes. I much prefer welcoming people.' He kissed the tip of her nose. 'The car will be downstairs now.' And he took her arm and led her to the elevator. All the way down he held her hand tight as if loath to see her go.

She slipped into the back of the Cadillac. He stood on the sidewalk waving to her and she leant out of the window blowing him kisses, until the car disappeared around the corner and she could not see him anymore. She sat back, thinking of what he had said. Could she ever live with him again? Suddenly she thought of Harry: here was a chance to have him back with her again. Why shouldn't they be a real family at last?

She was halfway to the airport when she ordered the car to turn around.

The small elevator swept up to her penthouse. She got out, the salon was empty. She kicked off her shoes, smiling to herself; he must be taking a shower, she would surprise him. She tiptoed along the corridor to his room.

She had no need to snoop or spy; she could hear the voices long before reaching his open bedroom door.

'And she agreed to marry you again?' She heard the

amused voice of John Robinson, the youngest of the accountants.

'Of course she did. What did I tell you?' Hal too was laughing.

'I did begin to wonder if you weren't playing it a little too cool.'

'Juniper has always enjoyed a challenge. Show her something she thinks she can't have and she'll want it. It would have been a disaster if I'd spoken too soon, she'd have lost interest.'

'Women are weird.'

'Stupid, more like. Do you know she even believed my story about having a dicky heart – very touching.'

The two men laughed loudly. Juniper stood rooted to the spot, not wanting to hear but unable to stop listening.

'And you're sure she has no inkling that you were in league with Charlie Macpherson?' John asked.

'Absolutely. You were smart to find out yourself. She never will, she's too thick.'

'You know me, Hal. I won't tell a living soul,' John said softly.

'I know you won't, John.'

They spoke like lovers. Juniper felt she was going to faint. She turned on her heel, forcing herself to walk back along the corridor, her face white with shock and grief. She let herself out of the penthouse, took the lift and went back to the car.

'The airport,' she said, like a zombie.

When the car was halfway there she ordered it to turn round again.

'Take me to a hotel. Any hotel.'

6

Juniper sat in the bar of the hotel and drank. She was deep in thought and unaware of the men about her, who were trying to attract her attention, delighted by the unexpected sight of a beautiful woman drinking alone. As she drank she smoked, angry short puffs on the cigarette which she stubbed out long before it was finished, immediately lighting another one, ignoring any proffered lighters from her uninvited attendants.

She was angry and full of bitterness and hate. She did not like this feeling. All her life she had avoided rows and arguments; there had been too many in her own childhood for her ever to be phlegmatic about them. Now she could not help herself. Over and over in her mind she kept replaying the scene she had overheard in the penthouse. Over and over again she kept berating herself for being a fool, for allowing Hal to deceive her one more time.

This was when she needed Polly, she thought, gripped by a sudden longing for that particular friend. Polly would have had some sensible advice to give her. She was always down to earth and sane. She would have made Juniper feel better about it all; she would have had a plausible explanation. Why had they rowed and over something as unreliable as a man?

Juniper drained her glass and looked around for the waiter to order another. One of the men beside her intervened, telling the waiter that this drink was on him. Juniper swung round to stare at him, the venom in her look making him retreat along the banquette away from her as if he had been scalded. She ordered her own drink and then settled back wrapping her anger around her like a cloak, that made her, once again, impervious to her surroundings.

The person she thought she was would have walked away from this situation, thrown herself into other amusements, anything to make her forget and stop this growing rancour. But this past month in New York had seen a change in her; too much had happened for her to turn her back this time. She wanted revenge, she could feel it welling up within her and knew that she would find no peace until she did. But what to do and how?

'Juniper? It is Juniper, isn't it?' A woman paused by her table.

She looked up, masking her anger at being interrupted, not wishing for company, not wanting to have to pretend that all was well.

'Maddie.' She frowned. Seeing this particular woman, at that moment, redoubled her bitterness.

'Mind if I join you?' Maddie said brightly.

She wanted to refuse, but innate politeness made her move along the banquette, making room for Maddie to sit beside her.

'Drink?' Maddie asked, once she was settled.

'Double brandy,' Juniper said shortly.

'My, are you in the dumps, or what?' Maddie smiled but with kindness and concern, as she clicked her fingers for the waiter.

'I'm planning revenge, if you must know,' Juniper said, and then wished she hadn't as she saw the curiosity in Maddie's face.

'Hal?' she asked simply.

'Among others.'

'I can't say I'm surprised. You were married to him once, weren't you?'

'Yes, unfortunately.'

'You could have knocked me down how friendly you both were. All the divorced folks I know would rather kill each other than share an apartment.' Maddie lit a cigarette. 'A bit of an odd cove, isn't he?'

'You should know,' Juniper said, shortly.

'Me? I hardly know the man,' Maddie shrugged.

'But I thought . . .'

'Then you thought wrong, honey. He hired me.'

'What for?' Juniper found herself sitting up and leaning forward with interest.

'My instructions were to keep telephoning the apartment. If a woman answered I was to use my sexiest voice and ask to speak to Hal. It didn't work, the problem was you never answered the goddamn phone. It was always a man answered except for that one time.'

'I stopped answering it. I was afraid it might be my husband.'

'Another one? My, you're some sort of girl, aren't you?' Maddie chuckled, Juniper didn't. Instead she wondered where in the States this woman came from. She had a strange accent and one she could not place.

'And the other night when he took you out, what happened then, where did you go?' She found herself despising herself for asking, but curiosity had taken control of her.

'He didn't. I arrived at the apartment, I'd been told to be a bit . . . you know . . . sloppy, over him. Then we left you, and in the foyer he gave me fifty dollars and I went home for the night. No point in working with that in my purse.'

'And he went where?'

'I don't know. He got into a car, there was a guy waiting. I'd noticed him when I went in, but he looked like a fairy – a young blond fellow, good-looking in a soft sort of way. I thought at the time what a waste.'

'John.' Juniper said softly.

'You know him?'

'One of my accountants.'

'Not any more, honey. Not the way those two greeted each other.' Maddie laughed.

'God, I've been such a fool.'

'Haven't we all, my friend?' Maddie shook her head with good-humoured resignation.

'You two luscious ladies fancy a night on the town?'

The women looked up to see two men swaying rather unsteadily above them, leering unpleasantly.

'Buzz off,' Maddie said sharply.

'No need to be like that, little lady. My buddy and I just thought . . .'

'Well, you can think again. Now bugger off and leave us in peace.'

'You're English?' Juniper said with surprise as the two men, their bonhomie turned sour, moved away.

'How did you guess?' Maddie grinned.

'Your quaint turn of phrase,' Juniper laughed for the first time.

'You've got a lovely laugh, like rich chocolate,' Maddie said admiringly.

'What are you doing here then so far from home and sounding so like a Yank?'

'I always pick up accents, they seem to stick to me like glue. If I'd gone to Australia, I'd sound like an Aussie now. Wish I had. I was a GI bride, only it didn't work out.'

'What happened or would you rather not talk about it?'

'Doesn't bother me. I'm from Cambridge, there were a lot of Yanks around there in the war and I had the misfortune to meet one. No, that's not fair. I'm sure lots of the girls who married are living in heavenly bliss. Me? I picked a wrong un. Oh, he was lovely to look at. Big and handsome and flashing the money about – very generous he was, then. Told me all this bull about his wonderful home and life in America. We married and I couldn't believe my luck, I thought I had really landed on my feet and bye bye boring Cambridge and never having enough money.

'When I finally got here after two years of paper-work and slog with the authorities, it was the letdown of all time. They were dirt farmers living in the back of beyond – the nearest decent town was fifty miles away. His lovely home was a shack. We were sharing with his parents and four brothers and sisters – one little room we had. Bloody useless it was. I might have adjusted to that, but then they expected me to work on the bloody farm too. I don't mind working, but I don't know one end of a cow from the other and I don't want to learn. I was worse than useless. They were real odd – church twice on Sunday – and the row when I wouldn't go!' Maddie rolled her eyes at the memory. 'They didn't like me wearing make-up or pretty clothes. They didn't drink, disapproved of my smoking. He was a different person to the man I'd met. I stuck it for a year but when he found he couldn't bully me into conforming he began to beat me up. That was that, no one shoves me around. So I did a bunk in the middle of the night and I've been here for nearly a year.'

'I'm sorry. It must have been hard for you.'

'I'm all right. At least I've seen a bit of the world. Now all I want is to get back home. That's all I work for.'

'What sort of work do you do?'

'In England I was a shorthand typist, but here I couldn't find a job, so, I work in Macey's – on the perfume counter. It's not bad, but the money isn't much. That's why I started moonlighting.'

'Doing what?'

'You can't guess? On the game, love.'

'Oh, I see,' Juniper said calmly.

'That how I met your ex-husband, in a bar down town. In fact he did me a favour. He gave me some money to buy these expensive togs for when I met you. I suppose they were to make you think I was well off. But the clothes meant I could move up town and charge more. So if it did you no good, at least it helped me,' she laughed. 'Do you mind?' she asked suddenly anxious. 'I mean, now you know what I do, if you want me to go . . .' She half-rose in her seat.

'No, don't go.' Juniper put up her hand to restrain her. 'It's all most interesting,' and then she giggled at the incongruity of her words. 'What's it like?' She leant forward and spoke in a whisper, consumed by the curiosity of many women upon meeting one of their 'fallen sisters'.

'To tell the truth, it's pretty grim, but I just lie back and think of England – literally.' Both women collapsed in giggles.

'Have you dined?' Juniper asked once she had stopped laughing.

'No, I usually wait to see what I can pick up, some of the nicer ones like to take you out first.'

'Fancy joining me for dinner?'

'I'd love to.' Maddie replied quickly; she was not about to explain to Juniper that she had not eaten for two days – apart from an apple and a small piece of cheese. Food was expensive and the less she ate the faster she would be able to buy her ticket. Nor was she about to confide what an amateur she was in this profession, and that in fact she had only been with three men and one of those had been Hal and he did not count since he had not wanted to sleep with her. But having started the bravado and seeing how fascinated Juniper was by her story she could not yet tell her the truth.

'Let's go up to my room, we won't be disturbed there,' Juniper said as she saw another two men approaching their table with a purposeful air.

'Creeps!' Maddie said loudly, with satisfaction at not having to be polite to them.

Juniper's room was not large. All the suites had been taken and this room, situated at the back of the hotel, over the kitchens was noisy and hot. But, when she had arrived she had felt too demoralised to be bothered to go to another or better hotel.

They rang down for room service and ordered their meal. Once it had arrived and the table had been set up, there was hardly room to swing a cat.

'This is a bit different from Hal's gorgeous apartment, isn't it?' Maddie said looking around the cluttered room.

'It's not Hal's apartment, it's mine,' Juniper explained.

'Then what the hell is he doing there and you here?'

Juniper looked up at Maddie and smiled. 'Of course. How right you are.' She poured them both more wine. 'Do you want a job?'

'What sort of job?' Maddie asked with the suspicion that her year alone in New York had taught her.

'In the next few days I shall need a secretary, in the bar you said that was your work in England. I have some scores to settle which you could also help me with. That done, I intend to return to England and I'll take you with me, if you want to come – all expenses paid, of course.'

'I don't believe it. You're not joking are you?' Juniper shook her head in reply. 'You're on. Crikes, it's almost too good to believe. And all because of dear old Hal.'

'Yes, dear old Hal,' Juniper repeated but again she was not smiling.

7

By eight the following morning Juniper was bathed and dressed. By eight-thirty she had telephoned Chuck Gouzenko, a friend from her childhood on Dart Island, whom she had heard was now a successful lawyer. On the dot of nine, Juniper and Chuck swept into the entrance of Wakefield Towers.

The salon was deserted, only the debris of the night before remained, Hal had evidently been celebrating with champagne. Juniper rang for Romain.

'Wake Lord Copton. Tell him I'm here and that I wish to see him immediately. When you have done that you will pack all Lord Copton's possessions – everything. Do I make myself clear?'

Romain did not reply, but dashed from the room. Juniper looked at Chuck, one eyebrow raised inquisitively as they heard a muffled scuffling in the hall and a conversation which, though whispered, was heavy with urgency. They heard the lift gates open and the whine of the lift as it descended.

'There goes the boyfriend,' Juniper said to Chuck with a twisted smile on her lips that looked as if it could, too easily, become a cry of sadness.

A moment later Hal appeared, sleepy-eyed but with hair immaculately combed and silk dressing gown neatly belted.

'Good morning Juniper,' he said in such a normal tone

that Juniper found she had an almost uncomfortable urge to hit him. 'What a wonderful surprise. And I thought you would be in Europe by now. What brought you back?' He advanced on her, arms outstretched, as if he were about to kiss her in welcome.

'I want you out of here this minute,' she ordered coldly, backing away from contact with him.

'My darling, what's the matter? You look so angry.'

'I came back last night. Really, Hal, you ought to learn to shut your bedroom door.'

Juniper had to admire him. Hal did not even pause. 'Juniper, my sweetie, what are you talking about?'

'Don't try to bluff me – not ever again. I heard you and John – I know everything.'

'Juniper, my darling, we must talk. I don't know what you think you heard, but I'm sure I can explain.'

'No, you can't. And stop calling me "darling". I'm not and never have been, have I?' There was a slight catch in her voice as she spoke. 'I've nothing further to say to you, Hal. I want you out of my apartment, out of my life and, if it can be arranged, out of my country.'

'Bitterness doesn't suit you, Juniper. You know you're not a vengeful person.'

'People change. I've changed. Get out.'

'Now, hang on a moment, I've stuff here, expensive stuff which I paid for.'

'I suggest you make an inventory, Lord Copton, then we can negotiate.' Chuck stepped forward.

'And who are you?' Hal sneered. Juniper knew then that he was rattled.

'I'm Chuck Gouzenko, Juniper's attorney.'

'Polack?' Hal's sneer had increased.

'Russian, actually,' Chuck said, with a slight bow.

'Just go, Hal.' Juniper turned her back, a look of distaste on her face. 'Right, Chuck. These papers here are the work we've been doing, which I want checked. Hal hired the firm of accountants and as far as I know they could all be bent too.'

'Who's being insulting now?' Hal's drawl was artificial, that of a man who, feeling he was in a losing position, was trying to take the initiative.

'If you don't go, I'm calling the police and I mean that, Hal.' Juniper looked at Hal's sleek black hair, his superior expression, the neat moustache, and shuddered. She must have been momentarily mad, she thought.

'Have I missed all the fun?' Maddie strolled into the room, ignoring Hal. Seeing her, Hal seemed finally to realize he had lost. Suddenly his shoulders slumped, he pushed his fingers through his hair with an uncharacteristic gesture and hurried from the room.

'What do you want me to do, Juniper?' Maddie asked.

'Telephone these people, there's a dear,' Juniper said handing Maddie a notepad. 'Make the appointments I've suggested. Chuck will deal with the accountants for me. Now I need a drink.'

About an hour later Hal returned with his inventory written hurriedly on four sheets of paper which he handed to Juniper. She did not even bother to look at them.

'Arrange for the whole goddamn lot to be removed – everything. I want nothing of that man left here. If he doesn't have anywhere for you to take it, then dump it in the East River. Maddie, get onto a furniture shop, order us two beds and then get me a list of interior decorators. I want this whole apartment redone, I want all trace of that louse removed.'

Juniper set out for revenge. By four she had had tea with Pearl Macpherson, when she amazed the woman by insisting on paying for, not part, but the whole of Charlie's funeral. Pearl had relaxed immediately, just as she had planned. She was at pains to tell Juniper her husband was innocent of whatever Hal had accused him of. Hal was the culprit. 'Blackmail,' she vaguely hinted. Once at ease with Juniper, the two of them talking as if they were long-term friends, it was entirely natural for her to accept Juniper's invitation to dinner the following week.

Six o'clock found Maddie and Juniper in a taxi travelling to a bar on the lower East Side for an appointment set up by Maddie that morning.

'What are the names of these men again?' Maddie asked.

'Larry and Rolly Macpherson. You shouldn't have any problems. Apparently they both loathe their wives. Larry's in politics: he's very ambitious, no doubt has his sights set on the White House. Rolly works for the Dewart Trust, he's married to one of the daughters. Have you heard of the Trust? It's a very rich Calvinist organization for fallen women.'

'How apt,' Maddie spluttered.

'Where's your friend meeting us?'

'Gloria? She'll be there. She knows what to do. I told her, we don't leap straight into bed with them, but play it straight just like two regular girlfriends.'

'That's right, string them along for a few days. I'll tell you when. Tell me, Maddie, you don't know any young men who do this sort of thing, do you? It's just I'm giving a little dinner party next week and I'd like a particularly handsome partner for a friend of mine – Pearl. She's just widowed and is very rich and cultured.'

'I know just the fellow. Humph Roth. He genuinely likes older women and does a lot of escort work. Officially he's an actor, more often out of work than in it. And he's terribly intellectual. I can't understand what he's saying half the time.'

'Sounds like a union made in heaven,' Juniper chuckled as the cab pulled up in front of The Tearaway Bar.

Juniper and Maddie swept in, greeting Gloria with the high-pitched squeals peculiar to young American women meeting old schoolfriends. The Macpherson brothers were waiting for Juniper. Aware of their father's activities, they were on edge at meeting her. Neither had wanted to come, but fear of what she might know had persuaded them. Juniper's friendly greeting and the beauty of her companions soon lulled them into a false sense of security. So taken were they with Maddie and Gloria that they hardly seemed to notice when Juniper quietly took her leave of them, giving Maddie a secret smile as she did.

In the subsequent two weeks the yellow press of New York had a field day. Starting with an anonymous telephone tip-off, quickly followed by an input of juicy snippets of information, the editors' interest had been speedily aroused and their investigative journalists put on the case. Quickly tracked down, Gloria and Maddie were quite happy, for a consideration, to speak to the reporters at length of their friendship with the Macpherson brothers and were surprisingly straight about themselves and their occupation. For his part, Humph would now be able to retire for life if he wanted with the very large cheque paid by one of the more scurrilous papers for the explicit photograph of himself in bed with Pearl the 'merry widow' Macpherson. Insinuations appeared about the circumstances surrounding Charlie Macpherson's death. The relentless campaign, notable for the high moral stance taken by these newspapers on the behaviour of prominent members of New York society, was finally taken up by *The New York Times* and the *Herald Tribune*. While these two were far more circumspect in their reporting, it was undoubtedly their involvement that sounded the death knell of the Macpherson family's standing on the East Coast and, with the help of syndication rights, further afield.

By the middle of October Larry's political career had become an impossible dream. The people he had counted as friends, with the same aspirations as himself, avoided him as though he carried something contagious. Rolly, after a far from pleasant interview with his superiors at the Dewart Trust, in which he was left in no doubt of their appalled reaction to his lamentable lack of moral fibre, had been summarily sacked.

Both men's wives had gone together to the best divorce

lawyer in town and had initiated proceedings. Their alimony demands were so high that New York society had an excuse for more delicious gossip for a long time to come.

Pearl, aware that her telephone did not ring as frequently, that the elegant invitations embossed on thick card no longer fell on to her doormat and that long-standing appointments were suddenly being cancelled, felt obliged to make the gesture of resigning from her many charitable committees. To her mortification not one begged her to reconsider. Overnight she packed her bags and was last heard of making speedily for the Mexican border, her young lover in tow. Of Hal there was no news.

Juniper's apartment had changed dramatically. Gone were Hal's innovative colour schemes and stark furniture; now it looked like an English country house with chintz covers, comfortable sofas and good English furniture. Juniper sat in what had once been a salon and could now only be called a drawing room, and thought that it was all probably an expensive mistake; perhaps she should have stuck with modern furniture. She felt indecisive, as she did about everything at the moment.

She felt empty too. Ever since she had first learnt of the way she had been cheated, the ruination of the Macphersons had been her ambition. She had longed for this moment, planned it, had known exactly how sweet it was going to be, and how happily she would savour her revenge, how triumphant she would feel. But there was no sweetness, no happiness, no sense of triumph. Instead she felt an emptiness and, far worse, a deep sense of shame.

She wished her grandfather was alive, he would have approved of her actions. There had been days in the past weeks, while she had been instructing Maddie and the others, when she could almost believe that he had been guiding her hand. His approval might have made her feel better about what she had done.

But it was too late for remorse. There was nothing she

could do to put the clock back. Careers once broken so dramatically could not be mended. Reputations, shattered as she had shattered theirs, could not be reinstated. The worst thing she had discovered in her ruthless pursuit of revenge was that it made her feel as despicable as those who had cheated her.

'Why are you looking so glum?' Maddie entered the room with a tray of champagne and glasses. 'I thought you would want this to celebrate. Looking at your face I'm not so sure.' Maddie placed the champagne bucket on the table. They had known each other such a short time and yet an easy familiarity had grown between them, they were more friends than employer and employee.

'I'm not very proud of what I've done. I wish I hadn't.'

'Juniper, that's rubbish. You're not feeling guilty, for goodness sake?'

'Yes, I suppose I am.'

'That's silly. You didn't make those two louts go to bed with Gloria and me. And once she had set her beady eyes on handsome Humph, nothing would have stopped Pearl from yanking him into her boudoir. You handed them on a plate what they were all longing for. It's hardly your fault if they took advantage of your generosity.'

'But I ruined them.'

'No, you didn't, they ruined themselves. Those two men had been cheating on their wives for years – they told us as much. And in public life they were so sanctimonious and superior. Two-faced creeps, it makes you sick. They were frauds, just as their father was, if in a different way.'

'But I used you and Gloria, and Humph.' Juniper was determined to punish herself.

'What a load of nonsense. Gloria was grateful for the money and clothes you gave her, and Rolly lavished presents on her. Thrilled to bits with her little haul she is. I did just as well out of it, I'm certainly not complaining! And Humph's as happy as a sandboy. He's gone to Mexico with Pearl. He likes her and he reckons he's set up for life. Come on, Juniper, cheer up and have some

307

champagne. It'll all blow over. No doubt Pearl will be back as the queen bee of charity in a few years. As for Larry, I think it was a good idea he was found out before he got anywhere in politics. You've done the people of America a favour.'

Juniper had to laugh. 'You know, you're so like Polly, a friend of mine. She always managed to see the good side to everything. Mind you, I think even she might have had a struggle this time to explain it all away. It must be wonderful to see everything in black and white as you two do.'

'Grey's such a boring colour.' Maddie grinned mockingly at Juniper, who was dressed in a fine grey cashmere dress. She poured the champagne, forcing a glass on Juniper. 'What about Hal?'

'What about him?' Juniper sipped the wine.

'He stole from you too. What are you going to do to him?'

'Nothing. I wouldn't be able to prove anything even if we found him. I'm sure everything was in cash and untraceable.'

'After all he's done to you, I don't think I could look at it in that way. I'd go for the bastard, tell everyone he's homosexual.'

'And ruin our son Harry? Imagine how cruel the children at his school would be. And what if Harry ever wanted to be a lawyer or something like that? He wouldn't stand a chance. You must know the hypocrisy of the English – you can have the most appalling secret in the family, so long as it remains a secret. If it comes out in the open, everyone abandons you.'

'You're right. Of course you could never harm your nipper. Then it looks as if you're stymied.'

'Best to try and forget him, that's what I've decided. I think I want to get away from here, put it all behind me,' said Juniper after a pause. 'I've got to go to Europe anyway. Chuck and an old senator friend of my grandfather are going to look after things for me here. There's safety in numbers; if one cheats, the other will find out. If they both cheat, then I give up!' She laughed. 'So, Maddie, my dear, I want to go back to England. Do you still want to come?'

'Oh, please.' Maddie's eyes sparkled with excitement. 'I've been so afraid that you'd forgotten your offer, or that it might just have been one of those things people say after a few drinks.'

'Why on earth didn't you ask?'

'I didn't like to. You hardly know me.'

'But I feel as if I've known you for years, Maddie. I'm so glad you came into my life. I need someone like you.'

Maddie suddenly looked shy at Juniper's compliment.

'Gosh, Maddie, I reckon I'm homesick.' Juniper stretched her arms over her head. 'England has always felt like home. I want you to see Gwenfer – it's the most magical place on earth. When it's mine, I'll never want to leave England ever again.'

'Shall we go straight there then?'

'No. I have to help my husband get elected. But that done, then I'm leaving him.'

'Why bother?'

'He could never get elected if we were divorced. He made me very happy once. One of my greatest regrets is that it didn't last.'

'You know what the Chinese say? "To regret the past is to forfeit the future."'

'There are times, Maddie, when I'm convinced that my past is the only thing that is worthwhile.'

8

Their flights were booked and packing commenced. While Maddie did most of the work, Juniper set out on a hurried round of lunches and dinners given by friends from her youth, with whom she had originally planned to spend more time, and hadn't.

At one such dinner where she was the guest of honour, Theo Russell stepped forward to be introduced. Juniper looked up at the tall man and as far as she was concerned, everyone else in the room could disappear. Before her stood the most handsome of men. His hair was the sun-bleached blond of someone who spends hours in the open air. His eyes were intensely blue, but not the cold blue of some eyes but a deep, warm colour. His cheek bones were well defined, his jaw firm, his teeth were perfect in the well tanned face. He was broad shouldered, with thighs as thick as tree trunks and if he turned, Juniper knew that his buttocks would be firm and tight. His large hands had unexpectedly slim, tapering fingers. His expression was intelligent, and his smile was sublime. Juniper felt herself holding her breath until he spoke, and then she relaxed, for his voice was deep and pleasant. From that moment she wanted to hear only him talk, no one else.

Warning bells of caution should have rung in her head, for experience should have told her that any man so apparently perfect must be dangerous. If they rang, Juniper either did not hear or chose to ignore them as she stretched out her hand in greeting.

'I'm so sorry this is your farewell party,' he said.

'It isn't.' She looked up at him, her head tilted to one side as if assessing him. 'I've changed my mind, I'm not leaving.' She smiled, an intimate smile, as if she was acknowledging the interest she had seen in his eyes, exactly mirroring her own excitement. 'Not yet . . .'

Juniper laughed at the surprised expressions of the group standing around her and she basked in the pleasure of hearing everyone say how pleased they were she had changed her mind. But, though they pressed to be told, she would not tell anyone the reason for her sudden decision to stay.

The rest of the evening was an agony for Juniper. Popular as she was, everyone wished to talk to her, when all the time she wanted to be alone with Theo. At dinner they sat opposite each other; being able to watch him, hear him so clearly had, in a way, made the longing worse. She felt restless. She would have preferred to leave as soon as the meal was over. Always impetuous, that was what she would normally do, with no thought of manners and custom or what people would think of her. But tonight she did not for fear that he might not follow.

As the evening wore on, from being certain that he had reacted to her as dramatically as she to him, she began to doubt her confidence. From experiencing that wonderful tingling feeling of anticipation, of like meeting like, the recognition that here was someone different, someone who was to loom large in her life, she began to waver. She noticed with a sinking heart that he was equally charming to every woman in the room. He listened attentively and she saw how solicitous he was to their needs. He treated everyone the same, she concluded despondently.

The party began to break up. Juniper, instead of being one of the first to rush off, collecting a group to take to a night club with her, held back. She was almost one of the last to leave, yet still he lingered as if waiting for everyone else to go. Finally she reluctantly decided to collect her coat, unaware, as she turned her back to go into the hall, that he had crossed the room to follow her.

'Would you think it presumptuous, Ma'am, if I asked if I might escort you home?' he asked, as he took her coat from the maid and helped her into it.

'I should be delighted.'

Her apartment was only two blocks away, so to prolong their time together, she said she had no car and would prefer to walk. She passed by her own car and chauffeur without a flicker of recognition. She felt an excited jolt as he took her hand and linked her arm through his. She was hardly conscious of what they talked about as they dawdled along.

At her apartment block, she found she could not let him go and invited him in for a nightcap. In the lift to her penthouse she felt suddenly shy and tongue-tied and they rode up in silence. The lift slid to a halt and they stepped out into her hall. Juniper had meant to flirt, to sparkle, to ensnare him with her charm. Instead she found herself, like an iron filing attracted by a powerful magnet, sliding into his arms.

They kissed with a hunger for each other that left them both shaken. Their clothes were an impediment to their needs; quickly they plucked at them, pulling, tearing away. They stood naked, clasped tightly together as if afraid they were about to lose each other. Only later did they move to Juniper's bedroom.

The next morning Juniper was devastated. She sat up in bed, sipping her coffee, looking soulfully at Maddie sitting on the end of the bed.

'Maddie, what have I done?' she wailed.

'What any healthy girl would do in the circumstances, it sounds to me.' Maddie grinned.

'You might, I know I do – too often for my own good. But the sort of woman Theo would like wouldn't, I'm sure. God knows what he must be thinking of me this morning. I've been a total fool, Maddie. He was perfect and now I've ruined everything.'

'You don't know that for sure. From what you've told me it sounds as if neither of you could help yourselves.'

'Have you ever met a man who doesn't despise a woman who leaps straight into bed with him? I haven't. They like to feel they have to do a bit of hunting first. Good God, we barely knew each other . . .'

'You do now . . .' Maddie giggled.

'I'm being serious, Maddie. He's the genuine article. Pure Ivy League. He'd want to court a woman, do everything properly. He won't take me seriously, not now he thinks I'm a whore. That's if I ever see him again.' She slid from the bed, looking woebegone. 'We might as well get on with the packing.'

An hour later Juniper countermanded her instructions when a large bouquet of roses arrived accompanied by an invitation to lunch.

*

'I didn't think you would want to see me again.' Juniper smiled shyly at him across the restaurant table.

He took hold of her hand. 'What on earth made you think that?'

'After last night . . .' She looked down modestly.

'My darling, I was afraid you would not want to see me for the same reason.'

'Oh Theo, how silly . . .'

'There you are then, we were both thinking the same thing. I'd like you to know I don't normally behave quite so . . . impetuously.' He paused, and looked at her ruefully, 'the fact is I couldn't help myself.'

'Yes. That's how I felt.' She was smiling happily now, but she did not lie; she did not claim it wasn't something that she normally did.

'Did you mean what you said, last night, about not leaving?' He was looking at her anxiously.

'Yes.'

'What made you change your mind?'

'You.'

'Right at the beginning?' he said, his tone revealing his wonder. 'It was the same for me. I walked into that room and there you were – the most beautiful woman I'd ever seen in my life. And I fell in love with you, Juniper. It doesn't seem possible, but it's happened.'

Juniper felt her eyes fill with tears of happiness that this should be happening to her. But she felt also a shudder of fear.

'Why are you shivering?' he asked, concerned.

'I'm frightened, Theo. Everything's happening so quickly. I can't ever remember being this happy. And I'm scared of it, scared it will all go away.'

'Dear Juniper. I'm not going away. I know it's all happened in a rush but that's the way it is, now all we have to do is enjoy it and each other.' He squeezed her hand reassuringly. 'I've never felt so convinced about anything or anyone in my whole life. I'm going to marry you, Juniper – if you'll have me? We'll have a football team of sons and live happily ever after.' He was laughing but there was no mistaking his determination that all this should be.

A frown flitted across her face. She looked down again, but this time it was because she dared not look at him, and watch the expression of disappointment when she told him the truth.

'Theo, I'm married.' She spoke so quietly it was almost a whisper.

She felt his hand beneath her chin and he gently lifted her head, forcing her to look at him.

'I know, my darling. Someone told me last night. They also said you were unhappy and that you've already decided to get divorced. I shall have to wait a while, that's all. We'll wait together for your divorce to be finalised.'

She looked up at him intently for some time before she spoke again. 'He's my second husband. I've already been divorced once. I have a son who doesn't live with me. The English courts wouldn't allow me to have him; they said I was unsuitable as a mother.' She spoke quickly this litany of shame, averting her eyes, terrified of what she might see in his. 'And I drink too much,' she added, almost as an afterthought.

'Don't we all?' To her relief he was laughing. 'As far as I'm concerned you could have murdered your first husband and I wouldn't give a damn. That's all in the past. It has nothing to do with us. You haven't told me the answer: will you marry me?'

'Please, Theo.' She could smile broadly now and he signalled to the waiter for champagne to seal their promise to each other.

9

If Juniper's grandparents had been able to choose a husband for her, Theo would have fitted all their requirements to perfection. Alice would have approved of his sensitivity, his gentleness, his intelligence and love of the arts. Lincoln would also have approved of his intelligence, the fact that he was American, that his family was one of the oldest in this newest of countries, that his character was strong and, lastly, that he was rich.

Juniper could not believe it when she discovered how rich he was. For the first time in her adult life she could be certain that a man loved her for herself alone, her money was of no importance to Theo. For the first time in any relationship she was showered with gifts that she had not, in a roundabout way, paid for. Now she never picked up a bill as she so often had in the past. And now, they were house-hunting in the city and it was Theo who was going to pay for the property. It was a novel experience for her and one she found she enjoyed. It made her feel cherished for with Theo she already felt safe, cocooned in his love and adoration. She felt once again as she had as a child with her grandfather – secure.

Juniper blossomed. Maddie watched as her friend became even more beautiful, something she would not have thought possible. Her contentment made her put on a little weight which suited her better than the rakish thinness of the past few months. Her skin glowed, her eyes shone and even her hair seemed to have changed its texture to become even finer. She hardly drank – only a little wine and champagne when with Theo. The gin and brandy were never touched. She had more vitality, she was enthusiastic about life once more. Her happiness was infectious and touched everyone who came near her. To Maddie, this happiness, this change in Juniper made up for her disappointment at the cancellation of their trip to England. It looked to her as if this relationship was likely to be permanent.

The lovers spent every possible moment together. They explored New York, walking until they could walk no further, and Juniper discovered whole areas of her city which were new to her. They went to museums, art galleries, the opera, to the vaudeville and to the cinema.

Everything she saw she liked better because she saw it with Theo. She made herself beautiful and she shopped only for him now. Every frock, suit, hat, handbag was chosen with him as consultant.

Now Juniper, in the way of all lovers when they fall in love anew, wished that her past had not happened, that there had been no Hal, no Dominic, nor all the men in between. She wished, illogically, that she had been a virgin for Theo. She now regretted every single time she had said 'I love you' to other lovers. She hated the thought that the letters she had written full of her passion for other men had ever seen the light of day. Even worse, that some still probably existed. She felt reborn and so turned her back resolutely on her past.

She knew she should write to Dominic to explain everything, and to ask for a divorce. But she kept delaying. She had little time to herself and anyway she did not want to contact him. If she did, she would have to think about him, someone from that past she was determined to blot out. She would do it eventually, she promised herself, but for the moment nothing was to mar their happiness.

Inevitably, this happiness she guarded so assiduously could not last, at some point the rest of the world would intrude. And then she met Theo's mother.

They motored to Boston so that his family could meet her. Theo might have been everything Juniper's grandparents could have wished for her; sadly, Juniper was not what Joan Russell had hoped for, for her eldest son.

Juniper felt as nervous as any young teenager as they approached Theo's family home. It was a glorious winter's day, the light blinding as the sun glistened on the snow surrounding the white colonnaded house set in its own park, the many leafless trees etched black against the whiteness.

For once Juniper's infallible charm totally failed her. From the moment she stepped over the threshold of the house, Theo's mother's attitude to her was as chill as the winter outside.

Joan Russell was one of those deceptive women who, with her petite body and pretty doll-like face, the breathless little-girl voice and laugh, dressed in frilly pastels, appeared soft and feminine. In fact she was made of steel. When, with little preamble and minutes after meeting her, she told Juniper she was an unsuitable match for her son, it was even more chilling to be told so in her soft voice with its impeccable Bostonian accent.

Juniper had resolved to be quite open and honest with Theo's parents about her past but she need not have bothered, Joan Russell had taken it upon herself to learn everything there was to know about Juniper and she was appalled by her findings.

Juniper listened, embarrassed, as Joan told her son about Hal, about Juniper's revenge on the Macpherson family and about her drinking, she even knew about her illness. Theo allowed his mother to finish before telling her that Juniper had already told him of this, that her concern was unfounded. But worse was to follow. Juniper was forced to stand and be mortified as her family's history was laid before Theo. Facts that had happened so long ago she had not thought it necessary to tell him. But Joan Russell lectured her son relentlessly in the spiteful tones of an advocate convinced of the rightness of her case.

Lincoln Wakefield's humble origins were stated. His dubious business dealings were listed. Alice's name was dragged in and her courageous struggle to survive, alone, in New York with a child to care for was reduced to sly innuendo at how that survival was achieved before Lincoln had rescued her, married her and adopted her daughter Grace. Juniper, by now, was resigned to Theo's learning of her mother Grace's illegitimacy '. . . Father unknown . . .' the soft voice hissed. Her father Marshall's suicide was told with relish and embellishment of his state of mind. To be followed, to Juniper's distress, by the information that her mother too had killed herself. This latter raising a query of the family's mental stability was thrown in rather as a gauntlet, final proof of her unsuitability.

Theobald Russell the third, Theo's father, was more phlegmatic, but then he was a highly successful business man. When he heard who his son wished to marry, his one thought had been that the joining of the two fortunes would make them one of the richest families in the western hemisphere. He admonished his wife as she attacked Juniper's credentials, but to no avail. He was silenced by a look of such loathing that Juniper found herself reaching for Theo's hand to hold for comfort.

'Mother, nothing you tell me makes any difference to me. I love Juniper,' Theo answered when his mother finally stopped to draw breath.

'Well, it makes all the difference in the world to me. You cannot, you shall not, marry this young woman. If you persist with this nonsense, then I shall never speak to you again and your father will disown you.' Joan's voice remained gentle and soft as silk as she gave her ultimatum.

Juniper did not dare look at Theo, but gazed instead at the carpet, studying its pattern intently, determined not to lose her temper.

'Then that's it, Mother. I'm thirty-four. I'm not a child. I shall marry the woman I love, and if you never wish to see me again then that's your choice.'

Juniper peeped up and relished the look of shocked astonishment on Joan's face.

'You've taken leave of your senses, Theo.'

'Probably, and it's wonderful,' Theo said, encircling Juniper's waist with his arm and holding her tight. Juniper could have burst with pride.

'You'll lose everything for a woman who'll probably be divorcing you in a couple of years as she has the others.'

'No she won't, Mother. She loves me as insanely as I love her. This is for ever, Mother, and there's nothing you can do about it. And, frankly, I think it's up to my father to decide if he's to disown me, not you.'

Three pairs of eyes turned to look at Theobald. He had heard various rumours on Wall Street that all was not well with old Lincoln Wakefield's holdings. But recently he'd heard counter rumours that this young woman, pretty as a picture as she was, had stemmed the haemorrhage and all would be well. He was certain that with Theo to guide her – and himself of course – there was little doubt that a merger of the two families could lead to even greater wealth and power for the Russells.

'Of course I shan't disown the boy, Joan. What dramatic nonsense. He's of an age to make his own decisions,' Theobald said firmly. At which Joan let out a pretty little scream and rushed from the room in a flutter of frills and flounces.

Theo and Juniper left. There seemed no point in staying. Father and son embraced before they climbed into the car.

'Theo, my darling, I'm sorry. I don't want to come between you and your mother. I never wanted to cause all this trouble.' Juniper snuggled deep into her mink coat which made her look even smaller and almost lost in its folds. Theo glanced across at her and smiled indulgently.

'Nonsense. My mother is a silly woman who lives only for society. I don't give a damn for Boston. Why do you think I live in New York? You wait, when we have our first son then she'll come round.'

He kept talking about having sons. Each time he did so Juniper tried to ignore it. She could still remember how awful being pregnant had been, how much giving birth had hurt, how she had vowed never to have any more children. She was a dreadful mother, everyone knew that. She had pretended to Theo that losing Harry had been the greatest tragedy of her life. She could not bring herself to tell him the whole truth about it for she realized that her attitude might shock him, and drive him away. Despite her original wish to be totally honest with him, there was going to have to be the odd scrap of rewriting of her past, she thought. But maybe with him, with his love to support her, she would feel differently about a child. Everything else about him and her together was different, maybe that would be too.

He pulled the car over to the side of the road.

'You're very quiet?' He looked at her, one eyebrow raised questioningly.

'I was thinking about babies,' she answered truthfully.

'Oh, my sweet darling, I can hardly wait.' And he pulled her towards him and showered her face with kisses and she felt safe.

In the following weeks her happiness, incredibly, grew. Theo had finally insisted that something must be done about a divorce and they had decided to travel to England together in the New Year. He would be with her when she faced Dominic and asked for a divorce.

One day he surprised her with the news that he was buying back the estate at Dart Island for her. This news shocked her. She was not at all sure that she ever wanted to live there again, in that place of sad memories.

'But the man who bought it from me can't have lived there for more than a few weeks. We can't disturb him, it wouldn't be fair.' She spoke quickly, desperate to find a reason to cancel the sale and yet not to hurt Theo's feelings.

'He's more than happy. I made him such an offer he nearly knocked my hand off to agree. Everyone has a price, you know, my darling.'

It was that expression – everyone has a price – which she had heard her grandfather say so many times, that made her leap up, fling her arms about him and thank him for his generosity. He had sounded so like Lincoln. Of course, with Theo beside her she could live there, be happy there. With Theo everything was different.

Theo reawakened in Juniper that burgeoning of interest in her businesses that had faded with the discovery of

Hal's deceit. He taught her to negotiate, he taught her the importance of a poker face in all dealings. He taught her to read her own balance sheets, how to follow the market each day, noting the progress of her many shares. He began to help her to rebuild her fortune, to consolidate her position on the markets. He fired interest in her.

They had been to Wakefield Town. Juniper had set herself the task of buying back one by one all the properties that Charlie Macpherson had lost her. One day, the whole town would be hers again. Today another two buildings on the Main Street were hers and negotiations on the cinema were in their last stages. Juniper was jubilant.

She was driving, a new car, a grey Cadillac which Theo had given her for Christmas.

'Darling, you drive too fast,' Theo complained.

'I love speed.'

'Well I don't. I'd like to think I might get to journey's end.'

'You're a coward,' Juniper said laughing.

'When you're driving I'm the first to admit I am. Pull over, I beg you.' He was grinning broadly at her.

With reluctance and muttering half heartedly Juniper complied.

'I'll drive the rest of the way, if you don't mind.'

He opened his door and she slid across the bench seat He settled himself behind the steering wheel and they set off again. Juniper found their favourite radio station and they sang as they drove through the winter landscape.

They had gone only ten miles when a lorry approaching from the opposite direction skidded and sliced along the side of the car.

Juniper awoke in the white room of a hospital. She did not know where she was or why she was there. Not until Maddie arrived – then she remembered everything. Three days had passed. Three days Theo had been dead and she had not remembered him and had not known.

'My poor darling. I'm so sorry.' Maddie said once she had, at the doctor's request, broken the news to her.

'It was my fault.'

'No, it wasn't. You must not think such a thing even for one moment. The police are satisfied that it was an accident – black ice. It could have happened to anyone.'

'No, not anyone – just me. I loved him, anyone I love leaves me.'

'That's no way to talk, Juniper. It's the last thing that Theo . . .'

'Don't say his name. Never speak of him to a living soul. Never mention his name to me, do you understand? He never happened, it was all a dream . . .'

And then she began to scream.

10

Juniper discharged herself from hospital, insisting there was nothing wrong with her. There was not, physically.

They picked up where they had left off the night she had met Theo. The packing was done again, berths were booked. But this time Juniper did not embark on a round of farewell dinners and parties, she could not, someone might have mentioned *his* name.

She had not cried nor did she appear to grieve. She had buried within her the memories of her short happiness with Theo. She had interred them so deep in her mind that it was as if the affair, just as she said, was a dream. But such a loss, not faced, but so purposefully ignored, existed, despite her neglect of it, and it festered.

So successful was Juniper that, soon after her return from the hospital, Maddie felt sometimes as if the past three months really had not happened. Logic, however, told her they had and she feared for Juniper. Many times, at night when she could not sleep for worry, Maddie would resolve that the next day she would insist they talk about him. But each time she decided this, in the morning, she was afraid to mention his name, afraid she might court more damage by doing so.

It all puzzled poor Maddie. Certainly Juniper appeared as if she did not have a care. Maybe she was right to behave in this way, perhaps it was her way of keeping her sanity, her method of survival. As the days passed Maddie decided that perhaps it was best to leave well alone.

Juniper decided to keep to her original plan to return to London, to see Dominic and to help him become a Member of Parliament. There was not much time, only six weeks, for on January 10, the day she arrived back in England, Clement Attlee, the Prime Minister, had announced a general election. There would be so much to do.

Sitting in the drawing room of her house in London, Juniper cursed herself for behaving responsibly for once. Dominic was in full flood, listing her shortcomings, pacing up and down the hearthrug, thumbs thrust into his waistcoat pockets and looking, to Juniper, insufferably smug.

She was tired, her head was pounding and she had arrived even more depressed. After the bustle and prosperity of New York, England, already in the grip of bitter weather, looked bleaker and even more defeated than she remembered. As the train rattled through the countryside she had felt her depression increase with each passing dull grey mile.

She looked about the room; she loathed this house. It was too big, but Dominic had insisted he needed a large house for entertaining. It looked more like a men's club than a home. When she had first bought it, she had been full of suggestions to lighten it, make it prettier, but all her ideas had been vetoed by Dominic. She wondered now why she had allowed him to overrule her and to create this dour, dark, masculine environment. She supposed it was a monument to how much she had once loved him.

'You're so ridiculously extravagant: it's not good enough in these times of austerity. It won't go down well with my electors. You should be setting an example.' He paused long enough to light his pipe. 'There's that huge house in Hampstead: when are you going to do something about it? There is a housing shortage, you know.'

Juniper burrowed into the chair as Dominic let rip as if he were already on the hustings. She should have sold the house in Hampstead years ago; ever since her father died she had hated the place. Not that he had ever been there, but it was where she was the night she learnt of his death. The house was tainted now, very much as the Dart Island house had become. She could never keep a house where anything awful had happened, she decided, and she wondered why she hadn't reached that conclusion a long time ago. She was suddenly aware that the room was silent. Dominic was leaning on the mantelshelf gazing into the fire. He had finished at last.

'I'm sorry I was away for so long, it couldn't be helped,' she said. He turned round to look at her, as if surprised to find her sitting there, so carried away had he become with his own oratory. 'As soon as I arrived in New York I discovered that a large portion of my fortune had been embezzled. I had to stay until the problem was resolved.'

'Good God, Juniper, why didn't you tell me? I would have flown over immediately and helped,' he said, his whole expression changing from anger to concern.

'I had excellent accountants and lawyers assisting me.' She looked up at him and wondered whether to continue now or wait for the morning, then she lifted her chin in a defiant little gesture. 'To be totally honest, I was also afraid that if it turned out that I had lost everything, you would leave me.' She puffed deeply on her cigarette. He stepped towards her as if to reassure her. 'No,' she went on, realising he had misinterpreted her meaning, 'no, you don't understand. I was afraid of being left alone – not of losing you.'

'But you didn't lose everything, did you?' he asked. Then added hurriedly and disjointedly, 'I would never leave you.'

'No, I didn't lose everything, but it was bad enough.'
This was hopeless, she thought, he was not listening, to
what she was saying, but then did he ever?

'That's all right then.' He turned back to the fire as if
the conversation were at an end.

'Not quite, Dominic. You see, I'm sure you would have
packed your bags ages ago if it hadn't been for your
career,' she persisted.

'That's a diabolical thing to say.'

'Not really, when it's the truth,' she said, helping
herself to another drink.

'Aren't you drinking rather a lot? I thought you weren't
supposed to.'

'I don't think it's any of your business, Dom.' She stood
facing him now. 'I've learnt a lot on this trip. I've learnt
that the fear of loneliness is no basis for a relationship.
And, if I'm honest, that one can be lonelier in a marriage
that isn't working than out of it. As our marriage isn't
working, Dom. We're two people with nothing in
common but a shared name, some memories and the
house we live in. So, I shall leave you, it's fairer to both of
us.'

'But you can't, you wouldn't, I'd never get elected if
you left. I . . .'

'You needn't worry. I'll stay with you until you're
elected and for a while afterwards to give you time to
make yourself irreplaceable to your constituents. Then
we'll see how things go. If you decide you want a divorce
you can sue me – I'll give you grounds – then you won't be
criticised. Everyone will blame me. People will feel sorry
for you, having such an impossible wife. It might even do
you some good.'

'You've met someone else?'

'No, there's no one,' she said briskly. She did not speak
for some time, but stared into the fire. Then from
nowhere she heard his name echo in her head – Theo.
How different this interview should have been. With
shaking fingers she lit a cigarette and inhaled deeply. 'I

doubt if I shall marry again . . . Not now,' she added so softly that Dominic did not hear what she said. She laughed, a short, brittle laugh. 'There wouldn't be much point, would there? I don't seem to be much of a success at it.'

'But I love you, Juniper.'

'No, you don't, Dominic. We both adored each other once; that time was wonderful. But it's gone. There's nothing left.'

'I thought we had a good marriage,' he said sulkily.

'Oh come, Dom. Who do you think you're kidding?'

'I don't want you to leave.'

'Probably not, but my mind is made up. I'm not prepared for this second-best sort of arrangement. I've never liked second-best.' She threw the half smoked cigarette into the fire. No, she could not settle for that, not now, not after the perfect love she had experienced. She shivered and crossed her arms across her chest as if warming herself.

'I think you're being intolerably selfish, Juniper.'

'Do you? I think we've both been guilty of that – you as much as me.'

'But how would I live?' he asked, his forehead creased with a deep frown.

Juniper smiled to herself. Ah ha, she thought, here we go, money again.

'You can keep this house.'

'It's a damned expensive house to run. I don't think I could afford it.'

'Of course not, but your allowance can remain as it is.' Although her smile stayed on her face, inside her she was sighing at the inevitability of the conversation.

'But, hang on, I thought you said you'd lost a large part of your fortune.' He sounded suspicious.

'I have lost a considerable amount, but don't worry, Dom, I can still manage the odd pensioner,' she said, turning on her heel, suddenly wanting to be out of the room and away from him.

What could be sadder, she thought, alone in her bedroom, than the cold clinical business arrangements at the death of a marriage.

There was not time in the next few weeks to think of much but the coming election. Juniper and Dominic hurtled from one meeting to another. Her feet ached from the miles she tramped each day, knocking on strangers' doors, talking to the shoppers in the street, always smiling, always charming as she persuaded them to vote for her husband.

To everyone they seemed the ideal couple, to the world they appeared to be madly in love. It was a game, but it was one Juniper quite enjoyed playing. Their smiling faces appeared regularly in newspapers and magazines – the perfect couple, smiling, holding hands, looking lovingly at each other. Dominic was becoming famous, a situation he relished, but which made him even more pompous.

Maddie was proving to be indispensable in Dom's electioneering, working as his press officer. The only person in the household who did not appreciate Maddie was Ruth, Dominic's secretary, but Maddie was quite capable of holding her own in any inter-office war.

'You're so good at this work, Juniper, you can't still be serious about leaving me?' Dominic said one night, as they travelled back to London from the north.

'I quite enjoy it, if I'm honest.'

'Well then?' In the dark of the car she felt his hand feel for her knee. Quickly she moved out of reach.

'I enjoy the people. I still find the meetings dull.'

'I need you, Juniper. Not just now but in the future. We're achieving this together. I want you beside me always.'

'No, you don't. Once elected and established you won't need anyone, be honest. In any case, I know myself, I should soon tire of my Lady Bountiful act.'

'Why won't you believe that I still love you?'

'Because it's not true. I bore you to tears, we have nothing in common.'

'I wouldn't say that.'

'I would. You bore me as well, so it's all right, it's mutual.'

'Juniper!' No one had ever told this rising star of the Labour Party he was boring.

'You've bored me for ages, Dom. It's best my way.'

On 24th February 1950 Dominic was elected to parliament with a hugely increased personal majority. The rest of the party had not fared so well, but then they had not had Juniper to help them. With a majority of only five, the Labour party clung to power by the skin of its teeth. Juniper found herself feeling oddly proud as they stood in the fusty town hall in the small hours of the morning, while the Returning Officer, relishing his moment of glory, read out the results. When later, back at their hotel, she wandered into the sitting room for a nightcap and found Ruth in Dominic's arms, Juniper felt a twinge of unexpected regret as she closed the door on them softly and went undetected to bed.

She lay in the dark looking at the ceiling. Stupid of her not to have guessed his involvement with Ruth, but she had made the mistake of many a beautiful woman before her of ignoring the quiet, plain little mouse in the background. It was silly to have felt that momentary sadness. She did not want him and now she knew he had someone else it would make her leaving easier. No, she knew her sadness was for her own lost chance of happiness. What was that Chinese saying? she thought as she turned and buried her face in the pillow wishing she could cry, knowing it would help if she did but still unable to set her grief free.

For a year Juniper was the perfect wife and hostess, charming everyone she met and cultivating the right contacts for Dominic. It was not always easy. She was appalled at the 'Gung-ho' attitude towards the Korean War. How could they be satisfied and excited over more war, more killing? Dominic's was one of the loudest voices, yet had she not held him, comforted him, when he had cried out his fear of dying? He had changed, how he had changed.

At the same time she slowly began to put her plan into action. First she went away for a week, then a fortnight. Then for a month she went to Paris. There she set up an office for Wakefields' European holdings, employing as its head the husband of a friend from her debutante days. Her grandfather, she learnt, had collected businesses as other people collected works of art or stamps. She owned a perfumery in Grasse, a vineyard in Burgundy, another on the Rhine and a watchmaking enterprise in Switzerland. Profits from these European operations had been channelled into a bank account in Switzerland. An account that Charlie evidently had not known about, for the funds had remained there intact, growing with interest over the years. Satisfied with the team she had chosen to manage these matters she returned to England to continue her strategy of distancing herself from Dominic. People became used to her absences. Finally she was planning three months out of his life and politics.

She would begin by going to Gwenfer. The election had been a full-time job, consolidating Dominic's position and what with that and her trip to New York, she had not seen her grandmother for two years. This was an important turning point in her life and, as in the past, she wanted to be at Gwenfer while she decided what to do. It had always been so. There in the peace and quiet, with the security the house always gave her, she could think more clearly than anywhere else.

After that? She did not know. She had had enough of politics, of the stunning boredom of official dinners, of listening to self-important town councillors, of complimenting mothers on the beauty of their hideous babies.

Most of all, she had had enough of marriage. Juniper fancied a spot of adventure.

'How well do you know this young woman, Juniper?' Alice asked her granddaughter as the day after her arrival they sat alone in the small parlour, having a drink before their dinner and waiting for Maddie to appear.

'I told you, we met in New York and she's been working for me ever since as my secretary. Why do you ask?'

'I worry about you and some of the friendships you make.'

'But Maddie's a sweetie. I can't see the problem.'

'The problem, my dear Juniper, is that you seem happy to discuss anything, including money, in front of her. I fear it is somewhat indiscreet of you.'

'Why, what's Maddie going to do, run away with all my money?'

'Don't be obtuse, Juniper. You know exactly what I mean. You're too trusting, you always have been.'

'Maddie's got courage which I admire. And she makes me laugh – which I need.' Juniper stood up and went to the drinks tray. 'Do you want a top-up, Grandmama?'

'No, thank you, and I think you've had enough. You seem to have forgotten that you were so seriously ill; the doctors warned you about excessive drinking.' Even as she spoke, Alice knew it was a mistake. She could sense Juniper bristling at what was after all natural concern. What was she supposed to do, she thought, just ignore the problem and hope it would go away?

'I don't think two gins before dinner excessive, Grandmama. In any case I'm almost thirty-two years old and I think I can decide for myself how much I drink.' Juniper spoke pleasantly but the look she gave her grandmother should have been warning enough.

'I was only concerned . . .' Alice began.

'Grandmama, if I'm to stay here happily I would appreciate your treating me like an adult and not a child. I wish you would realize it's my life and I can do with it what I want . . . Maddie?' she called out, in answer to a gentle tap at the door. Maddie came in, rather shyly for her. 'You don't have to knock, Maddie, treat this as your home. That's right, Grandmama, isn't it?'

Alice looked uncomfortable and her assent was an almost inaudible mumble. Juniper busied herself pouring Maddie a large drink and, looking pointedly at her grandmother, topped up her own glass.

'Is that little girl you?' Maddie asked, pointing to a photograph of a child on Alice's bureau.

'Good Lord, no. That's Annie Budd, a waif and stray of my grandmother's. Do you ever hear from the child?' She turned to Alice.

'Not any more.' A sad expression flitted across Alice's face, and one of satisfaction across Juniper's. Sharp-eyed Maddie wondered why.

'We all tried to warn you, Grandmama, Gertie Frobisher included.'

'I've somehow lost touch with her. After she left I received quite regular letters and then they stopped. When I was in London one time I decided to go and visit but Annie's father had moved and none of the neighbours could tell me where they'd gone. I got the impression they didn't care overmuch, that none of them had liked Mr Budd. I often think of her and wonder how she's turned out.'

'Probably married by now with a couple of screaming brats.'

'Don't be silly, Juniper, she's not sixteen until next year.'

'So? Then she's probably pregnant,' Juniper said, enjoying herself, until she noticed Alice's expression. She put down her glass, and rushed to hug her grandmother. 'I'm sorry, Grandmama. I'm sorry you miss her – I really am. I was being horrible. I . . . well, you must have realized, I was always so jealous of that child.' Juniper felt better once she had made this confession, although it wasn't her fault. If Alice had not been so besotted with the child she would never have felt jealous in the first place.

'Jealous of Annie? Good gracious, I had no idea. You wouldn't have felt so jealous if you'd met her father – an uncouth man, to say the least.'

'Poor Maddie, you look quite perplexed. Annie was an evacuee my grandmother doted upon. She even talked of adopting her, didn't you? But at the end of the war her father turned up and claimed her, and off she went back to London.'

'Mrs Whitaker, I'm so sorry, it must have been awful for you,' Maddie said, her voice full of concern.

'Yes, Maddie, it was hard.' Alice looked at Maddie with interest; the woman had sounded genuinely concerned. 'Annie was such an intelligent child. I offered to pay for her to go to boarding school, but her father wouldn't hear of it. Juniper is probably right. In a couple of years she'll be married and that'll be the end of all my dreams for her.'

'I saw a lot of Hal in New York,' Juniper said, changing the subject. She felt there had been enough talk of Annie.

'Really? Did you?' Alice said, glancing nervously at Maddie, wondering what was coming next.

'He's still a homosexual.'

'Juniper!'

'It's all right. Maddie knows all about it, don't you?'

'He gave me the creeps.' Maddie shuddered.

'Do you see Lady Gertie now? Is the row over?'

Alice stiffened perceptibly. 'No, I don't.'

'Gertie Frobisher was my grandmother's best friend, Maddie, but they quarrelled over me,' Juniper said blithely, apparently unaware of the distress she was again causing Alice. 'But you must hear news of her.'

'I gather she's living quietly with Polly now. Her son

Charles died of polio soon after the war. Both the houses in London and Mendbury had to be sold to meet the horrendous death duties. Mendbury, I gather, is going to be turned into a hotel. Gertie will hate that. The family managed to keep the Dower House, but of course it wasn't big enough for Gertie to share with her daughter-in-law and family.'

'Polly will look after her.'

'I'm sure she will. It seems so ironic to me that Gertie, with her radical views, is ruined by the Labour government. How's Dominic?' It was Alice's turn to change the subject. All talk of Gertie made her sad. She missed her friend desperately, but she would never admit it.

'I'm leaving him,' Juniper stated baldly, studying her nails as she did so.

'Oh, Juniper, no!' Alice exclaimed, her hands searching for the pearls about her neck, which she twisted with agitation. 'Why? He's such a nice man and so successful.'

'He's boring.'

'Juniper, you can't divorce someone just because they are boring.'

'I didn't say I was divorcing him, I said I was leaving him. It's up to him if we proceed with a divorce. I couldn't care less.'

'They sound very much the same to me, Juniper.'

'No, there's a world of difference, separation's cheaper.' Juniper's laugh sounded hollow.

'You seem to have become so hard, what has happened to you?' Alice's concern overcame her distaste at discussing family business in front of Maddie.

'New York happened to me. Too much happened there . . .' Juniper paused. Maddie held her breath – was she at last going to talk? Was being at Gwenfer, with Alice, helping Juniper come to terms with her tragedy?

'First I had to contend with Hal.' Juniper began and Maddie sighed with disappointment. 'Dear Hal, wheedled his way back into my affections. I was ready to go back to him.' Juniper spoke in a clipped tone completely different to her normal pleasant voice. She lit a cigarette. 'Then I learnt that good old Charlie Macpherson had been embezzling from me for years. As if that wasn't enough, I then discovered that Hal had been in cahoots and had been doing the same – only I can't prove anything.'

Alice's face turned ashen. 'Juniper, this is dreadful news. Why did you not write and tell me?'

'What was the point in worrying you? It was my problem.'

'How much?'

'Millions.'

'Dear God.' Alice's hand searched for her pearls, but this time her agitation was so great that the string broke, pearls cascading over the floor. Juniper and Maddie dived to rescue them, both giggling like small children as they crawled about the room, chasing the recalcitrant pearls, competing with each other to find the most. Alice watched them, her face a mask of shock, her hand clutching her bare neck. This was worse than Juniper knew. The sum of money left to Alice by Lincoln Wakefield had been more than generous at the time – in the thirties. Now, with inflation and taxes, Alice was struggling to make ends meet. Her own requirements were modest but the upkeep of Gwenfer was considerable. The day to day running of the large house was proving a burden but there was more; a large section of the roof needed attention – though still watertight, it would not be long before it began to leak. The wiring, installed by Lincoln, was antiquated and, Alice feared, dangerous. And the gardens sadly neglected. She had hoped that Juniper, loving Gwenfer as she did, and being aware of the situation, would want to help and she had planned to talk to her during this visit, to ask if it were possible not only for her allowance to be increased considerably but also for a sizeable sum for work needed. There was no question of asking her now, she could not possibly add to Juniper's undoubted worries.

'Leave the pearls,' she said briskly, 'we can find the rest in the morning. Dinner will be ready.' She led the way to the door. She had been so pleased last month to find her new and competent cook. Staff were almost impossible to find these days; the war had changed so many things irrevocably. Now she would have to let her go – salaries for staff would be out of the question.

'Why are you so hard on your grandmother? She seems such a sweet woman,' Maddie asked later, as they sat in the parlour, a bottle of wine between them, huddled over the log fire while the wind began its overture to the storm it was planning that night.

'She is sweet. I'm not hard on her, what a dotty idea.'

'Perhaps "sharp" would be a better word.'

'I wasn't aware that I was.' Juniper looked away from Maddie's keen gaze. It made her feel uncomfortable. 'Well, sometimes she irritates me.' She was finding it necessary to justify herself and did not know why. 'But that's inevitable, isn't it? She's like all parents, always interfering. She thinks she knows best.'

'She probably does,' Maddie said quietly, but not so quietly that Juniper did not hear. Maddie was rewarded with a cushion hurled in her direction.

'I love this house. If it were my home I don't think I could ever leave it. Just listen to that wind and the sea. I've always dreamed of a house where you go to sleep to the sound of the waves.'

'Ha! Some nights you can't get any sleep for the sound of the sea. And the spring storms, like this one blowing up, can be the worst.'

'And she lives here all alone? Don't you worry about her?'

'Alice Tregowan doesn't need anyone to worry about her, she's a survivor.'

'Tregowan? Is that her maiden name? Gosh, if it were mine I'd go back to using it. It sounds so romantic, doesn't it? Wreckers and seafarers . . . all the magic of Cornwall.'

'It's sad really. She's the last Tregowan, the name dies with her,' Juniper sighed.

'If you had another son you could give him Tregowan as a Christian name.'

'Don't be daft, I had enough trouble with the last one, I've no intention of having more children.'

'How old is she?'

'Grandmama? She must be seventy-five.'

'That's amazing. She looks ten years younger.'

'She's still a fine-looking woman. I don't know why she didn't marry again when her second husband died. Then I wouldn't have had to worry so much about her.'

'If you want to know the truth . . .'

'I don't, but I'm sure you're going to tell me.' Juniper grinned at Maddie.

'I think, after this holiday you're planning, if you're going to leave Dominic, you should live here. It can't be much fun for her on her own and you wouldn't need to worry, would you?'

'Wouldn't you mind living here? I'd want you to stay.'

'I'd love it.'

'It takes hours to get to London.'

'I hate London.'

'We'd never meet any men here.'

'Who wants men? I don't and I should think you've had your fill.'

'You know, Maddie, it's not such a bad idea.'

12

Having slept on the idea and thought about it for an hour when she first woke up, Juniper could not wait to tell Alice of her plan to return to Gwenfer permanently. Alice sounded pleased, although she secretly thought that nothing would come of it. It was probably another of Juniper's short-lived crazes. She felt duty-bound to point out that they might be bored, but both young women strenuously denied the possibility. Alice also, in the nicest way possible, hinted that Juniper hardly needed a social secretary in the depths of Cornwall. Juniper quickly insisted that Maddie would, and could, do anything and somewhat to Alice's surprise, Maddie agreed that Juniper was right, she would do anything, provided no one asked her to milk a cow.

Juniper made a long trunk call to her lawyer in London, outlining her plans, asking him to set in motion a legal separation and telling him what arrangements she had made with Dominic. She then telephoned Ruth to ask her to have her possessions packed. Maddie volunteered to go to the London house to supervise the packing.

While she waited for Maddie to return, Juniper became restless, a situation that Alice dreaded, for she could never be sure what she would get up to. But this time Juniper surpassed herself. She returned from a long walk to announce that she was opening up the Bal Gwen, the Tregowan tin mine that had lain dormant for over sixty years.

'I hope you haven't said anything to anyone, Juniper,' Alice said anxiously.

'Of course I did. I told whoever I met. I went to the mine, the machinery is still there. Then I found the old maintenance crew you used to employ and I spoke to them. Everyone's very excited.'

'It's out of the question, Juniper. Too much time has elapsed and too much damage has been done to the structure.'

'The flooding? That can be sorted out. We get the best engineers available – and Cornwall must have the best. The Americans have enormous pumps now that will do the job.'

'It would cost a small fortune, and it seems that is something you can no longer afford,' Alice argued.

'But this is important. I shall arrange money, I can sell things. My apartment building, for a start – I never want to set foot in the horrid place ever again. We can borrow money until I have raised my own.'

'Oh, Juniper no, that always leads to problems.' Alice felt for her pearls but they were still at the jeweller's being re-strung. Her hand, with nothing to occupy it, fell listlessly to her lap. 'Engineers inspected the mine back in 1939. The cost was thought prohibitive then, it would be worse now. All you will succeed in doing is raising the hopes of the people in the village, and that's not fair.'

'Grandmama, you are always so pessimistic. It will be such fun, something worthwhile for me to do. You can't object to that, surely?'

'No. I am just being realistic. I've seen people lose fortunes trying to re-open mines, and Bal Gwen was almost worked out when I was a child.'

'No, you're wrong – there's tin and copper there, you just have to listen to the old boys talking – I'd rather listen to them than a gaggle of experts with degrees.'

Alice sighed and returned to the sewing she had been doing. It was a mad scheme and yet she could still remember how she, as a young girl, had pleaded with her own father to re-open the selfsame mine. And what had he said? That the old miners would promise her gold if they thought it would make them do something. She should speak more to Juniper, but she couldn't bring herself to, the young woman's enthusiasm was too joyous to spoil further. And she seemed happy again. The experts' assessments would prove to her she could not afford the venture now that she had lost so much. Better that she spent what little she had left on ensuring Gwenfer's survival.

Alice saw little of Juniper in the following days as she rushed about, consulting one person then another over the subject of the mine. All contacts exhausted, she had to wait for results and began to moon about the house. Partly as a distraction Alice suggested she should have her own set of rooms. She realized that the generations rarely live happily together, and in any case she had her own routine and was not sure if she was ready to have it disrupted even by Juniper. Juniper chose to have the top floor. The old schoolroom, which was pleasant and large, would make an excellent sitting room. The night nurseries would be the bedrooms, and there was already a bathroom. Juniper enjoyed clearing out the space and planning further bathrooms and a kitchen. As to the latter, Alice could only hope that Maddie could cook.

Alice had not enjoyed the changes as much as her granddaughter. It pained her to see the schoolroom denuded of its desks and blackboards and the old cupboards torn out. The familiar cream walls, on which her own childhood paintings and those of the evacuees were still pinned, were stripped and repainted. This room had been left exactly as it was when she was a child. It was hard to watch its transformation, like watching part of her life being destroyed. Of course, she reasoned with herself, this was all sentimental nonsense; Juniper needed space to herself and this was the most practical solution.

Finally a large pantechnicon inched its way down the steep slope of the drive, laden with Juniper's books, paintings, clothes and personal treasures. The removal men were not happy with the long climb to the top floor, but once Juniper's purse was opened they set to willingly. By mid-afternoon Juniper's cases were on the top floor waiting to be unpacked.

Maddie had returned by train and was helping an excited Juniper. Much of what she was unpacking she had not seen for years. Her taste had been different from Dominic's and most of her personal belongings had been relegated to the attics. Now she was enjoying the pleasure of rediscovered possessions that had been half-forgotten, like lost friends.

Alice joined them with a tray of tea. Juniper was delving into another packing case. Her hands emerged clasping a bowl, wrapped in several layers of tissue paper. Carefully she unwrapped it.

'Good heavens, Juniper, where did you get that?'

'I found it in some rubble after an air raid. It struck a chord in me, I don't know why. I rescued it and had it mended.'

'It's la's azure bowl.' Alice's voice was barely a whisper as she tentatively put out her hand and stroked the side of the bowl, cracked now and with a small piece missing, but there was no mistaking it.

'Your la's? Then what on earth was it doing in a London street?'

'She left it to her daughter, Francine Frobisher.'

'Then it is hers. I picked this up outside Francine's block of flats.'

'And Francine?'

'The building received a direct hit. The workman said everyone must have been killed.'

'Poor Polly,' Alice said inaudibly.

'She didn't like her mother.'

'No but . . . if she's dead . . . Poor bowl.'

Juniper watched curiously as her grandmother continued to stroke the bowl, tenderly outlining the roses on its side, a suspicion of a tear forming in her eyes. 'Would you like it, Grandmama? I don't really want it. I'm not even sure why I rescued it.'

'I'd love to have it, if you're certain.'

'Positive. It's rather nice, isn't it; it's come home, just like me.'

A fortnight later, Juniper and Maddie set out on their planned holiday. They had asked Alice to join them, but she had wisely declined.

Once across the Channel, Juniper sat at the wheel of her car and asked Maddie where she wanted to go.

'Wherever you want. You're driving,' Maddie replied with her usual reasonableness. 'I presumed you would want to see to your business interests.'

'Business is boring. I'm not sure where we should go. You know, I've a house here somewhere – I'd forgotten about it.'

'Another one!' Maddie exclaimed, laughing. 'You amaze me. How can you forget about a house?'

'Easily, I was only there for a short time. It's rather nice, it's called the Manor of Buttercups. Lovely name, isn't it?'

'Let's go there then.'

'No. I don't want to see it. I was unhappy there, it doesn't do to return, I might be unhappy again.'

'You are funny, Juniper. Most people are unhappy sooner or later but it doesn't mean they sell up. Yet you're selling up everything.'

'It seems perfectly logical to me. Other people don't sell because they can't afford to. Luckily for me I don't suffer from that particular trap. In any case, I've decided, no more houses – they bring me bad luck. Now we're at Gwenfer there's no need for any more, Grandmama will leave it to me,' she said, as she put the car into gear. 'Let's just see where we land up, shall we? Let's just go.'

They had got as far as Paris when the cylinder head gasket went. France was on holiday. Frustrated by the delay while it was being mended, Juniper suggested they caught the next train out.

'But what about the car?'

'The head porter at the Ritz will take care of it for me. We'll collect it on the way back,' Juniper said airily.

Maddie was entranced with such an idea. When her parents travelled it had always been after weeks of careful planning; she adored Juniper's hit-and-miss methods.

That was how the two women found themselves on a train for Greece. They both agreed it was a fortunate choice. Maddie had never been further east than Southend and Greece had always been a dream. And Juniper, recalling a trip with her father years before, remembered how happy that holiday had been, how beautiful the country, and had merrily bought the tickets.

They stood on the platform at Athens railway station in the May heat. A taxi took them to the Grande Bretagne hotel, to a suite and long baths. That night they could not sleep for the heat, they agreed to leave the city. The next morning found them at Piraeus, choosing which island to go to by the same method they had chosen Greece – they would get on the first boat sailing.

The ferry approached the island across an azure sea – far more blue than the sea at Gwenfer. The houses of a small village appeared to tumble down the steep hillside to nestle around the bay. All the buildings were painted a blinding white, which together with the blazing sunlight reflecting upon them made it almost impossible to look at them. The air was heavy with the smell of jasmine. Crickets chirruped as though they would burst from the sound. Red geraniums bloomed in great pots of all the colours of the rainbow. The shadows were a deep shimmering green, as if they were under water.

'Juniper, it's perfect.' Maddie gasped with pleasure.

'Like a Shangri-la,' Juniper said, leaning against the rail of the boat.

They watched in silence as the ferry slid into its berth; unbeknown to both of them they were becoming bewitched by an island.

13

Juniper's First love affair on the island was with a young German archaeologist who lasted three weeks, her second with a young Greek fisherman who lasted three days. This second lover was sacrificed to the excitement of finding her third love – a house.

In the sun-parched brown landscape, the house, with its lush vegetation and bright green lawns, was like a cool oasis in the arid land.

It was a large, low, white house built into the side of the hill, five miles from the village, across a dusty plain. At the front was a wide terrace stretching the full length of the house, with whitewashed arches wreathed in creeper. The windows were pointed, protected by lattices of decorative iron bars screwed to the outside walls. The roof was constructed of strange blue tiles.

'The grass is so green,' Maddie exclaimed when she first saw the house.

'It's got its own stream. The lawns are irrigated.'

The terrace stretched around the house. 'Look.' Juniper pointed. 'Isn't that the most wonderful view you have ever seen?' she said with pride.

From the high position they could look down across the plain to the sea far away. The sun glistened on the water. On the horizon could be seen a string of islands, brown and white, like wooden beads scattered on the sea.

'Come inside and choose your room,' Juniper said, swinging around and literally skipping into the house. Maddie followed at a more sedate pace.

After the heat of the garden, the coolness of the house was in dramatic contrast. The rooms, all floored in marble mosaic, stretched one after the other through arches, so that the ground floor offered one long vista. The decoration was blue and white; on the walls wonderful tiles of intricate design added to the coolness.

'It's so Moorish, isn't it? I quite expect to see Othello appear. And look at this!' Excitedly Juniper led the way to an enormous bathroom where steps led down into a sunken bath tiled in lapis lazuli and gold. 'Have you ever seen a bath like that in your life? We could hold a party in there.' Excitement was bubbling out of her. 'I had to buy it, Maddie. I simply have to own it, it's so perfect.'

'You've already bought it?' Maddie sounded amazed, Juniper had kept the finding of the house secret from her, to surprise her she supposed.

'With difficulty. The owner didn't want to sell – his dead wife designed it, apparently. But then, everyone has a price . . .' Juniper stopped speaking and suddenly began to wring her hands together. 'That's what they say, don't they?' She laughed, a short burst of sound, not at all like her usual laugh. 'In the end he was like everyone else. He could not refuse my offer – dead wife or no.'

'But I thought you said you were never going to buy another house as long as you lived.'

'That was before I knew this one existed.'

'It's certainly beautiful,' Maddie said, crossing the empty room and flinging open the shutters. She leant on the windowsill staring out at the view, listening to the almost deafening chirping of the crickets, trying to adjust to this new turn in events.

'What's the matter?' Juniper asked.

'Do you really want a house on an obscure Greek island? What would you use it for?' Maddie turned back into the room to face Juniper.

'To live in, of course. I didn't know it until I came here, but this is what I've been looking for all my life. I knew I loved Greece, I didn't know how much until now. This past month I've felt such contentment. It's like coming home – maybe I've got Greek blood in me. Now, that's an idea.'

Maddie smiled at Juniper's childish enthusiasm, with her fine blonde hair, hazel eyes and slim figure anyone looking less Greek was difficult to imagine.

'What about Gwenfer?' she asked seriously.

'What about it?'

'You told your grandmother you were going to go there to live. She's expecting you back.'

'Oh, I couldn't now, I couldn't possibly. She'll understand, she always does.'

'And the mine?'

'Out of the question, far too expensive,' Juniper said dismissively. 'There's a swimming pool too, empty, of course and cracked, but I'm sure it could be mended. It needs more bathrooms, naturally, and decent plumbing,' she added, with an echo of her American upbringing.

Bemused Maddie followed Juniper through the villa. With rising enthusiasm Juniper told her of her plans, the exact pieces of furniture, paintings, mirrors she had in mind to buy for it.

But Maddie could not share in her excitement. She was concerned. This island was not the easiest place to reach. The boats frequently did not sail as the timetable said they would. There was no landing field for aircraft. To make a telephone call could take half the day from the one telephone in the Post Office, with most of the village hanging around showing intense interest in one's private affairs. It was summer now and paradise, but what would it be like in winter, the sea stormy and transport even more difficult. Worst of all was the lack of medical facilities.

'But what if you're ill? There's no hospital. What if your appendix blew up?'

'Why should I be ill? I shall refuse to be ill.' Juniper chuckled. 'There's a doctor, who seems very nice. You don't sound very keen any more. You needn't stay if you don't want to. I'll pay your fare back.' There was a noticeable sharpness in Juniper's voice.

'I'll stay, see you settled. I'm not too sure about after that.' Maddie felt relieved to have said finally what she had been thinking.

'That's fine by me.' Juniper turned to look at the boats out on the bay. 'You've given me an idea, though. I shall have to buy a boat as well.' And Juniper was off on another search, another set of negotiations.

Maddie had lived with Juniper long enough to have seen a pattern to her drinking. Provided Juniper was active and had an interest, such as now, she drank very little. But if there was a problem, even a minor one – perhaps a builder had not followed her instructions to the letter – then, the first thing she would do was open a bottle. Maddie could not imagine that Juniper would remain content on this island for long and then what would happen? How much would she drink?

It was a frenetic time and Maddie was quite happy for Juniper to leave her when she went to Athens to shop for furniture. The contrast, the peace, without Juniper made Maddie wonder how long she would have the patience or the will to cope with Juniper's ever changing moods and enthusiasms.

When Juniper returned it was with the hold of the ferry packed with the results of her shopping. There was enough to furnish the house instantly, and with loads to spare.

Even with the wind from the Aegean, July was not the best month to set up house and each night the two women fell exhausted into bed. August came and the heat increased, bringing with it visitors – those Athenians whose ancestral island this was, escaping from the searing heat of the city. Juniper and Maddie were introduced to Greek hospitality and night after night they collapsed into bed, overfed, having drunk too much and tired from the endless dancing that was part of every party.

'Feel bored here? You were joking, weren't you?' Juniper said one night, as shoes in hand, the cool marble soothing their tired feet, they said goodnight.

September came and with it a slight lessening of the heat. Letters arrived from Alice, including several forwarded from Dominic demanding Juniper's return. After less than two years in office the government had called a general election. Dominic needed her help. Had he asked, rather than demanded, it was still doubtful whether Juniper would have agreed, for it was as if nowhere in the world existed for her but this island. Alice wrote suggesting that it was 'her duty' to return to her husband – not the best phrase to use to Juniper. Consequently she replied to neither of them. Maddie wrote instead, but felt she should not mention the villa.

Maddie was the first to compliment Juniper on the villa. She had taste and skill and the house looked magnificent. It was no exaggeration to say that Juniper was lavishing love on the house as if it were a living thing. Maddie began to wonder if in fact all this, all the activity, was Juniper's way of substituting for Theo, her way of filling the void.

In October the house was nearly finished.

'Why don't we return to England for the winter and leave the builders to finish?'

'Good gracious, no. They might do things the wrong way. I want it perfect for the spring and then I can invite loads of friends to come and stay for as long as they like. It's going to be one long party next summer.'

'And your grandmother?'

Juniper looked away from Maddie's keen gaze. 'I know. You don't have to say,' Juniper said with exasperation. 'I should have written. I don't want to hurt her. I just don't know what to say.'

'The truth might be a good start.'

'God, you sound more like Polly every day. I promise I'll write tonight, tell her I'm staying here for the time being. That should make it better.'

In November more letters arrived from Alice. To Juniper she wrote that she quite understood about the house and Greece, and wished her every happiness. A home was always waiting for her at Gwenfer. In a postscript she mentioned briefly that, while Labour had lost the October election to the Conservatives, Dominic had been re-elected, though with a reduced majority. To Maddie she wrote confidentially, explaining Juniper's past medical history and how at risk she was if she drank too much. She should never be far from a hospital and could Alice rely on Maddie to stay with her, to look after her? Maddie sent a reply by the next boat. She gave her promise reluctantly, but she was sure that Alice would never realize it from her letter.

That month, Juniper flew to New York. Although her initial enthusiasm for looking after her business affairs had waned, she was never going to repeat the errors of the past and neglect them totally. She had not wanted to go and had had to force herself to do so. To return to the city which was now full of such unhappy memories for her was hard to do. But she did and she survived. When she returned, just before Christmas, she had a guest with her.

'Maddie, come and meet Jonathan Middlebank, an old friend. I found him signing books in a shop in New York. Isn't that marvellous? He's come here to write his next book. I'm so excited – this house will be famous. Nearly as famous as darling Jonathan.'

That night, over a long dinner, they had to apologize to Maddie a dozen times for boring her with their endless reminiscences, their talk of times and places and people she did not know. Maddie finally went to go to bed, not because she was tired or bored, it had all been fascinating, but because she felt certain that she was in the way.

The next morning, passing the guest-room door which was wide open, she could not help but notice that Jonathan's bed had not been slept in.

Chapter Five

1

'About time too, I've been ringing that damn bell for the last hour.'

'Not exactly, more like ten minutes, I'd say.'

'So you heard me? Then why didn't you come?'

'I was busy. I do have other things to do. Now, what is it you want?'

'I can't find my pen.'

'Oh really! Is that all you called me for? What's wrong with this one? It looks perfectly adequate to me.' Polly picked up a fountain pen from the desk, unscrewing it to check for ink. 'It's full.'

'It's not the one I like best. I like my gold one.'

'You're going to have to make do with this one today.' Polly slapped the pen down on the pad of paper. 'I'm not going to waste time looking for the other one.'

'You're a bad-tempered bitch, Polly.'

'Probably,' Polly replied without interest.

'I expect it's been stolen. That gold pen is valuable you know, it came from Asprey.'

'Yes, you've often told me.'

'That vulgar char you employ has stolen it, no doubt. I saw her looking at it the other day.'

'Mrs Tyman would do no such thing. She's as honest as the day is long. Don't you say a word to her about the flaming pen. If I lost her, I'd . . . I'd . . .'

'Kill me? Is that what you were going to say? You'd like that, Polly, wouldn't you? Me dead and you with all my money.'

'Don't be silly.' Polly bent to pick up a pile of magazines which had slipped to the floor.

'I'm writing to my bank.'

'How nice for you.' Polly straightened the magazines on the table.

'I want Clara back.'

'Clara will be back in a week.'

'I want her back now.'

'Well, you can't have her. Clara deserves, and needs, this break. You're not the easiest person to care for.' Polly plumped up the cushions on the old knole settee. She loathed these petty arguments, she despised herself for getting caught up in them, and even more so for the pathetic satisfaction it gave her when she did. 'I suppose you want some tea? Shall we have it on the terrace? The sun is surprisingly warm for March.'

'You know I hate the sun. I'm not like you, with skin like old leather. Bring it in here.'

'No. I'll serve it in the morning room. You can walk there.' Polly ignored the insult as she ignored many such.

'I can't walk, you know I can't.'

'The doctor says there's no reason why you can't. There's nothing wrong with your legs, I don't know how often you have to be told.'

'I'm crippled, you know damn well I am.'

'I know no such thing, but if you don't exercise more you will become a cripple for sure.' These words were said as if by rote, as if it were an oft-repeated conversation.

'You're so hard. I don't understand why you're so hard with me.' Tears began to form in the large green eyes. Polly looked away, hardened by years of such practised and effortless distress.

'For your own good, Mother.'

'There are days when I wish that that doodlebug had killed me, then I wouldn't have to suffer this misery.'

'What misery? You normally have Clara at your beck and call. We all try, but you refuse to allow yourself to get better.'

'What have I got to get better for? Scarred for life, my

career in ruins. But what would you care about that? You never cared, you're too selfish to care.'

'Yes, Mother,' Polly said automatically. 'I'll get tea,' she went on in an even voice as she let herself out of the room.

She shut the door and leaned with her back against it as she took a deep breath to calm her nerves. In the room with Francine she had appeared icy cool, but it was an act. Inside she was seething with irritation. Her mother always had that effect upon her. For all she knew, her mother annoyed her on purpose just to amuse herself, it would be in Francine's character to do so. She pushed herself away from the door with her hands, crossed the hall and went through to the kitchen. She hauled the large kettle on to the Aga, moved to the dresser, laid the tea tray, took the fresh bread from the bin and began to make sandwiches.

Polly wanted to feel sorry for her mother; she had tried all ways to do so, and had failed. The truth was that she resented her mother being here and as each year passed the resentment was growing. It seemed so unfair that she should have to care for her; unfair because there had never been any love between them.

Francine was not the only one who wished that the doodlebug had killed her – Polly stopped slicing the bread, the bread knife poised in the air. Each time that thought came into her mind she was swamped with shame. She never consciously summoned it, on the contrary she actively fought it. But if she relaxed her guard, it would wriggle its way into her mind, unwanted, unasked, and leave her racked with guilt. She shook her head, trying to rid herself of such unnatural ideas, and continued to slice the bread.

If only Francine would listen to the doctors. They had seen specialists in London, Polly had even taken her to Paris, to the world expert on nervous disorders. They were all of the same mind. Francine was not paralysed, she was suffering from a psychosomatic disorder which

351

made her imagine that she was. Polly now resented bitterly giving in to her mother and letting her have the wheelchair. Her grandmother had been right, when Francine had first come here Gertie had warned that, if Polly allowed the wheelchair into the house, then Francine would never get out of it – and she hadn't.

There was no doubt that Francine had been through a dreadful trauma. Surviving the direct hit to her block of flats had been little short of a miracle. Every other occupant had been killed. Clara, her maid, was only alive because Francine had sent her out on an errand. The fact that, at noon, Francine had still been in bed had probably saved her.

For four years Francine had been in hospitals and nursing homes seeking a cure for her lifeless legs, making the lives of the doctors and nurses a living hell. As each establishment finally reached the conclusion that there was nothing physically wrong with her, Francine would discharge herself and move on to the next medical expert. Then four years ago, she had, surprisingly, begged Polly to allow her 'to come home, please'. She had asked so sweetly, so disarmingly, she had even told Polly she loved her. Since it was the first time in her life Polly had heard such a declaration, she had agreed. And ever since then, Francine had endeavoured to make the life of everyone at Hurstwood hell.

Polly and Andrew had at first rejected, even been shocked by, Gertie's prompt opinion on the subject. Her theory was that Francine, already middle-aged when the bomb fell, could not face the loss of her fading beauty. All she had ever had were her looks; with their disappearance she had no other resources on which to fall back. Instead she had chosen to become a cripple, blaming the bomb for her non-appearance on the London stage. As Gertie had pointed out, in the eighteen months prior to the bomb Francine's appearances on stage had become fewer and fewer, and the revues in which she had appeared had been getting tackier and tackier. Even ENSA had turned her down, Gertie reported with, it had to be said, an unfortunate glimmer of glee.

Despite Polly's and Andrew's doubts about this theory, Gertie had more to say on the subject.

'I think she gets out of the wheelchair when no one's about,' she had declared with conviction.

'Oh, Grandmama, what a thing to say.'

'Have you looked at her legs? After all this time they should be wasted away. She's got muscles there. Mark my words, at night she's up and about and exercising.'

'Clara has never said anything. Her room adjoins Francine's; she would know,' Polly countered.

'Probably in on the conspiracy, probably paid to keep quiet.'

'But why, Grandmama? What good would it do her to play such a charade?'

'Who could ever unravel the Machiavellian threads of your mother's mind, Polly? I don't know when, but we shall see her rise again in all her relentless vulgarity.'

Such theories were shocking, but with the passage of time and given Francine's attitude, they began to appear less and less far-fetched. If true, it was still sad and surely evidence of a sick mind, Polly thought. She knew she should feel nothing but pity for a woman who could not face the loss of her youthful looks and had chosen to become a virtual recluse. She would have pitied her, had Francine been more pleasant. There were times when Polly wondered if her mother, seeing her daughter happy, was going out of her way to make Polly miserable. The conundrums were endless.

So Francine remained petulantly in her wheelchair, making impossible demands on everyone, endlessly playing the records of her past triumphs to the point where all of them would happily have smashed every record she owned – if they had dared.

Her disappearance into her daughter's home had fortuitously brought Francine new fame, though Gertie had serious doubts as to how accidental this was. Why had she hidden? Why would she give no interviews? The rumours in the newspapers and magazines abounded: that her face was horrifically scarred, that her legs were mashed to pulp and had been amputated, that her voice had been wrecked, rendering her speechless. When she read that particular theory, Polly would smile wryly; if only it were true. Hardly a month went by without an article on the mystery of Francine. She pretended that such press attention was distressing, but it did not stop her cutting out every item and sticking it into her large scrapbooks.

'She's pretending to be Garbo,' Gertie had sniffed dismissively.

None of her old friends from the days of her fame had visited her, so the truth had never become known. Once again Polly should have felt sorry for her, but having met most of these people, was not surprised. They were not friends, they had been opportunists, all of them. Polly found herself thinking that it was her mother's own fault, she should have realized she had been cultivating the wrong people all her life.

Polly looked up at the clock. Twenty to four. Should she delay tea until Andrew returned? He had gone to see the bank manager in Exeter to try to negotiate a short term loan. If they could not get the farm onto a profitable basis in the next couple of years then, they were both agreed, they were going to have to sell. To lose Hurstwood was something she could not bring herself to contemplate. She knew that she could never accept its loss, never get over it.

She sat down in the Windsor chair. She would wait until four, he should be here any minute and he would need tea when he got back.

The failure of the farm was no one's fault, especially not Andrew's. No one could have worked harder than he had done. Sheep farming was the mainstay of the moorland farmer, but the returns were so poor that Andrew and Polly had decided to diversify and that was when their problems had begun to multiply.

Pig farming seemed a better alternative, until the price of pork dropped; then swine fever devastated their animals. The small dairy herd they had started with the idea of supplying milk locally had been hit by foot and mouth disease. But worse was to come when, that spring, a mysterious disease had resulted in the ewes dropping their lambs before time and had left the vet baffled. The ministry were coming any day now to decide whether their whole flock should be destroyed. Polly and Andrew were teetering on the brink of bankruptcy. Such endless bad luck seemed almost as if it were preordained, as if there were no point in trying to continue, whatever they did they would fail.

Everything was mortgaged to the hilt. Polly could not remember the last time she had bought a new frock. If it were not for the contribution made by her grandmother, there were months when she would not have known how they were going to eat.

Chickens, they now hoped, were going to be their salvation. The demand for eggs never lessened. Andrew was hoping for a loan from the bank to enable them to build the sheds necessary to house the number of chickens they would need to be viable. The loan would only be short term because Andrew's father was old and while not rich, Andrew could expect a reasonable inheritance. To borrow money on this expectation had been distasteful to both of them, but there was no other way they could turn. Gertie would have loaned them money, Polly knew, but they preferred not to ask her. So far, they had managed to keep from the old lady how dire their financial position was.

Polly looked at her hands which were worn rough from hard work. She did not mind how worn they looked, how short her nails were – they were her badge of office really. Strange to think how pale they had once been, how neatly polished her nails. She smiled at her hands. How times changed.

Ten to four. She hoped he would not be long.

Whenever Andrew went out she missed him. Since their marriage they had spent every day together, every night. It was not surprising that she felt only half of her was there when he was away, for Polly loved Andrew far more now than she had on the day they were married.

It had not been easy reaching this point in their relationship. The first few years had been difficult as Polly, gently and with boundless patience and consideration, had nursed him back to normality, years in which his dreadful nightmares were common. She had lost count of the nights he woke, screaming, clawing at the air, bathed in sweat. She would hold him close to her, murmuring words of encouragement, rocking him as she would a small child until he calmed and fell exhausted into a deep sleep. The nightmares had faded.

They were years in which the fearful depressions to which he was prone to would suddenly arrive as if a dark and awful bird had settled on him, wrapping its evil wings around him, and he would slip away into a world of pain and sadness she could not enter. Then she had to run the farm alone, but she was always ready, waiting for him to return to her. For four years now there had been no black moods.

He had emerged finally very much like the Andrew she had known in Paris, fun to be with, kind, considerate. If there was any change it was only that perhaps he seemed a little quieter.

Their marriage appeared perfect to everyone, for no one knew that in the eight years she had been married, Andrew had rarely made love to her.

Polly longed for him to make love to her, ached for it and some days wanted to scream because he didn't. Yet she felt these longings were something she should be able to control and was appalled at herself when she could not.

At the beginning, it was easier to accept. What could she expect after all the horrors she imagined he had suffered? He still had not spoken of them to her and she doubted if he ever would. But she hoped that, given time, his desire would return, but it had not. Each time they had made love was etched on her memory to be dreamt about when the longing was at its worst. Those times had been when they had been out celebrating and had returned a little the worse for drink. Every time she hoped that the problem had resolved itself, that the next night he would want her again, but he never had. She had longed to find she was pregnant, then perhaps the lack of sex would not matter so much, but always she had been disappointed.

There was no one to talk to about her problem. She could never confide in her grandmother and her mother was out of the question as a confidante. There were many times when she wished that Juniper was still her friend. She could have talked to the doctor, but she felt that it would be a betrayal of Andrew. The doctor was a personal friend; how could she sit opposite him at a dinner table, knowing that he knew? And she did not like or trust his receptionist. If she read Andrew's notes, everyone in the village would know.

In the past she had once or twice tried to take the initiative in bed, but this had only led to them both being embarrassed so she had ceased trying. Often at night she would lie beside him in the dark, her body tense and ready for him, willing him to take her into his arms. She would have liked to talk about it with Andrew, she felt if only they could discuss the problem they might go some way towards solving it, but the only time she had tried, Andrew had stormed from the house in a fury.

Nothing was said ever again. She assumed that Andrew thought she had come to terms with the situation – she hadn't, it filled many of her waking hours and certainly most of her dreams.

She sat up with a start. In the distance she could hear the persistent ring of her mother's bell. She glanced up at the clock. Four. Andrew had obviously been delayed. She made the tea and carried it to the dining room. Then she returned to her mother and wheeled her through, ignoring the litany of complaint that accompanied them.

Andrew did not arrive home until nine and it took Polly only one look to see that all was not well.

'Oh, dear, they obviously said no,' Polly muttered to herself, jumping to her feet the moment Andrew entered the drawing room.

'Andrew, my dear, you look dreadful. What can have happened?' Gertie asked, equally concerned.

'He's drunk,' Francine said, with spiteful satisfaction.

'Are you hungry? I've saved your dinner.'

'I don't want any bloody food. I want a whisky,' Andrew said aggressively.

'Come, Francine, it's time you and I retired,' Gertie said briskly, crossing the room and taking hold of Francine's wheelchair.

'Take your hands off my chair. I'll go to bed when I damn well want, not when you tell me.'

'These two young people need to be alone, don't you see,' Gertie whispered. 'Let me call your nurse.'

'I hate that nurse, she's rough with me.'

Gertie began to push the wheelchair. 'I told you, take your bloody hands off my chair.' Francine swung the wheelchair around violently, barking Gertie on the shin. She winced with pain.

'It's most interesting how you can move this contraption when you want, Francine, pity you can't do the same with yourself.'

'Shut up, you miserable old crone,' Francine snarled at her mother-in-law. Gertie took hold of the chair again, immune by now to Francine's insults. Her indifference, as she intended, invariably reduced Francine to frustrated anger. 'Watch where you're pushing me, bitch,' she hissed.

'Isn't it extraordinary, Francine, that with all your advantages in life you still manage to retain a total lack of manners and charm.' Gertie spoke in measured tones, continuing to wheel the chair towards the door.

'I told you, leave me alone, I'm not going to bed like some brat you want out of the way when it suits you all.' Francine's voice was ugly and shrill.

'For Christ's sake, shut up, both of you! Get out of my sight, leave us alone.' Everyone jumped as Andrew bellowed.

'Andrew, that's hardly fair . . .' Polly said defensively, glancing anxiously at her grandmother.

'Please, Polly, I understand,' Gertie said gently.

'That's where you're wrong, Gertie, you don't understand a bloody thing. None of you does.' Andrew crossed to the drinks tray and poured himself a large whisky to which he did not add water.

'Goodnight, both of you,' Gertie said with quiet dignity.

'See the thanks you get for interfering . . .' Francine said, as she was wheeled away and the door closed behind the two women.

'Andrew, that was so rude. You know how punctilious my grandmother is about leaving us alone. She never intrudes if she can help it.'

'Don't you bloody start, I've had enough.' He had downed the drink in one and was now pouring another.

'Darling, don't you think you've had enough?'

'I'll drink what I bloody well want, I don't need you to tell me how much.'

'Andrew, come here.' Polly patted the sofa beside her. 'Tell me what happened. I assume the bank manager said no.'

'I didn't go.' He slumped on the sofa, easing one shoe off with the other.

'You didn't go?' Polly repeated with astonishment.

'That's right. I went to the Exeter and County Club and got drunk.' He sounded almost boastful. 'What have you got to say about that?'

'If you felt like going to the club, why not? And if you felt like getting drunk, why shouldn't you? But I wish you'd telephoned, I'd have come to pick you up. As to the bank, I'm sure you had a good reason not to go.' Polly put her hand out to take his. He snatched it away.

'Not really. I didn't want to go. I felt like a ghoul if you must know. How could I go and ask for money, when my father's still alive? It would have been a disgusting thing to do.'

'Of course you couldn't, I understand.'

'I knew you would. You always understand.'

Polly looked at him closely. There was no mistaking the bitterness in his voice.

'I'm sorry,' she said, unsure of her ground and what he expected her to say. She was alarmed, she had seen him like this once or twice before; the depression was coming back, she was certain.

'You always bloody understand. Aren't I so lucky, the luckiest man in the world, don't you agree? I have the most understanding wife. They'll have to write it on your tombstone, won't they?' He swigged at his drink. 'Mind you, there wouldn't be much else to put, would there? Precious little else you've done.'

Polly could feel the skin on her face stiffen at his bitterness, at the anger in his voice, at the betrayal she was beginning to feel.

'I realize you've had a bad day, Andrew. I'm sorry and I've said I think your reason for not going to the bank perfectly understandable.' Polly weighed her words as she spoke, feeling that she had to watch everything she said. She knew she was dealing with someone who any moment could burst into an ungovernable rage.

'There you go again *understanding*. Why can't you be normal? Why can't you be angry with me for failing you yet again?'

'My darling, you've haven't failed me, you've never failed me . . .' she started.

'I fail you all the bloody time. I'm not a husband, I'm nothing. And I can't even make this bloody place pay. I come home, loathing myself, to listen to those two crabby old women and to you being so bloody reasonable I want to scream.' He was shouting now, looking at her wildly and then, to her astonishment, he hurled his glass into the fireplace, where it smashed into fragments.

'Andrew, I don't know what else to say to you.' Polly was white-faced with shock.

'Forgive me as you always do. Go on, you must be longing to say it. You always say it, making me loathe and despise myself more and more.'

'Andrew, I love you,' she almost wailed.

'How can you love me? You married me out of pity, don't you think I know? I've always known.'

'That's not true.'

'It is. We live a lie most of the time, but tonight let's be honest with each other.'

'I married you because I loved you, I wanted to help you, obviously I've failed . . .' Polly could feel tears forming and looked away so that he should not see.

'Why aren't you looking at me? What are you hiding? Crying? Are you crying, at last, have I made you weep?' He grabbed her shoulders and turned her round, forcing her to look at him.

'I love you,' she whispered.

'Don't lie to me. I can't stand your damn pity . . .' His voice was like a cry of pain and she put her hands out towards him, to hold him, to take the pain from him, to feel it for him. 'Your bloody understanding bores me rigid,' he shouted, his face twisted with anger.

She stepped back, her hands dropped to her side and she stood rigid with shock, silenced by his words.

'How dare you speak to me like that, how dare you!' she said suddenly, her voice raw with anger. It was his turn to be shocked. 'You're bored? I'm bored too. I'm bored with all the bloody self-pity in this house. If it's not my mother whining, then it's you.' She was shaking now, oblivious of his pained expression. 'I'm sorry for what happened to you, Andrew, but that was a long time ago. No one can help you any more, least of all me. But for once, just once, think about me, will you? Think what it's like for me. I'm in a prison too, but one of your making, not mine. I've tried patience and understanding and now I'm told I bore you. Fine, then damn well sort yourself out.' She turned abruptly to walk from the room.

Andrew had been standing as if in a trance, but as Polly's hand reached for the handle of the door, he came to life, lunging towards her, grabbing her wrist and yanking her back into the room.

'Let go of me, Andrew.' She tried to pull away, but he dragged her further into the room. 'Let me go,' she shouted.

He pushed her towards the sofa and pinned her against the back of the knole, kneeling astride her.

'Don't threaten me like that,' he said urgently.

'I wasn't threatening.'

'I'd die without you.'

'Oh, Andrew . . .' But she didn't finish the sentence for his mouth crashed on to hers and they were clinging to each other with the desperation of their frustrated love. In the light from the flickering fire they loved each other with an intensity fuelled by their need.

Later, they sat a long time and talked to each other as they never had before and should have done long ago. Polly bared her heart to him and he to her. Together they faced their problems and this time they were determined to resolve them.

The next morning Andrew stood by the bed, a tray of tea in his hands.

'My, we are reformed,' she teased, smiling up at him from the comfort of the pillows, feeling the strange and happy lethargy of a body well loved.

'I've got to change,' he said, suddenly shy with her.

'We've both got to change,' she replied. 'You're right. I am too understanding – it must be infuriating to live with.'

'I didn't really mean that. I don't even know what made me say it.'

'Because it was the truth. After all, *in vino veritas*.'

'I don't think so – that's just a meaningless saying.' He laughed nervously.

'Well, I do. We have too much on our plate at the moment, Andrew.' She patted the bedcover inviting him to sit beside her. 'We talked honestly last night, but we must not expect too much too soon. I don't think we'll ever be completely physically relaxed until we can sort out some of our money problems, the pressure is intolerable. And we need to be alone more.'

Andrew nodded agreement as Polly told him her plans. For a start she was going to ask her mother to contribute some money – Gertie did, so why shouldn't Francine? And she was going to suggest that her mother bought a cottage in the village which was for sale.

'God, I don't think I want to be around when you tell her,' Andrew managed to laugh.

'It's the only solution. My mother and I have never got on, never had a good relationship, but living as we do, it's all turning into hatred, certainly on my part.'

They agreed that Gertie was no problem. She was sensitive to their need to be alone and she was frequently away.

And then Polly turned to the thought uppermost in her mind and one they had not touched on the previous night. She was quietly determined.

'I want children, Andrew, I've always wanted them. I'm thirty-four, time is running out for me. I should have explained to you before how strongly I feel about it. I need motherhood.'

Andrew looked down at his shoes, pushed his hair back from his face, looked as if he wished he was anywhere but in this room.

'We've nothing to fear. We love each other – we proved that last night,' Polly continued – 'We'll make a success of it all my darling, I promise you.'

Polly was not to know that this new found optimism and determination in herself was to be the solution to many of their problems.

Telling her mother that she thought it better if she no longer lived at Hurstwood was something that Polly dared not delay. She knew herself and she knew her mother. If she hesitated she was likely to lose her nerve.

It had to be today. After her early-morning talk with Andrew, Polly felt full of a new confidence that she feared might be short-lived. She waited until breakfast was over, when Andrew was on the farm, Gertie out on her morning walk and Francine would be alone in the drawing room, listening to her records while her nurse tidied her room.

'Mother, I want to give you this.' Polly started by handing a piece of paper to Francine, not sure even at this late stage how best to broach the subject.

'What is it?' Francine held the paper at arm's length, moving it up and down on invisible rails in an effort to bring it into focus. She should have had spectacles ages ago, but when Polly had suggested a visit to the optician she had been met by a tirade of abuse. Francine would have been far too vain to wear glasses even if Polly had managed to get her to have a sight test. Since she never read anything, Polly had not bothered to insist.

'It's the bill from the agency for your temporary nurse.'

'The what!' Francine exploded with anger, just as Polly had known she would. 'You expect your own mother to pay for a nurse?'

'Yes, Mother, I do. You can afford her, I can't, it's as simple as that. You pay Clara's wages without complaining; why then, when she goes away and we have to get a nurse in, am I expected to pay?'

'Clara's my maid, that's why I pay her. It's a different situation. I don't see why the agency bill is my responsibility. I never asked you to get the wretched woman in. In any case she's a dreadful nurse, I was going to suggest that you didn't pay the full amount anyway.'

'It's a bit late in the day to start arguing with the agency about her suitability. She's been here nearly three weeks. But that's not the point. She had to come. You wouldn't like me seeing to your personal needs, would you? And to be quite honest, Mother, I'm glad you have never expected me to.'

'If you refuse to look after me and have to get someone else in, then, I'm sorry, Polly, but the responsibility for the payment rests with you.'

'No, Mother, I'm not paying it. You'll have to.'

'You ungrateful bitch, Polly. I'm your mother, for God's sake. You're only in this house because of me. If I'd wanted to make a fuss I could have had your father's will overturned and Hurstwood would be mine.'

'That's a lie, Mother, as well you know.'

'To think it has come to this. I'm not wanted here, you've made that painfully clear to me, I might just as well be dead.' On cue the tears began to form in the extraordinary dark green eyes.

'Mother, your tears don't work with me, they never have.'

'You're selfish, Polly, you always have been. Oh, you appear sweetness itself, but I'm not fooled like the rest. I know your type, seen them all my life, sugar and spice on the surface, but hard as nails underneath and always get exactly what they want.'

'This is getting us nowhere, Mother. Andrew and I can no longer afford the expense, it's as simple as that.'

'Oh, now you're throwing me out.'

'There's no question of throwing you out. We can't keep paying the bills involved, that's what I'm talking about.'

'And what about that dried-up old prune Gertie?'

'My grandmother pays for her keep and has done since the day she joined us.'

'Your grandmother is as rich as Croesus and can afford to, I can't. What little I have will have to last me the rest of my life now I'm a cripple.' There was a dramatic catch to her voice as she spoke.

'That's where you're wrong. The war has changed a lot of things – including Grandmother's income. Times have changed, these days everyone must pay their way.'

'Why should I pay to stay in my own daughter's house, the house which, I would like to point out, used to be mine? I've never heard of such meanness in my life. You talk like a boarding-house keeper, Polly.'

'It's not meanness, Mother. Andrew and I are nearly bankrupt – that's how bad things are.'

'Well, I'm not helping you, that's flat. You don't think I'm going to waste my hard-earned capital on a failure like Andrew?'

'He's not a failure, he's had the most appalling bad luck.' Polly leapt spiritedly to her husband's defence.

'Rubbish. One makes one's own luck in this world. Blaming bad luck is indicative of a useless failure.'

'Then I failed miserably right from the start choosing you as my mother,' Polly's voice snapped and she shocked herself by her unpleasantness. She clenched her hands into tight little balls. She did not want to be like this, disgruntled, bickering and carping all the time, but this was the result of her mother living with them. Something had to be done if she was to stop becoming a shrew. 'Mother . . .' she started, looking shamefaced.

'I'm not staying here, that's for sure. Not where I'm not wanted – only my money. When I think what you owe me! When I discovered I was pregnant with you and I didn't know who your father was, I could easily have got rid of you. That's what my friends advised, and I knew where to go too. Like a bloody fool, I felt I couldn't destroy the life inside me. You're only alive because of my unselfishness.'

'What did you say, Mother?' Polly was looking at her mother now, staring at her. 'When you *didn't know* who my father was? Is that what you said? I thought you were always certain who my father was.'

'I was, of course I was.' Francine was flustered, moving things in and out of her bag with nervous haste. 'I'm leaving this house. I've been insulted enough to last anyone a lifetime,' she added quickly, too quickly.

'I want to talk about this.'

'Well, I don't. Hand me my telephone book. Ring for that dratted nurse, tell her to pack. I'm going today.'

Polly looked at her mother with exasperation. Francine had never said a word to Polly about her parentage and just as Polly thought she might be about to learn something concrete her mother had clammed up. She would hear no more from her. 'Look, I don't want this ill-feeling, I'm sure you don't. But, be honest, you're not happy with the present arrangement either. It's probably a good idea if, as you say, you go somewhere else. There's a very nice cottage in the village where I could come and see you every day. That way, we might get on better, become friends, you never know.'

'Friends? You and me? Ha! You're the last person I would choose as a friend, Polly. And a cottage? Me? You must be mad. Someone like me living in a cottage? I shall return to London and find a flat. I've always hated it here. You've done me a favour, Polly, showing me just how little you care for the woman who gave you life . . .' Francine threw her head back and spoke dramatically; Polly wondered which of her many plays that line came from.

There seemed nothing left to be said. Alone in the kitchen Polly tried to feel ashamed at how easy it had been to manipulate her mother into leaving. Instead, she realized that had she known how easy it was, she would have done it years ago. She felt almost lightheaded with success.

She got out the ironing board and began the week's ironing. When she had something to think about she liked to iron – the smooth rhythm seemed to lull her, made all other thoughts go away. It was interesting, her mother saying she had doubts who her father was. Yet when Juniper had told her that her father was Marshall Boscar, she had said it as if it were a fact. But now, she discovered, even Francine had doubts. Richard or Marshall, it was fifty-fifty either way. Her conviction that it was Richard – the man she thought of as her father – had more substance now. Previously she had thought that perhaps she was being sentimental, now she had a statistic to go on.

Gertie bustled into the kitchen.

'Coffee?' she asked, crossing to the Aga.

'Um, please,' Polly answered, folding the shirt she had been ironing.

'You work too hard, Polly. Why don't you send Andrew's shirts to the laundry?'

Polly bent down to the basket of linen, avoiding answering her grandmother.

'Too expensive?' Gertie persisted.

'It's not that. I like ironing his shirts.'

'Don't fib, Polly. No intelligent woman likes ironing shirts.' Gertie hooted at the idea.

'Well, I do, even shirts,' Polly said, shrugging.

'Then you're an oddity.' Gertie smiled and then her face was suddenly serious. 'I'm not a fool, you know, Polly.'

'You're the last person I would think that of, Grandmama,' Polly said lightly, but with the feeling that a conversation was about to begin which she would prefer not to have.

'Things are bad on a financial level, aren't they?'

Polly remained silent.

'As I thought. I've been aware of your struggles, Polly, for some time. I had hoped you would confide in me. I should like to help. I'm fully aware of the expense of keeping this house going, let alone the recent catastrophes on the farm.'

'But you help enormously. You give me enough to keep a dozen ladies.'

'I've expensive tastes and at my age there are certain things I refuse to give up. But you're sidetracking me, Polly. Please let me assist you and Andrew. I really would be honoured to.'

Polly set the iron to one side. 'Thank you. But this is our problem. Andrew wants to solve it himself. He has to, don't you see?'

'I do, but then, how long can you go on without assistance? Money worries are, without doubt, the most destructive to a marriage. I've seen it happen time and again.'

'Then we wouldn't have much of a marriage, would we?'

'Promise me one thing, Polly. If things get really desperate and your home is at risk, Andrew or no, you will come to me?'

'Yes, Grandmama, I promise,' Polly said and looked down hard at the board so that Gertie would not see the tears in her eyes. How easy it could be: she knew her grandmother would give her her last penny. But at the back of Polly's mind, and she knew at the back of Andrew's, was always the fear that one day that is exactly what they could so easily end up doing – it was out of the question.

'My mother's leaving. She's going back to London,' Polly said casually, as they settled at the kitchen table for their coffee, but she was barely able to hide the grin on her face.

'Well, well. And what brought that about? I can't say I'm sorry. In fact I have to admit to a great degree of elation.' Gertie beamed with pleasure.

'You've been wonderful the way you've put up with her these past years. I know it hasn't been easy for you, there was so much in the past you could never forgive. I shall never forget the night I had to tell you my mother was coming here, after she'd discharged herself from hospital yet again. The expression on your face was a picture. And yet I never doubted that you would agree to her joining us.'

'This is your home and she's your mother, it really was nothing to do with me. And she was family even if I could have preferred she wasn't.'

'Well, anyway, she's going. I left her on the telephone

to Harrods' property department. I don't think she's speaking to me any more.'

'Poor Polly, you don't deserve the mother you have.'

Her coffee finished, Polly returned to her ironing and Gertie to *The Times* obituary column, her essential morning's reading.

As Polly ironed she looked across at her grandmother with affection. The changes in her life would have destroyed many women, especially one like Francine. Once she had lived in mansions with armies of servants, travelled in a private train or her husband's steam yacht. And then the war had come and it had all disappeared – a whole way of life, over, gone, never to return. She had learned to dress herself without the help of a maid, when never before in her life had she so much as put on her own shoes. She had learnt to cook, to make do and mend. She had buried two sons, seen her homes sold, watched her own income more than halve, and yet Polly had never once heard her complain. This woman who had hosted glittering balls and dinners, whose company was sought by statesmen, by great writers and painters, who had counted royalty among her friends, was still able to sit in Polly's kitchen beside the Aga, sipping coffee from a mug, and appear content with the way of the world. How Polly loved and admired her.

Gertie had been engrossed in the births, marriages and deaths for a good ten minutes before moving on to the personal column. She had barely started reading it when she suddenly shouted so loudly that Polly nearly dropped the iron.

'Grandmama, what is it?'

'Listen to this: "Famous Cornish Elizabethan manor house of great beauty, now ready to receive visitors of discernment. Reasonable terms. Half and full board. Brochure available. Write in the first instance to Mrs Whitaker, Gwenfer . . ." Well,' said Gertie, removing her spectacles and laying them on the table, 'what do you think of that?'

'Oh dear, what has happened?'

'No money, that's what that means. That's desperation, my dear Polly. Who has strangers in their house unless they need the money?'

'Maybe she's lonely.'

'Never. Not Alice. She's on Queer Street.' Gertie sucked in her cheeks and pursed her lips in concentration.

'Juniper would never allow her to do something like that, she would make sure she had enough.'

'Maybe she doesn't know. Maybe Juniper has lost her fortune. She always struck me as the sort of person who shouldn't be let out alone with a cheque book.'

'No, Juniper had too much money. You can't lose the amount she had, it would be impossible.'

'Money can always slip through careless fingers, my dear Polly. Juniper spent money like water and never seemed to have a care or a notion what her financial position was. A prime candidate for unscrupulous people to exploit.' She shook her head. 'But this is sad, this is serious. My poor dear friend.' And Gertie's face looked immeasurably sad.

'Why don't you write to her, Grandmama? Ask her if all is well.'

Gertie sat ramrod straight, and thought. 'No, I can't do that. I was accused most unfairly.'

'But a long time has gone by. Couldn't you reconsider?'

'Would you forgive Juniper?'

'Easily. I wouldn't have Andrew now, would I, if she hadn't done what she did? And you know Juniper. She always acted without thinking of the consequences – just like a child.'

'Alice never did, though. But maybe I'll send her a Christmas card and we'll see where we go from there.'

'But Christmas is nine months away, Grandmama.'

'So. These matters should not be rushed,' Gertie said with dignity, put her spectacles back on and returned to her newspaper. 'Maybe we could send for a brochure, under assumed names of course. What do you think?' She looked up at Polly with a conspiratorial air.

Francine had not been able to leave quite as dramatically as she would have wished, that is, on the day she had argued with Polly. The nurse refused to budge: there were only three days of her contract left and, since her home was at Torquay, she had no intention of rushing off to London, only to return almost immediately. Clara, sensibly, could not be contacted on holiday. With the acute housing shortage in London, a legacy of the bombing, the purchase of a flat to suit Francine's exacting standards was going to take time. For two weeks the air was thick with unspoken resentment, artificial courtesy and unresolved confrontation. This situation might have gone on indefinitely had Andrew not remembered a friend from his schooldays whose mother, before the war, had a small business renting luxury flats to gentlewomen. She was contacted, her agency was flourishing and suitable accommodation was quickly found which would do until Francine found a flat or house to buy.

'If she deals with gentlewomen, for God's sake don't tell her the truth about Francine,' Gertie had whispered to Andrew as Francine could be heard screeching at Clara for failing to do something fast enough.

When Francine's final day at Hurstwood arrived, the 'goodbyes' were not as easy as had been anticipated. Gertie surprised everyone by being upset by Francine's departure. But Gertie knew that the enmity between them would now never be resolved; it would go to their graves with them. Polly felt a sadness too, but it was the sadness of the child who knows it will never know its parent. Andrew felt sorry for Polly but, in an odd way, for Francine too, who suddenly seemed a rather pathetic, lonely, middle-aged woman.

Such emotions were short-lived, however. They thought they had been aware of the effect Francine had on them, but none of them was fully aware of the extent of her destructiveness until she had gone. Overnight the atmosphere relaxed, tensions disappeared. It was as if even the building sighed with relief. In the first days after her departure there was almost a holiday feeling in the old house.

The next evening, Polly cooked a special meal and acknowledged guiltily that she supposed it was in celebration, but how wrong that made her feel.

'If we're glad to see the back of your mother, Polly, she has only herself to blame,' Gertie had reassured her. 'I know how you feel, though. How sad that we should be celebrating. Life is so short and family enmity such a waste of energy – as useless as revenge, I fear.'

Andrew had brought up the best wines from the cellar in honour of the occasion, those bottles Polly's father, Richard, had laid down years before the war. And champagne was required, they were all in agreement upon that.

At about midnight, Gertie confessed to feeling 'somewhat disguised' and lightheartedly weaved her way to bed. Andrew and Polly sat on in the drawing room, the lights low, the log fire burning down in the grate.

'I've been wondering about going to night school to learn upholstery. Something should be done about this knole and we can't afford to have it done professionally.' Polly lay back on the sofa, her hand wandering over the faded velvet.

'Oh no, you must not do that. I love it as it is, all shabby and worn. Please don't ever change it.'

'I wish you had known my father, you'd have got on so well.' She smiled across at Andrew, sprawled contentedly in the wing chair opposite. 'He and my mother nearly came to blows one day over this sofa. She wanted to cover it in chintz. He hit the roof, said she was never to touch a thing in this house.'

'A man of discernment.' Andrew felt for his glass on the small table beside him. 'Do you know your face lights up when you talk about your father? He was obviously a wonderful man, the complete opposite of Francine. I wonder why they married when they were so badly mismatched.'

'Gertie maintains she tricked him into it by being pregnant. But I don't think that's the whole story. He'd been wounded in the Great War, he'd lost many friends, it was a time of upheaval and snap decisions, a bit like our war, I suppose. And I'm sure he was besotted by her. She was so beautiful when she was young. You only have to look at the old photographs; even with the changes in fashion you can see that her face would have been beautiful in any age.'

'She still is, though she can't see it, poor woman.'

'But it soon went dreadfully wrong. I'm told she started playing fast and loose the minute I was born. And my father was such a proud man that he would never leave her, never admit to the family that he was wrong, even though they disowned him.'

'Were he and Gertie ever reconciled? You never hear her mention him.'

'Yes, but too late, literally a day before he died. She must regret so much.'

They lay back, he in his chair, she stretched out on the sofa, in that easy contented silence of people who know each other well, both looking dreamily into the dying flames. Polly was too comfortable to find the energy to go to bed.

'Darling . . .' Andrew said.

She looked across at him. There was no need to say anything, the longing was in his expression. She held up her arms to welcome him.

Two days after Francine's departure, Gertie had left for what she called one of her grand tours. She went on these trips twice a year, staying in the houses of old friends. She never stayed longer than three nights, maintaining that any longer put an unforgivable strain on one's hosts. Her itinerary was planned with a general's precision. She had so many friends, and so many invitations, that it necessitated two trips a year; even then she never saw the same family twice.

For the first time in four years Polly and Andrew were alone in the house. Their love-making started tentatively – sometimes they were successful, sometimes not. But the failures no longer mattered to Polly. At last they were trying and this time she was certain they would succeed. With Francine gone it was as if a cloud had disappeared from the house and their lives.

When Gertie returned after a month it was to find Polly radiant, almost certain she was pregnant. She had not meant to confide in anyone until she was one hundred per cent sure, but she found herself telling her grandmother the moment she arrived back in the house.

'Don't say a word to Andrew. I don't want to disappoint him. I'm seeing the doctor next week, then I'll tell him.'

'Not a word,' Gertie promised and began to remove her hat. She stood, hatpin in hand, her head on one side, her bright brown eyes smiling at Polly. 'It's all very exciting, but at the same time I can't help feeling it's a pity. When at last you've found each other, it seems almost a shame to have a baby coming so quickly. I always thought that about honeymoon children: it never gave their parents a chance to have fun and really get to know each other.'

'You knew?' Polly said with astonishment.

'Yes, my dear.'

'But how?'

'You loved each other, that was plain to see. But you were never physical with each other in the way one expects lovers to be – a lingering touch, a look.'

'Grandmama, you are amazing.'

'No, I'm not. I love you, Polly. Every nuance of your life affects me. But I couldn't be happier about this news. You both deserve happiness.'

There are times in life when words become redundant. Gertie and Polly stood in the kitchen, holding each other close for several minutes, each savouring the precious moment that would never return.

Gertie trumpeted into a very large white linen handkerchief while Polly looked away, knowing how loath her grandmother was to show emotion.

'Did you find out about Alice?' she said briskly, when Gertie had recovered.

'Oh dear, what a muddle that all is. It would seem that Juniper has lost a fortune.' Gertie sat down at the head of the kitchen table and suddenly looked weary.

'Oh no!' Polly also sat down with a bump.

'Not all her money, but quite a lot. That unspeakable catamite Hal Copton, who else? She's gone to live in Greece. I suppose it's cheaper there and one can live like a queen on a couple of thousand a year. But she's left poor Alice with not enough money, and the mine.'

'The mine?'

'Juniper had some madcap idea about opening the mine at Gwenfer. She's had engineers crawling all over it, she called in mining experts from America, can you imagine? Well, of course they all want paying, don't they? Poor Alice is left to foot the bill. Hence the paying guests.' Gertie sucked in her cheeks with disapproval.

'Oh, Juniper.' Polly's sigh was heartfelt. 'She probably wanted to help the local people. I can just hear her – "it'll be such fun" – I bet that's what she said. But poor Alice, how can she manage when she's . . .' She paused. She had nearly said 'too old,' but had stopped just in time. Alice and Gertie were the same age and Gertie would not take kindly to being called old, others were old, not her. 'Does she have help to run her . . .' She stopped again, unsure how to describe Alice's venture.

'Boarding house, I think, is the only way to describe it.'

'But the idea of somewhere like Gwenfer as a boarding house seems ridiculous.' Polly shook her head in dismay.

'The size of the place is irrelevant. It's not a hotel, is it? What about "guest house", do you think that has a nicer ring? Shall we call it that, Polly?'

'Is she on her own?'

'As far as my friend could make out. She's booked herself in for a week in June. We should know more after that.'

'I love you, Grandmama, you'd make a wonderful spy with all your contacts.'

'I can't sleep for worrying about her, Polly.'

'Then write.'

'I have.' Gertie looked dispirited. 'I wrote from Augusta Portley's. I wished her well in her venture and said that you and I would dearly like to book in one day. I've heard nothing. There's nothing here from her, I suppose?'

'I'm afraid not, only the bundle of mail I gave you.'

'I fear she might think that I'm gloating.'

'Alice? Surely not.'

'I don't know what else to do. But I think someone should tell Juniper.' Gertie looked pointedly at Polly with the expression that always reminded Polly of a severe headmistress who has no intention of being thwarted.

'But I don't know where she is, Grandmama.'

'I do.' Gertie grinned widely, delving into her commodious handbag and producing a slip of paper with an address upon it.

'I'll think about it.'

'Before I went away you said you had forgiven her.'

'I know, but this is, well, it's interfering. I'm not sure if it's any of our business. They might have had a row for all we know.'

'Alice and Juniper? I've never heard such rubbish. That would be like you and me falling out, unthinkable.' Gertie shuddered at such a notion.

'I'd have said the same about you and Alice. And look what happened, and on my wedding day.' Polly was laughing.

'If only one could turn stupid clocks back. If only saying sorry wasn't always so incredibly hard – when you're not in the wrong, I hasten to add.'

Polly did not write to Juniper immediately. She decided

to wait until after Gertie's friend had been to stay at Gwenfer. They might be able to glean more information. Gertie agreed.

Nor did she keep her promise to herself not to tell Andrew about the baby until she was certain. She was too excited and blurted it out about two hours after she had told Gertie. To say that Andrew was thrilled was an understatement. He seemed to change in front of her eyes. He stood taller, held his head erect, he was full of pride; they were normal, they were going to be a real family.

'I have something to say to both of you,' Gertie said across the dinner table. 'I don't wish to be interrupted and I request that you listen to everything I have to say.'

When Gertie spoke thus there was no one who dared contradict her. Andrew and Polly sat expectantly on their chairs, sitting up straight like young children in school. Neither dared look at the other in case they made each other laugh.

'I have always respected your courageous stand over financial matters, Andrew, and . . .'

'I say, I didn't realize . . .' Andrew interrupted, but was silenced by a withering glance from Gertie. He slumped back in his chair looking agitated and trapped.

'I realize this is a subject that you find distressing, Andrew, and one you would prefer not to be discussed in the open. But you have responsibilities approaching, you can no longer afford the luxury of such sensibilities. Consideration for your child must be your top priority. Now, I have spoken to my bank manager in London and have set aside twelve thousand pounds, which will be at your disposal when you give my manager the details of your bank.'

'Grandmama, that's a fortune. We couldn't possibly.' Polly found she was wringing her hands, she feared how Andrew might react to this.

'Yes, you can. Of course you can. Now, this is not a loan . . .' As they both started to protest Gertie held up her hand for silence. 'If it makes you any happier you can make me a partner in your chicken venture and you can share the delicious profits, which I'm confident you will make, with me. There, you may speak now.'

'No!' They said in unison.

'And why not?' Gertie sat ramrod straight. It always fascinated Polly how her grandmother could sit on a chair for hours, her back never touching the backrest.

'I couldn't, Lady Gertie, for the simple reason that if I lost everything, how would I pay you back?'

'I don't want to be paid back, even if it fails. Did I not make myself clear, Andrew?'

'You can say that now, but you might not feel that way if it happened.' Andrew looked embarrassed.

'Rats! I only ever say what I mean. The moment the money is in your account, it's out of my possession, gone, no more.' And Gertie rubbed her hands together as if washing the money away.

'But it's such a lot of money, Grandmama.'

'And what am I to do with it? I'm seventy-six, I don't expect to go on forever.' She laughed her loud hooting laugh. 'I have plenty of money for what's left of my life. I would only have left it to you in my will, Polly, far better that it helps you now. And I shall have the satisfaction of seeing you enjoy it.'

'It's not that easy, Lady Gertie. I could have gone to my own father, but I felt I couldn't make such demands. I nearly went to the bank and asked for a loan on my expectations.'

'Well, I'm glad you didn't. A friend of mine, Primrose Potter's son, did just that; it was dreadful for everyone concerned. Poor Humbert Potter felt he shouldn't carry on living, that his son was just waiting for the black-edged telegram. He lived another ten years, by which time the amount of money he left did not even cover the interest on the loan. A totally unsatisfactory situation all round.'

'Grandmama, you are wonderful, you always have a friend who fits any situation.'

'No I haven't, I don't know anyone who has committed

murder or who has been murdered – ah, but wait a minute, that's not strictly true. There was the most appalling talk and mystery about young Phillip Masterman's nasty accident with the gamekeeper on his father's grouse moor. I'd quite forgotten.'

Both Andrew and Polly burst into laughter.

'Well, Andrew, what have you to say?'

'There's not a lot I can say, except thank you, Lady Gertie.'

'Most satisfactory.' Gertie beamed at them. 'It's rather unorthodox at this time of night, Andrew, but do you know, I think I would quite like one of Juniper's wonderful martinis – so uplifting I always find them.'

5

In July, Gertie received a long letter from her friend Prunella Smeeton, who had been to stay at Gwenfer as a paying guest. While the letter was full of praise for Alice, the beauty and comfort of Gwenfer, the excellence of the food, the peace and tranquillity, the writer felt that Alice was a worried woman. 'Detached,' was the way she described her, 'as if her mind were always on other matters.' The mine had not opened, though the correspondent had been unable to find out more '. . . the local population being obsessively secretive about the matter. A characteristic of the Cornish, I gather . . .' Juniper had finally sold her house in Hampstead, the letter continued, and two old dogs, the remaining pets that Juniper had bought before the war, had been delivered to Alice to care for. The level of comfort would imply that financial matters were not Alice's greatest concern.

'It doesn't make sense,' Gertie said, pushing the letter back into its envelope. 'If she has no money worries, then why do it? Alice is too private a person to enjoy having total strangers in her house. And what about the dogs. Does Alice like dogs – I don't think she's ever had one herself. Poor creatures. Really, Juniper is so irresponsible. First her child, then her dratted dogs, just left scattered about the country for others to care for, as if she had tired of them.'

'Oh, Grandmama, that's a bit hard. Juniper suffered over Harry, you know. I always think that's why she was such a problem in London with the drink and things. She wanted to be a good mother, she just couldn't. I hope I can.'

'Piffle. One cannot compare you and Juniper. Your little mite will be a most fortunate child to have you as its mother, Polly.'

'I do understand Juniper better now, though. Sometimes at night if I can't sleep and I think of the awesome responsibility of having a child, I find it quite frightening, Grandmama. And I shall be thirty-five when I'm a mother. Juniper at twenty was still a child herself when she had Harry. She must have been petrified.'

'You've always had such understanding of people, Polly. A tolerance beyond your years.'

Polly looked bashful. 'I think it's time I wrote to Juniper, don't you?'

After such a long time, it was not the easiest letter to write – eight years had gone by since she had last seen Juniper. As she sat at her desk, chewing the end of her pen and trying to find the words, Polly marvelled at how much had happened to her. Andrew was well again, they had almost been bankrupt, but now their chicken venture went from strength to strength; and she was pregnant – all monumental happenings in her life, but of little interest, she was sure, to Juniper with her glamorous lifestyle. One thing was certain, Polly thought, for all their problems she would not change places with Juniper for one minute, nor would she have wanted the smallest percentage of Juniper's wealth. As far as she could see, so much money only led to unhappiness and problems.

'Well,' she said aloud to herself, and grinned. 'Maybe a little bit of her fortune would not go amiss.'

She started to write, having decided that apart from the news that she was pregnant and happy the rest would bore Juniper. Since she did not know how Juniper would react to hearing from her, she decided to keep the letter fairly short, reserving the bulk of it for Gertie's concern about Alice.

After the letter had been posted, Polly put the problem from her mind. Until they heard there was nothing further they could do and she got on with her own life.

Gertie's birthday was in August and she had treated herself to a present. She was very mysterious about it and tended to giggle uncontrollably if it were mentioned – most uncharacteristic of Gertie.

The day it arrived in the van, work at Hurstwood stopped. Gertie had bought a television set.

'If they decide to show the coronation next year, and I gather from friends of mine that it's being discussed seriously at a very senior level,' Gertie whispered behind her hand to Polly, 'if they do, you won't get a set for love nor money. So I thought we should have one now. What do you think?' They were standing on the front drive watching the men set up the aerial. The worry was that the reception might be impossible because of the hills. 'Nonsense, young man,' Gertie announced to the bemused engineer, 'of course it will work. We shall make it work.'

'I think it's a wonderful machine, but so expensive, Grandmama.'

'Tush. I think I've earned a treat, don't you? And do you realize that this will be the first coronation that I haven't personally attended this century?'

'Of course. Which one was the best?'

'The most opulent? Why, I think I must say Edward's, though I barely knew him and all we young gals were, to be honest, quite terrified of him. But Queen Alexandra was ethereal, no other word for it. The most moving undoubtedly was dear Bertie's – after all the awful trauma of the abdication and that unspeakable American adventuress – well, it was all such a relief, don't you see?' Gertie paused and looked up at the roof. 'Why have you stopped?' she shouted to the man.

'Sorry, Ma'am, I was listening to you, fascinating. You wait till I tell my kids.' The workman resumed his task, listening out for the instructions of his mate whose head kept popping out of the small parlour window as they tried to align the large H of the aerial to tune the set.

'You know, Polly, I think one of the nicest things that came out of the war is the easy familiarity of people. That man wouldn't have dared admit to eavesdropping before the war.'

'I'd have thought you'd hate that.'

'Me? Gracious no, only a reactionary old stickler would object and that's the last thing anyone could call me,' Gertie said, sweeping into the house to tell the engineer in the parlour how best to do his job.

Overnight Gertie became a television addict. She watched everything: the quizzes, documentaries, household hints, the children's programmes, right through to the epilogue. There were short films inserted to enable viewers to make a cup of tea – not Gertie. She remained rooted to her chair watching the potter's wheel turn on the small flickering screen. Her greatest frustration, and frequently voiced complaint, was that there was too little of it, she wanted programmes all day. In consequence Polly and Andrew might just as well have been alone in the house in the evenings for, after the initial excitement, there was little either of them wanted to watch. They even dined alone since Gertie insisted on having her meals on a tray rather than miss a programme.

'Do you think it's good for her?' Polly asked one evening. 'You don't think it'll hurt her eyes, do you?'

'I doubt it, not now she's got the light rigged up correctly. It's given the old girl a new lease of life, if you ask me.' Andrew laughed at Polly's worry.

The summer passed and Polly, not hearing from Juniper, wondered if her letter had gone astray somewhere in Greece. Though she had scoured the large atlas in her father's study, she could find no reference to Juniper's island, so it must be very small. The letter might have offended her, of course, which would explain why she had not had a reply. Consequently she had almost given up, when, one October morning, in the pile of mail Andrew brought in from the postman, Polly recognized Juniper's large looped writing on an envelope. She felt a ridiculous surge of excitement at the sight of it and was almost reluctant to open the letter in case it was a disappointment.

The letter was typical of Juniper, sprawling, needing eight pages of airmail paper when anyone else could have crammed the letter into two sheets. The way it was written was almost like hearing Juniper speak. She was 'overjoyed' to receive Polly's letter. 'Gee, it's the best thing that has happened in years' . . . The congratulations over the baby took up a whole page, together with exhortations that she hoped, 'no insisted,' that Andrew tell her the moment it was born. She would ask to be godmother, had she not been such a miserable failure as a mother, but she would not embarrass them. Several pages were taken up with a description of her 'paradise'. Polly and Andrew must come the moment they could. Life was 'wonderful', 'blissful', 'delirious', 'divine'. Masses of friends had been to stay and all asked after Polly. She enclosed photographs. Reply 'immediately, please, please, please' . . . There was a small postscript that went along the bottom of the last sheet and up the side. Alice appreciated their concern, but she was fit, fine and happy, Juniper had scrawled.

Polly delved into the envelope for the promised photographs and they tumbled out on to the table. The first one made her go cold. There was Juniper on the terrace of her house, glass in hand, and with his arm about her waist was Jonathan.

She scanned the other photographs closely for any sight of Jonathan among the smiling faces, but she could not distinguish him in the slightly out-of-focus prints. She quickly put the offending one back in the envelope and left the others out for Andrew and Gertie to see. She did not want Gertie to see that one. Offending, that was the word. Why should she feel offended? What was it to her that Jonathan was once more with Juniper? It was none of her business what they did. It didn't matter to her – only it did.

Andrew and Gertie were puzzled when she did not sit down and reply immediately. And after a week or two they gave up asking her if she had.

In the first days of February 1953, Polly finally went into labour. She had reached that point where she thought she was going to be pregnant for ever. She had wanted to have the baby at home, but in view of her age the doctor would not allow it. So Andrew, in a fine state of excitement and gear-crunching inefficiency, drove her into the nursing home in Exeter.

It was a boy. Richard Andrew Frobisher Slater, they decided to call him.

Two days later Gertie was allowed to visit. She popped her head round the door of Polly's room and to her consternation saw Polly sitting in bed, holding her baby and sobbing her heart out.

'My dearest Polly? What has happened? Is there anything wrong with the child?' Gertie was across the room with the speed that always surprised in one of her age.

'Grandmama, look, oh look . . .' Polly hiccuped through her sobs. 'Just look at his hair.'

Gertie searched for her spectacles and scrutinised the baby's scalp. The child had a fine head of hair, as yet golden but, unmistakably, not the golden hair of a blonde to be, but that of a redhead.

'My hair, my Richard's hair.' Gertie's voice caught with emotion.

'You see what it means? I was right all along. I was Richard's child. You really are my grandmother.'

Gertie put her arms round mother and child, and Polly was not the only one who was crying.

6

The year 1953 had begun happily enough. Gertie had insisted that she pay for a baby nurse for Richard, to enable Polly to get back on her feet. Although she had said nothing, Gertie was appalled at the speed with which Polly had been discharged from hospital and was expected to cope. Ten days was a scandal in Gertie's eyes. A woman needed at least three weeks' rest in bed to recover from the trauma. Gertie approved of all things modern, but she felt strongly this was a retrogressive step.

All was well with the baby until, after a month, the baby nurse left for her next patient's confinement. Polly was convinced Richard knew she had gone, for the taxi could not have been halfway down the drive before he began to scream. It seemed he would never stop again.

There were days when Polly felt ill with exhaustion, when she did not know how to put one foot in front of the other. After several disturbed nights she suggested that for the duration of this colic she would sleep in a separate room. Andrew, working as hard as he did, needed his sleep. It was a mistake. Within three days Andrew had a nightmare of such intensity he was afraid to risk going back to sleep. Polly moved back in and the strain of trying to keep the baby quiet so that her husband could sleep took an additional toll of her strength.

She loved the baby and yet there were days when she resented him and hated herself for such unnatural emotions. Gertie had been right, she began to think, it was in a way a pity he had come. The wonderful intimacy she and Andrew had begun to enjoy was wrecked by this screaming child in their midst.

Gertie was a tower of strength. She insisted on taking over the cooking so that at least Polly did not have to

386

worry about getting meals on the table. And Gertie would pace the floor for hours at a time, trying to comfort the baby so that Polly could grab a precious hour's rest.

The house, despite the efforts of Polly's charlady, Mrs Tyman, began to look dusty and neglected and even the garden which Polly had worked so hard at trying to restore to its former glory began to slip back.

Before the baby's arrival, Polly had spent many happy hours dreaming of how motherhood would be. She had imagined herself, calm, placid, nursing her child. She had seen Andrew and herself, hand in hand, with love in their eyes gazing down into the crib on their blissfully sleeping child, or, if not sleeping, he was smiling and gurgling at them. The reality made her think she was a complete failure as a mother. It did not matter that both Andrew and Gertie spent hours reassuring her and telling her that the crying would end. She was sure she was hopeless: bad tempered and exhausted to the point of desperation.

One day the dreadful tiredness caused her to make a remark of such insensitivity to Andrew that she knew she would never forgive herself and she would not blame him if he couldn't either. In one of those rare, snatched moments when Richard was asleep, she had gone to find Andrew, busy with the chickens, to ask him when he was next going to Ashburton, as she needed more gripe water.

Andrew was in one of the long sheds. The noise of the chickens pecking and squabbling was deafening, the heat intense, the smell awful. She did not like these sheds; they often made her feel so claustrophobic that she avoided them when she could. She had never said how she felt since Andrew was understandably proud of his success.

'Richard asleep?' Andrew asked, looking up from filling the water trays.

'Yes, at last. He looks like a little angel, now.' She laughed ironically. She looked around her, not bothering for once to hide the expression of distaste on her face. 'I don't know how you can spend the hours you do in here,' she said, shuddering, pulling her cardigan close about her despite the warmth.

'I like it. I've grown very fond of these little ladies.' He smiled.

'It's so unnatural. I feel sorry for the poor things. It's cruel. It's like a concentration camp in here.' The words seemed to slip out of their own accord, but worse, she knew she had said them on purpose. She knew that she wanted, in some twisted way, to punish Andrew for her own tiredness, for her own failings.

The look he gave her made her feel chill. She put her hand to her mouth, already beginning to regret. 'I'm so sorry, Andrew. I didn't think.'

'Evidently,' he said coldly, turning abruptly on his heel and striding down the long avenue between the cages of birds.

Polly ran from the shed, raced across the field and garden to the house. She bounded up the stairs two at a time and, with no thought of the sleeping child, slammed her door shut with a crash. She flung herself on her bed and began to cry. Once started, she found she could not stop. She did not hear Gertie enter the room and cross towards her. Only when Gertie sat on the bed and put her arms about her was she conscious of her.

'There, there.' Gertie stroked her hair. 'Do you want to tell me about it?'

'I've just been absolutely foul to Andrew.'

'He'll understand. You're tired.'

'No, not this time. I was so cruel. But what's worse, Grandmama, I was cruel on purpose. I wanted to hurt him and yet I love him. What's happening to me?'

'Hush.' Gertie continued to stroke her hair, soothing her. 'Polly, this is all too much for you. You and Andrew are too proud, at this rate your pride is going to make you ill. Let me pay for some help, you can't go on like this.'

'Other women manage. Why can't I?'

'Not every mother's got a little monster like Richard. When I think of the army of nannies we had, and maids and cooks, and you are expected to do everything and still be a loving wife! A woman's role seems to get harder, not easier. I can assure you I would have walked out, I could not have coped with such pressures.'

'Oh, Grandmama, you are so sweet. I bet you wouldn't have, you'd have stuck it. In any case your babies wouldn't have cried.' Polly smiled weakly. 'I'm being so wet.'

'There's a young girl in the village who's willing to come here to help you. I think they call it being "a mother's help". And I've spoken to Mrs Tyman, she's quite happy to come in every morning for an extra two hours at my expense.'

'That would be wonderful.' Polly looked at her grandmother through tear-dimmed eyes, too tired to protest.

'Then it's done.'

And Andrew forgave her. That evening she apologized and confessed that she thought she had acted deliberately. She was even more ashamed when he kissed her and told her he loved her.

The mother's help had barely unpacked when Richard stopped crying. One day he was screaming, the next cooing and blowing contented bubbles. All the trauma was over, now Polly could concentrate on loving her baby as she had dreamt of doing. Although calm was restored and sleep had become possible again, Gertie insisted that the extra help be maintained.

And then in May Gertie became ill for the first time in her life. The doctor questioned them closely and announced that Lady Gertrude had been doing too much and needed complete rest. The slight cold she had caught from sitting in a draught became heavier and then developed into bronchitis, the bronchitis into pneumonia. Polly was devastated as she watched her grandmother's condition worsen. Each day she seemed to shrivel and age in front of her horrified gaze, and finally slid into a coma. Polly had to face the prospect that her grandmother was going to die.

Polly pestered the doctor for a prognosis. They employed a nurse immediately and Polly shadowed the woman, asking her at every opportunity what she thought about her grandmother's chances. Both reassured her with those fatuous and empty remarks, delivered woodenly by members of the medical profession, that never convince anyone for one moment. The fact that they had decided not to move her to hospital filled Polly with dread, she was sure they had given up hope. The exhaustion of looking after the baby was now replaced by the strain of staying up at night holding her grandmother's hand.

'Darling, you must sleep, you'll make yourself ill. I'll sit up with her,' Andrew volunteered.

'I can't leave her. I'm sure she knows I'm there. What if she opened her eyes and I wasn't?'

Polly nursed her grandmother through the night: checking the oxygen for the tent, keeping her warm, watching for any change, taking her pulse as the nurse had taught her. She would sleep restlessly in the chair beside Gertie's bed, holding her hand, waking at the slightest stir.

Unknown to Polly the doctor had given up hope and could not think of what else to do. He said as much to the nurse one evening over Gertie's recumbent form. Gertie, deep in her coma, heard every word he said and, furious at such a defeatist attitude, fought back.

A fortnight into her illness, Gertie opened her eyes, asked how the baby was and slipped into a fitful sleep. The danger was over.

They managed to persuade her to go to a convalescent home in Bournemouth for a fortnight with her nurse to recover. She was back in less than a week. The residents were 'old', she complained, and boring – and they talked when the television was on. This was the last straw. Home was best, she announced, settling into her favourite chair in front of her beloved small screen.

The Queen was crowned. Polly had invited a good

twenty people from the village to watch the ceremony on television at Hurstwood. With so many spectators they had to move the set into the drawing room and arrange the chairs and sofas in rows like a cinema. Gertie sat front row centre, wrapped in a quilt and with her feet up. She watched from first thing in the morning until late at night, every repeat was checked with an eagle eye, 'In case they leave something out,' she informed them, helping herself to the canapés and champagne that Polly had set out for their visitors.

The fact that her grandchild was an Elizabethan seemed to fascinate Gertie more than anything else.

August came and with it, at last, the Korean war was over. Two young men who had worked for Andrew before doing their National Service returned safely. Polly and Andrew gave a large welcome-home party for them in the largest of the barns.

It was one of those perfect nights when everyone was in accord, a pleasant warm evening after a miserable summer. There had been no arguments, no one was terribly drunk, the young mingled with the old and the fiddler played for the dancers as if possessed.

'Mr Slater. Look!' A child from the village had grabbed Andrew by the sleeve and was pulling him towards the door of the barn. Over the tops of the trees in the garden was a bright red glow.

'But we had the bonfire over . . .' Andrew did not finish the sentence. 'Call the fire brigade,' he yelled as, stripping off his jacket, he raced towards the glow, the rest of the party in hot pursuit grabbing buckets and brooms as they ran.

They were too late. Both chicken sheds were too well alight. There was nothing anyone could do. Andrew slumped to the ground, his head in his hands, unable to speak, unable to watch.

Polly found him.

'Oh my poor darling – all that hard work. But we'll start again.' She knelt on the ground on the grass beside him. Andrew turned his face away from her. 'It was an accident. The insurance will pay . . .'

And then Andrew looked at her, his eyes once again full of despair and she knew, without his telling her, that there was no insurance.

Polly stood up with Richard in her arms, the heat from the burning sheds hot on her flesh, and stared ruination in the face.

Part III

Chapter Six

1

The street lights reflected on the film of drizzle that was falling. Despite the weather, the young girl was dawdling through the park. Although it was only fine rain she was rapidly becoming soaked. She appeared to be in no hurry to get home – she never was.

The girl walked with her head bowed as if intent on the sodden leaves in her path. Her shoulders were hunched almost to the point of deformity. With her posture and in her oversized navy-blue raincoat, her thick black stockinged legs in ankle-length boots and her hat pulled low on her head, she could have been a woman of any age. But the satchel clutched closely to her chest showed her to be a schoolgirl.

She paused for a second under one of the lamps which had recently been placed at intervals on the wider paths in the park. She wedged her satchel between her legs, standing knock-kneed so that it did not slip, and removed her spectacles. She breathed on both lenses, wiping them dry with a handkerchief from her pocket. Replacing them on her nose, she peered into the gloom in the direction of the main gate: no one was there. More upright now, she walked towards the gate, adjusting her glasses which had begun to slip down her nose which was glistening with rain. The perfectly round frames were of gilt wire and made her face look equally round. They were the most unattractive style in the National Health Service range; that was why she had chosen them.

A lank strand of hair slipped from under her hat. Again she stopped and wedged her satchel between her knees. Hooking her hat over her arm by its elastic, she quickly removed the band which held back her hair. She retwined the band, catching the loose lock and making a neat ponytail of the fine hair, nearly white in its blondeness. She crammed her hat back in place and, with her satchel once more held tight to her chest like a shield, she went through the gate, turned left and froze. Ten yards along the road was a group of young people. They stood under the street lamp so she could see them clearly. Most had bicycles, some of them leaning against the wall, the owners sat on others their feet firmly planted on the road. One or two, more adept than the rest, balanced without appearing to move. Others sat astride the park wall where the railings had still not been replaced. There were about a dozen of them.

Abruptly the girl turned on her heel and scurried back into the park. Once more with bowed head she walked quickly along the labyrinth of pathways beneath the dripping trees. The bell announcing the closure of the gates began to ring. She knew she had only five minutes to reach the side gate before one of the park keepers locked it for the night.

She was parallel with the group now, but felt secure, shielded as she was by the wall and the thick shrubs between them.

'Annie,' she could hear them calling. 'Annie.' They called in a sing-song way like small children rather than sixth-formers like herself.

'Come on, Annie. Let's see yer.'

'Why don't you come and join us?'

'What we done wrong, Annie?'

'Stuck up cow . . .'

'Annie Budd . . .'

She broke into a run and carried on until she could no longer hear the voices of her tormentors. When she eventually stopped she could feel the breath rasping in her throat. She gulped, forcing herself to calm down, to walk normally.

That had been unfair of them, she thought, standing

where she could not see them, thinking they were going to trap her, making sure she would have to walk past them, giving them the chance to hurl abuse. Her route home was always circuitous for there were several places where the girls from her grammar school met the boys from the boys' school. She had to avoid Watling Street because there was a large gang from the fifth form who met outside the cinema. And she had to cut down side roads, adding to her journey, so as to avoid The Blue Top Coffee Bar crowd. And then there was the group which should have been standing in the gateway of the park, not halfway along the avenue.

When the weather was fine she did not mind the longer walk home for she was never in any hurry to get there. But when it rained, she resented having to go the long way round the park. But she had no choice. Annie doubted if anyone would ever understand what she suffered if she had to walk past any of those boys, aware of the remarks, of their eyes upon her, feeling her flesh burning with shame and embarrassment as she did so.

Annie pulled her mackintosh closer about her as she continued to plod through the rain. In some ways she preferred winter and autumn to spring and summer. As spring approached she would sit in assembly and would feel herself sweating with fear that this morning was the one the headmistress would order them into summer uniform. In the pale cream silk shantung dress, it was harder to disguise her figure. In hot weather, in the pale dress, she would walk with head held even further down, shoulders more hunched, arms clutching her heavy satchel in front of her, anything to hide the feminine form beneath.

The figure beneath the mackintosh was, unfortunately for her, a good one. She had slim hips, a small waist and full, well-rounded breasts. Her face too, if she let anyone see it without the ugly spectacles, was pretty. She was fully aware of her figure and her face and had done everything she could to minimize them. The clothes were easy, the rest had proved difficult. She ate cream buns, too much chocolate, anything unsuitable, in the hopes that it would give her spots and make her fat. But her skin remained perfect and her weight constant, much to Annie's distress, for she longed to be overweight and ugly. If she had been, then she would be able to pass boys and men unnoticed. She was terrified of men – all of them, irrespective of age, colour, looks. She wished she could hate them as well. She had tried hard enough, but memories, vague and misty with time, kept getting in the way of the hatred. She had one strong memory of a kind and gentle man with a beard who had helped her to draw and who smelt of paint. She could not remember his name or who he was, but he must have belonged to Gwenfer. All her best memories came from Gwenfer.

Annie heard the swish of bicycle wheels on the damp leaves and oved quickly to the side of the path. Head averted, eyes downcast, she walked like a woman in purdah.

'Your name's Annie, isn't it? Annie Budd?'

The bicycle halted and her way was barred by a tall youth who sat astride the saddle. His arms had outgrown the sleeves of his jacket and the school cap sat incongruously on his head – incongruous because he was no longer a child even if he wasn't quite a man.

Annie did not answer, but stepped on to the grass, ignoring the 'Keep off' sign, and skirted him and his bicycle. He followed, she could hear the sound of the tyres behind her. She quickened her pace.

'Come on, Annie. Talk to me. I won't hurt you. Why are you so shy?'

Annie walked blindly in the direction of the gate. The bicycle shot from behind her, weaving in an arc across the grass and into the darkness. Annie could feel her shoulders slump with relief as she broke into a run to get to the gate in time.

The park keeper was there holding the gate open for her.

'That was a close shave, miss. You shouldn't cut it so fine.'

'No, I'm sorry.'

'Luckily for you this young man said you were coming along, otherwise you'd have been in trouble.'

'What young man?' She raised her head, looking anxiously to right and left.

'Me, who else? Right little Sir Walter, that's me.' He was grinning at her; she looked away and hurried along the pavement. She stopped at the clatter of the bicycle mounting the kerb and swinging round in front of her.

'Look, Annie, I know you get teased a lot. I'm sorry about that. But I promise you, it hasn't been me. I really want to be friends, honestly.'

Almost imperceptibly Annie's head turned a little towards him.

'Come on . . . won't bite.' He laughed and put his hand out towards her. She lifted her head sufficiently to see his hand. He had long fingers with clean nails, she noticed the nails immediately. The rain was glistening on his hand in the light from the street lamp.

'Can I walk a little way with you?' He cupped his fingers, gently urging her towards him as he would a wild animal. She took a step, but she did not reply. 'I just want to be your friend.'

This time she lifted her head and looked at him. She saw an intelligent face, brown eyes full of humour and a mouth that twitched into a smile.

'My name's Chris.' With practised ease he swung his bicycle around with one hand which he rested lightly on the drop handlebars. The light from his dynamo lamp dimmed as he fell into step beside her. 'I'll walk you to the main road, shall I?'

She nodded reluctantly. He had been in that group, she was sure. Maybe he was sorry, perhaps he really did want to be friends. But how could she ever have a male friend? She shuddered, it wouldn't make sense.

'You cold?' he asked, noticing her shudder. 'A real Sir

Walter would have a coat to lend you, wouldn't he?' He was grinning now.

'I suppose so.'

Chris leapt a couple of feet in the air. 'Success. She speaks,' he shouted. 'What "A" levels are you doing?'

'English, History and Art.'

'Going to university?'

'Art college, I hope.' She looked away with embarrassment, aware she was staring at him.

'I want to be a doctor – Chemistry, Physics and Maths.'

'That's going to be difficult.'

'I'm not worried. I'm brilliant.'

'Oh, I see,' she said quietly, full of admiration for anyone with so much confidence.

'Well, here we are. See you tomorrow?' She nodded. He was on his bicycle and she could see the red light growing smaller as he sped down the hill. Suddenly, and to her surprise, she felt very lonely and she wondered why.

It had begun to rain in earnest now so she walked much faster. Within fifteen minutes she was letting herself through the front door of her home.

'It's only me,' she called out in the direction of the kitchen. She slipped out of her raincoat and hung it on one of the pegs in the passage where it began immediately to drip on to the highly polished linoleum. She frowned as she mopped up the rain from the floor with her hanky, took the coat down again and made along the passage towards the kitchen door. She normally slipped straight up to her room when she entered, on the pretext of work to do. Because of the coat she would be caught in chatter.

'My coat was dripping on to the floor.'

'Dreadful weather. Still, what else can we expect for February? Give it here, I'll hang it with mine. I've put out some newspaper to catch the drips.' Annie's stepmother held out her hand for the coat which she put carefully on a hanger and then hung it up at the back of the door. 'What a size this coat is. You could get two if not three of you in there. Why you always need your clothes several sizes too big beats me,' Doris said.

'It's warmer. Traps the air,' Annie replied. It was the usual excuse she gave.

'So you always say. Want a cuppa?'

'I've got a lot of homework . . .' she began.

'Nonsense. You've got time for a cuppa, surely. They work you too hard, if you want my opinion.' Doris bustled about making the tea.

Annie did not want Doris's opinion. She had never asked her opinion on anything, there was no point. Doris was nice, kind, a good woman, but she was not very bright. Annie knew the woman would have liked to be friends with her but, try as she might, Annie had never been able to think of what to say to her, nor had she felt anything for her in the six years Doris had been her stepmother.

She was a good stepmother, not at all like the ogresses in the story books. She had never shouted at Annie, nor lifted a finger against her. She had cared for her as well as any mother. But that was the crux of the problem: she was not Annie's mother and never could be.

'You'll never guess what happened at work today. Laugh? I thought I was going to blow a gasket.'

'Really?' Annie smiled willingly enough as she accepted the cup of tea in the rose-patterned cup, part of a tea service which was Doris's pride and joy, given to her as a wedding present. It was used every day even if it did mean the odd loss. 'I didn't come through that bloody war without realizing a thing or two. And one thing is, enjoy today. No point in having this nice china and not using it,' Doris was wont to say.

'What was I saying?' Doris asked, settling on the wooden chair and cutting herself a large wedge of fruit cake.

'Something funny happened at work . . .' Annie switched off. She had yet to hear of anything that had happened in the shop where Doris worked part-time that was even halfway amusing. While Doris chattered on, Annie thought.

Annie felt quite sorry for Doris. She did not know her exact age, but Annie doubted whether she were more than twelve years older than herself. And yet her life was set in its boring routine and rituals. Nothing ever happened, nothing was ever likely to happen. Doris's youth and excitement were dead and gone for ever. Annie did not want to live like Doris. She could remember clearly being introduced to her future stepmother. It had been her eleventh birthday and it had not been a success. The failure of the day had been a good week in the making, starting with Annie announcing that she did not want a party and was compounded on the actual day when she refused pointblank to wear the yellow taffeta dress her father had bought her specially.

'Of course you want a party,' her grandmother had said. 'All little girls want parties.'

They had told her she could invite six friends, and Nanny Budd and her Aunt Joy had spent the day before her birthday making buns and jellies and icing the birthday cake. On the day itself they had made sandwiches – a choice of salmon paste or sandwich spread, her grandmother's favourites.

Four o'clock came and went, and no guests. By five the family was sitting dolefully looking at the piles of food, the corners of the sandwiches already beginning to curl.

'Well, where's everyone got to?' said Nanny Budd, looking at the clock for the umpteenth time.

'I didn't invite anyone, Nan,' Annie finally admitted.

'You what?' Her grandmother stood up, pushing back her chair so violently that it toppled over.

'I did tell you I didn't want a party. I meant it,' Annie said in an uninterested tone.

'Why, you ungrateful little cow!' Aunt Joy was on her feet, leaning across the table. 'A good slap, that's what you need. Spoilt you are, and hateful with it.'

Annie looked unblinking at her aunt, a short woman,

prematurely embittered and prematurely fat, whose longing in life was for a man, but for a man who had never materialized.

'I told you. Even yesterday I said don't do all this for me, it won't be necessary. I can't help it if you don't listen.' Annie, even at eleven, spoke to the two women as though they were the children.

'Who the hell do you think you are, speaking to me like that? I could hit you, I really could.' Joy was screaming at her now.

'Hullo, everyone. Are we having a lovely time?' The door was flung open and in the doorway stood Annie's father with a pretty peroxide-blonde woman clinging to his arm. 'Where's everyone?' Stan asked.

'There's no party, the little bitch here didn't invite anyone.'

'What's this, Annie? Why ever not? What made you do a thing like that?'

'I don't like parties. And I don't have any friends.'

'Of course you've got friends, lovely little girl like you.' Stan Budd moved around the large table and Annie backed away from him. 'Come here, Princess. I've got a new friend for you here.' He put out his hand to the young woman who sashayed forward, giggling. 'This is your Aunty Doris.'

'Hullo, Annie.'

'Hullo,' Annie said, standing awkwardly, her hands at her sides.

'Give Aunty Doris a kiss, then.' Her father pushed her in the small of the back. 'Go on, kiss her.'

'I don't want to.' Annie stood firm, her hands clenched now into small fists.

'What a grumpy old thing you are, then, and on your birthday! Sorry about this, Doris girl, but Annie's gone and got the hump.'

'Don't matter, Stan. We'll make friends, I'm sure.' Doris giggled inanely, her red painted lips parting to show nicotine stained teeth.

Nanny Budd fussed over the guest. 'Sit you down. Joy, get that there kettle on. As for miss here, I think you'd best go to your room until you're in a better mood.'

'Oh, come on, Mum, it is her birthday.' Stan smiled placatingly at his mother.

'She's gone too far this time, Stan. I've been worked off my feet all day. She should be punished. This is my table and I decide who sits at it.'

'It's all right, Dad,' Annie said, as she squeezed between the chair and the sideboard on her way to the door.

'Take this then. Can't have my princess starving, not on her birthday.' Stan hastily piled cakes and sandwiches on a plate which he handed to her, giving her a huge conspiratorial wink as he did so.

Annie did not go to her room nor did she eat but sat on the stairs, her elbows on her knees, her chin resting on her hands, and listened to the conversation from the living room, something she often did.

'Well, Mum, since Doris and I are getting wed I can have who I want at my own table,' Stan said pointedly.

'I didn't mean it like that, Stan,' Nanny Budd whined. 'I just felt she should be taught a lesson.'

'Perhaps there's too many of us teaching her lessons. Once Doris and me have got our own place . . .'

'You're not stopping here then? You're more than welcome, Doris. We've got the room, and with you working . . .' Nanny Budd was wheedling now, Annie noticed. She listened without interest, whether she lived here or there was of no consequence to her.

'Your little girl seems a bit shy, Stan.'

'She never got over her poor mother, Doris, that's for sure,' Stan said in the lugubrious tones he reserved for talking about his dead wife.

'Rubbish, Stan, she never even mentions her mother. She's stuck up more like, thinks she's too grand for the likes of us and Clapham. That's why she hardly ever speaks. Shy be blowed!' Joy interjected.

'Poor little mite.' Doris sounded truly shocked at the bitterness in Joy's voice.

'She is stuck up, Doris,' Joy continued staunchly. 'She was evacuated to a big house in the country in the war and got spoilt rotten, she did. It shouldn't have been allowed. Came back here with such highfalutin ideas.'

'Go on, Joy, you're too hard on the kid. Don't listen to her, Doris. My Annie's the sweetest child God put life in. The light of my life she is.'

'It don't help, Doris, but that woman she lived with still writes to her. I've told Stan it should stop, it really should. I think it's sinister. You know she wanted to adopt her if Stan hadn't come back? What does she want with the likes of her? She's got family of her own. It's not natural, that's what I say. What do you think, Doris?'

'Well . . .' Doris sat thinking, quite puffed up with pride that her opinion should be sought. 'Certainly letting your poor mother do all this food for nothing, that wasn't nice – as if she was punishing her for something. If you're going to get her to snap out of it, Stan, you'll have to stop the letters, Joy's right. Write and tell the woman she's not to write to Annie no more,' Doris said sagely.

'There won't be any need for that. When we move from here, I'll just tell Mum to throw the letters away.'

Annie stood up and went to her room. They could try, she thought. Even if she didn't get letters from Alice, they could not stop her writing to her to let her know she was well.

'What you say to that?' Doris's voice, still laughing, burst into Annie's reverie. Annie shook herself, wondering what had made her remember all that after such a long time.

'Very funny,' Annie said, vaguely.

'I thought you'd see the funny side. There, listen, that's your dad and I haven't even started his tea.' Doris leapt to her feet and turned towards the sink into which she emptied a bag of potatoes. 'We're out here, love,' she called.

Stan Budd entered the kitchen. 'Cor, what a night,' he complained, pulling off his greatcoat.

Annie stood up and sidled towards the door.

'You going?' he asked.

'I've got homework to do.'

'Ah, I see. Let your dad give you a kiss then.' He leant his face forward and she moved her head slightly towards him. He kissed her cheek. Annie moved to the door, fumbled with the knob. When she was safely on the other side she leant against the woodwork and shuddered, rubbing forcefully the place on her cheek where his lips had touched her.

2

Annie did not sleep well and during the following day found it difficult to concentrate on her lessons. She was puzzled. All she could think about was Chris. To be so intensely interested in anyone was a new experience for her, that he should also be a boy amounted almost to the miraculous.

The minute she entered the park on the walk home from school she was glancing everywhere, fearing she might miss him. It was not until she had dawdled her way halfway across the park that she saw his bicycle leaning against the bandstand. She slowed down, peering through her spectacles, trying not to appear as though she were looking for him. But she could not see him. She wondered whether to stop and wait a minute, but felt that might seem too forward. Reluctantly, she continued to walk towards the path that led to the smaller side gate. Inexorably the gate came nearer: she had missed him.

'Annie!'

She swung round at the sound of her name. He was pedalling furiously towards her. Reaching her, he cycled round her in large swooping circles. 'I thought I'd missed you.'

'I saw your bicycle,' she said shyly.

'Did you?' Round and round he went, guiding his bicycle nonchalantly with one hand, the other in his pocket. Today his cap, set jauntily on the back of his head, did not look at all incongruous. Watching him she began to feel giddy. 'If you saw my bike, why didn't you come looking for me?'

'I didn't like to,' she replied, finding to her fury that she was blushing. She could have kicked herself. She must be the only girl in her class to blush when talking to a boy.

'Fancy sitting down over there and having a talk?'

'Have we got time?'

'Plenty. I know a way out when the gate's locked.'

'All right then,' she replied, a little unsure. His bicycle whooshed around her again and then shot off across the grass towards a park bench. He leapt off and, using his cap, dusted the seat for her with exaggerated sweeps. 'Fit for the Queen.'

Annie found she was giggling, just like Doris, as she took her seat. But when he sat down beside her she found herself inching along the bench as far away from him as possible without appearing rude.

At first she did not know what to say to him, desperately searching her mind for topics that might be of interest. She was confused; she wanted to keep him here with interesting conversation and yet she wanted him to go.

Ten minutes later she could not imagine why she had felt such confusion. There was so much to talk about, so much they had in common. She had never sat and talked with anyone before who liked exactly the same things. She had never until then experienced that excited feeling of discovering that here was someone else who thought just as she did.

He liked the same poets, but that was just the beginning. He liked the same artists. He had a Toulouse-Lautrec poster on his bedroom wall, but did not much like Van Gogh either. He had enjoyed *Brighton Rock*, hated Jimmy Young . . . the list was endless.

'What about Stan Kenton?' he asked.

'I'm afraid I don't know him,' she said, wishing the ground would swallow her up at having to admit to such ignorance.

'Then you'll have to come round to my place and listen to my records of him. He's the world's greatest.'

'I'd like that,' she said, aware that she could hardly breathe with excitement.

The park keeper's bell had rung a good fifteen minutes before.

'I'd better be going,' he announced, to her disappointment. He led her to the back of the park, past the long rows of greenhouses, past the gardeners' sheds and out to the street. 'See you Monday,' he called and she felt that same desolation as the previous day as she watched the red light on the rear of his bicycle fading as he sped down the hill.

She was glad when she got home to find the house was empty. She had quite forgotten that it was Friday; Doris always went to tea at her sister's in Rochester on Fridays.

Annie made herself a pot of tea and looked in the biscuit barrel for her favourite Garibaldi biscuits. She put the tea and plate of biscuits on to a tray which she carried carefully up to her room. There she took down the latest record she had bought – Yehudi Menuhin playing Beethoven's Violin Concerto. She put it on the turntable. She unpacked her homework, but the books remained unopened. She sat on the bed, oblivious to the music, and thought of Chris.

What was happening was the last thing she had expected to happen to her, of all people. With her fear of men she had resigned herself to a future without a man of her own. The decision had always been one that filled her with sadness, it seemed so unfair that she should feel this way, but she had educated herself to reject the prospect of marriage and children. Yet here she was mooning like any other girl in her class. She hugged herself at the thought.

It was not quite the same, though, she realized that. She did not really think like the other girls, she couldn't. She could remember how horrified she had felt when, as the girls in her class grew older, so their interest in boys developed. As she listened to their conversations, she realized with horror that these girls were discussing and planning and wondering about the very thing that had blighted her life . . . She covered her face with her hands, the book on her lap slipping to the floor. No, it could never be like that with Chris. He was a friend, a friend of the soul, nothing more – ever.

She suddenly remembered her tea and poured herself a cup, grimacing as she tasted it and found it tepid. What if she invited Chris here to listen to records? She would prefer that to having to meet his parents. Annie did not like meeting new people. What if her parents were here, would it be all right to invite him to her room? It was not as if they would do anything, they couldn't, but would her parents believe that?

Annie looked about the room. Certainly there was nothing to be ashamed of here. Her room was perfect, her father had seen to that. They might not have much money, but Annie had never wanted for anything. The room was redecorated every other year, always with the prettiest paper her father could find. The curtains at the window were changed each time to go with the new paper and Doris would spend hours sewing the frills, which Stan insisted upon, on to the bottom of the curtains. The furniture was the best he could afford with a divan, the latest thing in bedding. The desk was brand new and good enough for any office, with an angle poised lamp. The armchair was covered to match the curtains and the dressing table had a frilled white net skirt to it. The wardrobe was crammed with clothes she rarely wore and her bookcase was piled high with books. Annie wanted for nothing, Stan saw to that.

'Fit for a princess, our Annie's room,' Doris would boast. 'Pity she doesn't appreciate it more,' she invariably added with a sniff.

No one else ever saw the room. If Chris came he would be the first. She did not have any girlfriends, she did not dare risk being invited to their homes. It would mean that she would have to invite them here in return, and she couldn't, that was the problem.

The music came to an end and she turned over the record. This time as she sat on the bed she hugged a large misshapen, home-made teddy bear. Her father would have loved to get rid of the bear, to him it was an eyesore that marred the perfection of his little girl's room, but Annie would hear of no such thing.

As she held the bear she had a deep longing to be at Gwenfer with Alice. She frequently had these feelings. They invariably occurred when there was something important in her life which she wanted to discuss with someone, someone who would understand her and whom she could trust – Alice.

There were days when her longing for the woman, and the house, were almost too much to bear. She had assumed that as time went by, the longing would get less, but instead it seemed to get stronger.

She wished she could remember everything far more clearly, but she had only been nine when she left Gwenfer and the memories were fragmented. But what remained was the distinct knowledge that then she had been happy in a world of sunshine and laughter. A clean life and a safe one. Always, safe.

That world had been snatched from her so suddenly. One day she had been happy, safe and loved at Gwenfer, Alice the pivot of her life. The next day the stranger had come. She had approached him willingly enough, for Alice had taught her to be polite to strangers. And he was a handsome man with hair as fair as her own and with blue eyes that twinkled kindly. But she had not expected him to grab her, to hug her to him so tightly that it hurt, to shower her face with kisses and to tell her he was her father. She had not meant to anger him, but she had told the truth when she said she did not want to go with him, that she wanted to stay at Gwenfer: her 'home', she remembered calling it that. It had never crossed her child's mind that there could come a time when she would have to leave this haven, the only home she could remember.

Gwenfer and Alice. She had panicked at the thought of losing them. She had begged and pleaded. She had wept and screamed. She had clung to Alice's skirt in desperation. But it had been Alice who had prised open her small hands and had led her to her father and the waiting taxi. It was a fearful betrayal and there had been a time when she thought she would never be able to forgive Alice's desertion.

The next thing she remembered was the long train journey with this stranger in army uniform who was quickly irritated by her tears. Annie had finally sat silent, thumb in mouth, retreating into her mind as she had done once before. She sat feeling reproachful, unhappy, and far from safe.

That night she had gone to bed in the unfamiliar room of a house she did not know, full of people who were strangers to her, but who insisted that they knew her. They kept kissing her and saying how she had grown, and they all tried to get her to speak. She had lain in the dark, listening to the strange noises of the city, wondering what Alice was thinking, whether she was missing her, noting that there was no smell of lavender as there had been on the sheets at Gwenfer. The door had opened slowly and a shadow had unfolded across the ceiling towards her bed. The shape of a man was silhouetted in the doorway of the room for a second before closing it and stealthily tiptoeing to the side of her bed.

'Now then, let's see what we got here.' Gently he lifted the sheet and blanket back from her body. 'Let's see Annie's little Rosebud then,' said her father.

From that moment Annie knew she had seen the last of happiness. As she recoiled physically, so she recoiled mentally. She became silent and withdrawn in the house that was not her home, with the people who said they loved her and whom she did not want to know – her own family.

This family consisted of her paternal grandparents, her father, and Joy, her unmarried aunt. Joy and her mother worshipped Annie's father, in their eyes he could do no wrong. Annie saw it daily in little acts towards him; the way their faces lit up at the sound of his key in the lock, how they gave him the best slice of meat, the biggest cake, the largest strawberry. As she witnessed this love she knew she could not tell them what was happening to her. They would not have believed her, they would have hated her. Her grandfather was a kindly man, newly retired from the railways, despised by his wife and children, living an isolated life in his own home, ignored in favour of his son. He held out a welcoming hand with longing to Annie, seeing in her the end of his own loneliness. But he was a man and she could not go to him, she could never trust him.

Withdrawn at school and yet of higher than average intelligence, teachers began to wonder what could be the problem with Annie. Annie would watch her teachers and imagine what it would be like to unburden herself to them, to feel the weight of guilt lift off her. But she could not. Her father had warned her of the consequences if she told. Her father was called to the school. He retold the sad tale of his wife's death, of how she had shielded the little Annie with her own body, no doubt sacrificing her own life for that of her child. Tears welled not only in his eyes, but in those of his listeners. Was it any wonder his little girl was as silent as she was, he asked, his head in his hands with despair. The young teacher, straight from college, sympathised. 'How brave that Mr Budd is,' she told her colleagues, 'such a lot he's had to bear.' And wasn't he handsome, in a rather common sort of way, she confided to herself.

Annie's father swamped her with presents. She had the best clothes of any child in her street, the smartest shoes, the best dolls, the finest toys, the latest books. Annie wanted for nothing. She was, as everyone agreed, the luckiest little girl in the street, they all said so . . .

As she thought of the child she had been, Annie clutched the old teddy bear so tight that her knuckles showed white from the effort. Often in the past she had talked to it, telling the toy of her shame and pain. There had been no one else to tell of her unhappiness, her feeling that things were very wrong, fearing that somehow she had been to blame.

Then she had believed everything her father told her. After he married and they moved away from her grandmother's house, he had found her writing to Alice and had taken the letter from her, tearing it into shreds, and had threatened her with the police. He told her that she would go to prison for what she allowed him to do. Was that what she wanted? Stop writing to Alice or else, was the ultimatum. By the time she had learnt the truth it was, she felt, too late to write to Alice, she doubted if she would even remember her.

When she met Doris she had not particularly liked her, but within days of the wedding she could have gone down on her knees and thanked God for her stepmother. Now she was left alone, the night-time visits ceased, but even though he no longer bothered her, she continued to hate her father.

She had passed the scholarship to the grammar school. She worked hard at school, aware that here was the key to escape from her world. Now she was seventeen and she wanted to go to art college. There was no fear that her father would not pay. Whatever his little princess wanted she got, he was proud of boasting to all and sundry. She had two ambitions: to go to art college and never to see her father again.

The scraping of a key in the front door lock brought her

back to the present. She slipped off her bed and ran down the stairs.

'Hullo, Doris,' she called out. She had always called her stepmother by her Christian name even though, at first, they had tried to get her to call her Mother.

Doris looked up with surprise at Annie on the stairs. There was something expectant in her voice. 'You sound excited.'

'I was wondering . . .' Annie followed Doris into the kitchen. 'I was just thinking I might like to invite a friend to tea next weekend. Would you mind?'

'Why on earth should I mind? I wish you brought more friends home.'

'Thanks.' Annie turned towards the door.

'It wouldn't be a boy by any chance, would it?'

Annie felt herself begin to blush. 'Does that make a difference?'

'None whatsoever, provided you don't get up to any hanky panky.'

'Oh, Doris!' Annie rushed from the room, crimson with confusion, and raced up the stairs to her bedroom. She swung open the wardrobe door and wondered what she should wear when Chris came to tea.

3

Having planned what she was going to wear, what they would eat and what they would say to each other, Annie was devastated when, on the way home from school on Monday she did not meet Chris. It was the same on Tuesday and Wednesday. On Wednesday she was almost tempted to do the unthinkable, to approach the gang by the park gate and ask the other boys if he were ill or if they knew where he lived. She didn't; when it came to it, when she saw them standing gossiping with their easy confidence, she had ducked back into the park and the safety of the little-used paths. By Thursday she had given

414

up hope of bumping into him and decided that either he was avoiding her, or she had imagined his interest in the first place.

Dressed as always in the too-big mackintosh, she walked quickly through the park and pretended to herself that she did not care if she never saw him again. She tried to concentrate on what she was planning to write for her English essay. When she heard the swishing of a set of bicycle wheels she realized she was holding her breath. Cycling was banned in the park and he was the only person she had ever seen dare to break the council's rules.

'Hi.'

'Hi.'

'Missed me?' He was grinning.

'Yes.' She was blushing. She wished she could have lied and been blasé, pretending that she did not care whether she saw him or not.

'I've been away.'

'Really,' she said, longing to ask him where, but not liking to appear nosy.

'Newington. My nan died.'

'I'm sorry.'

'I'm not.' He looped his bicycle away in a wide curve. 'I didn't like her,' he said, as he returned.

'Really?'

'Can't you say anything but "really"?'

'I'm sorry. I don't know quite what to say.'

'You could congratulate me for being honest.'

'I do.'

'Do you like your nan?'

'I can't remember. It's ages since I saw her.' She wondered why she lied; she loathed Nanny Budd and always had done.

'Got any brothers or sisters?'

'No.'

'Lucky you.' The bicycle swooped off again and she wished she had the nerve to tell him to stop riding huge rings around her, that it annoyed and unnerved her. 'What about your parents?'

'My mother's dead.'

'God, that must be awful.' He braked and leapt off his bicycle. 'I mean, I couldn't imagine life without my mum.'

'I can't remember her and so I don't even remember what it is I'm missing.'

'What about your dad?'

She stopped walking. She stood, her head on one side, and looked at him. He began to look away, embarrassed by the intensity of her stare.

'I hate him,' she said finally. She surprised herself with the vehemence with which she spoke. 'Hate him,' she repeated, as if unsure she had really said it, disappointed that, having done so, she did not feel any different.

'Join the club,' he grinned. 'I don't know a living soul who likes their old man.'

'Is that so?' she said, surprised and delighted. Having never had anyone close to talk to she had assumed her hatred for her father was unique, that she was alone in her wickedness.

'Let's sit down on our bench.' He leant the bicycle carefully along the back of it and patted the seat beside him.

'I wondered if you would like to come to my place for tea this weekend, bring your Stan Kenton records if you like,' she said shyly, not daring to look at him.

'When?'

'Saturday or Sunday, it's all the same to me.' She congratulated herself then on how nonchalant she sounded, as if inviting people to her house was an everyday occurrence.

'Saturday then. And I'll bring the records. I want you to hear them and at the moment, what with my nan, my mum doesn't like me playing them.'

'Of course not.'

'It's got nothing to do with respect for the dead, she's frightened what the neighbours will say, that's all.'

Annie threw back her head and laughed.

'You know, you're very pretty, especially when you laugh,' Chris said, and it was his turn to blush.

'Me? Don't talk so daft.' She pushed him gently and snorted with derision, but was secretly pleased.

Annie took all Saturday morning to get ready. She cleaned her room so that there was not one speck of dust left. She pressed the dress she had chosen: a jersey wool in royal blue with a polo neck. She baked cakes, made sandwiches and asked Doris if she could borrow her favourite tea cups. Saturday was the ideal day, Doris would be shopping in the High Street all afternoon and her father would be at the football match. They would have the house to themselves until at least five-thirty.

By three she was waiting. She had experimented with her hair, wondering if she should wear it loose. But at the very last moment she had lost her nerve and tied it back into a ponytail again. To her surprise he arrived on time.

'A Grundig! They're the best. Is it your dad's, will he mind us using it?' Chris was fingering the soft grey leather of her record player with admiration.

'No. It's mine, my father gave it to me for Christmas.'

'Fancy swopping dads?' he laughed, slipping a record out of its cover and placing it reverently on the turntable.

'Happily,' she laughed, and busied herself at the table with the tea things. They were in the front room, which was only used at Christmas or on the rare occasions when guests came. It had been a last-minute decision on her part. She had looked at her bed and had known a moment of panic. She could not entertain him in her bedroom, they would be alone in the house. So she had carried the record player and one or two books she wanted him to see down to the front room.

'What records have you got?' he asked, as he carefully read the instruction booklet that Annie had taped to the lid of the record player.

'Mainly classical.'

'Boring.' He pulled a face.

'Yes, they are.' She loathed herself the minute she said it. How could she deny Bach and Beethoven so glibly? 'For some,' she added quickly and felt immeasurably better for doing so. 'Is that a Stan Kenton? Put it on, let's hear it.'

Sitting on the floor, the skirt of her dress spread out around her, she closed her eyes and tried to listen intelligently to the record. But as the complicated modern jazz unfolded, she hated it. The music was repellent to her, a noise she found painful to listen to. With eyes still closed she wondered what on earth to say about it when the record finished.

'You don't like it, do you?'

Annie jumped at how close his voice was. He had been sitting at the other side of the room when they began, now here he was beside her on the rug.

'Your face had such a pained expression, it was awful to watch.' To her relief he was laughing.

'I'm afraid not. Perhaps it's the sort of music you have to listen to lots of times before you can appreciate it. Tea?' she asked brightly.

'No thanks. Would you prefer to put on something you like, then?'

'Please,' she smiled and got quickly to her feet. She selected a Debussy and put the machine on automatic.

'You must have a cake even if you don't want tea. I made them specially.' She gave him a plate and then perched on the edge of the sofa.

'Don't be unfriendly. Come here.' He patted the floor beside him.

'Sandwich?' She pretended to ignore the action.

'No thanks. Smoke?'

'No, I don't,' she said, and wished he didn't, tobacco smoke reminded her of her father.

'Come on, sit here, let's listen to this lovely music together.'

'You like it? I thought you said it was boring.'

'I didn't mean that. I just said it for something to say.'

'I'm so glad,' she almost sighed with relief and gracefully sank to the floor beside him. They sat side by side listening to the music and Annie felt she had never known such contentment before, this was true companionship. She went rigid as she felt his hand touch her shoulder and remained so as she felt him fiddling with the band holding back her hair.

'That's better,' she heard him say, as her hair fell loose about her shoulders. 'You've got such lovely hair,' he said in a whisper.

She turned to face him. 'Chris, I can't . . .' she began, but he silenced her by placing his finger on her lips.

He put up his hands and slowly took her spectacles off. 'I knew it. I just knew you had the most wonderful eyes. Crikey, Annie, you're bloody beautiful, why do you hide it all?'

'I . . .'

But she could not speak, did not want to speak, for he was holding her face cupped in his hands. 'Bloody beautiful,' he repeated, as he leant towards her so that all she was conscious of was his full lips so close to hers and the pounding of her heart.

'You filthy little sod. You dirty tyke. You get your mucky hands off my little girl.'

The door had burst open and her father stood for a second looking at them, then, with a roar like a mad bull, he rushed across the room, lifted Chris by the collar and hauled him to his feet. 'Get out, you scum!' he shouted.

'Dad, what the hell do you think you're doing?' Annie had rushed to the two men and was ineffectually trying to pull her father away from Chris. Stan threw Chris on to the sofa.

'What do you think you were up to? You think me and Doris is stupid? I knew you'd be up to no good.'

'We weren't doing anything,' Annie protested.

'Oh no? Then what did I see with my own eyes but him snogging with you.'

'It wasn't anything,' Annie persisted.

'Look, Mr Budd . . .' Chris was getting to his feet. Stan pushed him back again.

'There's nothing you can say, young man. Pawing my daughter . . .'

'But I wasn't . . .'

'God knows what would have happened if I hadn't come in when I did.'

'Dad, I'll never forgive you for this.'

'Mr Budd . . .' Chris was attempting to stand again and this time took the precaution of twisting round so that the arm of the sofa was between himself and Annie's father.

'Get out. You needn't think I don't know who you are. You molest my daughter again and I'm straight round to see your father, understood? Now get out of my house.'

'Annie . . . ?' Chris looked at Annie helplessly.

'Best go, Chris. *Jusqu'à lundi, d'accord?*' she called, as he slipped out of the door.

'What you say to him?' Stan grabbed her by the arm and twisted her round. 'What you say, you little whore?' He was screaming, his face a mottled puce, his eyes bulging with rage.

'Ha!' Annie laughed, ignoring the pain in her arm. 'I thought I was your little princess. Now I'm a whore.'

'You won't see that boy again, do you understand? I don't want no one messing about with you.'

Annie twisted free from her father. She stood rubbing her wrist where he had held her. 'I'll see him whenever I want, Father. Every day of the week if that suits me.'

'You bloody well won't.'

'I bloody well will. Otherwise, do you know what I'll do? I'll tell Doris and your mother – best of all I'll tell the police, everyone. I'll tell them what a loving father you were. I'll tell them why you don't want anyone else messing with me. I was a child then, now I know and understand everything. You can't fob me off with lies any more. You're an evil, dirty old man – prison's too good

420

for you. This is no threat, I mean it. Now get out of my way, I'm going out.'

4

The two young people met on Monday and every evening after school. The first time she saw him after the incident with her father, Annie was filled with embarrassment, but Chris was surprisingly philosophical.

Each evening they sat on their park bench for half an hour and talked. Several times Chris had tried to kiss her, but Annie could not allow him to, not in the open, not where people could see, not for something as beautiful and precious as a first kiss.

During the whole week she had not spoken to her father once. It was fairly easy not to. She made certain she was in her room when he returned from work and by taking an apple and a piece of cheese up with her she could stay there until they had gone to bed. Then she would steal downstairs to make herself a sandwich. Since she normally avoided her father as much as possible Doris saw nothing strange in her behaviour.

Twice her father had tried to speak to her, tapping on her locked door, and twice she had told him to clear off and leave her alone or else . . . In a way there was a strange satisfaction in it, she realized, it was he who was frightened now, he who lay awake at night sweating with fear. The revenge had been a long time coming; she wished she had done something about it before.

The following Saturday Chris invited her to tea at his house. She felt uneasy as she opened the gate. The house was near the park, a large solid house built between the wars, with deep bay windows and a large garden, far superior to her own terraced house at the bottom end of town. At least she knew she looked fine. She had taken a long time getting ready. She had scraped her hair back so that not a wisp flew free, and she had put on a full red felt skirt with a black polo-neck jumper, black stockings and shoes. It was a strange thing about her father – the clothes he bought her were always fashionable and smart. Even though she was never with him when he bought them, they always fitted. She had taken pleasure in the past by not wearing them, just to annoy him. Now she was taking pleasure in wearing them to meet Chris, something that annoyed him even more.

'You must be Ann,' said the thin, smartly dressed woman who answered the door.

'Annie, actually.' Annie smiled and peered shortsightedly at the woman, wondering if she had made a mistake in not wearing her spectacles.

'Chris has just gone on an errand for me. Do come in.'

The door was held open, Annie stepped in and took off her coat. Mrs Mason looked her up and down from head to toe. If this was done to make Annie feel uncomfortable it had the opposite effect; it put Annie on her mettle. She was led into a large sitting room full of well-stuffed furniture, with French windows through which she had a hazy impression of a lot of trees.

'I'll just go and put the kettle on,' the woman said and the door slammed shut. As soon as she was alone, Annie whipped her glasses out of her handbag and, holding them up to her eyes rather than putting them on, looked quickly about her as if taking her bearings. The room was far grander than she had anticipated, with several good watercolours, a fine radiogram and a chest that Annie, from her time with Alice, recognized as Jacobean. She quickly slipped the spectacles back in her bag as she heard the clatter of a tea trolley coming along the hall. She stepped across and had the door held open in time.

'Why, thank you, Ann,' the woman said with deliberation and Annie felt it better not to correct her.

She was told to sit while the tea was poured with great show and ritual.

'I'm glad we've got these few moments alone, Ann. I'm a little bit worried about Chris.'

'Are you?' Annie said, not sure how she was supposed to respond.

'He has a lot of work to do.'

'Yes, this second-year sixth is hard.'

'He so much wants to be a doctor.'

'So I gather.'

'I hear you hope to go to art college.'

'It's all fixed, provided I get my "A" levels, of course.'

'As it is with Chris. He has a place at University College, provided, of course . . .'

'Oh, Chris will pass, you've no need to worry about him, Mrs Mason. He's so clever.' Annie smiled reassurance.

'That's not quite what I meant, Ann. I feel he should not be bothered at this time . . . he needs to be free of encumbrances, to study . . .'

'I'm not bothering him. And I don't think he regards me as an encumbrance,' Annie said sharply.

'Any girlfriend is likely to be.'

'I'm not his girlfriend, as you put it. We're simply good friends with the same interests.'

'Yes, well . . . these things . . . Ah, Chris, there you are.' Mrs Mason smiled as her son entered the room.

'Hi, Annie. That was a wild goose chase, Mum. They said Dad had picked up the joint this morning and you must have known since you were with him.'

'Oh silly, me.' Mrs Mason laughed genteelly. 'Tea, my darling?'

Annie would have been foolish not to realize she was far from welcome and equally slow not to realize she was not approved of. Despite Chris telling his mother several times that her name was Annie, Mrs Mason continued to call her Ann. 'So much prettier than Annie,' she had fluttered. 'Surely you weren't christened that, were you, Ann?'

'I wasn't christened,' Annie said with satisfaction.

Mrs Mason had quickly ascertained where Annie lived, that her father worked in the dockyard – a word she seemed unable to repeat without a slight shiver – that her step-mother worked, received with another shiver, and that Annie had been born in Clapham, at which the shiver was almost convulsive. By the end of the interrogation Annie had concluded that the woman was a snob, and if she did not like Annie the feeling was entirely mutual. What perplexed and, as the tea progressed, obviously began to annoy Mrs Mason was that Annie did not seem as overawed with the house as she anticipated when Chris had told her where this girl lived. Nor did she seem particularly afraid of Mrs Mason but appeared quite relaxed, as if dealing with an equal. What was more she appeared strangely knowledgeable for one of her upbringing: she was aware of the period of the Jacobean chest, she correctly identified the watercolours as Laura Knights. And when Mrs Mason asked her to be so kind as to pour the tea, while she pretended to rearrange the sandwiches, the girl had without pause poured the tea in first. Her dexterity with the cake fork only added to the puzzle, and Mrs Mason's vexation.

'What do you use on your hair, my dear?' Mrs Mason suddenly asked, like a bolt from the blue.

'My hair? Why, nothing.'

'Annie was born with that fair hair, weren't you Annie?' Chris was glowing with pride.

Mrs Mason said nothing and Annie was convinced she was fighting the urge to sniff, just like Nanny Budd when she showed disapproval. She said nothing but instead stared Mrs Mason straight in the eye until she looked away.

'Your mother doesn't like me,' she said, as Chris walked her home.

'Don't be silly, of course she does.'

'She was trying to catch me out all afternoon. I must have been quite a disappointment to her.' Annie smiled, thanking Alice for all her lessons over the years, knowledge which she had not even been aware she had absorbed until today.

'Why should she do a thing like that?' Chris said defensively.

'She probably thinks I'm not good enough for you.'

'What a load of rubbish. My mum's not like that.' Annie was aware that Chris sounded affronted. Not having a mother it had not crossed her mind that she could not speak her mind about Chris's. Annie made a mental note not to criticize the woman in future, she did not want to antagonize him. Chris stopped walking. 'I don't think I'd better go any further. I don't want to meet your father.'

'I don't care if you meet him.'

'Well, I do. I don't fancy getting beaten up.' He laughed. 'One of these days I'm going to kiss you, Annie Budd. We didn't have any luck today either, did we?'

'No. Your mother makes a good chaperone,' she said, with a smile, unable to resist it. 'See you Monday, then?'

'Fine.' He swung his leg over the saddle of his bike. 'Annie, is that the real colour of your hair?'

'Yes, as a matter of fact it is. Did you doubt me, did you think I was a peroxide blonde?' Annie said, smiling but feeling real anger inside.

'No, of course not. Monday then?'

On Monday Annie was unwell with a sore throat. The doctor was called and although it was nothing serious he gave her some antibiotics and told her to stay off school for the week. Annie was disappointed. She had become used to seeing Chris each day and she missed him. On Thursday a letter arrived from him. There was to be a dance at St Augustine's Youth Club on Saturday, could she come?

Annie's first reaction was blind panic. She had never been to a dance in her life, the only dancing she had done had been at school and since she was tall she had always been made to take the male role. She would be all feet, she would be a laughing stock, she could not possibly go. And yet . . . maybe she could persuade him not to dance. She missed him, she wanted to see him more than anything else.

That evening she wrapped up warmly and slipped out to the telephone box in the next street. She found his number in the book and dialled it. As she pushed the button and the copper coins clattered, she prayed it would be him at the other end. It was his father. There was nothing she could do but leave him a message that she would meet him on Saturday outside St Augustine's church.

Since she was not speaking to her father she did not have to explain anything she was doing on Saturday. She polished her nails, pressed her clothes, had a bath, washed her hair. She did not have to tell Doris either. Doris's sister had gone down with a bad case of flu and Doris had gone to Rochester to look after the children for a couple of days.

At seven Annie was waiting in the dark outside St Augustine's. She stood in the shadows so that nobody would be able to see her, just in case he failed to turn up. Her heart jumped into her mouth as she saw his tall figure striding down the path. She watched him, admiring him and thinking how handsome he was, waiting till the last minute before she took her spectacles off and her world became all hazy again.

'Chris, I'm over here.'

'Annie, I'm so glad you could make it. My father says you were ill.'

'Just a bad throat. It's better now.'

She felt so proud as he linked his arm through hers and led her to the church hall where the Youth Club dance was being held. Inside she went to the Ladies' cloakroom and left her coat. She looked at herself in the large mirror: without her glasses she had to stand close. She had risked a little make-up tonight and was still wondering if it looked all right. She smoothed down the tartan taffeta dress with the white Peter Pan collar, looking slyly at the girls who had followed her, checking if the dress was suitable. She felt a huge relief, her dress was better than all right. She felt far more relaxed as she tripped out to the hallway to find Chris.

'Annie, you look wonderful.' He looked at her admiringly. 'And you've let your hair loose.'

'You seemed to like it that way.'

'You have to be the best-looking girl here, Annie. And that's no exaggeration.'

Annie did not know it was possible to be so happy and still live. The evening sped past in a whirl of foxtrots, waltzes and half a dozen quicksteps. She need not have worried, the dancing lessons at school had stood her in good stead. And she realized that she had been the talking point of the evening. No one could believe that here was shy Annie Budd. She even talked to other girls and they were sweet to her. She began to think that her whole life was changing, that on Monday even school was going to be different.

'Annie, get your coat now. It'll soon be the last waltz and there's always a scrum.'

'Right. I'll meet you back here.'

She weaved her way through the dancers to the Ladies' cloakroom. The coats were in racks, full now since she had come, acting as a barrier between the entrance and where the basins and lavatories were. She gave her ticket to the attendant and waited for her coat.

'You sure you left it?'

'Positive. It's navy blue wool.' Annie leant on the counter while the woman searched.

'You could have knocked me down with a feather when I saw her. Who'd have thought she could look like that?' Annie idly listened to the conversation on the other side of the coats.

'I still think there's something odd about her. I think she's hiding something.'

'What, for goodness sake, Sylvia? You have got an imagination.'

Annie felt her shoulders stiffen; instinctively she knew

they were talking about her. She did not want to listen, but on the other hand found herself almost hypnotized.

'Has Chris won the bet yet?' She heard a third voice ask.

'What bet's that?'

'Didn't you hear? Peter Watts bet him five shillings that he wouldn't get to kiss her within two weeks. And Colin bet him ten shillings he won't get his hands in her knickers before the end of term.' The trio shrieked with laughter. Annie felt herself go ice cold.

'Is this the coat, love?' the attendant was asking.

'Yes. Yes, that's mine,' Annie said automatically. She took the coat and trailing it along behind her walked back into the hall. She barged through the dancers, not saying excuse me, saying nothing. Her myopic eyes focused on Chris talking to a crowd from school. She tapped him on the shoulder. He swung round.

'Here,' she said, grabbing his face in her hands and kissing him full on the lips. 'At least you got the five shillings, sorry about the ten shillings. You bastard!' she screamed.

She turned on her heel and, blinded now by tears as well as her short sight, she blundered across the dance floor, the others making a path for her as she did so. She tripped on the steps leading from the hall, but oblivious to the pain in her ankle ran as fast as she could down the hill.

'Annie.'

'Oh, no,' she groaned. And pushed herself to run faster.

'Annie, stop. Listen.'

She could hear his footsteps pounding up behind her. There was no escape, her high-heeled shoes would not allow her to run faster. She felt his hand on her arm.

'Don't you touch me. I hate you,' she hissed at him.

'Please listen to me. It's not how you think.'

'Oh no? Then you explain it to me. Those girls I overheard didn't even know I was there. Are you telling me they were lying to each other? Why would they make it up?'

428

'I admit that's how it started: it was a bet. I made it the first night I spoke to you. It was just a bit of harmless fun. You were a challenge, you must admit.' He tried grinning at her, but she turned her head away in disgust.

'You amaze me, Chris. I thought you were a decent human being, not the sort who could play games.'

'I wish you'd listen, Annie. It didn't work out like that. As I got to know you everything changed. It's not the bet any more, it's you.'

'You lying bastard.'

'I'm not, Annie. I mean it.'

'How could you be so cruel? How, Chris? I liked you, I really liked you. Do you realize what you've done?'

'I love you, Annie. I do.'

'Don't make it worse. For God's sake, don't patronize me . . .' She twisted out of his reach. 'I never want to speak to you again – ever. Do you understand?'

Chris found himself backing away from the anger in her face, the hatred in her eyes. 'Annie, I'm sorry . . .' he said. But Annie did not stop to listen, she was running pell-mell down the road.

Blinded by her tears she could barely get the key into the lock. She stumbled into the house. The door to the kitchen opened and her father appeared.

'What's happened? Good God, Annie, what's the matter?' He stepped towards her, his face concerned.

'It's nothing. Leave me alone,' she sobbed.

'Come, Annie. Who's upset you like this? Come on, girl. I've just made a pot of tea. You can't go upstairs like this. Come and have a nice cuppa. Tell your dad all about it.'

He took her arm gently and she felt she had no resistance left in her. She allowed him to lead her into the kitchen. He poured her a cup of tea which he loaded heavily with sugar. 'There. You drink that, it'll make you feel a lot better. Was it that Chris?'

She nodded.

'The scum. Snotty-nosed little bugger. I knew he was up to no good. What did he do to you, Princess?'

It was like an avalanche of words. Through the sobs she told of their friendship, her hopes for it, her hopes to make other friends, her need for them. And then she told him of the humiliation of the bets. And then she flung her head onto her arms and sobbed until she ached.

'My poor Princess,' he said soothingly, putting his arm on her shoulder, playing with her hair. 'There, don't carry on so. You'll make that pretty face all ugly and red. Come on.' He put his hand under her chin. 'Look up at Daddy now.' Through her tears she did as he told her. 'Nasty boys,' he said, as he gently rubbed the tears away from her eyes. 'They're all the same, Princess. You should stay with your daddy, I'll look after you.' Slowly he lifted her from the chair so that she was standing in front of him. 'There, there,' he said soothingly, his hands moving slowly to the buttons of her dress. She stood rigid, she felt she could not move, she was in a dark tunnel, walls of pain pressing down upon her, and she felt there was nothing she could do about it. 'There, my little Rosebud,' her father whispered in her ear.

'Rosebud'. The word echoed in her mind. It was the one word that could shake her from her paralysis.

'No!' The word was a scream. 'No.' The scream was more animal than human. 'No!' She pushed him away from her, her face distorted with horror. He followed her across the kitchen. She was at the sink; from the shelf she took a heavy saucepan and with all her strength lifted it and crashed it down on his skull. He crumpled to the floor, groaning. She stood over him, still clutching the pan, poised ready to hit him again. His body twitched and there was silence. Nervously she approached him and checked that he was breathing, but how long before he woke up?

Annie looked wildly about her. She went to the shelf where Doris kept her best cups and saucers. There was an old teapot there, cracked and unused. She shook the lid off, it smashed on the floor. She delved into the teapot and took from it a pile of banknotes. Her mind was racing now, crystal clear. She went from the kitchen and ran to her room. From the top of the wardrobe she took a small case and piled as many clothes into it as she could. From the dressing table she took her Post Office savings book which she pushed into her handbag. Into a duffle bag she stuffed the old and worn teddy-bear.

She ran down the stairs and away from the house, not pausing even to shut the door. She did not stop running until she reached the railway station and there, out of breath and almost incapable of speech, bought a single ticket for the last train to London.

5

Annie was tired. The previous night she had managed little sleep, huddled as she was in the Ladies' waiting room on Victoria Station. In the morning, not thinking clearly, she crossed London to Paddington and found herself buying a ticket for Penzance.

Once on the moving train she began to wonder what she was doing and why. It had not been a sensible decision to go to Cornwall. She could ill afford the fare to a destination so far away and what was she to do when she got there? Work would have been easier to find in London, so would anonymity. In the circumstances, would she have the nerve to search out Alice? Would Alice even remember who she was? She wondered if she had chosen this action because in the back of her mind there was a collection of faded memories of a place where she thought she had been happy. But it was all so long ago now and maybe her memories of happiness were nothing but dreams?

She wondered, almost in passing, if she had killed her father. She found the thought that he might be dead was of supreme indifference to her, nor did she feel any concern about what might happen to her as a result. It was as if the whole incident had happened to another person in another place and time.

During the journey she kept falling asleep from exhaustion, only to be woken at each stop, when the relentless thinking would begin again.

At last the train was approaching Penzance station. Annie, looking out of the window, suddenly pressed her face close against the glass. Appearing to float on a sea tinged pink from the setting sun was the large mass of St Michael's Mount silhouetted against a fiery sky. She remembered that place, she thought excitedly. She remembered visiting it with Alice: the long climb up the hill in the baking sun to reach the house perched on the summit. She clearly recalled what fun the day had been. As the memories materialized – ones she could now acknowledge were real and not dreams – she suddenly felt she was coming home.

The train slowed to a halt. Annie stepped on to the platform as the locomotive subsided in a last hissing burst of steam. So strong was her feeling of homecoming that she looked about her, quite expecting to see Alice or Lady Gertie emerge from the waiting crowd. Such a silly notion, she thought, and began to walk up the long platform, enjoying the feel of the keen wind from the sea on her cheek and smelling the sweet air – familiar memories again.

For some time she wandered aimlessly about the small town, searching for other sights that would jog her memory further. In Market Jew Street she stopped at a café for tea and seeing the saffron cake on display ordered a slice. She remembered the bright-yellow cake from special occasions. As the memories piled up they were like a child's toy bricks building up the past in total clarity.

She took a long time over her tea knowing full well she was delaying making decisions, frightened of Alice's possible rejection of her.

It was dark when she finally emerged from the café, apologizing to the waitress for being the last to leave. At the bus station she discovered she had missed the last bus to Gwenfer by ten minutes.

Glad that she had little luggage, Annie walked up the hill through the town. She wondered, as she walked, if she had been meant to miss the bus, if it were a sign not to go to Gwenfer. She had cleared the town and paused at the crossroads on Mount Misery. Which way should she go? To St Just? Back to Penzance and the night train to London? Or this road, which would take her eventually to Gwenfer?

Annie stood huddled under the signpost trying to make up her mind, knowing she was being irrational. If the circumstances had been different she would quite happily have picked up the telephone to announce her arrival in Penzance and it was probable that she would have heard a welcoming response. Because she was upset she was imagining that Alice had forgotten her. What was more, she was assuming that her father was gravely hurt, but maybe he wasn't. Maybe once she had left the house he had got to his feet, shaken himself and had already made up some plausible story as to why Annie was not there. There was no reason why she should try to hide. Happier now and with a determined stride Annie took the road to Gwenfer.

'Would you like a lift?'

She had been so deep in thought that she had not even noticed the car draw up beside her. Anxiously she peered into the interior, but relaxed on seeing a plump and smiling woman leaning over and opening the door for her.

'I'm going to Gwenfer,' Annie said and smiled back broadly. She was saying the very words she had often dreamt of saying.

'You're in luck. I'm going that way myself.'

Annie settled back in the car seat, half listening to the woman as she talked non-stop. Even though she looked hard out of the window, it was too dark to see where they were, or to recognise any landmarks.

'By the way, I'm Mrs Penrose, my dear,' the woman said after ten minutes of chatter, mainly about the lecture she was on her way to attend at Gwenfer Community Centre.

'My name's Annie Budd.'

The car swerved on to the wrong side of the road. Mrs Penrose righted it.

'Good gracious! I'm sorry about that, but you gave me such a start. Not the Annie Budd? The little evacuee who stayed at Gwenfer?'

'Yes, that's me.' Annie found herself tensing, unsure why Mrs Penrose had reacted so strongly. What did she know? Were there reports about her father in the newspapers?

'Well, I'll be blowed and no mistake. What a lovely surprise. I was your billeting officer in the war – a sad little thing you were, to be sure. Why, Mrs Whitaker will be so pleased to see you.'

'I hope so.' Annie felt the muscles of her body relax. 'She doesn't know I'm coming. I acted on an impulse, you might say.'

'Mrs Whitaker won't mind. She's never been one to stand on ceremony.' In the dark Mrs Penrose looked closely at Annie. 'Are you going to be here long?'

'I don't know.'

'Well, I hope you are. Mrs Whitaker needs a strong girl like you to help her out, that's for sure. Poor woman . . .' Before Annie could ask why, the car ground to a halt. 'I'd take you right down to the house, my dear, but my lecture starts at eight.'

'No, no, Mrs Penrose. I wouldn't think of it, I can easily walk. Thank you for the lift and enjoy the lecture,' she said, climbing out of the car.

As Mrs Penrose's car started down the street, Annie stood a moment getting her bearings. There was the church and the little school she had attended. There were the Ia Blewett Almshouses. Gwenfer was across the scrubland, past the cottages, she was certain; everything was coming back. She set out, the forgotten feel of the cobblestones beneath her shoes. She was tired, but as she crossed the scrub the tiredness began to fade until, when she entered the large gateway, its pillars topped with the stone falcons, and started down the steep drive, she was almost running.

It was dark, the wind was lashing in off the sea, a cold cutting wind, one which she was certain meant a storm was coming. She could hear the sound of large waves booming as they pounded the rocks far below at the end of the valley. She felt exhilarated as she sped, surefooted, down the curving drive. At last, there was Gwenfer. She paused, looking at the great house of granite, lights shining warmly at the mullioned windows. She crossed to the nearest wall and touched the stone as if assuring herself it was real. And then she was running again, past two cars on the driveway, across the terrace and round the corner to the side entrance. The iron latch of the door lifted easily; she pushed, it opened. She had known it would: the doors here were never locked, were always open in welcome. In front of her lay the long stone-flagged corridor, flanked by white walls, with an oak settle halfway along; on the windowsill stood a large copper pot full of dried beech leaves. Annie stood a second – it was exactly as it had always been. This was the comfort of Gwenfer, this was what had brought her here – the overwhelming feeling of permanence and security the house possessed.

Quietly she walked along the corridor towards the door behind which she was sure was the kitchen. That was where she expected to find Alice, for that was where Alice and Gertie had spent most of their time during the war years. There was a sliver of light under the door. She would have liked to creep in, put her hands round Alice's eyes, play the child's game of 'guess who'. But she was afraid it would give Alice a fright, she was afraid she might be too old now for such childish games. Instead she knocked on the door and waited for the familiar voice to tell her to enter. There was no reply.

Gingerly she opened the door. The large room was empty. Annie leant against the door hungrily taking in every detail of the scene. It looked as it had always done. The copper jelly moulds stood in regimented rows on the long dresser. There also were the plates patterned with blue flowers, the kitchen plates they had used every day, unlike the best china. That china was stored in a room called a cupboard, stacked on shelves, each piece separated with crinkly tissue paper. It was next to the silver room where spoons lay in felt-lined boxes and where there was always the nose-tingling smell of polish. The wooden clock on the wall, which had ticked relentlessly towards so many of Annie's bedtimes, still ticked and tocked noisily towards twenty past eight. The huge black and brass range had gone, replaced by a large cream Aga – the only change. The big wheelback chairs stood sentinel on either side of the Aga with the cushions, faded now, worked for Alice and Lady Gertie by May, one of the other evacuees. The blindingly white runner towel with the blue border hung on the door that led to the stillroom and pantries, just as it had always done. On the kitchen table was the debris from the preparations of a meal, on the draining board was a pile of neatly stacked dishes. Alice must be entertaining guests for dinner: first the cars on the driveway, and then all this washing-up.

Annie removed her coat and hung it on the back of the door. She would make Alice really pleased to see her, she thought, as she slipped on a pinafore she found hanging there and turned back to the sink to begin to wash up. From the passage which led to the still room she heard a noise. The door was kicked open and a young girl walked in, laden with a huge basket of vegetables. At the sight of Annie she dropped it with a loud shriek.

'Oh my, who are you? Why you'm gave me a start.'

'I'm sorry. I was looking for Alice,' Annie apologised as

436

she scuttled around the floor collecting the fallen vegetables.

'Mrs Whitaker to you, if you don't mind,' the girl said in a shocked tone.

'Yes, of course. Mrs Whitaker,' Annie replied, flustered, remembering the fuss Juniper had made at her calling Alice by her name.

'Her'll be through in a minute. Her's serving the pudding.'

'Oh, I see.' The vegetables retrieved, Annie returned to the washing-up.

'That be kind of 'ee, doing that there washing-up.'

'While I'm waiting . . .' Annie shrugged her shoulders. 'By the way, my name's Annie Budd. You don't know if there have been any telephone calls about me?' As soon as she said it she wished she had said 'for' rather than 'about'. The latter word, she felt sure, would alert this girl to her being a runaway.

'Not as I know. I'm Rose Penrose.'

Annie wiped her damp hands on the pinafore and they solemnly shook hands.

'A Mrs Penrose gave me a lift from Penzance – a nice lady. Is she perhaps a relation of yours?'

'Cor love 'ee, there be hundreds of we Penroses hereabouts. Maybe her was, and then maybe her weren't.'

The door opened and an elderly woman came in carrying a tray. Her hair, which was completely white, was neatly pleated at the back. Her carriage was rigid, that of a person in pain from arthritis, but who will not give in to it. Her face bore more lines than the last time Annie had seen her and her eyes had an expression of extreme sadness.

'Have you laid the coffee tray, Rose? I think I can persuade them to have it in the drawing room, then we can get the dining room cleared and you can be off.' She looked up as she placed the tray on the table. 'I'm so sorry, I didn't see we had a visitor.' She peered towards the sink where Annie stood, her face half in shadow. She

437

wished the whole of her was in shadow now. This was the moment she dreaded.

'Surely, it's . . .' Alice took a step towards her. 'It's Annie. You're Annie Budd,' Alice's voice rang out with pleasure. 'Oh, please, say you're Annie.' Alice advanced with hands stretched out in welcome.

Annie had to fight an almost uncontrollable urge to cry, to bury her head on Alice's shoulder and let her deal with everything for her. 'Yes, I'm Annie,' she said, her voice stilted with a control she knew she could easily lose.

Alice moved quickly, taking Annie into her arms and holding her close. 'Oh Annie, what a wonderful surprise. I can't tell you how many times I've dreamt of this moment. I've missed you so . . .Oh Rose, this is so exciting. Young Annie here lived with me in the war. And she's come home . . . I can't believe it. Have you eaten, are you hungry?'

Annie laughed. 'You were always like that, worrying about our stomachs. I had some saffron cake in Penzance.'

'Not enough for a young woman like you. You've grown so tall, look at you.' Alice's voice was brimming with pride. 'We've some pie left – you used to love my pies, once Lady Gertie had got you over your fads and fancies. Rose, get Annie some pie, there's a dear. You look tired, Annie, desperately tired.' Alice frowned, aware that there was more than tiredness in Annie's expression. Her hand moved to the pearls at her neck and she began to twist them. 'Have you come a long way?'

'From Chatham.'

'In one day?'

'No, I left yesterday. I slept the night at Victoria Station.'

'Oh, Annie, what a silly thing to do. You could have been attacked, anything could have happened to you.' Alice's hand went back to her neck, fingering her pearls. Annie remembered the gesture so well.

'Ah, here's Rose with the pie. You eat, I'll just take the coffee through and then we can really talk.'

As Alice left the room, Rose set a plate in front of Annie. 'It's still warm. Do you want me to heat it up more?'

'No, that'll be fine. To tell you the truth, Rose, I don't really want anything.'

'You'd best eat it up, Mrs Whitaker will fret else.'

By the time Alice returned, Annie had finished the meat pie and was now eating a bowl of stewed apples and custard.

'At least there doesn't appear to be anything wrong with your appetite,' Alice said, smiling. 'Rose, I think it would be best if you went home now. It's beginning to blow up out there. I'll manage here.'

'There's an awful lot to do and I haven't started on they saucepans.'

'Never you mind, I've got Annie to help me.'

'You want me in for breakfasts?' Rose asked, as she struggled into her coat.

'I don't think so, Rose. There are only three guests.'

'Right then. Well, goodnight, Mrs Whitaker and Annie.' She paused at the doorway. 'Now you sure you'm all right?'

'Perfectly, Rose. Thank you.'

Alice got two cups and poured them both coffee from the pot on the Aga. She crossed to the dresser, opened one of the cupboards and took out a bottle of port. She took down two glasses and returned to the table.

'You look as if you could do with this.' Alice carefully poured the port. 'A habit left over from the good old days with Lady Gertie. I presume you're old enough to drink legally?'

'I'm not eighteen until June.'

'Annie nearly eighteen. How time flies.' Alice sat down at the table. 'So, what's happened? Do you want to talk to me about it?' she said, seriously.

'Alice, I thought I did . . . I thought that was why I had

come here . . . but I can't . . . not yet.' Annie looked away, feeling the heat on her skin, knowing she blushed. She had wanted to tell someone and that person was Alice, but now she found she was too ashamed, could not tell, maybe would never tell.

'Very well. When you want to, when you think I can be of help, I shall be here.'

There was a light tap on the door. Alice, tutting with annoyance, levered herself up and crossed to the door, opening it a little way so that whoever was knocking should not see the muddle in the kitchen.

'Yes, Mr Thornton?'

'I wonder if my wife could have a hot-water bottle? She feels the cold so.'

'She'll find one in her bed, Mr Thornton, and should it have cooled too much for her liking, just ring the bell and I'll bring you a hotter one.'

'I'm so sorry to bother you, Mrs Whitaker.'

'Not at all, Mr Thornton, it's what I'm here for.' Alice smiled sweetly as she closed the door. 'I do so enjoy it when I've pre-empted their requests, so silly of me,' she chuckled, crossing back to the table.

'What's going on, Alice? Who was that man?' Annie asked, puzzled.

'Of course, you don't know, do you? I run a guest house here, now.'

'Gwenfer? I don't believe it.'

'Neither could I at first. But I needed to make some money. The only way I knew was by cooking and turning my home over to the public.'

'But when?'

'I started in the spring of nineteen-fifty-two – two years ago. It was slow the first year. But last summer was wonderful, I was fully booked for most of the season. And as you see, it's only late March and yet I've got guests. I never turn anyone away, mind you.'

'But it must be hard work . . . I mean . . .'

'At my age? Is that what you wanted to say?' Alice

laughed. 'When necessity bites it's amazing how one can forget one's aches and pains. I'm as fit as a flea. I've got dear Rose, who helps me in the evenings and early mornings, and there are two women who come in for the beds and cleaning. I do the cooking and serving mainly.'

'You're wonderful, Alice. There aren't many ladies of your background who would knuckle down like this.'

'Oh, you'd be surprised, we're a hardy breed, we Victorians. And I have a distinct advantage over anyone else, I'm a daughter of this granite land. It gives us a strength denied to others, you see.' Alice laughed lightly.

'Can I stay?' Annie asked, her face strained with worry.

'Of course, my dear Annie, For as long as you like.'

'I'll help you.'

'That's very kind of you, I should like that.'

'Where's Juniper? What does she say about all this?'

'She doesn't know. She's living in Greece. She wrote to me some time ago; some busybody was interfering, saying I had opened a boarding house. I wrote back and said I was fine and had had rather a lot of friends to stay. I don't want her to worry. Luckily she believed me.'

'Can't she help?' Annie asked.

'No, I never asked her. I'm sure she would if she knew,' Alice said, in the tone of voice that warned her listener she did not wish the subject pursued further.

The two women sat late into the night talking. When they finally went to bed, Alice felt happier than she had for some time. With Annie here, she had companionship, someone to turn to, someone who loved the house as she did. She had made light of how fit she was. She was seventy-nine, and tired. There were days when she did not know where she found the energy to get out of bed, let alone be polite to her guests and cook for them. It would be wonderful to have Annie, young and strong, to rely on, she thought. And how strange that she did not mind Annie knowing of her predicament and yet would go to any lengths to prevent Juniper knowing. But Juniper had financial worries enough of her own without burdening her with her own was her last thought as she drifted to sleep.

In her room Annie was lying in the bed grinning at the ceiling, she could not stop. She was home, that was what this place was to her, her real home. She burrowed her head in the pillow, inhaling deeply the scent of lavender she had known would be there. It was a good job she had come: Alice looked so tired. What was Juniper thinking about, letting her grandmother toil like this at her age? It was disgusting. But then Juniper only ever thought of herself. Annie realized that while she had been thinking of Juniper the grin had disappeared from her face.

6

How Alice had managed before she arrived was a mystery to Annie. As the weeks and months passed Annie's respect for Alice grew. She herself was eighteen, she was fit and she was agile, yet most days she found herself tired out. Annie quickly found that running the guest house was hard work. At first she went to bed every night with throbbing feet, aching calves, frequently a headache and her patience in tatters from dealing with guests who were invariably demanding in their requirements. Annie had to force herself to be polite to them and she could only marvel at Alice's smiling and gracious patience.

At the outset Rose Penrose had been rather suspicious of Annie. Annie assumed it was jealousy, that Rose resented anyone else usurping her position with Alice. She was wrong. The suspicion was caused by Rose's wanting to protect Alice from someone she feared might use her mistress. As the days slipped into weeks and Annie continued to work as hard as ever, Rose relaxed and, on Annie's eighteenth birthday in June, it was she who had made the most fuss.

Alice had been adamant right from the start that Annie must have a wage.

'Just my keep, Alice. I don't want anything else,' Annie had argued.

'Nonsense. Never undervalue your worth, Annie, no matter what it is you're doing. If you work for me and refuse to take a wage, how can I ask you to do things, perhaps tasks that none of us likes particularly? No, I'm sorry, either you take a wage, or you can't work here. Of course you can stay, I don't mean you should leave . . .' Alice added hurriedly.

'I don't like doing it. I feel I owe you so much. But, if you insist, there doesn't seem much I can do about it.' Annie smiled as she looked at the determined set of Alice's shoulders; when she sat like that no one could win the argument.

The season was a success. The house had been full of guests for the majority of the summer. Since the only other local place which sold food was the pub in the village, whose pies, once eaten, were never requested again, all their guests booked in for dinner and they had begun to take bookings from people staying elsewhere. Given her success and her growing reputation as a cook, Alice was seriously considering applying for a licence so that she could serve wine with her excellent food.

Despite the hard work and long hours, as the money flowed in Annie could see Alice relax, the sad expression beginning to disappear. One day in late autumn, Alice called Annie into the small parlour which she had kept as her private sitting room and office. On the table stood a half-bottle of champagne and two glasses.

'I'm not sure if the champagne will be any good. It was laid down by my first husband. Do you know how long champagne lasts, Annie?' Alice asked, as she carefully uncorked the bottle.

'It's not the sort of information you pick up in my part of Chatham.' Annie grinned as she accepted the glass. 'What are we celebrating?'

Alice held her glass aloft. 'To the end of debt,' she said triumphantly.

'No debts.' Annie raised her glass. She took a sip.

'What do you think?' Alice asked anxiously.

'It's very nice. I'm not sure if it tastes much like champagne, are you?'

'No, but I should think it gets one just as tiddly.' Alice was giggling already.

'May I be rude and ask what debts we're drinking to?'

'I shouldn't have said that, but unless I tell you, you'll worry unnecessarily. When Juniper was last here she decided to come to live here permanently. She also had a plan to open up the mines. Everyone told her it would be no use, that she would be throwing money away. When she went to Greece – on holiday, you understand, she didn't mean to settle there, I'm sure – she left the engineers and men working in the mine. They had to be paid, of course and, well, you know Juniper, she obviously forgot all about their fees.'

'You're not going to say you paid them, Alice?' Annie said aghast.

'I had to. The men were dependent upon me. I sold my house in London, but it wasn't enough to meet all the bills and the debts I'd already accrued on Gwenfer. My allowance had long ago ceased to cover my expenses. There was nothing for it but to borrow from the bank – though I'm sure my late husbands would have been horrified. And to repay the bank, I decided to do this. There was no other way for me to earn money.'

'But why didn't you contact Juniper?'

'I couldn't. I wasn't sure of her situation and she was happy. For the first time in years she was deliriously happy – it was in her letters, it sprang from the page. I couldn't spoil it with silly old money worries. The bank have been kind to me and I've really enjoyed what I do. This house was far too big for one person to live in, it should be shared with others. But now I've repaid all the money to the bank and for the first time in ages, it seems, I feel quite lightheaded and deliriously happy myself. And next year we need not work as hard. Isn't that wonderful news?'

'Juniper doesn't deserve you,' Annie said, before she had given herself time to think.

'You don't know all the facts,' Alice said sharply and, since she never normally spoke in such a tone, the effect was far more dramatic.

'I'm sorry, Alice. It's none of my business.'

'Quite.' Alice said, thin-lipped with disapproval.

A week later the Atlantic unleashed one of its worst storms at Gwenfer. The sea was whipped into a white frenzy, the spray leaping up the jagged sides of the cliff. The wind assailed the old house viciously. Sleep was out of the question and when, in the middle of the night, there was a loud crash of masonry, both women feared the whole house was about to fall around their ears. In the first light of morning, the two women looked out and were appalled at the devastation. The driveway was strewn with balustrading from the top of the house. There was also a large hole in the roof where a huge section had been blown away.

Alice and Annie stood huddled in their coats, scarves round their heads, amongst the debris and the broken branches of trees.

'Oh Alice, it looks bad. The poor house. Still the insurance will pay for it, won't it?' Annie said, trying to see things in the brightest light.

Alice said nothing for some time. 'There is no insurance. I couldn't afford it,' Alice said in a quiet voice, so quiet that Annie had to strain to hear it.

'Oh dear. What do we do then? It'll have to be mended, the rain'll get in.'

'You bitch!'

Annie swung round with an astonished expression, not believing her ears at such language from Alice and wondering what she had said to cause such an unprecedented outburst.

'You greedy bitch, what more do you want of me?'

Alice was screaming and shaking her fist at the house, her face distorted with rage.

'Alice, please . . .' Annie said ineffectually. She tried to take Alice's hand to calm her, but she shook it away.

'I thought everything was going to be all right. I thought she was protected now. I thought I was free of worry and debt – and now she's done this to me. Why?' Alice appealed to Annie. 'How could she?'

'Alice, I don't understand,' Annie said, perplexed, not knowing what Alice was talking about.

'The house, that's who I mean. She's the cruellest mistress in the land. My stone mistress, I long ago learned to call her. She demands everything from me, every last penny, every last effort . . .' And to Annie's horror, Alice began to scream at the house as the wind whirled about her and the house, as if laughing at her and dancing triumphantly at the damage it had achieved.

The bank was consulted again. Further money was borrowed. The repairs began. Alice would have to continue to work hard for many years to come.

'Annie, shall we go for a walk?'

Annie looked up from the book she was reading. It was January and cold and bitter for this part of the world. It was too early in the season for guests and they were sitting comfortably in Alice's parlour in front of a large fire. The last thing Annie wanted to do was to leave the warmth and comfort and go for a walk. She looked at Alice quizzically.

'We should get out more while we have the opportunity,' Alice said briskly, as if reading Annie's thoughts. 'In any case I always seem to think better in the fresh air.'

Reluctantly Annie went to her room to kit herself out with gloves, scarves and a woollen hat as well as her coat. She met an equally well wrapped-up Alice in the hall.

Once they were walking they forgot the cold as they climbed up the steep drive. They walked the cliff path for a couple of miles and then turned back towards Gwenfer.

The whole way Alice walked in silence, head down in deep thought. Annie trudged along beside her wondering what it was Alice wanted to think about and why she had insisted on her coming. As they returned to the house, Annie turned to go inside, but Alice went the opposite way to the steps that led to the valley.

'I need to talk to you about something, Annie. Would you be patient with me a little longer?'

Annie, who could never refuse Alice anything, forgot the fire, the crumpets she had planned and the steaming cups of tea, and followed Alice down the valley. She knew where they were going, to the large rock at the entrance of the cove, Ia's Rock, Alice called it. It must be something serious, for this was where Alice always came when she had things to think about, problems to solve. Annie began to feel apprehensive as they settled themselves on the rock.

'I fear I'm being dreadfully selfish, Annie. It's wonderful to have you here and helping me, but I don't think you should stay any longer.'

'But, Alice, you need me,' Annie protested.

Alice smiled at her. 'What I need is irrelevant. We must think about you. You have such artistic talent. I think you should finish your education and go to art college. You can't waste time helping an old woman run a guest house, you're far too clever for that.'

'You don't want me here any more?' Annie felt her face stiffen. She had not expected this. She had imagined she would stay here for ever now, that she was safe.

'No, that's not what I said. I'm thinking of your future. I am aware that you're happy here and for the time being want nothing more. But what about the future? What about when you wake up one morning and see all the time you've lost? What then? You might be angry with me because I didn't point out to you what you should be doing. You might resent the lost years spent here.'

'No. I'd never do or think any such thing. I'm not a child any more, Alice. I know what I'm doing and why. I

447

need to be here, I don't just *want* to be. I couldn't go out into that world. I'm not ready for it and if you make me, then I don't know what would happen.'

'Oh come, Annie. You sound so melodramatic. You're the most stable young woman I've ever known.'

'Maybe you don't know me then,' Annie said quietly, so that Alice did not hear.

'Of course I'm happy for you to stay here and you could finish your education in Penzance.'

'And live on what?' Annie managed a wintry smile.

'Perhaps if we wrote to your father. The fact is, Annie, I've been worried that you've not been in touch with him and I feel you should. He must be very worried as to your whereabouts.'

'No.'

'Then let him help with your education.'

'No. I don't want to accept another penny from that man,' Annie said, her voice rising with panic. She gazed out over the sea feeling the old fears and resentment rise again. 'I hate him. He's not my father any more.' Annie turned and looked at Alice who was horrified by the desperation she saw in the young woman's face. 'You don't understand, Alice, I tried to kill him.'

Alice gasped and looked at Annie, shock etched on her face. 'Kill him? Your own father?'

'You see now why I can hardly ask him to help me, even if I wanted to.'

'But why, Annie? I don't understand. Did you argue, young people often argue with their parents . . .'

'Nothing like that. I think I want to tell you now, Alice. I think perhaps I should.' And she began.

Once started it was as if nothing and no one could stop Annie talking. The words poured out as, to Alice's mounting distress, she told of her first night away from Gwenfer and of the subsequent nights until the arrival of her stepmother rescued her. Alice sat in shocked silence as the tale unfolded. She felt her flesh creep with horror, she felt anger as she had never experienced it in her life before, and she felt tears on her cheeks for the lost innocence of this child so dear to her.

'But why didn't you tell anyone? Your teachers, your grandmother, the vicar? There must have been someone you felt you could trust?' Alice eventually said when Annie had stopped talking and sat slumped back against the rock as if she had no energy left in her. Annie laughed, a strange little laugh, full of irony.

'I couldn't. You told me not to.'

'I what? What do you mean Annie? I was hundreds of miles away.'

'When you argued with Lady Gertie, you told me then. You said, "Loyalty to your family is the most important thing. You must protect them at all cost." That's what you said, Alice, when we were feeding the birds in Trafalgar Square. Don't you remember?'

'Oh, my God, Annie. Oh, my dear God.' And Alice looked aghast at Annie. 'But not this, I didn't mean you should hide all this. I'm so sorry, please forgive me.'

'There's nothing to forgive, Alice. I was a child and as a child I misunderstood. Your words stuck in my mind. And then, by the time I was old enough to understand how evil he was, he stopped bothering me. Until my last night in his house. He started again and I tried to kill him.'

'But you didn't, you couldn't have, we'd have heard – the newspapers, the police. They would have searched for you, I'm sure . . .'

'The worst thing was, I found it didn't matter to me if I had killed him. I really frightened myself thinking like that.'

'I should like to see the police informed, have him arrested and sent to prison.'

'No, it's all over and buried in the past. I've resolved I shall never see him again. And my stepmother was kind to me, I'd hate to see her hurt and humiliated.'

'Perhaps I could help with your studies . . . ?'

'Oh yes, how?' Annie was really laughing now. 'Alice,

you're so sweet, with all your problems . . . How would you pay for me? Take in washing on top of everything else? That would make me feel wonderful.'

'I feel so inadequate.'

Annie leant over and kissed Alice gently on the cheek. 'That's not a fair thing to say about yourself. But can I stay now? You do see my position. And I'm happy here, I enjoy knowing I'm useful to you.'

'Dear Annie. I have to admit I'd been dreading this conversation. I feared that perhaps you were staying because you felt sorry for me. How I was to manage without you, I just did not know. It was something I preferred not to think about.'

'Now you needn't give it a thought.' Annie squeezed her hand.

'No, but I wish the circumstances, for you, were different. But, at least out of all your suffering, we have each other.' Alice sighed. 'Oh look, the sun will be setting soon. Perhaps tonight we'll see the green flash. Let's wait.' And Alice put her arm around Annie's shoulders and held her close, feeling the love she had always had for her since that first day. She wished there was some way she could erase the past for her and she vowed to protect Annie from all harm for as long as she was permitted to live.

7

Juniper lay on the silk-cushioned sofa idly leafing through a magazine. By her side was a glass of champagne, in her hand a long ebony cigarette holder. 'Rock Around the Clock' was booming out of the radiogram. The record stopped spinning. Suddenly she sat bolt upright, the ash from her cigarette cascading down the front of the white pyjama suit she was wearing.

'Come here quickly,' she shouted excitedly.

From the bathroom came a muffled response, taps were turned on and water gushed. Juniper turned back to the magazine and studied the illustrated advertisement with interest. She stubbed out her cigarette and lit another one. 'Did you hear?' she called, her voice full of exasperation. He was always so long in the bathroom, she was sure he spent more time there than she did. What he did in the bathroom once he had bathed was a mystery to her. He had a beard so he did not even need time to shave.

Juniper lazily slipped her legs off the sofa and went towards the bathroom. She opened the door without knocking. Jonathan was sitting on the bath stool reading a book.

'Is this what you spend all your time doing in here?' she asked. Her voice was light enough, but those who knew her well would have identified a slight edge to it.

'Getting away from you and that infernal music, if you must know.' Jonathan grinned back.

'The trouble with you, Jonathan, is that when you make little jokes like that you're invariably speaking the truth. Look . . .' She handed him the copy of *Country Life*. 'Isn't that awful?'

Jonathan took the magazine in one hand and with the other kept one finger marking the place he had reached in his book. Juniper noted the gesture with irritation. It was rude, she had told him time and again. It was a sign that she was being allotted only a moment of his time, that he was eager to return to the book as soon as possible.

'Poor Polly, she must be devastated,' he said finally, when he had read the copy and had handed the magazine back to Juniper.

'We must do something.'

'What?'

'Give her money, of course, so that she doesn't have to sell Hurstwood. She adores that house.'

'I know she does, but I doubt if giving her money is likely to help. If they're selling, then it means they're in a serious mess. They've probably mortgaged the house up to the hilt and now the banks are calling the money in. So any money you gave them would be gobbled up by the bank. It's a pretty house, though. They will have no trouble selling it.'

'But it would kill her, Jonathan,' Juniper protested.

'Do you really think that Polly would accept any money from you? She must have heard about us.'

'That's ancient history, don't be so silly. She's happily married, everyone knows that. She adores Andrew and obviously loved him far more than she loved you, otherwise you'd be the one selling the house, poor as a church mouse, and not here with me, wouldn't you?'

'Miaow . . .' Jonathan stood up, carefully putting a bookmark into place and closing his book with the resigned expression of someone who knows he is not going to be able to return to it for some time.

'You really would rather read your stuffy books than talk to me, wouldn't you?'

'Juniper, that's not fair.'

'Isn't it? If it weren't for Maddie I'd have gone mad this past couple of years. You've always got your nose in a beastly book.' She spoke sharply. For some reason, ever since they had arrived she had felt edgy and bad-tempered.

'Well, I've put it away now. Where are we having lunch?'

'I thought the Ivy?'

'Fine by me. Is that the telephone?'

Juniper ran ahead of him to take the call, her face alight with interest. The expression on her face changed as she listened.

'It's your agent,' she said sulkily, handing him the instrument.

'Peter, hullo . . .'

As Jonathan began his conversation Juniper drifted into the bedroom of their suite. In the dressing room she studied the rows of clothes and wondered if they weren't all a mistake. On the island she had evolved her own style of dressing, which had looked right there, but she was not so sure now. This was the first time she had been back in

London for three years. They had travelled extensively – India, Malaya, Indonesia, Japan, but always East, never West. It had all been fascinating and necessary for Jonathan's research. Juniper had collected so many artefacts for her house that she had had to enlarge it by several rooms. There had been times, though, when she had longed to be back in London or New York. Her enthusiasm for her business had waned as did so many of Juniper's passions. With her affairs now in the hands of trusted advisers there was less reason to make frequent trips across the Atlantic. She had never let Jonathan know she yearned for her old haunts, not since he had announced one evening that he never wanted to live in the West again. And Juniper needed Jonathan; she had quickly realized that. She could not survive alone, and she dreaded that he might one day leave her for someone younger, someone more in tune with his writing. She knew that it was her fault his book was late – it should have been published a couple of years ago – but she was jealous of his writing. She felt her money did not tie Jonathan to her as it had tied others. He'd never seemed to be interested in it. Provided he had his typewriter, paper, a bottle of wine and pipe tobacco, he frequently told her, he was content. In the beginning, Juniper had found his disregard for her money attractive, it had made him different from other men. But now she wished it mattered more to him: she wanted him to need her too.

Juniper picked out a black jacket with large bell shaped sleeves and heavily embroidered in green and scarlet, which she had found in Belgrade. She held it up against herself and studied her reflection. A small pied-à-terre in London would be nice. Surely Jonathan would welcome that; it would not be returning to live full-time in the West. She could always suggest it and say how convenient it would be for him to have a base close to his publishers.

She looked up as Maddie quietly entered the room.

'Maddie, do you think I shall look a complete fool if I wear this to the Ivy?'

'I don't even know what the Ivy is, but if it's a posh restaurant, then I think you'll be a smash hit.'

'Really?'

'Yes, I've just got back from Bond Street – your necklace will be ready in a week, by the way, they said at Asprey's – I think the women all look the same, no originality, not like you.'

'Very well then. On your head be it.' Juniper slipped on the black velvet jodhpurs and the Yugoslav jacket. Maddie helped her into the highly polished black riding boots from Hermès. 'Hat?'

'Yes. The black floppy beret.' Maddie dug it out from the hat box on top of the cupboard and twitched it into place. 'There.' She stepped back to study the effect. 'You look bloody wonderful,' she said with genuine admiration.

'Are you sure you don't want to come out to lunch?' Juniper asked.

'No, honestly. I want to save myself for tonight. I'm going to spend the afternoon doing my nails and hair.'

'Don't get too excited. Launch parties for books are bound to be dreary. Just think how boring all those writers and publishing types were who visited Jonathan on the island. It'll be like that, only worse – hundreds of them instead of ones and twos.'

'Crikey. Nothing could be worse,' Maddie said, pulling a face at the memory of endless evenings spent listening to the conversation of Jonathan and his friends, devoid of even a smidgen of interesting gossip to lighten it.

'You could do me a great favour, Maddie. There's a *Country Life* magazine in the sitting room. You'll see a house called Hurstwood, about halfway through the advertisements. Could you call the agents and ask them to send round details by messenger, but to you, not me. Whatever you do, don't mention my name.'

'You're buying another house, then? In England? That would be super,' Maddie said with feeling. She liked Greece and nothing would make her leave Juniper now, but there were times when her longing for England was almost painful.

Juniper ignored the question. 'When it appears you've had time to study the details, telephone and make a provisional booking to view the house, using your name again. We can go on Saturday afternoon on our way to Cornwall.'

'We are going to Cornwall, then?'

'I have to. My poor grandmother will begin to feel I don't love her. And I'd like to be at Gwenfer for a while, I've things to think about. Could you call and tell my grandmother we'll be arriving on Sunday?'

'Can't you do it. Juniper? Shouldn't you speak to her yourself?' Maddie said in her usual forthright fashion.

'I will, I will. Don't nag me. I just want her to have plenty of warning and I'm already late for our luncheon. Do it, there's an, angel, please. Tell her I'll call later. Must fly . . .'

Juniper was not too happy when they arrived at the Ivy to find Peter Quilt, Jonathan's agent, waiting for them. From the sheepish expression on Jonathan's face, he had obviously invited Peter deliberately, although he had known Juniper wanted time alone with him before the fuss with the press began.

'Peter, dear,' she kissed the air either side of his cheeks. 'What a wonderful surprise.'

'Kind of you to invite me,' Peter beamed.

'Wasn't it?' Juniper smiled sweetly and, smiling brightly at the waiter, ordered her drink.

Maddie had been right, she thought, noticing the admiring glances directed at her, the clothes did work in London. She basked in the pleasant awareness of being the centre of attention and began to feel less scratchy.

'I'm sorry I was cranky back at the hotel,' she suddenly said to Jonathan.

'You weren't cranky.'

'I was, about you always having your nose stuck in a

book. So selfish, but you know me . . .' She chuckled. 'It's the thought of seeing my dreadful boring husband that made me horrid.'

'Dominic's doing well for himself in his party. A friend heard him speak the other day on the economy . . .'

'No politics, Peter, I forbid it, I had enough to last me a lifetime with Dominic.'

'Sorry, Juniper, okay, no politics. Mind you I wouldn't be surprised to see him Prime Minister one day,' Peter continued.

'Good job you left him, Juniper. You'd have made a lousy Prime Minister's wife,' Jonathan teased her. 'Just imagine if some head of state bored you!'

'As bad as a novelist's wife?' She looked at him slyly.

'Not at all, you're wonderful. I only wish you really were my wife.' Jonathan looked at her wistfully.

'That's not what you said a couple of months ago. You said I was hopeless and frustrating and ruining your great opus.'

'*I* was being cranky then. I was under pressure . . . months behind on my schedule, that was all.'

'Which reminds me, Jonathan. I was talking to Nigel this morning. Turnhills want the next book finished on time. They were, to say the least, a little put out by the delay this time. All publishers expect late delivery, but over two years . . . ?'

'It's living in paradise that does it, makes work a most unattractive proposition.' Jonathan grinned apologetically.

'It's my fault, Peter. I hate him writing, I resent every minute he spends with it rather than me. Can you imagine, I get jealous of the books? Isn't that the silliest thing you ever heard, so childish?' Juniper said softly, entwining her hand into Jonathan's. 'It's because I love him too much, I suppose.' She smiled at both the men.

'I understand the difficulty, old boy,' Peter laughed, looking with envy at Jonathan and the beautiful woman by his side. Someone had told him she was thirty-six: it did not seem possible, she hardly looked a day over twenty. She had the fine bone structure that he realized would always ensure she had good looks, but her tanned skin had no lines. Her blonde hair she wore unfashionably loose and it swished as she moved her head animatedly in conversation. But perhaps, he thought, her most striking feature was her hazel eyes, flecked with gold, which had all the innocence of a child which was quite extraordinary given her reputation. He envied Jonathan his success with his previous two novels but most of all he envied him for having this beautiful woman so obviously in love with him.

Juniper, despite her misgivings, enjoyed the party in the evening, given by Turnhills publishing house to celebrate the publication of Jonathan's third novel. Everyone agreed that *Eastern Idylls* was even better than the first, which had been heralded as a work of genius and far superior to the second which some had found disappointing. As she watched people fêting Jonathan, the cameras clicking and women flocking to him, she felt immeasurably proud of him. Forgotten was her frustration on the island, the isolation she had felt, the continual rejection when he had turned to his work and not to her. Now she felt ashamed of her petulance, her frequent tantrums. She should be honoured that he chose to live with her. She would mend her ways, she resolved. Smiling brilliantly she gave all her attention to the reporter who wanted to interview her as well and agreed with alacrity to be photographed with Jonathan.

Two days later she felt she could delay no longer and went to see her husband. It was not an interview she had been looking forward to. But it was silly to continue as they were. It was not that she wanted to marry Jonathan. She knew he would like to marry her, but Juniper could not see the point. They were happy as they were, why change anything, she argued frequently. It was not as if they wanted to have children. But it would be tidier to be divorced. Juniper was tired of having to explain herself and her relationships to people. No doubt it would be an expensive exercise, but Juniper was used to that now. Hal had taught her how expensive divesting oneself of a husband could be.

Dominic welcomed her at the House of Commons with a kiss. She was impressed by the size of the office he ushered her into and in retaliation gave him a signed copy of Jonathan's book, pointing out with pride that it was dedicated to her. Dominic made some fulsome remarks about Jonathan's talent. While they were both agreeing how clever Jonathan was Juniper looked closely at him. Dominic himself bore little relation to the young pilot she had married. His shoulders were still broad, but he had grown soft-looking and plump. He had large bags beneath his sombre brown eyes and an unappealing six o'clock shadow. Sitting opposite him, she marvelled that she had ever lusted after him.

'Dominic, I don't want to cause you any trouble, nor to stand in your way, but I think it's time we got divorced. It would be so much neater, wouldn't it? And one day you might want to remarry.' Juniper opened the subject when it was obvious that Dominic was not going to bring it up himself.

'What gives you the idea I should ever want to remarry?' he asked gruffly.

'A handsome man like you and still so young? I'd have thought you'd want children.' She had planned that bit and watched carefully for his response. She saw him glance in the mirror, enjoying the flattery.

'It may be nineteen-fifty-five but the electorate don't like divorce, you know,' he said ponderously.

'Being divorced hasn't stopped Anthony becoming Prime Minister and being happy. Of course, he is very clever and of course he has remarried. Maybe that's why the voters have forgiven him.' She smiled her sweetest smile. She was lying, she had never met Anthony Eden and hadn't the vaguest idea if he was happy or not.

'It could affect my prospects . . .' He thoughtfully

fingered his chin. 'There's another election on the twenty-sixth of this month.'

'I know, but nothing would happen that quickly. I'm happy to give you grounds. I don't give a fig for my reputation. And I would ensure that it wouldn't hurt you financially, if you wouldn't be insulted? I'm happy to continue the allowance.' Again she smiled. Sometimes she wondered at how shallow and how stupid most men were and why it was necessary to go through this charade of protecting the male ego.

'It puts me in a difficult position. I mean a chap doesn't like to be labelled a gold-digger,' he blustered.

'Oh good, Dominic. I knew you'd understand. Shall I get my lawyers to contact yours?' Juniper said gaily, knowing she had got what she wanted – at a price. So much for all those wonderful principles about money he had once had.

Outside the Houses of Parliament she dismissed her driver and decided to walk back to the hotel. It was a lovely May day and she felt elated. It was ridiculous to feel so lighthearted. She had not thought of Dominic in years and being married to him was hardly a serious tie to her, but it would be wonderful to be free of him – like clearing out an untidy cupboard and throwing out the unwanted rubbish. Seeing him today she almost felt ashamed that she had ever loved or wanted him.

She stopped at Garrard's and bought Maddie a pretty pearl bracelet with a diamond clasp. She crossed to Jermyn street and in Turnbull and Asser ordered enough shirts and ties to keep Jonathan clothed for years. In Fortnum's she bought a huge hamper of food to be delivered for their trip to Cornwall. At Hatchards she bought a pile of the latest books, half for herself, the other half for Jonathan. In a small exclusive shop she bought Maddie and herself huge bottles of bath oils. By the time she reached the Ritz she felt as if she were walking on air.

She let herself into the suite and called out. 'It's me.'

She swept into the sitting room. Jonathan was standing

by the window, a young man at his side, very tall and slim with jet-black hair. He was dressed casually in slacks and blazer which he wore with an easy elegance. He turned and she saw that he was handsome. There was something familiar about him, she felt she knew him.

'Hullo,' she said, unsure of herself.

He stepped towards her, an apprehensive smile on his face, hand held out in greeting.

'Hullo, Mother.'

8

'Harry!'

Juniper sped across the wide room, scattering her bags and parcels in all directions as she did so, holding her arms up to the young man. Blushing furiously he took a step back and looked about him as if trapped. Juniper stopped running and stood, her arms still held up in front of her, feeling foolish. Then, as if sensing her confusion, Harry stepped forward and she was holding him, kissing him, crying his name until she realized he was standing as stiffly as a lump of wood. She let go of him.

'This is the most marvellous surprise,' she said, spinning around the room, collecting together her discarded packages. She had to do something to cover her disappointment that he had not responded to her warmly. She returned to where the young man still stood and took his hands in hers with a deliberate movement, as if taking control of the situation. 'Champagne, Jonathan, we must celebrate. Let me look at you.' She studied Harry at arm's length. He looked relieved to be spared more hugs for the moment. He looked so like Hal that it made her want to shiver. There seemed to be nothing resembling her in him, except perhaps his eyes. They weren't dark, almost black, like Hal's, but had flecks of gold in the brown, closer to her own hazel. He was so tall: when she had hugged him she had been standing on tiptoe to reach him. She had last seen him as a little boy of six and now here he was, a man.

'You should have come yesterday – your birthday. We could have had such a party.' She was smiling at him brightly, willing him not to look so scared.

'You remembered?' he asked shyly.

'I always remembered,' Juniper said softly. 'Over the years I always sent you presents.'

'Did you?' He appeared to be puzzled.

'Ah well,' she said, more as a sigh. 'What could I expect?' She turned her face away so that he would not see the bitterness of her expression. It was as she feared, they had kept her gifts from him. She had always hoped she was wrong, that Leigh would have insisted he receive them, that Harry would have known she had never forgotten. 'Such a celebration we could have had,' she said vaguely.

'I was with Uncle Leigh. They had planned a big dinner for me.'

'How nice for you. Was it fun?' Juniper could not look at him when he spoke of his guardian; she resented the affection for Leigh that she saw in his face.

'It was cancelled. Uncle Leigh said it wouldn't have been proper, in the circumstances, to celebrate.'

'What circumstances?' Juniper asked.

'My grandmother died last week. Lady Copton,' he added for Jonathan's benefit.

'Ah ha!' The happy exclamation escaped before she could stop herself. 'Poor grandmother.' She turned towards the waiter, who had entered with the champagne, to hide her broad grin from her son.

'I hadn't heard. We've been travelling for ages. Jonathan doesn't like to fly, do you, my darling?'

'I can swim if the ship sinks, I can't fly if the aeroplane falls.' Jonathan was pouring the drinks.

'Sounds reasonable to me, sir.' Harry smiled at Jonathan. Juniper noticed it was a different smile from the only one she had received so far: relaxed, without fear. Why he should be afraid of her was mystifying.

'Did you like your grandmother?' She wondered why she had asked.

'Very much. She was very kind to me.' He seemed embarrassed at her question.

'I'm so glad,' Juniper said with heavy irony.

Jonathan served the flutes of champagne. 'A toast, I think,' he said. 'To what? To refound friends? Renewed acquaintances? How about that?'

'Long lost sons.' Juniper raised her glass and the others repeated this toast, both looking slightly bashful.

'Well, let's sit, everyone looks so uncomfortable.' Juniper sank gracefully on to the sofa, patting the seat beside her for Harry to join her. 'So, what made you suddenly come?' She said the words in as gentle a voice as possible, she did not want Harry to think that there was any criticism implied.

'I couldn't come before because . . . well, my grand-mother wouldn't have liked me to . . . I didn't want to hurt her . . . I didn't want to hurt anyone . . . It wouldn't have seemed right, somehow.' Harry was obviously finding it difficult to explain himself.

'Quite,' Juniper said, with almost superhuman control, all her past hatred for her mother-in-law rising like bile inside her.

'You were put in a difficult position, old chap.' Jonathan smiled encouragingly at Harry.

'Yes, sir. It did get a bit perplexing at times.' Harry smiled back with gratitude. 'Of course I didn't know you were here. You haven't been to England for ages, have you?' Harry asked, as if justifying himself. 'Then, yester-day, I saw your photograph in the newspapers. I tele-phoned Mr Middlebank's publishers. They were very stiff and at first they wouldn't tell me where you were staying, but luckily a cousin of my aunt's works there and he told me. I hope you don't mind.'

'Them telling you, or your coming? Neither. I think it's

the most marvellous thing that's happened to me in years.' Juniper was beaming at him. Harry looked at his mother, at her smile, and like so many before him he sat as if hypnotised.

'Have you seen your father recently?' she asked, in an off-hand way.

'Not for years. Last time he was here, about four years ago, he had a frightful row with my grandmother and uncle. He went back to America.'

Juniper would have loved to ask what they had rowed about, but refrained. She was not going to become like them. He would hear no ill of his father from her.

'Father married again. But you must know that?'

'No, I didn't. How odd. I usually manage to learn most things on my little island.'

'It was a very quiet wedding, I don't think he told many people.'

'Who's the blushing bride?'

Harry looked up at the obvious bitterness in his mother's voice. 'I haven't met her. She's an American, a widow – from Connecticut, I think.'

'Well, let's hope she's rich,' Juniper said with brittle sounding amusement. Jonathan almost imperceptibly shook his head at her, willing her not to spoil this reunion for herself.

'How old were you yesterday, Harry? Seventeen? So you're still at school,' Jonathan asked, trying to steer the conversation away from the Coptons.

'No, I'm waiting to go to Cambridge. I got a scholarship last year. I left school at Easter, they said there was no point in my staying. So I've got time off. I'm not sure what I'll do with it. Travel, I hope, learn another language, perhaps.'

'What about your National Service?'

'Everyone says it's going to come to an end, sir. By the time I leave university I hope it'll be done with.'

'A spell in the army never hurt anyone.'

'Don't be so stuffy, Jonathan. Why should he waste

two years for nothing? I told you he is brilliant. What's the point of him doing National Service when he can be at university? I'll tell you what you can do with your free time: you must come and stay with me . . . Oh dear, that sounds so dreadfully bossy, doesn't it?' Juniper chuckled. 'Please come and stay with me, I'd love you to,' she added, a little less gushingly.

'I'd like that. I've never been to Greece.'

'And now? You haven't got to rush off anywhere, have you? You'll come to dine with us? Stay with us? We're off to Cornwall at the weekend, your great-grandmother would love to meet you. There's so much to find out about each other, so much talking to be done. And we could go shopping before we go and I could buy you everything you want, anything . . .'

'Juniper, calm down, my darling. You'll frighten this young man witless.'

'Oh dear, I'm sorry.' She leant across and took his hands in hers. 'Forgive me, Harry, but I've dreamt of this day for years, the day you would search me out of your own accord. You'll never know how happy I am.' There was a suspicion of tears in her eyes as she spoke. Harry looked away with embarrassment. Jonathan sat himself on the arm of the sofa and laid his hand on Juniper's shoulder. Through the thin silk of her blouse he could feel her trembling.

'I think we should go to the theatre tonight and then have supper? A quiet evening rather than racketing about. What do you say?' Jonathan looked from one to the other.

'That sounds wonderful, sir.'

'He'll be bored rigid.'

'No, I shan't, Mother. I love the theatre. And I'd like to come to Cornwall but I think it would be best if I went home tonight and saw my uncle and aunt. They've bought a small flat and are down from Scotland. I'm not sure what to do about Greece: I have to get permission from the courts to leave the country. I don't know whether I should say it's to stay with you.' Harry blushed even deeper.

'Lie. It'll be safer. Say you're staying with an old friend. Oh please, Harry, lie for me. I don't trust the Coptons, they'll try and stop me seeing you, I know they will.' She snapped open her handbag looking for a handkerchief. Jonathan handed her his. Harry, appalled at the prospect that his mother might be about to cry and anxious to rescue her from her tears, asked permission to use the telephone. With satisfaction Juniper heard him telling his aunt that he had met up with a crowd from school. They were going to the theatre and he would be home late. The same crowd were motoring to Cornwall, he continued. They had invited him and he had accepted, and was that all right?

'It's only half a lie,' he said, grinning sheepishly as he replaced the receiver. Juniper rushed across the room and, throwing her previous caution to the wind, hugged him tight, showering him with kisses.

'Juniper, I do think you should try and control your excitement with the boy,' Jonathan was saying to her later as they changed for the theatre.

'What do you mean?' Juniper bristled.

'You know exactly what I mean. He was quite happy to borrow a dress suit of mine, but you insisted on Gieves sending a man round to fit him out. The boy was flummoxed at all the fuss.'

'He's not a boy.'

'Of course he is. And if you keep gushing over him, swamping him with kisses and all that guff, you'll frighten him away. He's had a conventional English upbringing, with little overt affection, I should think.'

'Oh, the poor darling. I must make up for lost time,' Juniper said brightly, spraying on more scent than she needed with an almost violent squeeze of the spray.

'No, Juniper. There you go again. Treat him as he's used to being treated. Stand back a little.'

'Goddamn it, Jonathan, there are times when I find you

totally insensitive. Unbelievable in a so-called writer,' she said, her voice tight, lips pursed. 'In any case, what do you know about it? You don't have any children, you couldn't possibly know how parents and children feel about each other.'

'With all due respect, Juniper, I wouldn't say you had much idea about that either.'

Jonathan was rewarded with a savage glare from Juniper.

During the next two days Juniper spent a fortune on Harry. Savile Row was visited, Turnbull and Asser again, Lobb's to have several pairs of shoes made. Since all these clothes would take time to make they then had to go to other shops to fit him out temporarily. The more Harry objected and tried to stop his mother, the more she spent. Amongst the ever increasing pile Harry had boxes of gold cufflinks in all shapes and sizes, a crocodile briefcase and a matching set of Vuitton baggage, a gold cigarette case and lighter, even though he did not smoke – but within a few days he was learning. Juniper bought him a Patek Philippe watch and would have bought him an MG TF motor car except, as he pointed out, he could not drive yet. So she had to content herself with arranging lessons for him and the promise she would buy it for him the moment he passed his test. Finally, even an inspired present-giver like Juniper had to admit she was defeated, she could not think of another thing to buy him, unless . . .

'He'll need somewhere to stay in the vacations from Cambridge. He's not going to want to travel to dreary Scotland every time, is he? No doubt those awful Coptons bore him as much as they bored me. So, I thought, Jonathan . . .' She was massaging the back of his neck, which she knew he liked; she had forgiven him his remarks of a few days before. 'I think I should buy him a flat, what do you think? Something quite small and central. And then I thought – best idea of all – that you and I could always use it when we're in town.'

'You don't have to excuse yourself to me, Juniper, my sweet. If you want to buy him a flat, then buy him one. And if you want a flat of your own in London, then get one. Why consult me? By the way, have you telephoned your grandmother about this weekend?'

'No.'

'Good, I think I shall be a few days late. I need to go to the British Library to do some research.'

'Oh, Jonathan.' Dutifully she injected disappointment into her voice, but she did not feel it in the least. Nothing could be better, now she need not share Harry with him on the trip to Cornwall.

9

They had left Juniper at the Royal Clarence Hotel in the Cathedral Close in Exeter, claiming she was simply 'dying' to see inside the cathedral. Maddie had never seen her visit a church, cathedral or museum in all their travels; a sore point with Maddie, who would quite often have liked to explore a bit more. Maddie doubted whether Juniper was really bound for the cathedral. She had probably said it to impress Harry, who had raved about the building. Maddie feared that she was far more likely to settle down at the hotel with a book and a bottle of champagne. All Maddie's efforts to curb Juniper's drinking had come to nothing. When Jonathan joined them matters had got worse, the two seemed to goad each other into greater excess. Maddie, outnumbered, had given up trying to control Juniper, but it did not stop her worrying.

Maddie and Harry set off in the back of the chauffeur-driven Rolls-Royce.

'What is this Hurstwood?' Harry asked, as the car streaked off the A38 and plunged into the narrow lanes of Dartmoor.

'It belongs to an old friend of your mother. They fell

out, but I don't know why. Now the house and farm are for sale, she thinks they must be in financial trouble. Whether she's thinking of buying it or not, I don't know, she hasn't said, just that I'm to pretend to be interested in it myself and that we're not to introduce you as Copton. What shall we call you?'

'My aunt's maiden name was McForbes. Shall I use that?'

'Fine. You don't look particularly Scottish. Still, I suppose lots of Scotsmen don't.'

'It doesn't seem a very nice thing to do – buying this house if her friend is in a mess, does it?'

'Not particularly, but then we don't know what the friend did, do we? Your mother has been badly let down, and cheated – by experts,' Maddie said loyally.

'Really, who?'

'No one you would know.' Maddie turned her head sharply and looked out of the window at the passing scenery.

Polly was waiting at Hurstwood to receive them. She loathed the whole business of showing people around her house. However illogical, she found it difficult to be polite to prospective purchasers who might one day be living here rather than herself.

When the first would-be buyers had come, Polly had gone through the house rigorously tidying and dusting, but after three weeks of so many viewers she had given up. If they could not see the beauty of her home because of a few out-of-place magazines and books, a bit of dust, or the odd pile of washing-up waiting to be done, then they did not deserve to own it.

'Who are these people? Do you know anything about them?' Polly asked the young man from the London estate agent. So much interest had been shown in Hurstwood that he had been obliged to take up residence in the local inn. That week they were going to have to decide if it would not be better to go to auction.

'This one is a Mrs Huntley. I gather she's recently

returned from travelling abroad and is looking to settle down in the West Country.'

'There have been so many this past week, Mr Smedley, I begin to wonder if some of them just come to get a look at the house. Quite honestly, I'm getting fed up with the lot of them.'

'We try to ascertain that everyone is a bona fide buyer, Mrs Slater. But this Mrs Huntley sounded very pleasant on the telephone.'

'Then I hope she's more suitable than the majority so far. I will not let my house go to anyone who wants to turn it into a hotel, a country club, a health spa, or who wants to alter anything in it.' Polly tossed her head defiantly.

'It might be hard to find the right person then, Mrs Slater, few people want to be bothered with these large houses as homes any more.' The young man smiled at her kindly. They both knew that Polly had no choice over who was to buy her home. It was up to the bank and if someone wanted to turn it into a striptease club, provided they had the money, the bank cared nothing.

'At least it looks as if she's got money,' the young man said approvingly, as Juniper's Rolls drew up outside.

Maddie stood on the forecourt for a moment, looking up at the house, quietly absorbing the atmosphere of the place. It was the prettiest house she had ever seen and she regretted she was not a genuine buyer. If she had Juniper's sort of money she would snap it up there and then. The estate agent stepped forward and introductions were made. That done, Polly excused herself and went to her grandmother's sitting room.

'More viewers?' Gertie asked.

'Yes. A woman and young man. They look quite pleasant. They came in a brand-new Rolls-Royce.'

'Umph, that means nothing these days, what with hire purchase and such character-sapping arrangements. In my day you had what you could afford and that was that.'

'Yes, Grandmama.'

'It leads to ruination, all this borrowing. Look at you and Andrew. If you hadn't borrowed from the bank when I told you not to, you wouldn't have been in this mess now.'

'That's not strictly true, Grandmama. If we hadn't borrowed, we'd have been in Queer Street sooner. In any case, we couldn't keep borrowing from you.'

'I'm finding these perfect strangers clumping about the house insufferable, Polly. It's undignified, as if they were rootling about in my cupboards. It's like being burgled, I should imagine. They are all so awful, so vulgar,' Gertie said belligerently.

'I know, Grandmama. It can't be helped though. I just hope that somebody sympathetic to the house comes along.'

'I feel so wretchedly useless.' Gertie banged her fists on the arms of her chair. 'When one thinks of the great possessions our family had – and to come to this. I can't adjust to it and I don't even know if I want to. I'm reaching the point, Polly, when I wake up and think, oh dear God, not another day.' There was a break in Gertie's voice as she spoke and, as if aware she was letting go, she tossed her head. 'I should think it will be a good season for the roses,' she said, forcing her voice to sound normal.

Polly quickly crossed the room and put her arm around her grandmother's shoulders, pressing her cheek to hers. 'Oh, darling Grandmama, don't talk like that. What would I do without you? We're all feeling low, it'll pass. It's harder on you. You've had too many changes in your life.'

'But I've always been able to help. Now I can't. I don't understand anything. I had so much money and now the bank manager says I shouldn't help any more, but I want to, Polly. I can't bear to see you lose your home.' Gertie was becoming agitated.

'The bank is right, Grandmama. You'd be throwing good money after bad. And if you did any more for us I'd have an even worse conscience about you.'

'But to lose Hurstwood. A Frobisher has owned this property for centuries.'

'You lost Mendbury and recovered from its loss. I'll get over this. As Andrew says, it's just sentiment. As he pointed out to me, looked at logically, we're losing bricks and mortar, that's all.'

'What a stupid thing to say. I'm surprised at him. Where is he?'

'He's gone to Exeter about some fertilizer. We've got to carry on.'

'He's never here when people come, have you noticed that, Polly? Why?'

'I think he feels ashamed. As if the people who come here will know we failed.'

'I know Andrew suffered greatly in the war, but so did many others. I hate to say this, Polly, but I do sometimes wonder if he's not lacking in moral fibre.' Gertie sat stiffly.

'I don't wonder any such thing. In the circumstances I think he's made a remarkable recovery. We've had bad luck and that could happen to anyone, war or no.' Polly spoke patiently. Even if she did not agree with Gertie, she was not going to upset her further by arguing with her. 'In any case, Andrew thinks he's found the ideal smallholding on Exmoor, and with quite a nice house.'

'I don't like Exmoor. It rains even more than Dartmoor. When I was a gal I used to go and stay at Pixton Park and it never stopped raining,' Gertie was complaining as the door opened and, with apologies, the agent, Mr Smedly, entered followed by Maddie and Harry.

'Lady Gertrude, might I introduce Mrs Huntley and Mr McForbes?' The agent was walking backwards, stooped, and wringing his hands continually; such an obsequious stance made Gertie sit even straighter and peer down her nose at him.

Gertie next looked directly at Harry who, under such close scrutiny, wished he had followed his first inclination and not come.

'Are you any relation to the McForbes of Inverness-shire – from Glen Bucket?' Gertie asked briskly.

'No.' Harry found he stumbled over this one small word.

'Odd. Not that you would have been a McForbes, but odd all the same. The Coptons?' Gertie virtually spat the name out.

'No . . .' Harry coughed on his lie.

Gertie swung round to face Polly. 'Who does this young man remind you of, Polly?'

Harry found himself wishing the floor would open and swallow him up.

'I'm sorry, Mr McForbes, it's so rude of us to stare.' Polly said apologetically, giving her grandmother a pointed look. Harry smiled weakly back.

'I just asked you, Polly, who does he remind you of?' Gertie persisted, with the old person's ability to ride roughshod over others' sensibilities.

'I don't know, Grandmama.' Polly spoke in a resigned way, fully aware that her grandmother was going to tell her, whether she wanted to hear or no.

'Don't be silly, of course you do, Polly. He looks like Hal Copton – he could be his double, the dreadful cad. And Hal's sister-in-law – Caroline Copton – you remember, Polly, a perfectly charming woman, though why she should get involved with that awful family is beyond comprehension – she was a McForbes from Glen Bucket. No doubt that . . .'

'Yes, well, Grandmother, that's enough. Poor Mr McForbes has told you he's not related to them and I'm sure the last thing he wants is a rundown on the London society of years ago, long before he was born.' Polly smiled kindly at Harry, who was standing uncomfortably, apparently unsure what to do with his hands and feet. It was odd, though, he could easily be a young Hal, but with a pleasanter face. As if to make amends for Gertie's rudeness she offered to show them the rest of the house herself.

Outside the door of Gertie's room she apologized to Harry.

'I'm sorry about that. My grandmother says whatever comes into her head, it can be so embarrassing.'

'Oh, please, Mrs Slater. My grandmother was just the same. My uncle always said we should lock her up in the east wing when guests came.'

'And she's forever seeing likenesses in people.'

Harry laughed. 'My uncle says it's a sure sign of age when you do that.'

'Oh, not in my grandmother, she's always been the same, young and old.' Polly laughed, hoping no lasting damage had been done. Of all the people who had been to view these two were the ones she had warmed to the most. The young man was charming and had been so understanding about Gertie. She had liked the woman immediately, she had such an obvious feeling for the house. To the agent's astonishment, she offered them tea.

'It must be very hard to leave such a beautiful house,' Maddie said, once they were settled in the drawing room with tea and cake.

'It will be hard,' Polly admitted. Maddie looked at her sympathetically. 'We had a fire, you see, in the chicken houses. It was a disaster and the bank, you know. Fair weather friends . . .' she laughed half-heartedly. She wondered why she was explaining their affairs to these strangers, wondering what on earth had got into her.

She was saved from further explanation by a gentle tap on the door. It was her son, Richard, brought down from his afternoon nap by the young girl from the village who helped her with him. Richard took to the visitors immediately. Polly set great store by her son's instinct where people were concerned.

'Of course,' Gertie had said when Polly had sheepishly confided this theory to her, quite expecting her grandmother to tell her what rubbish it was. 'Children have an extra sense to adults. Always watch your child and your

473

dog where people are concerned – if they don't like them there's something wrong with them. I've found it infallible.'

Polly was therefore gratified to see Harry on all fours playing trains and Maddie with scant regard for her elegant suit taking Richard on her lap to look at his story book. She would have liked them to stay on to meet Andrew as she was convinced these were the right people for Hurstwood, but they explained that they had to return to Exeter where a friend was waiting for them.

'Well?' said that friend as they entered the residents' lounge of the Royal Clarence to find Juniper, as Maddie had feared, sunk deep into one of the large leather chairs with the meagre remains of a bottle of champagne standing on the table beside her.

'It's a beautiful house. You could look for years before you find another one like that. It's a gem,' Maddie enthused.

'I know that,' Juniper said dismissively. 'What about the people? What does Polly look like, and Andrew?'

'Andrew wasn't there. Mrs Slater was charming, very sweet, wasn't she, Harry?'

'You can say that again,' Harry said enthusiastically, 'especially when she shut her old grandmother up.'

'Lady Gertie? She's still alive then?'

'Very much so. I could have died for poor Harry.'

'Why? What did she say?' Juniper swung round to face her son.

'She recognized me. She said some frightful things about my family.'

'Did she?' Juniper could not suppress a smile of triumph. 'She was always forthright. I adored her. But you didn't let on who you were?'

'No, I didn't want to after I'd heard the old lady, she might have had me horsewhipped or shot,' Harry laughed. All the same he wished he had the courage to ask Juniper why Lady Gertrude had spoken about his family as she had, but he still felt too shy of his mother.

474

'You haven't said what Polly looked like.' Juniper was almost jumping up and down with impatience.

'If you could erase the worried look, I should think she's a fine looking woman. She's got such a strong face and yet still has a sweet expression. It was as you thought – money. The bank is foreclosing,' Maddie explained.

'Poor Polly.' Harry saw a sad expression flit across Juniper's face.

'Her little son's a cracker. He'll break some hearts in the future,' Maddie continued.

'Of course, her son. I'd almost forgotten about him. Polly would make a wonderful mother. Not like wicked old me.' She chuckled.

'Oh, Mother . . .' Harry was not sure if she was joking or not.

'How old is he, do you think?' Juniper asked with genuine interest.

'About three, I'd say, wouldn't you, Harry? But oh, you should see his hair, it's glorious.'

'What about his hair?' Juniper was smiling.

'It's the most glorious colour I've ever seen.'

'What colour?' Juniper was almost snapping, no trace of a smile now.

'The most wonderful auburn. Apparently the old lady had hair like that and so did Mrs Slater's father.'

'No.' Juniper was almost shouting. 'You must have made a mistake. The child must be adopted.'

'Oh no, they were talking about his hair. He wasn't adopted. She's dark as you know. No, the colouring came from her father's side of the family. Mrs Slater said so.' Maddie continued, blithely, to chatter on.

Without a word Juniper got up and walked out of the lounge, crossed the entrance hall and went out into the Close.

'What did I say, Harry?' Maddie was astonished.

'I don't know.' Harry shrugged his shoulders.

'Oh, Harry,' Maddie sighed, 'I love your mother, but sometimes she's so difficult, such an enigma.'

'Do you think I ought to follow her?'

'I think that would be a very good idea.'

Harry raced out of the hotel to see Juniper walking quickly across the green in the direction of the cathedral. With his long legs he soon caught up with her.

'Mother, what's the matter? What did we say?' Harry asked, his voice full of concern. 'Mother, why are you crying?'

'Oh, Harry, I'm so unhappy. I was sure that Polly was really my sister . . . But the hair, the baby's hair, it's the wrong colour for that to be.' Juniper turned and clung to him and began to sob. Harry hurriedly looked about him, frightened that people might notice. Gently he led her to a bench on the side of the green. 'Now tell me all about it,' he said quietly, as if he were talking to a child.

'I wanted her to be my sister so badly. I needed her to be. I felt I could make her if I tried hard enough. Now I've lost her. I thought we could forget the stupid argument we had, that I would go to Hurstwood tomorrow and I would help her as I always did in the past. But that was when I was sure she was my sister. Sisters forgive. A friend won't – not after what I did. Oh Harry, I've lost everyone I've loved in my life and now Polly.' She began to search in her handbag for a handkerchief.

'You're not alone, you've got Jonathan.'

'For how long? He won't last, men never do.' She wiped at her eyes with the handkerchief Harry gave her. 'I've never got one of my own,' she explained through her tears, trying to laugh.

'There's your grandmother. You spoke of her with such love and affection.' Harry was trying to coax her back to happiness when all the time he longed to know what she had done in the past to cause this storm. And why she should think Polly was her sister. It would seem that this side of his family was going to prove far more interesting than the Coptons.

'She'll die and leave me, just like my parents did, just

like Lincoln.' She began to sob again and he began to stroke her hair awkwardly.

'Ma,' he said, as the sobbing subsided, unaware that he had not called her 'Mother'. 'You've got me, Ma. I'll never leave you.' And the undemonstrative son gently kissed her.

10

Annie was almost speechless when, after Maddie's telephone call, Alice asked her to contact all the guests who were booked into Gwenfer for the last week in May and the whole of June to tell them they could not come.

'We can't do that,' Annie protested.

'We can and we will. I'm not asking you to lie. You will say that due to family matters I have, regretfully, had to cancel their booking. I shall write to them all personally, of course.'

'They'll be furious. You'll lose them. They won't come again.'

'I can't help that. I don't want Juniper to know what is going on here.'

'Why ever not?' Even as she spoke Annie knew that, since Juniper was involved, she was skating on thin ice. But she had worked too hard helping to build up this business to watch it damaged without protest.

'Because I don't,' Alice said firmly.

'You're not doing anything to be ashamed of.'

'Quite honestly, Annie, I don't think my reasons are any business of yours. Now, if you wouldn't mind telephoning these people for me . . .' She paused in the doorway. 'There's a dear.' She smiled sweetly before slipping out into the hall.

Annie took down the booking diary; when Alice spoke like that there was no arguing with her. Anything to do with Juniper was sacrosanct. Annie's memories of Juniper were dim, but not so dim that she had forgotten Juniper's coldness towards her and how frightened Annie had felt if she found herself alone with her. She remembered the unnerving way Juniper had of flouncing from the room if, having condescended to smile, Annie had not smiled back – as if the smile was a great gift, a gift that cancelled out her previous unpleasantness. Annie had not liked her, but it had obviously been mutual. This visit was not something Annie could contemplate with equilibrium.

Annie began making lists of addresses and telephone numbers to call. This would be a disaster to Alice's projected turnover and she wondered how the bank manager would react when he knew she had cancelled business so that Juniper would not be upset. It was a ridiculous situation. Why shouldn't Juniper know? Alice had hinted that perhaps she was not as rich as she had once been, but, if that were the case, was she likely to go into mental decline at the thought of Gwenfer as a guest house? She so rarely came here that it would not affect her and would she not rather that it was making money for itself? Of course she might feel guilty because her grandmother was having to work so hard. Perhaps that was what Alice was protecting her from.

It must be an extraordinary feeling to have someone love you so much that they would go to these lengths to protect you, she reflected, as she dialled the first number on her list.

Now it was Sunday and Alice's granddaughter was due at any moment. Annie checked the dining table to make sure everything still looked perfect. She had not laid a place for herself. They would not want her with them.

'Annie, the table looks beautiful. Thank you, my dear.' Alice had come quietly into the room behind her.

'You don't think I've overdone the flowers?'

'No, they're perfect. But, Annie, you haven't laid enough places. There are only four place settings . . .'

'Yes, you and Juniper, and her two friends.'

'But I want you to eat with us too.'

'Oh, I don't think so, Alice. You won't want me and Juniper certainly won't.'

'What on earth makes you say that? I've never heard anything so silly.' Alice crossed to the sideboard and took more cutlery from the drawer. She quickly rearranged the other settings and laid another place. 'There, that's better. Now, should we put the apple pie in now or later?'

'Later. I suggest we sit down and have a glass of sherry,' Annie said kindly. Alice looked exhausted. She tired far too easily these days, yet she stubbornly refused to see a doctor and chided Annie for worrying.

The drive from Exeter had been subdued. Juniper had spent most of it looking moodily out of the window and Harry was unsure how to deal with her. His efforts at conversation as they left Exeter had not been a great success and he too had lapsed into silence.

'I say, look . . .' Harry pointed excitedly at the signpost. 'Look, it says to Boscar. Isn't that your father's place, Mother?'

'Yes.'

'What's there?'

'A house,' she said frowning and then, as if realising she was being too abrupt with her son, added. 'It's a centre for natural healing now, that sort of thing.'

'Can we go and see?'

'No. They're all peculiar people, not our sort at all.' She lit a cigarette.

Harry watched her for a moment, trying to gauge her mood, wondering if he could enquire further.

'It's very beautiful. We'll go there one day, I promise.' She patted his hand and smiled at him which gave him the courage to ask,

'What was my grandfather Boscar like?'

'Odd,' she said, the smile disappearing from her face, and she turned from him and stared out of the window again.

Harry slumped back on to the leather cushions of the

car, disappointed. This was what always happened. As soon as he began to think he was about to find out something about his family, the mental shutters would come down and he could learn nothing. It seemed a strange state of affairs to be meeting this side of his family now, at seventeen. He was curious to know them, to know what, if anything, of them he had inherited either physically or in his personality. At the moment it was as if he only knew half of himself.

He was glad he had found the courage to seek out his mother. It had been a spur-of-the-moment decision; no doubt if he had thought about it he would have chickened out. But she had made everything so easy for him with her welcome and the presents. What presents! He almost wished he were still at school so that he could flash them around.

He had always known his mother was rich, but not this rich. He had heard rumours, which were imparted with a marked degree of glee by his Aunt Caroline, that she had lost money, but she still appeared to have plenty left and he thought it was about time he saw some of it.

Not that his mother had ever been mean to him. He had always been well-clothed and educated. Leigh had given him an allowance which he honourably explained was from Juniper. It had been adequate, but not over generous. But still, none of it made up for the fact that she had deserted him, dumped him with his uncle and aunt, or so he had been told. She said she had sent him presents over the years, but had she really? Was she just saying that to salve her conscience?

There were so many things to which he had not yet found the answer. Why had she given him up? Why had both his parents been declared unfit to have him? Whenever he had asked, his uncle and aunt quickly indicated that everything had been Juniper's fault, but they had never filled him in on the details.

He glanced at her. She was certainly beautiful. It seemed incredible that someone looking that young and glamorous could be his mother. He liked her. She could be enormous fun to be with, wanting action the whole time. He knew she wanted him to love her. He wished he could oblige, but he doubted it. He did not think he loved anyone. The closest he got was with Leigh and Caroline. But the more time he spent with her, the more he was aware how attractive he found her way of life: money certainly smoothed the path to forgiveness, he thought with a half-rueful smile.

As the car swept through Penzance, Juniper finally sat up and began to look interested. Approaching the village she became quite animated, pointing out to him the various landmarks. By the time the car reached the gates of Gwenfer she was clutching his hand with excitement.

At a bend in the steep drive Juniper ordered the car to stop. The great granite mansion lay below them, nestling between the tall cliffs, serenely beautiful.

'This is home, Harry. Wherever I go in the world I always take a part of Gwenfer with me,' Juniper said emotionally. 'You'll love it, I know you will, just as I do.'

The car started up again and Harry hung out of the window, watching the building grow larger and feeling a strange sensation, as though perhaps he too belonged here.

The car had not stopped before the large oak door swung open and Alice's upright figure hurried as fast as her arthritis would allow on to the terrace. 'Juniper, my darling,' she called and Juniper, having almost tumbled from the car, raced towards her. The two women hugged each other as if they would never let go.

'Grandmama, I'm delirious to be here . . .and I've a surprise for you. Look,' She pointed to Harry who stood grinning from ear to ear.

Alice looked closely at the young man. 'Is it Harry?' she asked, hardly daring to believe it.

'It's Harry,' Juniper replied, a lump in her throat.

'Oh, how wonderful! What a surprise!' Alice longed to

rush to him and engulf him in a hug, but knew she must not. She was a stranger to him, she must give him time to come to her. Diffidently, Harry crossed the terrace towards the old woman.

'I'm not sure what to call you.' He smiled shyly.

'Call me Alice. I'd like that.'

'Oh, I don't know . . .' He looked from one to the other of the women.

'Of course you must, if that's what my grandmother wants.'

'Thank you,' he said, somewhat surprised by her informality. The Copton side of his family were not like this. He leant down and kissed her on the cheek, for he thought that maybe he should.

'And Maddie, I'm so sorry, my dear, forgive me, I'm so excited to see these two.' Alice held her hand out to Maddie, who had been standing to one side, watching the scene. 'But where's Jonathan?'

'He might be coming later, he's held up with boring work in London.'

'Such wonderful reviews of his new book; you must be so proud of him,' Alice said politely with a smile. She had been shocked a few months back to discover that the 'friend' Juniper had mentioned in her letters during the past couple of years was in fact Jonathan Middlebank, the man with whom Juniper had misbehaved and had pretended was of no importance to her. The same man who had caused her breach with Gertie. She hoped he was not coming. She felt she would not like him. He seemed to be unreliable in the extreme, and was certainly not the man she would wish Juniper to settle for. She would also have preferred Juniper to be divorced from one man before living with the next. Alice felt that these were matters which she should discuss with Juniper, but they were matters, she knew, that would not be mentioned. Perhaps it was better not, for the subject of Jonathan might again cause an argument which both of them would bitterly regret.

'Ah, well, come in. Welcome to Gwenfer, Harry,' Alice said, holding the door open wide.

'What a stunning hall,' Harry exclaimed, looking up at the hammerbeam roof and admiring the stark simplicity of the great room. 'It doesn't look as if it's been altered since it was built.'

'It hasn't,' Juniper said. 'See the sconces on the walls? And all the furniture is original. There's never been anything else here, has there, Grandmama?'

'You like it?' Alice asked Harry almost urgently.

'I think it is the most wonderful house I've ever seen.'

'Oh good,' Alice said, putting out her hand as if about to touch him and then withdrawing it. 'Let's have a drink before lunch . . .' Alice began to usher them towards the small parlour.

'Glory be, Grandmama, why on earth have you put that funny old bowl on the refectory table? It looks ghastly.' Juniper laughed at the sight of the azure bowl she had found on the bomb site, in such grand surroundings.

'Really? I think it looks just right there,' Alice said firmly, going into the parlour, where Annie stood stiffly, as if she had been waiting for them.

'Annie, you remember Juniper, don't you?' Alice asked.

'I didn't know you were here. When did you come?' Juniper spoke sharply.

'Hullo, Miss Juniper,' Annie said, suddenly nervous.

'Annie's been here over a year, and without her I don't know what I would have done, especially last autumn when half the roof blew away.' Alice answered for her. 'Annie, this is Maddie, Juniper's friend. And this is my great-grandson, Harry,' Alice said proudly.

Annie shook hands with Maddie and smiled, but Maddie noticed that when she took Harry's hand there was no smile and she looked intently at the ground.

'Harry,' she mumbled and hastily removed her hand from his grasp. 'Would you like me to get the jug of martini, Alice?' she asked and when Alice agreed, she virtually bolted from the room.

'Good God, what a weird creature: I always thought she was going to be beautiful. Did you see those indescribable spectacles?' Juniper drawled, as she slipped a cigarette into its holder.

'She's shy,' Alice said.

'I thought she was rather pretty,' Harry added.

'Don't be ridiculous. Harry. She's ghastly. Plain as can be.'

'She's had a hard life,' Alice said, wishing she could explain and knowing she could not. 'She needs to be treated quite gently,' she added, looking from Juniper to Harry.

'I think she's hiding behind those spectacles,' Maddie said. 'I had a friend like that. She was afraid of men and tried to make herself as ugly as possible.'

'How bizarre,' Juniper said with an indifferent shrug. 'Well, Annie doesn't have to try very hard, does she?' But nobody answered her question.

Annie returned with the jug of martini and the glasses on a tray. Seeing her carrying such a heavy load, Harry quickly relieved her of the tray and placed it on the table. While everyone chatted he kept glancing at Annie. His mother was wrong; beneath those glasses her eyes were beautiful and he could just imagine how lovely her hair, so fair that it was almost white, would be if released from the clips that held it back in a pleat. She had a good figure too – full breasted women featured large in his fantasies.

Alice noticed Harry's sly glances in Annie's direction and she also saw the one shy smile Annie gave him in return. That was nice, she thought. In all the time Annie had been here she had never seen her smile at a member of the opposite sex. She was always polite to the male guests and spoke to them courteously, but it was as if there were a barrier between her and them. Today the barrier seemed to be slipping a little. In a way it was a shame Harry was so young. Had he been a little older he might have helped Annie get rid of her fear of men.

Juniper noticed Harry looking at Annie and did not like what she saw. She wished she were still a child and could have a temper tantrum, stamping her feet, making them notice her. She felt the same anger as in the past when she had seen her grandmother fuss over Annie. What was it about this girl that made her feel so threatened? And what made other people so protective and caring of her? She moved across the room and sat on the arm of Harry's chair. 'So, my darling, what do you think of these wonderful martinis?' She chuckled huskily, and stroked the nape of his neck.

'They're wonderful, Ma.' He leant back in his chair and smiled up at her warmly.

Oh dear, thought watchful Maddie, as she sipped her drink and watched everyone.

It was one of the longest meals Annie had ever endured. Harry kept looking at her, which she found unexpectedly pleasant. Juniper was also staring at her, but, in contrast to her son's look, there was a heavy resentment in her stare which filled Annie with foreboding. She found herself shivering. Across the table Maddie saw the strain on Annie's face. Something awful had happened to this girl, she felt certain. She hoped they would be here long enough to find out what: maybe she could help.

'Alice tells me you paint beautifully.' Maddie smiled encouragingly at Annie.

'Alice always exaggerates about me,' Annie smiled at Maddie knowing instantly that here was an ally, but against what or whom?

After lunch Annie banished Alice from the kitchen and refused Maddie's offer of help with the washing-up. As soon as it was finished, she slipped out of the back door and wandered down through the garden to the beach. She would keep out of the way while they were here, that was probably the best thing to do. She reached the cove and crossed to Ia's Rock, clambering on to its smooth surface.

It was a lovely rock, always warm as if it stored the sun within it.

She sat a long time staring out at the sea. She felt sad, knowing she had lost something precious. Here alone with Alice she could almost pretend that this was her home, that Alice was her flesh and blood. But with Alice's true family here she had to acknowledge that she was an outsider, that she would never truly belong. She was alone in the world and it was a frightening fact to have to acknowledge.

Maddie set about unpacking. Alice took her ledgers out of her desk and worried over the figures. Could she mention money to Juniper? Just a little would help so much . . . No. She slammed the ledgers shut. Juniper seemed edgy, but Gwenfer always helped her and it was Alice's duty to see that nothing marred her stay.

Juniper and Harry went for a walk too, up the drive and along the cliff path.

'It's lovely here, warmer than Scotland,' Harry said appreciatively.

'I hate Scotland.'

'Is that why you never came?'

'No.' She turned, looking at her son over the collar of her coat which she clutched to her. What on earth was she to say, how to explain the complicated emotions and fears that had accompanied her ideas of motherhood. She knew she loved him now but could she expect him to believe that? 'It was all too difficult . . . I didn't get on . . . I wanted . . . Oh, look, there are the Brisons. Don't they look like a rock galleon floating on the sea?' She changed the subject, unable yet to explain herself. 'I'm getting cold, let's go back. Let's hope there's saffron cake for tea.'

'We've just had lunch.'

'I eat like a horse at Gwenfer.'

Harry paused as they entered the gates. They were of intricately worked wrought iron that looked incongruous on the scrub landscape.

'Are those falcons part of the Tregowan crest?' He asked pointing up at the large stone birds.

'Good God, my darling, I don't know. You must ask Alice. I've always thought crests and titles and everything absolute guff. It's the republican in me.' She chuckled.

'Really?' Harry spoke calmly enough, but he was appalled. He had been brought up to regard his heritage with a respect bordering on reverence.

They paused halfway down the drive to admire the house, the granite warmed by the sunshine.

'What a house!' he exclaimed.

'Mm . . . it's a dream, isn't it? When Alice dies and it's mine, I shall never leave it. I shall find peace then.'

'What about Greece?' he asked.

'Oh, I'm bored with Greece. But I'm never bored with Gwenfer.' She linked her arm through his. 'We'll live here together, you and I, for ever and ever. We'll shut the rest of the world out. What do you think of that?' She looked up at him.

'Lovely,' he said, smiling broadly, not at all sure.

11

The friendship started slowly. Harry, newly released from public school, was not used to women outside his own family circle in Scotland and was unsure how to talk to them, let alone deal with them. Young women were particularly problematic and he tended to avoid them. But he found he did not want to avoid Annie. There was something about her that brought out the protective instinct that he had not even known he possessed until he met his mother. First Juniper, now Annie.

Annie, aware of Juniper's hostility, at first tried to avoid Harry, but she caught herself constantly thinking about him and was pleased when she bumped into him unexpectedly; finally she found she was dreaming about him. Of course, she told herself at regular intervals, it was all silly. To him she was little better than a servant and in any case he was so young – two years younger than she was. She would scold herself for even thinking along those lines. He was probably lonely among so many adults and searched her out because she was nearer his age. It was friendship he was offering her; she should not be such a romantic fool.

He had fallen into the habit of taking his breakfast in the kitchen alone with Annie. It had happened by accident. His mother and Maddie always slept late and never bothered with food until lunch-time and Annie had insisted that, with no guests to worry about, Alice should take it easy and have her breakfast in bed each morning. She had expected Alice to argue with her and was somewhat alarmed when she agreed. It was the first concession to age she had known Alice make. As a result they had the kitchen to themselves until well into mid-morning. Annie felt safe there. She realized that 'safe' was an odd word to use, but it was the one that had sprung to mind when she realized that Juniper was not the sort of person who ever went into kitchens or the back regions of a house.

During these mornings, over leisurely bacon and eggs, or while Harry helped her to prepare the vegetables for lunch, the two young people learnt a lot about each other. This had to be the best time in a new relationship, Annie thought, before you knew anything, when the other person was like a blank blackboard on which to write one's discoveries.

At night she tended to worry. With Chris she had been so young and what she had wanted had been vague, unformed – a kiss would have sufficed. Now what did she want, what did she expect? Now she was more a woman and she found that, in the safety of her bed, she could allow her mind to wonder, to imagine what his body was like, what it would be like for him to kiss and caress her – her imagination never allowed her to go further than that. That was what worried her, she wanted a physical relationship with him, but she doubted whether she could manage the reality.

Soon they were taking walks together. One morning she took him up the driveway and for miles along the cliff. But they never did that again, not after experiencing Juniper's annoyance when they got back.

'Where have you been? We thought you were lost. How dare you just wander off like that,' she said angrily.

'I'm sorry, I didn't think anyone would be worried. I know the area so well, Miss Juniper,' Annie said apologetically. She still addressed Juniper in this formal way and Juniper had never corrected her, although it was 'Alice' and 'Harry' and 'Maddie' with the others.

'It was my fault, Ma.'

'I know whose fault it was, Harry.'

'But . . .' he began impotently, looking appealingly at Annie.

'I've something I want you to see, Harry, come with me. We'll take tea in the hall, Annie,' Juniper ordered pointedly, as she swept from the room.

Harry sought Annie out as soon as he could get away from his mother. He was full of apologies for Juniper's behaviour.

'It's all right, Harry, I don't mind,' Annie lied.

'But it's so unlike her. She's usually so free and easy with people.'

'Not with me,' Annie muttered.

'Sorry? What did you say?'

'Nothing,' she lied again. One thing she had learnt from Chris was never to criticize a man's mother.

After that little incident they tended to gulp their breakfasts and walk when everyone was still safely tucked away in their rooms. Once Harry had seen the cove, that was where he most wanted to be. They spent many a happy morning beachcombing, shellseeking and just sitting and looking at the water.

Juniper, suspicious of the friendship obviously growing between her son and Annie, cast around for something to distract her son. She remembered the papers in the muniment room and the fun she had had with Alice tracing the family tree, unearthing the family scandals. She had not thought of them in years, but for one whole summer they had fascinated her to the exclusion of everything else. It might have the same effect upon Harry.

'Have you done any more with them, Grandmama?' Juniper asked as, with Harry, she waited for Alice to unlock the door to the small room off the great hall, which was packed from floor to ceiling with boxes full of family papers.

'Not for years, not since you and I spent that time sifting through. Would you really be interested, Harry?'

'I'd be more than interested. I love deciphering old documents, but with my own family it's going to be doubly fascinating.'

Juniper's plan failed. Instead of going for morning walks, Annie and Harry now spent their time poring over the papers. Years before, Alice had started to catalogue the archives and Harry took up where she had left off. It was, he said with satisfaction, going to be a task that would take several years, requiring repeated visits to Gwenfer. As he said this he had looked Annie straight in the eye, his expression serious. He smiled only when she said 'good'. Certainly it was a historian's delight. The papers went back to the sixteenth century. Amongst them were the marriage settlements and legal agreements of all his Tregowan of Gwenfer ancestors, their letters, their lawsuits, their wills.

'It must be odd to find out who you are in this way.' Annie looked up from the faded letter she was reading. 'This is a love letter, it's beautiful. How many people can possibly know what their ancestors thought of each other?'

'Only half my ancestors. The Coptons lost their papers years ago. I've always suspected they were rather a rum lot, but the Tregowans are much more interesting.'

'I know who my grandparents were and that's about it,' she said grinning at him.

'When we've done this, we'll trace your family.'

'Oh, don't be silly, that would be impossible.' But she was still grinning. These would take years and then they would make a start on her family – it meant he intended to keep seeing her.

'No, it wouldn't be. Once you know how it's quite easy. Would you like that?'

'I'd love it.'

'Great, but first you can help me with these. Can you sort this box – wills, settlements, all in different piles . . .'

They had been at Gwenfer for ten days when suddenly Juniper announced they were going back to London within the hour.

'But my dear, I thought you would be here for at least a month,' Alice said, her voice full of disappointment.

'I was, but Jonathan can't get here so I've got to return.'

'I don't see why, Juniper.'

'If he were my husband you wouldn't think twice about it, would you? You'd think it my duty to be with him,' Juniper said briskly.

'Well, yes, but . . .'

'He is my husband. All that's lacking is the marriage certificate.'

Maddie, who was a witness to this conversation, had to look out of the window. She knew perfectly well why they were leaving so suddenly: Juniper had seen a photograph of Jonathan in a newspaper gossip column, with a very pretty young woman on his arm – that was enough.

Harry raced to find Annie on hearing the news, but she had gone shopping in Penzance. He left without saying goodbye to her and worse, he thought, as he sat silent in the car, they had not even kissed each other.

Annie was devastated to find Harry had left. She should not have been such a fool and had stupid dreams, she told herself. She got on with her work and hoped that would help her forget such nonsense. She changed her mind two days later when a letter arrived from Harry, and all her dreams returned. Each night, after rereading it, she slipped it under her pillow before allowing herself to dream.

Two weeks later Juniper and Jonathan left England. They flew to New York, for Juniper to see her advisers. She might be bored by business but she was never to allow that disinterest to slip into neglect again. Jonathan was to see his American publishers. In August Harry would join them in Greece for a month once, as a ward of court, he had obtained the necessary permission.

12

Polly had never been the sort of woman who fainted, but the contents of the letter in her hand made her closer to it than at any other time in her life.

'Good God!' she exclaimed and sat down heavily in a chair. 'How wonderful.'

'Are you all right, Polly? You look ill,' Gertie said, with concern.

'It's from the agents. Do you remember that pleasant woman, Mrs Huntley, who came to view the house with the young man you thought looked like Hal? Well . . . it seems she wants to purchase Hurstwood.'

'I wouldn't have expected to hear you say that was wonderful news, Polly,' Andrew said, from the depths of his armchair where he was engrossed in *The Farmers Weekly*.

'Wait till you hear this: she doesn't want to live here, she wants us to continue just as we are. She's willing to pay the asking price – the agents never expected to get that – and she's paying us a retainer to run the place for her, but, and this is the really odd bit, she doesn't expect any income – she wants any profits put back into the estate. The only proviso is that it's taken off the market immediately – no auction, no other offers to be considered.' She looked up from the letter. 'Look.' She handed the paper over to Andrew. 'The bank will have to agree with that, surely.'

'Is she mad?' Gertie asked.

'Mad? I couldn't care less if she's certifiable so long as they don't lock her up until she's signed everything and it's watertight.' Polly was jumping up and down with excitement. 'It's the next best thing, isn't it? Even if we can't own it, we'll still be here.'

'There has to be a catch in it somewhere.' Andrew looked up from the letter.

'Why do you always have to see the worst side, Andrew? Perhaps for once something good is going to happen to us. It's about bloody time,' Polly said with exasperation. Andrew looked away from her, but not before she saw the hurt expression on his face. She was immediately across the room and kneeling at his chair. Gertie quietly left the room. 'Andrew, I didn't mean that.'

'I wouldn't blame you if you did. Let's face it, you've had a hard life ever since we married. Really, Polly, I didn't mean to upset you. I just didn't want you let down.'

'Tell me what you're worried about. We have to discuss this.'

'It's too good to be true. It feels wrong. I mean, why spend so much money on a house and land you don't intend to live in or farm, and then pay us that ludicrous sum to stay here? It doesn't make sense, does it? It's fishy.'

'We need legal advice.'

'Lots of it,' Andrew agreed, beginning methodically to fill his pipe.

A week later they had signed the papers. Their solicitors had gone over everything with a fine-tooth comb, there was nothing wrong in the offer, their advice was to accept. However, they recommended, and wrote to the buyer's firm of solicitors, that Polly and Andrew be given a tenancy of Hurstwood, for which they would naturally be prepared to forgo the retainer. The reply came back that there was no objection to the tenancy and that the additional money would be required by the Slaters to get the farm back on its feet. Their lawyers encouraged them to sign and quickly.

When the documents came they did not have Mrs Huntley's name on them but that of a company called Dart Properties, which sounded very strange to Gertie and Andrew, but Polly could not have cared less who was buying it. They could stay at Hurstwood, that was all that mattered.

Another week passed. Polly was alone one day when a delivery van turned into the driveway. No one ever sent Polly flowers so she was really more curious about the large basket of orchids than the big manila envelope also presented to her by the driver of the van. She sat at the hall table and made herself attend to the envelope first. Inside were a pile of documents and a letter from her solicitor asking her to sign where they had marked with a pencil cross. How dull, she thought. Putting the documents to one side, she turned her attention to the flowers. She opened the small envelope. She had to read the message twice before she could take it in. Feverishly she delved again into the envelope of documents and this time she read them. The words seemed to dance in front of her eyes.

The documents were the deeds of Hurstwood, but instead of Dart Properties as the owners she saw her own name. The house had been transferred into her sole name – Hurstwood was hers again.

She picked up the card again and fingered it thoughtfully.

'*Am I forgiven now, Polly? Love Juniper.*'

Polly had never cried over the impending loss of her house, she had always managed to control her anguish, but this was too much. Gertie found her still sitting at the hall table, her head on her arms, sobbing uncontrollably.

'Polly, what has happened?'

Polly could not speak, but slid the documents and Juniper's card across to her grandmother.

'Good gracious.' It was Gertie's turn to sit down heavily. 'Well what a surprise.'

'I was so happy, Grandmama. I thought Hurstwood was safe. But now . . .'

'What on earth do you mean?'

'Well, I can't accept, can I? You must see that, Grandmama.'

'I'm afraid I don't.'

'For a start it's too ridiculously generous, typical of Juniper, of course. But I could never take it, it would smack too much of charity. Why should she do this? What are her motives? After all that's happened between us . . .'

'Can't accept? What nonsense is this? After all the trouble that young woman has caused over the years? Obviously she is trying to make amends. As a gesture it could be regarded as a trifle vulgar, however, she is an American after all, and they always do things on a larger scale.' Gertie hooted with laughter. 'Of course you must accept, Polly. It would be churlish to refuse.'

Chapter Seven

1

Maddie wandered through the garden of the island house. Her throat felt tight and it ached from trying not to cry. She was hurt and despised herself for being so. She had lived with Juniper long enough to know how difficult she could be and it was stupid of her to let Juniper wear her down. When something upset Juniper she invariably took it out on the nearest person – this time it was Maddie.

Maddie sat on a stone bench placed between the pillars of a mock ruined temple Juniper had built. It was Maddie's favourite place; from here she could see the sea stretching into the distance. When she was hurt or upset, she often came here. She would look across the ocean and long to be the other side of it. Then why wasn't she?

Maddie took a packet of cigarettes from her pocket, lit one and inhaled deeply. She could not leave, that was what she told herself time and again. What would Juniper do without her? What would become of her?

She extinguished her cigarette with the heel of her shoe, picked up the stub end and wrapped it in a tissue. The place was too perfect to mar it with her litter. Smoking? She had not smoked for years, so what had made her pick up that packet? There had been plenty of other times when she had felt just as demoralised, so what was different this time? Maddie feared she knew the answer: she was reaching the end with Juniper.

She was a fool. She would be forty next birthday and she had no home, no husband, no children – nothing. She had devoted herself to Juniper, kidding herself that she was indispensable. But no one was that to Juniper.

Maddie had frequently seen her drop people without a thought. Friends who thought they too were loved by Juniper would suddenly find the invitations had ceased, letters were unanswered, telephone calls not returned. Maddie had often been part of the conspiracy. To her shame, if it was someone she did not particularly like, she had quite enjoyed the game. But why should she assume the same would not happen to her?

She supposed she should have seen this morning's drama coming, it was partly her fault – she should have kept her big mouth shut.

Maddie, recognizing Harry's writing on the envelope, had taken the letter straight in to Juniper, knowing she would want to read it before looking at anything else. She waited, tidying up some books on a side table for she was keen to hear its contents. For the past three years Harry had visited the island for up to two weeks at a time; they had also met up with him on several trips to Paris and a short visit to London. Juniper was happiest when her son was with her. She seemed to change, to scintillate, almost to glow when he was with them. That's why the letter was so important.

'Is he coming?' Maddie asked. Juniper was sitting up in bed, her head bowed, blonde hair falling forward hiding her face, her shoulders slumped. 'Oh, no, he isn't.'

'He thinks he should spend Christmas with Leigh and Caroline.' Juniper spoke in a tight, controlled voice. 'Ungrateful little brat,' she added, after a lengthy pause.

'Juniper, that's not fair. Harry is in an intolerable position. He has an obligation to them, after all.'

'What obligation?' Juniper said sharply.

'Well, they did bring him up. They must be like parents to him and he probably doesn't want to hurt their feelings.'

'What about my feelings? What about them? I'm his parent, they're not.'

'But he comes every summer.'

'I wanted to spend Christmas with him. Do you realize,

I haven't spent Christmas with him since he was a year old?'

'It must have been dreadfully hard, Juniper, but I see why he has made this decision. I'm sure you will too when you've calmed down.'

'Calmed down, what do you mean, calmed down? I'm perfectly calm.' But Juniper's voice had a dangerous edge to it. 'I'm amazed at his lack of gratitude, his inconsideration. They've had him every other Christmas. Is it asking too much to want to share it with him twice in his twenty years?'

'I know, poor Juniper,' Maddie said sympathetically.

'Don't be patronizing.'

'I didn't mean to be, I'm sorry.' Maddie felt herself stepping backwards, as if she were trying to escape from the bitterness in Juniper's voice.

'I think he's avoiding me. I think they've been poisoning his mind against me.'

'Don't be silly. He's his own master, he wouldn't listen to them.'

'Then why isn't he coming? And answer me this, why, when the varsity summer vacs are so long, why does he only come for two weeks? Why doesn't he come for the whole summer? A normal son would, with a mother living in a fantastic place like this.'

'He probably has a lot of work to do in the holidays. Some of the students even stay up in college during the vacs, to catch up.'

'What on earth would you know about it?' Juniper said dismissively.

'My father is a college porter, that's how I know,' Maddie replied sharply.

'You needn't snap at me like that.'

'I wasn't snapping.'

'You were, you're just like everyone else. You loathe me really, you despise me, I can hear it in your voice. You're only here for my money and what I give you.'

'Juniper, that is grossly unfair,' Maddie said angrily.

'Is it? Look at you. Nearly forty and still hanging on here when you should be out looking for a man. So, I have to ask myself, why are you here? The answer that comes winging back to me is dollars and the lifestyle I give you.' Juniper was not shouting, she never did. When she attacked, the very reasonableness of her tone made it all seem worse. Maddie looked at Juniper with disbelief, turned on her heel and walked out of the room. She wished she could walk out of Juniper's life.

Then why didn't she? Why stay and have that sort of insult hurled at her? Perhaps Juniper was right. Perhaps she had become addicted to this life of luxury, maybe she was scared she could not exist without it any more.

No, she shook her head in a determined way. Life with Juniper was not as easy as people assumed. The routine never varied – breakfast at eleven. A swim. Reading and writing letters. Lunch at three. Too much wine so that a siesta was needed. Martinis at eight. Dinner, by which time everyone was already drunk, was served at ten, followed by drinking until bedtime at two if she was lucky, but often later. Juniper had one strict rule: no one, no matter their age, could retire to bed until she herself did. If a guest chose to break this rule they were never invited again. If she had told Juniper the truth she would have said she understood why Harry rationed his time with her to a fortnight.

When they travelled things were little better. They rose at the same time and the period between breakfast and lunch would be filled by discussion as to where they should eat. Once this had been decided the next decision would be where they were to dine. Then they shopped. Juniper still loved to shop. Maddie had lost count of the countries she had visited where she had not seen the sights of the city she was in, merely the hotel, the shops and the restaurants.

As the years slipped by Maddie had watched Juniper change. She had observed a woman who fled from boredom become increasingly bored. Despite everything

Juniper had been determined to be happy, but too often now Maddie saw her slide into depression. She had once had a charming innocence and enthusiasm for people, but Maddie had seen her openness become cynicism. And the abundant self-confidence she had once possessed had been replaced by a sad vulnerability.

Maddie knew it was not surprising, given the way she had been treated by the men in her life. Juniper was still deeply hurt about Hal. A hurt exacerbated by the news from New York that Hal was deliriously happy with his new wife. There was no talk of other men in his life. His wife was now pregnant and, as if to add insult to injury, Juniper had learnt that she was not a rich woman, money had played no part in the marriage. Juniper tortured herself with the thought that Hal was perfectly capable of loving a woman after all, but not her.

Dominic, after Juniper had allowed herself to be cited as an adulteress, had banked her more than generous settlement cheque and waited no more than a day after their divorce was final before marrying Ruth, his mealy-mouthed secretary. Since then, he had taken every possible opportunity to blacken Juniper's name to the extent that those who knew her found difficulty in recognizing the woman he described.

Since that awful day in the hospital in America, Theo's name had never been spoken. Maddie still thought this was a mistake. There were times when someone would mention a particular restaurant in New York, or a certain piece of music would be played on the radio and Maddie would see an expression of such ineffable sadness cross Juniper's face that she longed to reach out to her, hold her, make her talk of Theo, but she never had.

And now there was Jonathan – a man who appeared incapable of fidelity. When they returned to the island after the visit to Gwenfer, Jonathan frequently claimed that he had to go to Athens on business, though what possible business it could be, he would never say. It did not take much intelligence to put two and two together.

Juniper hired a detective to follow him, something Maddie had warned her she would regret. The detective reported that Jonathan had a mistress – a young English woman, about twenty years old, the woman in the press photograph that had made Juniper cut short her visit to Alice.

Maddie supported Juniper through her anger and grief, and still did not know if they were caused by the woman's existence as Jonathan's lover or her youth. Juniper seemed to be obsessed with the thought that she was only twenty. Any woman would have found such a situation difficult to accept, but to a woman of Juniper's beauty it must have been unbearable. It did not matter how much Maddie told her she was still the most beautiful woman she knew, Juniper could not believe it. She would spend hours just staring at her image in the mirror with a lost, sad look on her face.

When Jonathan returned from Athens after the detective's report there had been a monumental row. It had washed through the house as they followed each other from room to room screaming at the tops of their voices. Maddie took a bottle of wine, a jar of olives, and locked herself into her room for the duration.

Jonathan eventually got rid of the girl in Athens and was rewarded with a speedboat and an E-type Jaguar. But he paid a price. Although this had all happened over three years ago, Juniper no longer trusted him. She would not leave him alone for one moment and trips to Athens on his own were out of the question. When she said she wanted to spend every moment of her day with him, Juniper meant it. When he went to the room he used for writing she would accompany him. They sat at matching desks imported from Paris, like Victoria and Albert, and as he wrote, she wrote. Or that was the idea. The problem was, Jonathan had more to write about and Juniper rapidly became bored and restless. She would begin to talk and then try to persuade him to leave the boring writing – come and swim, come for a drive, come for some olives, come and make love to me, come Jonathan, come . . .

His publishing house began to bombard him with letters and requests for the manuscript of the new book, now seriously overdue. The letters were pleasant to begin with, but slowly the tone began to change. Then his agent came to stay.

'I'm sorry, Jonathan, at this rate they're going to drop it altogether.'

'They can't do that, what about the contract?' Juniper said with spirit.

'They can and they will. They're very patient but . . .'

'But he's a genius. You can't expect a genius to work to order like any old hack.'

'Darling, I'm not a genius,' Jonathan said, looking sheepishly at his agent. 'I've been lazy. Too easily distracted, that's my problem, Peter. It's too much of a lotus land here.'

'What can we do to stop them?' Juniper asked.

'Well, they're unlikely to ask for the advance back, at least that's one good thing.' Peter looked worried, even so.

'There wouldn't be much point, I spent it ages ago,' Jonathan laughed.

'I'll give it back to them, then they won't have to keep bothering and nagging him. He can go to another publisher, one who understands. I'll buy a publishing house, what about that? Poor darling, how can he be expected to work with this pressure on him? How much is it?' she demanded, already getting her cheque book out of her handbag.

Jonathan looked at his agent and shrugged his shoulders. There was little he could do about it. It was a relief almost. These days he often doubted if he would ever finish this book, or even if he would ever write another one, or if he even wanted to. If he had married Polly there would have been no interruptions, he thought. He could just imagine how the whole house would have revolved around his work. Ah well, he sighed, picking up his glass and finding it empty.

'Best do as the lady says, Peter,' he grinned at his agent, and turned to open another bottle.

The problem, as far as Maddie could see, was that now the advance had been paid back, he did not have to write. Now there was no attempt at any discipline whatsoever. Jonathan did nothing. He slept late. He never went to bed sober. Although he appeared to have few distractions, Maddie knew otherwise. Despite Juniper's certainty that he could never be unfaithful since she deliberately spent nearly every waking moment with him, she had forgotten the times she was shopping or at the hairdresser's in the small town by the port, or when she was taking a leisurely bath. Maddie knew for certain of one lover, a young Australian who was living higher up the hill in an old shepherd's house. She never found out if Jonathan had arranged for the woman to live so conveniently close or whether they had met by accident. And she had seen him once too often creeping out of the guest wing when there were young women staying.

Maddie sighed and looked out at the sea miles away across the plain. She supposed she should have despised Jonathan, maybe she should even have told Juniper about him. But she did not. In truth she felt sorry for the man. He had such talent, yet Juniper, and the life he led, seemed to be sucking all that talent out of him.

Maddie wished Polly would come. It was not an empty wish. The two friends corresponded regularly now; Juniper's letters begging Polly to accept Hurstwood, Polly's rejecting the plan. A compromise had been reached: the Slaters now had a tenancy. Maddie knew they had been invited to the island. If only Polly came, maybe she would be able to have some control over Juniper, for Maddie had none. Juniper, when she was in the mood, drank compulsively. Maddie lived in fear that one night she would find her collapsed – another reason she stayed.

Almost wearily Maddie stood up and wandered back towards the house. It had grown now out of all recognition; there was a new guest wing and several guest bungalows in the grounds. Juniper had built a huge room with a wall of glass for parties. The swimming pool had been rebuilt so that now one could swim in the open or under cover in a huge palm house. It was all very grand and luxurious, the furnishings and wall-hangings like something out of the *Arabian Nights*, but all the same Maddie preferred it the way it had been when they first found it – a dead woman's Moorish dream. Now it was a sprawling, modern palace, beautiful but soulless.

As she reached the terrace, Juniper appeared.

'Darling Maddie, will you ever forgive grumpy horrible old me?' She smiled brilliantly. 'I let my disappointment get in the way.'

'That's all right, Juniper,' Maddie said. It was, she knew, inevitable that she would forgive her.

'I've solved it all. We shall go to England ourselves for Christmas. We'll go to Gwenfer. I shan't tell Alice, we'll surprise her. What do you think?' Juniper was jumping about with excitement, her earlier anger with Maddie completely forgotten.

2

They did not go to Gwenfer for Christmas. They had made a detour via Rome: Juniper needed some silk shirts made and Jonathan wanted to visit his tailor. They were staying in the Excelsior and their arrival had been duly reported in the *Rome Daily American*. Maddie had taken the telephone call, from a Signora Antonio.

'I don't know anyone called Antonio,' Juniper had announced, refusing to take the call.

'I'm sorry, but Mrs Boscar isn't here,' Maddie lied, stumbling over Juniper's maiden name. She was still having difficulty remembering it, even though Juniper

504

had been using it for a couple of years now. She said it made her feel finally finished with Dominic, as if by not using his name she could erase the marriage from her, and everybody else's, minds.

'Would you take a message then, please?'

Maddie mimed to Juniper for a pen and paper. Juniper handed her a pad.

'If you could please tell her that Tommy is in Rome until Wednesday and would love to see her. I'm staying at the Eden, just round the corner.'

'Tommy?' Maddie repeated, not sure if she had heard correctly.

'That's right . . .'

'Tommy!' Juniper shouted, diving across the bed and grabbing the telephone from Maddie's hands. 'Tommy, where are you? I thought you were dead. Why did you never write? Oh Tommy, Tommy . . .'

Within the half hour Tommy Antonio was seated opposite a Juniper who could not sit still with excitement.

'Maddie, Tommy was made my guardian when my grandfather died. But you were more than that, weren't you Tommy? You were my best friend.' Juniper explained. 'And my grandfather's lover.' She grinned slyly.

'You always were too knowledgeable for your own good, Juniper.' Tommy moved uncomfortably in her chair.

'Champagne, to celebrate.'

Tommy looked at her watch. 'A little too early in the day for me, Juniper.'

'Don't be so stuffy. Maddie, order some champers, there's a pet.'

Maddie looked across at the older woman who shrugged her shoulders in resignation. Maddie liked the look of her. Maddie had good instincts and was rarely wrong. There was an orderliness and calm to this woman she liked. She was beautifully dressed in a neat navy-blue barathea suit and expensive silk shirt, Pucci, she was sure. Maddie wondered how old she was, it was difficult to judge. She surmised that Tommy was the sort of person who had looked middle-aged when young and probably looked the same now she was verging on her sixties. She had to be at least that age, for Juniper herself would be forty-two in February. Yet with her fine head of chestnut-coloured hair swept back into a neat bun, her discreet but immaculate make-up, Tommy looked no older than her mid-forties herself.

Maddie opened the champagne and then discreetly left the room.

'Why did you never contact me, Tommy?' Juniper asked, pretending to sulk.

'My dear Juniper, how can you ask me that, after the letter you wrote me?' Tommy asked fairly sternly.

'What letter?' Juniper sat up straight with interest.

'I wrote to you that I was married to Stefan Antonio – he's a very successful doctor,' she added her face glowing with pride, 'and that you were always welcome at my home near Florence. You replied that you never wanted to see me again since, as you put it, I had gone behind your back and married – deserted you, you said.'

'Tommy!' Juniper sat back appalled. 'You must have been so hurt.'

'Of course I was. Maybe if you hadn't been married to Hal, I might have tried to sort it out. But I didn't like him and knew I never would. And if that was your attitude, there seemed little point. I couldn't ask Alice's help since it was obvious from her letters that she wasn't seeing you either. Then the war came and, well, one thing followed another. But yesterday I saw the name Boscar in the newspaper and thought, I wonder if that's Juniper and if the dreaded Hal is no more? It seemed worth the risk.'

'Tommy, I never wrote that letter. You must believe me. I admit I was very mixed up at that period and I did some silly things. But I didn't write that – never. I'll bet that was Hal's doing. He wouldn't have wanted you in touch with me. You're too clever and smart, you see.

You'd have got in the way of his embezzling a fortune from me.'

'Juniper. How awful! Oh, why didn't I persist? You can't imagine the times I've regretted not picking up the pieces and trying again. If only I had . . .'

'Well, you've found me now. I was going to England for Christmas. What are you and your husband doing? Join me. We can go to Switzerland. I'll book us into the Dolder Grand Hotel in Zurich, what do you say . . .?'

Tommy held up her hand at the torrent of words pouring from Juniper. 'Your grandmother, is she still alive?'

'Very much so, as fit as a flea. She'll be eighty-four in February.'

'She'll be expecting you for Christmas herself, surely? You mustn't disappoint her.'

'No. She won't be expecting me. Oh no, let's follow my plan. We've so much to catch up on.'

'I've a better idea. Stefan and I were going to our chalet in the Dolomites, just the two of us. There's masses of room. You and your party must join us.'

It was arranged. The following week they were installed in Stefan's chalet in the mountains.

Annie had been lurking in the great hall for a couple of hours. Her excuse was that she was checking the tree to make sure the decorations were secure. In fact she was in the hall so that she would be the first to hear Harry's car on the driveway, the first to welcome him.

'The more you listen the longer he'll be. It's like waiting for a kettle to boil,' Alice teased when she found Annie fiddling with a near-perfect tree.

'Alice, I'm so excited. It's weeks since I saw him.'

'I know, my dear. But think, you've got him here for a whole month now.' Alice leant on her stick as she spoke. The arthritis, which had been plaguing her for a good ten years, had begun a new attack with a vengeance. Alice was philosophical about it, what more could she expect at her age? She had been so healthy all her life that she could hardly complain. What bothered her was how useless she was becoming and how totally she relied on Annie. The young woman did nearly everything now as Alice slowed up, including most of the cooking for the guests. If Annie were to leave then Gwenfer would have to be sold. Alice was fully aware she could not struggle on alone. She had fought as long and as hard as she could, she had steeled herself so that when that day came – the day Annie left – so would she. She would close the house up, swathe everything in sheeting, lock the door and try not to worry about the house and its uncertain future with other owners. She had already secretly investigated suitable residential hotels in Cornwall she might go to.

If Juniper had cared more about the house, then things would be different. She had always believed that Juniper felt about it as she did, but in the past ten years she had come to accept that it was her own dream, not Juniper's. Juniper was only happy when she was free to roam as she wished. She would never make Alice's mistake of loving a house like a person, of allowing that house to dominate her life and entrap her.

Alice was beginning to feel guilty about Annie. She would be twenty-four the following June, time for her to be thinking of marriage and children, not running Gwenfer for Alice. Annie was as trapped as she was. Apart from the guests and the shopkeepers in Penzance, she never met anyone of the opposite sex. Their guests were always charming, but invariably middle-aged, certainly not one of them had been a young maiden's dream. Annie said she did not care, that she was happy, that she was content to wait for Harry's visits.

Alice liked Harry and she felt he would never knowingly hurt Annie, but she worried that he might do so unintentionally. For Alice had noticed in the young man a detachment, a degree of coldness that was not surprising given the circumstances of his upbringing, but which at the same time reminded her uncomfortably of his father.

Alice had watched the attraction and affection develop between Harry and Annie. To be young and in love . . . Alice had not forgotten what that was like. But had the past made Harry into someone who would never be able to love totally, just like his mother? Alice sighed at the idea. Annie would need to be deeply loved, anything less and she would be further damaged. And everything was happening for them too soon, too quickly. Apart from the two weeks he spent with his mother each summer and the occasional duty weekend with his Uncle Leigh, Harry spent every spare moment here at Gwenfer to be close to Annie.

Too soon it might be, but to see Annie emerging from her shell when he was here was lovely to witness. She shone, she changed, she became the beauty she really was. But the moment Harry left, back the girl would creep into that defensive carapace she had erected around herself.

Alice wondered whether she was worrying unnecessarily about them. Was she seeing ghosts where no ghosts existed? But, still, Harry lived in a different world when he was up at Cambridge, with friends more sophisticated than Annie. He was clever and educated whereas Annie, although bright, had never completed her education. Could such a relationship last?

'He's here,' Annie shouted, bringing Alice back into the present. Annie rushed to the door, mildly cursing the huge bolts as she pulled them back, and hurtled out into the dark of the windy night. When she returned with Harry on her arm and Alice saw the happiness on both their faces, she chided her worries and hid them away. She hobbled towards them and kissed her great-grandson welcome.

They had a perfect evening, talking and joking together with the easiness of great friends. Annie had cooked an excellent dinner and Alice discreetly went to bed early, leaving the young couple alone. They sat in the kitchen having a last drink.

'Alice looks exhausted Annie. Every time I come here she seems to have aged.'

'She's getting tired out, Harry. We need more help. I can do the cooking and check the housekeeping, that sort of thing, but then there are the books and all the correspondence and the ordering. No wonder she's tired. But, you know, sometimes I think that it's not just the work, I think she's getting tired of living.'

'What will you do if . . .'

'When she dies?' Annie shuddered. 'I can hardly think about it, I love her so. She's been more of a mother to me than a real mother could be. I just don't know, Harry. It's funny too, she worries about me all the time. I think she has convinced herself that I stay because of her, that I'd rather be away from here. Really it's the other way around; I don't know what I'd do without her.'

'You've got me, Annie. I'll always be around.' He grinned at her in the light from the lamp that hung low over the kitchen table.

'Will you, Harry?'

'You don't believe me?' He was suddenly serious.

'I believe you. I believe that's how you feel now. But how will you feel in the future?'

'The same,' he said defensively.

'Harry, my darling, I don't want you to think you have to make promises you might not be able to keep. We've got now. That's what matters to me. Today. I want to spend it with you, I want to make it as perfect as possible. Tomorrow? I'll face that when it comes.'

'I love you, Annie,' he said. He was not sure if he did, but he was certain it was what Annie wanted to hear. One thing he did know, he liked her more than any other girl he had met or bedded – and in Cambridge there were many. When he was with Annie he felt he did not have to act, he felt he could be himself. That was worth a lot. She was lovely and he wanted to make love to her more than anyone else in the world. 'Maybe we should get married,' he suddenly said, using the ploy that invariably worked.

'Oh, Harry,' she sighed, 'don't, don't spoil things.'

'I'm not. You talk to me sometimes, Annie, as if I were a child. I'm only two years younger than you and in some ways I'm a lot older. You're going to be my wife, I've decided.'

'I can just imagine your mother's reaction to that!' Annie laughed, not daring to take him seriously.

'I don't care what she says. It's not as if she's been like a real mother, is it?'

'She might cut you off without a penny.'

'So? I don't care if she does.'

'That's when you sound younger than me, when you say things like that. You'd hate me eventually if you lost your inheritance because of me.'

'You don't seem to think much of me.'

'It's not that, but you do seem to be scared of her. Why else did you ask us not to let Juniper know you were staying here for Christmas?'

'For heaven's sake, I'm not scared, I just prefer a quiet life. I don't see any point in making her angry if I don't have to. She was cross enough when I refused to go to Greece. Come on, Annie. What's the matter? You sound really scratchy.'

'I'm sorry. It's just that I think if anyone can separate us, it will be Juniper. She loathes me. I don't know why, but it's always been that way between us.'

Harry put his hand out and touched hers gently. 'I love you, Annie.'

'I love you too, Harry.'

'I want to sleep with you.' There, he had said it. He looked at her intently, waiting for her response.

Abruptly she withdrew her hand. 'Harry!' She looked up at him, her eyes wide with horror. 'Don't ask me, please. You know how I feel, you know I'm frightened.'

'Don't you think I'm frightened too? I don't make a habit of this, you know.' He lied easily.

'You know what I'm talking about. You know. You told me in the summer you understood.'

'I know I did. But I've been thinking about it. You love me, you like me to kiss you. Good heavens, Annie, we do everything else but sleep together – we get so close. Do you know what I think? I think you're imagining that there might be problems. I think we should sleep together and see what happens. We'll never know otherwise.'

'But what if I can't?' She felt desperately nervous.

'Annie, I told you, I love you. I can wait the rest of my life for you if necessary.'

Far into the night Harry argued, cajoled and begged to be allowed into her bed. Annie countered the arguments, tried to ignore the cajoling and put her hands over her ears when he begged. He touched her, caressed her, kissed her and she felt her resolve slipping away until exhausted from overwork and his cleverness she finally agreed.

They crept to her room. Before undressing she turned the light off. He lit a candle. She blinked as she saw his dark eyes glinting, his hunger for her blatantly obvious, as he looked at her naked body. He engulfed her in his arms and led her gently to the bed. She lay woodenly in his arms but her fear of him physically gave way to her fear that if she did not allow him to love her she might lose him.

As his hands began to search her body she closed her eyes prepared to feel a nausea rise in her. But it did not. Instead she found her body responding to his caress enjoying what was happening to her as if her mind no longer had any control over her, as if her body belonged to someone else.

And then her mind, with its dreadful memories and fears, like her body, changed too. The trauma faded and she heard herself moaning with pleasure. She realized she was pushing her body against him. Knew that she was longing for him to enter her and possess her and make her his forever.

That night each time he took her body she gave him more of her heart.

Christmas in the Dolomites was like celebrating the festival in a picture postcard. The snow was thick as if a plump white eiderdown had been thrown over the land; in contrast the sky was improbably blue and the sun shone every day. The normally cruel edges of the mountains were softened by the snow and looked their most beautiful and the chalet, traditionally built of wood, was perfect.

The house party had grown. Stefan's son from his first marriage, Giovanni, had arrived from Rome. Maddie, making her mind up immediately, found she didn't like him. He was too handsome, too charming, too smart. He reminded her of a crocodile with his white teeth flashing in his tanned face. Juniper, on the other hand, appeared to be entranced with the young man. Unknown to both of them, Giovanni was not liked by either his father or his stepmother. He had arrived uninvited. He claimed he was a painter, but Stefan, while conceding that modern art was frequently not appreciated and that the young should be encouraged even if it was not always easy to understand, had totally failed to see any talent in his son, except as a sponger.

Tommy's goddaughter, Bette, had arrived unexpectedly from New York. Maddie liked Bette, who like many young Americans she had met, had the lovable exuberance of a puppy demanding to be liked. She was tall and loose-limbed, always casually dressed, but with the effortless style typical of her race. She had a mass of black unruly curls, bright red lips and, when she laughed, she showed her perfect white American teeth. She was clever; despite her twenty-odd years, she had already established herself as a freelance writer for several magazines. Her passion was literature and her excitement and enthusiasm when she found that *the* Jonathan Middlebank was a fellow guest was, Maddie thought, endearing.

No one, Maddie had decided, could dislike Tommy's husband. He was a kind, softly spoken man, with eyes which looked at one with gentleness, and at Tommy with total adoration. Whenever Maddie intercepted that look she was envious and longed to be loved at least once in her life that way.

Everything should have been perfect: it rapidly became disastrous.

Jonathan seemed to start the rot by not reacting to Juniper flirting with Giovanni. It certainly appeared to goad Juniper into greater excesses of coquetry. She was also drinking heavily, not that Tommy or her husband were supposed to know. Juniper had followed her usual practice, when staying in somebody else's house, of taking her own drink supply with her. She had made Maddie store the bottles in her own room.

'Thanks. I just love the thought of the maid labelling me an alcoholic,' Maddie had laughingly complained as Juniper stumbled into her room burdened with a heavy case. When opened, it revealed enough gin, brandy and whisky to see Juniper and Jonathan through the holiday.

'Tommy would disapprove and then she'll lecture me. I'd hate that, it could ruin my Christmas.'

'Juniper, you're not a child, for goodness' sake. You can drink what you want.'

'No, I can't, not where my grandmother and Tommy are concerned,' she grimaced and Maddie reluctantly stored away the bottles.

What Juniper had not thought out was that neither Tommy nor her husband were fools. Juniper arrived downstairs in the evenings a little too excitable and effervescent. In the mornings she took far too long to get going for someone whose body and mind were completely healthy. Her breath also smelt suspiciously of peppermint. It was Stefan who saw her have a dizzy spell and who rushed to her aid.

'I'd like to take your blood pressure, Juniper.'

'Stefan, darling, I wouldn't dream of letting you.

Doctors need holidays too. You don't want to start treating dreary patients.'

'It would only take a minute and I think it should be checked.'

'Oh fiddlesticks, Stefan. I stood up too fast, that's all it was.' Juniper brushed away his offer.

Maddie spoke to him privately that evening before the rest had come down for dinner.

'Juniper often gets dizzy spells like that, Stefan. I worry about it.'

'As you should. Won't she see a doctor?'

'Every time I suggest it she says she'll only go and see her doctors in London or New York. But when we're there she never does. She always finds some excuse or other . . .' Maddie shrugged.

'Tell me, how much does she drink?'

Maddie looked guiltily towards the door. 'She drinks every day and a lot of the time it's at an acceptable level. But there are days . . .' Maddie paused, finding it difficult to betray Juniper.

'When she drinks like crazy?' Stefan prompted her gently.

'Yes.'

'Any drugs?'

'No. No, I'm certain of that.'

'Cigarettes?'

'Far too many. I'd hate to hazard a guess. You see, Stefan, when I first began to work for Juniper I got a letter from her grandmother . . .' And Maddie told the sympathetic doctor the details of Juniper's illness when she was in her twenties and in London. 'She must have drunk masses since then. At the beginning I tried hard to get her to stop, but she never listens, not to me anyway,' Maddie said half-apologetically.

'Tommy says she wouldn't listen to her either even if she spoke to her.'

'You're worried too?'

'Yes. She could collapse any day. If her drinking is as I

fear, and with her medical history, well, not to put too fine a point on it, she's slowly killing herself.'

'My God! I had no idea it was that serious. Oh, poor Juniper.' Maddie was too shocked to say more.

'Poor Juniper indeed. Perhaps when this holiday is over I can talk to her and try to persuade her to enter my clinic for a rest.'

Christmas Day went well; it was as if everyone was trying to make it a huge success. As usual, Juniper had surpassed everyone else with her presents. She might have some glaring faults, but her generosity was beyond question. Everyone was included, even the old woman who came in from the local village to help with the washing up. It was a mystery to Maddie how she even knew who worked there. She had never seen Juniper enter the kitchen of any establishment in all the years she had been with her.

Bette's admiration for Jonathan was becoming embarrassing. She followed him around the house hanging on to his every word. They could be found curled up in the large armchairs in front of the log fire in the library, discussing literature. All the others watched Juniper, nervously expecting a reaction, but she said nothing, did not even seem to notice, or if she did, she pretended not to. Once she had realized that Jonathan was not upset by her flirting with Giovanni she had stopped, much to Maddie's relief. She hated the games Juniper and Jonathan were playing with each other.

At first Maddie believed Jonathan was just enjoying the admiration of a young fan, one with aspirations to write herself, and one who seemed to know his three novels even better than he did. But it began to dawn on Maddie that Jonathan was spending so much time with Bette because he was interested in her and what she had to say. They had too much in common for comfort.

But the crunch, when it came, was not over Bette, even though she might have been instrumental in bringing it about.

A snow storm had been raging for two days and it was impossible to get out of the house. Skiing was out of the question, as was walking and shopping. There was nothing to do but to stay indoors, beside the huge fires, talking, reading, playing cards and waiting for the storm to abate. Bette had persuaded Jonathan to read from one of his books. He had a good voice and they enjoyed listening to him.

'It's a shame there are no other writers here, isn't it? Then we could have a really great reading evening,' she said, sitting at Jonathan's feet, her long legs pulled up, her arms about her knees. Looking innocently about her. Maddie was certain she was longing for someone to ask her to read something she had written. But it did not work out that way.

'But we do have another writer here. Juniper writes.' Jonathan announced. 'Don't you, darling?'

'Is that so, Juniper? Oh, how wonderful, might we hear some of your work? It'd be just great, a real privilege,' Bette said gushingly.

'Don't get excited, Bette. She won't read to you. No one is allowed to see what Juniper writes, are they?' Jonathan looked across at Juniper, one eyebrow raised quizzically.

'That's not true. I'll read to you.' Juniper got to her feet. 'If you'll just bear with me while I get my notebook.' She slipped from the room.

'Good God, I don't believe this.' Jonathan was grinning with surprise. 'She scribbles like crazy, but I've never been allowed to see a word.'

'I'm not surprised, Jonathan. Who would dare show their work to a major writer like you?' Bette smiled up at her hero, with an expression of guileless admiration.

Juniper returned, holding a large red-leather book which Maddie had never seen before.

'This is all I've got with me,' she said half-apologetically. 'They're just poems.' Juniper looked around at the upturned faces and the pages of the book rustled as she leafed through it. Maddie realized that she was nervous, her hands shaking.

'Even better, I just can't live without poetry,' Bette said. 'Now, everyone, quiet.'

Juniper stood in the middle of the room, the red leather binding matching almost exactly the red of her skirt. 'I wrote this some time ago, of course . . . It's called "Pain" . . .'

Juniper coughed, the others waited expectantly.

> She was twenty,
> She who caused me pain.
> He was forty,
> He who did the same.
>
> In the room
> Night shade falling,
> Anguish deep inside me
> Would not go away.
> Death then I longed for,
> Death my friend who
> Would cause me no pain.

In the ensuing silence, the snort from Jonathan was like the report of a small cannon. Bette, as if taking her cue from him, began to giggle. Jonathan's shoulders shook as he fought to suppress his laughter. Maddie and Tommy, more sensitive to Juniper's feelings than to the quality of her work, began to clap, but were silenced by Juniper's expression.

'I'm glad I've managed to amuse you,' Juniper said coldly. She held the book close to herself as if she were protecting it.

'I'm sorry . . . Juniper . . .' Jonathan was struggling with the laughter still bubbling up inside him. 'I didn't mean . . .'

'I'm sure you didn't. And I suppose your little friend didn't mean to cackle either?'

'Oh, come on, Juniper. You must admit . . .' But Jonathan didn't finish.

'Admit what? I want to know, Jonathan.' Juniper was speaking in a dangerously controlled voice. No one else said a word.

'Very well,' Jonathan said, as if squaring up to her. 'You must admit that takes the biscuit for bad poetry.'

'We can't all be geniuses like you, Jonathan. But some of us try our best to do as well as we can.' She snapped the red-leather book shut, turned on her heel and left the room.

'That was horrible of you both,' Tommy admonished.

'Well, she shouldn't have read such drivel,' said Bette defensively.

'As a matter of fact, I thought it was rather good,' Tommy said.

'Oh, Tommy, I don't believe you. It was awful.' Bette was laughing again.

'It's a darn sight better than I could do.' Tommy glared angrily at her goddaughter.

'You know damn well what that poem referred to, Jonathan, what it cost her to write it, let alone read it. That was despicable.' Maddie was on her feet now, hands on hips, standing over Jonathan who still lolled in his armchair, apparently oblivious to the damage.

'Mind your own business, Maddie.'

'Anything to do with Juniper is my business. I won't stand by and see her hurt.'

'For God's sake, what's the drama about? It was a stupid little poem, that was all.'

'Is a poem ever stupid to the person who wrote it?' Stefan asked quietly, as he knocked his pipe out against the side of the fireplace.

Jonathan did not have time to answer. The door swung open with a bang and Juniper came in, hauling a large suitcase behind her.

'I've packed for you and I've telephoned the local guest house. They're sending up a car. You can collect your stuff from my house during January. I won't be there then. Good night, everyone, and goodbye, Jonathan.' Juniper turned back to the door.

Jonathan was on his feet in a flash and racing to grab her by the arm. 'Juniper, don't be silly.'

She looked at him icily. 'I'm not being silly, Jonathan. Our relationship has been dead for a long time. I stupidly tried to ignore reality.'

'I won't let you do this to me.'

'You have no choice. I'm doing it.' She pulled away from his grasp. At the door she looked back. 'Let's leave it at that, okay? No more fuss.' She closed the door.

'You can't go, it's still snowing.' Bette gazed up at Jonathan; she was frightened now and avoided looking at Tommy.

'It's stopped,' Tommy said quietly.

'I think I hear the car. It's only five minutes, Jonathan,' Stefan picked up the case as if to speed him to the door.

'I see,' Jonathan said, looking from Tommy to Stefan, his expression a mixture of belligerence and fear, as the realization that he might have gone too far with all of them dawned on him. 'Okay. But I'll be back in the morning to speak to her – when she's calmed down and got over this tantrum.'

In the morning when Jonathan arrived Juniper had gone and young Giovanni with her. Maddie was never to see her again.

4

Tommy felt enormous guilt for what had happened and was not comforted by Maddie telling her that the writing had been on the wall for some time for Jonathan.

Jonathan, at the beginning, could not believe that Juniper had been serious and kept returning to the chalet to reassure everyone that she would turn up in a few days and the incident would not even be mentioned. He kept to this conviction for a week. And then, overnight, became resigned to his relationship with Juniper being at an end. The other members of the party could only assume that he had been helped in reaching this conclusion by Bette, since ten days later he left for the Greek island to collect his possessions in her company.

In many ways Maddie thought that perhaps it was the best thing that could have happened to him, for Bette seemed to have rekindled his creativity. He had begun to talk excitedly of writing the next book even before he had left the Dolomites.

Of Juniper there was little news apart from a short note to Tommy a few days after she had left, thanking her politely for Christmas, but with no mention of Jonathan. A letter from Giovanni was more forthcoming: he said he was going to Tahiti with Juniper, and he included an envelope for Maddie. Inside was a cheque for three months' wages. There was no letter, nothing. Maddie stood holding the cheque and felt a dreadful bleakness. The years with Juniper had been difficult, but she had loved and cared for her in the only way she knew. She had thought she was important to Juniper; this cheque told her otherwise.

'What will you do, Maddie?' Tommy asked with concern when she saw the expression on her face.

'I don't know. Go back to Cambridge, I suppose. I should be able to get a job in one of the colleges. I've managed to save quite a bit. Juniper was always very generous to me,' she said loyally.

'In money terms I'm sure she was. But of herself? A sad fact of life, Maddie, is that I fear the very rich are different to the rest of us.'

Maddie turned away, unable yet to discuss Juniper with anyone. It hurt too much.

'You could be of help to me,' Tommy said, 'if you don't want to go back to England.' Maddie looked up. 'I have a design company which I run from home near Florence. It's quite small, you understand,' Tommy continued. 'We do knitwear – a very exclusive range. I'm thinking of expanding and I need help in the office.'

'But I don't speak Italian.'

'You'd soon learn and anyway I wouldn't need you to. I'm expanding into the American markets: I need an English secretary. The pay won't be marvellous, nothing like the amount I'm sure Juniper was paying you. But there's a flat over the stables at home that you would be welcome to use and we have a profit-sharing scheme. When we hit the big time, so will you! What do you say?'

'I can't thank you enough, Tommy, it sounds just what I need – a new start. But I'll have to go to Greece first. I've got masses of stuff at Juniper's house and I'd rather collect it while she's away. I don't want to see her . . . it would be difficult . . .'

Maddie felt that returning to Greece and the house must be very much like returning to one's home after a divorce. She still felt shell-shocked by her summary dismissal. She and Juniper had lived together for almost ten years. They had shared this house for eight years, which was a long time to call one house home. The place was full of English workmen when she arrived, busily packing everything into large wooden crates.

'What are you doing?' she demanded of them.

'House is for sale, miss. We're to pack everything and store it.'

'Where's it all going?' she asked curiously.

'London. Harrods' Repository.'

Maddie packed as quickly as she could. She wanted to get off the island as soon as possible now. She longed to be away from it, to make a new start and try to wipe the thought of Juniper from her mind.

Settled in Florence with the Antonios, Maddie began to pick up the pieces again. News filtered back to them. Within three months they heard that Jonathan had been offered a visiting professorship at a university in the Mid-West of America, no doubt arranged by the adoring Bette who had travelled with him.

'I do hope your goddaughter will be all right with him, Tommy. Jonathan isn't exactly the faithful type.'

'My dear Maddie. My goddaughter is in seventh heaven just knowing someone as famous as Jonathan. No doubt she'll let him get away with murder, just so that she can be with him.'

Neither woman was too surprised to hear that within a month of arriving at the university Jonathan and Bette were married.

'At least his writing is secure. Bette will tie him to his desk,' Stefan said sagely, upon being told the news.

It was June. Tommy and Stefan's car inched down the driveway at Gwenfer. The door opened and somehow Tommy expected to see the slim elegant shape of Alice come rushing out to greet her. Instead it was a rather shy young woman, with fine blonde hair and large spectacles. Tommy looked at her and remembered herself all those years ago when she had first gone to work for the dynamic Lincoln Wakefield. She too had tried to disguise her own beauty behind a large pair of spectacles. She knew her own reason – fear of the world – and she wondered why this young woman was doing the same.

Annie showed them in and straight through to the little parlour where Alice sat waiting for them. Tommy was shocked by how old her friend looked. It was stupid to be so shocked, it was just that Alice was the sort of person one never expected to age.

'My dear Tommy, when I received your letter, I was so excited. And this must be your Stefan.' Hands were shaken, cheeks kissed, tea was drunk, reminiscences were exchanged.

'Have you news of Juniper?' Tommy asked eventually.

'Why, yes. She's been on Tahiti with a young artist. He sounded a bit of a rogue to me . . .'

Tommy did not dare look at her husband in case she felt obliged to explain about Giovanni. That would have mortified Alice too much.

'But she's left him now and is in New York – her business, you know. She has to go and see them every so often. Check all is well.'

'She told me she'd lost a lot of money some years ago.'

'A disaster!' Alice threw her hands in the air.

'She doesn't seem to have changed her lifestyle very much, from what I could make out.'

'She's probably putting a good front on it. You know Juniper, always so proud. She tells me she's bought a small house in Italy. I've put the address somewhere on my desk.' Alice began to look for it and then, appearing to tire of the task, shook her hands with annoyance. 'I'll find it for you before you go.'

'Please do, I can look her up. What does she think of you running Gwenfer as a hotel?'

'Oh, she doesn't know about that – she must never know.' Alice looked anxious. 'I don't want her worried, you see.'

'But your allowance from Lincoln? Surely you still receive it?'

Alice looked embarrassed. She did not know Stefan.

'Stefan, my darling. Be an angel. Go and explore the garden just for five minutes,' Tommy said hurriedly in Italian.

'Forgive my lack of manners, Alice, speaking in Italian, but I thought you would prefer my husband not to be here,' Tommy explained, once Stefan had gone. 'Now, what is all this?'

Alice explained her financial predicament to an appalled Tommy. 'But my dear Alice, I think you have misunderstood the situation. Juniper is still enormously wealthy. She could easily afford to give you more money. I can speak to her if you want.'

'No!' Alice almost shouted.

'Well, I still have the allowance that Lincoln willed me for my life. You must have that.'

'I couldn't possibly. Lincoln wanted you to have that

money. You were good to him when he was most alone,' Alice said truthfully, for she had never felt any rancour towards Tommy for having been Lincoln's lover. After all it had happened after she had left him; in fact she had always been grateful to the younger woman.

'And Lincoln never intended that you should want for anything. What on earth do you think he would say if he knew you were having to run your home as a guest house or hotel? He would be horrified.'

'But, Tommy, you must need it yourself.'

'No, I don't. Stefan is an enormously successful doctor and I don't think we are likely to get divorced at our age – at least I hope not.' She smiled kindly at the older woman. 'In any case, I have my own business which goes from strength to strength. I'm virtually independent. I don't need Lincoln's money. I'd much rather you had it, as he would.'

Alice looked at Tommy for a long time. She thought of the money, how it would be to come down in the morning and not be afraid to look at the post in case there were bills she could not meet, or a letter from the bank. With just a little more money they could have more help. It would be less worry. But, it was charity, she had never taken that in her life and to start now . . .?

'Tommy, you are too kind. It would mean so much to me. Just a little of it, not all,' Alice said, trying not to sound too eager, the thought of the pressure easing overriding her normal pride in such matters.

'All or nothing.' Tommy patted her hands gently.

'I don't like doing this, Tommy, you understand?' Alice could hardly bring herself to look at her, already she felt ashamed. 'But you see, there's young Annie, the girl who let you in. She's wonderful to me. She does so much work, but if she should get ill . . . I don't know what I would do. I would have to sell Gwenfer.'

'You couldn't do that, Alice. This place means so much to you.'

'It does. If I accept, you must realize, it's not for me, it's for . . .' But she did not finish the sentence for she doubted if anyone could understand. 'For Gwenfer' she had wanted to say. In the end, she realized, Gwenfer and her love for it would always outweigh all other considerations, even her pride.

'I had hoped Juniper would feel the same way, but she doesn't. Harry loves it – my great-grandson,' she said in explanation. 'But he's so young and clever and, though he likes it here and swears he'll never leave, I expect the world and a career will call, and would he want to stay here then? But, Tommy, do you know who loves it the most? Annie.' Alice paused as if deciding whether to continue. And then she leant forward, glanced at the door and spoke very quietly. 'I've left it to her, to Annie, in my will. Do you think that is terribly wrong of me? When it's my family home.' She sat back, her face set, as if she were preparing herself for censure.

'No, Alice, I don't think it's wrong of you. This house deserves the person who loves it most.'

In the time she spent at Gwenfer Tommy heard all the news. She heard of the row with Gertie, and she heard how Alice regretted it now. She was shocked when she discovered how little time Juniper had spent there. And she tried to persuade Alice to go to London to see a specialist about her arthritis.

'It's nothing.' Alice had dismissed Tommy's concern. 'I expect a few aches and pains at my age. It's worse at the moment because of this damp June. It'll be better when the proper summer comes.'

On the drive back to London Tommy was sad and angry for Alice. She must have been mistaken about Juniper's finances. She might have incurred losses but Tommy was certain she was still very rich. It was horrifying to think how hard the poor woman must work when there was no need. It seemed so unjust too, when she had given so much of her life to her granddaughter, that Juniper should be so neglectful of her. And yet she knew it was not really neglect, Juniper just had not thought about it. No doubt she expected her grandmother to live for ever.

'Is that the famous Dartmoor over there?' Stefan pointed to the purple haze of the moors in the distance. 'Where the Hound of the Baskervilles lives?'

'The very same.'

'Shall we stay a night or two?'

They booked into the New Inn at Widecombe. It was in the bar that she overheard two men, discussing horses, mention the name of Lady Gertrude Frobisher as the best judge of horseflesh in these parts. She made enquiries, telephoned Polly and the next day they set out to meet Gertie and Polly.

Tommy had quite expected an uphill task in trying to persuade Gertie to go and visit Alice. In fact she received the news with delight, confessing that for some time she had been thinking of writing. How stupid and undignified were feuds between people of their age, Gertie admitted.

Tommy remembered Polly from when she and Juniper had been debutantes together. Watching her so contented with her life, Tommy wished that Juniper had been as lucky. Alice had hinted there had been trouble between Polly and Juniper too. There was no need to pry. Now she put two and two together as she remembered that there had been a time when everyone had expected Polly and Jonathan to marry.

'How is Juniper?' Polly asked, shortly before Tommy was to leave, as if she had delayed until the end asking the question.

'Beautiful and unhappy.'

'She should be so happy, she has everything,' Polly answered wistfully.

'She doesn't have an Andrew,' Tommy said simply.

'She has Jonathan.'

'Not any more. He's in the clutches of my goddaughter. We shall hear much more of Jonathan the writer now, I think.'

'Did he make her unhappy?' From another woman Tommy would have interpreted this question as being malicious, but from Polly, she was sure, it was inspired by concern.

'I think they made each other unhappy.'

'Ah, I see.' Polly looked out of the window for a moment. 'She writes to me and asks me to go and stay. But I don't think I want to, not yet. I don't know why.' She turned to face Tommy as if she expected her to have the answer.

'Maybe she hurt you too much – once,' Tommy said softly.

'There was a time in my life when I almost hated her.'

'And now?'

'Who can hate Juniper for any length of time?' Polly smiled.

Stefan, who had been taken on a strenuous tour of the gardens by Gertie, returned and pointed out they must leave if they were to be in London for dinner. Tommy kissed Polly goodbye and silently wished they could have had a few more minutes alone. She sensed there was something bothering her and she might have been just about to confide in her.

Tommy had only been gone a few days when Harry arrived at Gwenfer. He was exuberantly happy, Cambridge was behind him and the future stretched excitingly ahead. He had secured a first in modern languages. He had also been offered a research grant and many a hint had been dropped that an academic life was his for the asking. He had turned it down.

'But what are you going to do, Copton?' Sir Henry Willinck, the Master of Magdalene, asked him.

'I'm going to run a hotel, Master,' he said with glee, as if he had planned the reply for a long time.

'But Harry, my darling, you're far too clever to run Gwenfer,' Alice said, when he related this conversation. 'You should have a career. I always assumed you would go into the Diplomatic Corps. You'd make a wonderful ambassador.'

'Me? I'd be bored to tears.' Harry laughed. 'I loathed university. Just because I'm clever everyone assumes I want an academic life. Well, I don't. I want to be free.'

'Perhaps you could help your mother. She's never had a man she could trust totally with her money affairs.'

'Me? In business? No, thank you, Alice. That would bore me more than diplomacy.'

'Then what shall you do?' Alice frowned with concern.

'I was being serious. I'm going to help you here until I make my mind up what I really want to do. There's plenty of time,' he said dismissively with the confidence of the young who imagine they will live for ever.

That night, as she lay in his arms, listening to his plans, Annie was almost too scared to believe he was telling the truth.

'You'll be bored to tears,' she said.

'No, I shan't. I love it here and I love you and Alice. You can both wait on me hand and foot.' He grinned.

She grabbed a pillow and hit him with it. He returned the compliment. They battled until one of the pillows exploded in a cloud of feathers and they collapsed with laughter.

'Shush . . . you'll wake Alice. She wouldn't like to know what we get up to.' Annie giggled. He leant over and scooped her into his arms. In their ensuing excitement and passion a few elementary precautions were forgotten. There at Gwenfer, in the land of granite, a child was conceived.

5

The aeroplane from Rome droned through the air. Juniper looked down on the earth far below and wished she could stay up here in the sky, need never touch down, need not face problems, nor have to acknowledge guilt and inevitably be blamed for everything.

Pietro, beside her in the next seat, stirred in his sleep. She looked at him, the finely tanned face smooth and unlined. It was the face of someone to whom so little had happened that there were no marks of life upon it. In sleep he looked even younger than he was. She wished she had not brought him with her. It had been a stupid last-minute decision on her part, but he had looked so lost and sad when she had told him she was returning to England. He refused to believe it was only for a couple of weeks, nothing she could say would convince him she would be returning to him. So she had given in and allowed him to come with her. What to do with him when they arrived, however, had been occupying her mind for most of this flight. She could not possibly take him to Gwenfer; her grandmother would never understand, nor accept, this boy only slightly older than her own son whom she had taken into her bed.

Other people. She was always circumscribed by other people. Was one ever free, could one ever be one's own mistress? Why at forty-two did she still worry about offending Alice? It was her life, why then should she not lead it as she wished? Instead she spent her time closeted away in other countries, Greece, now Italy, leading her life her way, but always as a secret. For some time now when she ventured from the security of her home it was as if she held a shield in front of her, hiding what her life was like, what she was doing. Had she been a man, her father for example, would anyone have raised an eyebrow at the taking of a beautiful young mistress? Her father had had an army of them. But she was planning to hide her lover, keep him away from her family and friends, as if she were ashamed of him.

Was she ashamed of him? She hated the all-too-frequent suspicion that people whispered and laughed about them once they had passed by. She often found herself wondering what remarks were made, what conclusions were reached. What people thought was not really the problem. What troubled her was that, in some way she had not yet worked out, their sneering tarnished what little she and Pietro had. That was what she resented.

She clicked open the mirror of her powder compact and studied her face. At least no one would be saying she was old enough to be his mother. She was, just, but she didn't look it, that was one great blessing.

Why Pietro? Because of his handsome face and beautiful, insatiable body? Because he was young, made her laugh, made her feel young again herself? All or even any of these? No, if she were honest it was because Pietro had found her when she was alone and lonely. It was chance, pure and simple. Sitting drinking a brandy at a café close to the magnificent Duomo in Florence, it had been Pietro who had walked by. If he had not happened to pass her table, it would have been the young man who sauntered by two minutes later and had looked at her in the same appraising way. And if not him, then the next, or the next . . . God, what a depressing thought.

Still, she thought more brightly, she did not love him and so what happened in the future would not matter in the same way as her other loves had mattered. She was employing him, really. When he misbehaved, or no longer fulfilled her requirements, he could go. It would be better that way, less hurtful; probably cheaper too, she told herself with a rueful smile.

Then with no warning, Theo's name echoed in her head. She sighed and sank back into the airline seat and closed her eyes. As much as she had tried, over the years, to forget him, to pretend he had never been, often, for no apparent reason, she would remember and long for him. Thinking of him never helped. The opposite happened, it accentuated the emptiness of her life, it made the bitterness that he had been taken from her harder to bear. Time heals, they said, but not for her. All that time had done was to form a scab over the agony of Theo's death. Aware that a tear was sliding down her cheek, she wiped it away, lit a cigarette and signalled to the stewardess for another brandy. Think of something else, she told herself, firmly.

She almost wished that Tommy had not come back into her life. Jonathan would not have met that unspeakable, squeaky-clean sophomore, Bette. But then, she realized, she was deceiving herself. If it had not been Bette, it would have been someone else. She had been out of love with Jonathan for a long time, as he had with her. She had clung to him because she was frightened of life on her own. And, no doubt, he had clung to her because life with her had become soft and easy. Perhaps he too had become afraid of life without her, or, more honestly, without her cheque book. Still, he should not have mocked at her poem. Her face twisted at the humiliating memory.

If she had not met Tommy again she would not have had to endure the uncomfortable interview of last week.

Juniper had been happy until then. She had Pietro and she had found a beautiful villa in the hills outside Rome – always one of her favourite cities. Juniper was always happiest when embarking on the conversion of a new house. And then Tommy had arrived and spoilt everything.

It was an angry Tommy and she could barely remember ever seeing her angry before. Juniper had argued that it was hardly her fault if her grandmother had not told her about her money problems, that she had misunderstood Juniper's financial situation.

'What am I supposed to be, a mind reader?' she had said, angrily for Juniper.

'You don't have to be to work it out. You know how much your grandmother was left by Lincoln all those years ago. It doesn't take much intelligence to realize that with prices as they are these days, it's no longer enough for the poor woman to manage.'

'I didn't think.' Juniper had looked sulkily at the floor, feeling like a child again.

'You should have thought. What the worry and the

hard work have done to your grandmother during the past ten years, I shudder to think. Thank God she has that nice girl Annie.'

'Oh, dear sweet little Annie. No doubt sleeps on a little truckle bed so as not to be a nuisance. I loathe little Annie Budd, I've always loathed her.' Juniper stood up abruptly, her fists clenched into tight balls, desperately trying to control herself.

'Oh Juniper, really!'

'I wish, Tommy, you would stop speaking to me as if I were a child. It's not my fault. Will you please get that into your head? I don't think about money. I never have done, I have no need to. It just comes, don't you understand? I don't even know how much one person needs to live. Those are ordinary people's problems, not mine. If my grandmother has been so silly as to struggle on without telling me, I'm sorry. But I didn't ask her to.'

'My God, Juniper. You've become so hard.'

'I don't think I have, Tommy. I'm just getting tired of always being blamed for everything.'

Tommy had stayed a while longer and they had managed to steer the conversation away from Gwenfer and Alice, but Juniper knew that their relationship would never be the same again. In fact, it nearly ended when Tommy mentioned that Maddie was working for her. Juniper's face registered irritation. Tommy dropped the subject.

The plane was well over France now. She looked down on the chequerboard of farm and woodland which was Central France. She wondered if she was passing over any of the roads that she and Polly had taken at the beginning of the war: that had been fun, she had felt really alive, with a point to her life. Then she had been happy, even if she had been afraid. She missed Polly desperately, she knew she always would. In a way Maddie had been a replacement for her old friend. But when the end came with Jonathan, it had also to be the end for Maddie.

Jonathan was the past now and Juniper could not bring any of the baggage from that past into her present, so the house in Greece, much as she loved it, had had to go. Despite her loyalty and sweetness, Maddie too had had to go. That was how she was, she could not help it.

Pietro stirred.

'Where are we?' His face was crumpled with sleep.

'Over France. Not long now.'

'Umm . . .' He twisted in his seat so that his head rested on her shoulder. She stroked his hair until he slept. She hoped he lasted, she liked him.

An hour later the aeroplane taxied to a halt. It was raining. Juniper smiled. Whenever she thought of England it was always perfect weather and yet invariably when she arrived it was pouring like this.

Pietro complained all the way into the city. The grey clouds, the rain, seemed to have extinguished his high spirits, changed him. He even looked different, the colour of his skin had changed so that he no longer looked tanned, but sallow, his eyes lacking their sparkle: he had become as dull as the day. Juniper certainly hoped, for his sake, that the sun came out soon.

The taxi drew to a halt. She had decided to take Pietro to the flat she had bought Harry in Ebury Street. If Harry was there she would ask him to look after the Italian while she went to Gwenfer. She trusted to luck that she would be able to explain Pietro to her son without embarrassing both of them too much. If he was not there, then Pietro would have to fend for himself for a few days. For all her annoyance at having to hide Pietro, she was not going to take him to Cornwall.

Harry was not there. Pietro made a scene. He hated the flat, it was too small, too old. He disliked the furnishings, the paintings. He hated London, England, the weather. He was homesick, he wanted to go home. Juniper, in exasperation, threw his return ticket and a wallet of money at him and walked out of the flat. She took a taxi and booked into the Ritz for a couple of nights. She had some shopping to do, her lawyer to see and then she'd take the train to Penzance – alone.

6

Alice was in such a state of excitement that Annie was worried. The old lady tired so easily these days and Annie liked her to be quiet, not to get over-excited and then exhausted. The previous week she had received a letter from Gertie asking if she and Polly might come to stay for a few days, as paying guests, of course, Gertie had insisted. Alice did not take offence, realizing it had been offered in the right spirit, but thought how nice it was going to be, thanks to Tommy, not to have to accept their money.

'Alice . . .'

'Gertie . . .'

A small kiss on each other's cheek, hands held warmly, a long studied look at each other and so ended the feud of too many years. Neither apologized, there were no recriminations, the matter was simply not discussed. There was so much to talk about, news to exchange, and so much time to be made up, something both women were short of.

The years had been kinder to Gertie than to Alice. In fact she had been shocked at the sight of Alice, a surprise she hoped she had managed to disguise. For Alice, always slim, was now thin, far too thin. She who had been so upright was now bowed. The woman who had had such energy was permanently tired.

'I think the worst thing about growing old is the creaking and the aches and pains, don't you, Gertie?' Alice asked.

'Undoubtedly,' Gertie had replied, for she had not the heart to tell her friend that, apart from her bout of pneumonia when she had given everyone such a scare, she did not know what illness was. As to aches and pains, she had none. She was a bit slower, but that was because she was much heavier now than she once had been. But she could walk with the best of them, still occasionally rode, if not to hounds, and would often stay up far later than Polly, with a decanter of port and a nice piece of Stilton to nibble, and never a hint of heartburn – even her digestion had not let her down despite her eighty-four years.

It was inevitable that Polly would seek out Alice to discuss Juniper and Hurstwood. Since the offer, the deeds still mouldering in her lawyer's office unreturned, Polly had incessantly solicited advice and opinions from everyone. Had she just had herself to consider there would have been no problem in her refusal to sign. But by being so proud, she knew that she was depriving her son of his family home. When he was an adult, would he sympathize with the stand she felt she had to make, or would he never be able to forgive her? Coming here was a godsend, who better to consult than Alice, a member of Juniper's family? Polly had decided she would do what Alice thought was best.

Both Polly and Gertie had been invited to stay longer than the four days originally planned. Gertie had accepted with alacrity, but Polly felt she must return to her husband and son. She had left consulting Alice until just before she was due to return to Devon.

When she heard of Juniper's gesture, Alice smiled, but Polly, watching her closely, noted that it was a very little smile.

'So typical of Juniper, such a generous child,' she said quietly and hoped that she was managing to cover up the hurt.

'What do you think I should do?' Polly asked.

'I can't help you decide, my dear. You must do what you think is right.'

'But I don't know what is right.'

'Why have you not grabbed at this opportunity already?'

'I think I understood Juniper's motives. It didn't seem right to take advantage.'

'That's a very interesting phrase to use, Polly, "to take advantage". Perhaps you could explain?'

'Well, I think she acted out of a strong sense of guilt. It's like the guilt of a child who's done wrong and thinks that if she gives her chocolate to the person she's hurt, everything will be all right again. But it isn't the action of an adult.'

'No? Juniper has always been a very generous person, you know that, Polly, better than most.' Polly could not help thinking that there was more than a hint of reproof in Alice's voice.

'Oh, I know. I know that very well, but all the time I'm afraid that there is this other factor, maybe something Juniper herself isn't even aware of. Then I think I can't accept. It would be like taking the chocolate from the child, but under false pretences. You see, Juniper did me a great favour, I've been so happy with Andrew, a happiness I'm sure I would never have had with Jonathan. It would be stealing.'

'I don't know why you ask me, Polly. You've obviously made up your own mind, and rightly too, I think. Why not just stay as you are? You have the tenancy. I'm sure Juniper will never want the house back. In any case she would never see you homeless, now would she? Keep faith with your conscience, Polly, don't listen to others. Now, you drive carefully! And telephone the moment you are safely home,' Alice said abruptly, giving Polly the distinct impression that she did not wish to talk about Hurstwood any longer.

But that night, after Polly had driven away, Alice found it difficult to sleep. How could Juniper, with all her financial difficulties, be so profligate? Alice remembered the hours she and Annie had worked to protect Juniper from having to pay a penny towards the upkeep of Gwenfer. Yet she would happily lay out that large sum of money for Polly, to assuage her conscience, it would seem. But, had she been fair to Polly, hadn't she let her hurt get in the way of an honest judgement? Why shouldn't Polly accept if that was what Juniper wanted? It was Juniper's money to do with as she wished – not as Alice wished. What if Polly listened to her and continued with this impasse? She would write to Polly about it, she should try to get the young woman to accept, she must make her accept, she must. She turned on her pillows. She would compose a letter and give it to Gertie to take home with her, it was too important a subject to put in the mail. That decided, she fell asleep immediately.

Annie was pleased Gertie had stayed on for a couple of weeks. They were usually very busy in September: people often took a second holiday in the hope of catching an Indian summer. With Gertie here, she need not worry about Alice. Gertie would entertain her, would stop her fretting about not helping enough, go for afternoon walks with her, leaving Annie to concentrate on the cooking and the running of the house. Now that Harry was with her she did not know how she and Alice had managed before. Harry had taken to the business like a duck to water. He was wonderful with the guests, having abundant charm, and it was a relief to be able to leave the ordering of the wine, the book keeping, in his capable hands. Harry had great plans for Gwenfer. He was going to ask his mother for a loan, he said, for he planned to make Gwenfer the most luxurious and exclusive hotel in the West Country. Both Alice and Annie, while applauding and encouraging his plans, agreed that they doubted if Harry would stay long enough to see them come to fruition.

'You're getting fat,' Harry said one day, laughing, as he encircled Annie's waist as she stood at the Aga making a sauce.

'I'm not. Don't be so rude,' she said, stirring her sauce with angry vigour.

'You're blushing,' he accused her, still laughing.

'I'm not. It's the heat from the stove.' She pointedly

removed his hand from her waist. 'If you've nothing better to do than to insult me, I have.'

'What's the matter with you? Why so grumpy?'

She ignored his question, bowed her head and attended to her cooking with exaggerated concentration.

Harry removed the pan from her hand, took the wooden spoon and laid it on the side, closed the cooker lid and led her to the kitchen table.

'Now, what's the problem. You're upset about something, what is it?' he asked.

'Can't you guess?' She looked away from him, appearing to stare intently at the copper pans on the dresser as if seeing them for the first time.

'No, what is there to guess?'

She turned slowly and looked at him for what seemed a long time before answering.

'I'm pregnant.'

Harry knew that his mouth hung open slackly, knew that the shock he was feeling was etched on his face, knew she was waiting for him to say something and found that no words came. She looked away from him again and went back to studying the contents of the dresser.

'Are you sure?' he said eventually.

'Positive.' Annie slumped back into the chair with a sad, resigned expression on her face. His reaction, that little question he asked, told her all that she needed to know.

'That's wonderful,' Harry said, regaining his composure, if a little late.

'No, it's not. It's the last thing you wanted to hear.'

'It is . . . why . . . bloody hell . . . We'll get married.'

'No, we won't. Not for that reason.'

'Don't be silly. Of course we will. We must.'

'No.'

'Oh, come on, Annie. Think about it. What else can you do? Have it adopted?'

'I couldn't give my child away.' Her voice wavered as she spoke, s if fighting tears.

'A friend of mine's girlfriend had an abortion.'

She swung round angrily. 'Never. I couldn't do that. How could you even suggest it?'

'I wasn't suggesting it. I was just telling you. If you won't marry me and you won't have it adopted, then . . .' He shrugged his shoulders helplessly.

'I'm going to have the baby. And stop saying "it".'

'Then if you're going ahead with it, that's settled. We get married.'

'I don't want to marry you, Harry. Now, if you don't mind, that sauce will be ruined.' And she pushed her chair back, its legs scraping on the floor, returned to the Aga and began calmly to stir her sauce.

Harry looked at her back, rigid from suppressed emotion, and was perplexed. Of course she was right, a baby was the last thing he wanted. He might originally have said he wanted to marry her to get her into bed, but it had not been part of his scheme of things. Not yet. He was too young, he did not want this sort of commitment, this responsibility, this trap, he thought with rising panic. But it was his fault too. He was fond of Annie, he couldn't leave her to cope with this alone.

'I think I've got a say in this too.'

'I told you, you haven't. It's my decision. It's my baby.' She turned from the cooker and was smiling at him. 'Don't worry, Harry. I meant it. I don't want to get married either.' She said it bravely, but all the while she felt her heart was breaking. He did not say anything, he did not need to, she could see the expression of relief flit across his face.

Alice guessed. When neither of the young people said anything to her, she finally plucked up the courage to speak to Annie.

'There's nothing to discuss, Alice. I made a mistake and it's a mistake I shall learn to live with. I shan't be the first. Other girls have managed, why not me?'

'But, Annie, I'm sure Harry would wish to marry you.'

'He's already offered – I wouldn't grace it by calling it a proposal.' Her laugh was meagre.

'And you refused?' Alice sighed. 'My dear Annie, you have no idea what the future will be. It's not easy managing a child on your own. I don't mean by that that you can't stay here, of course you can, and welcome. But a woman needs the support of a husband. There would be times when it would be so difficult for you without him.'

'I couldn't possibly stay here, Alice. It wouldn't be fair on you. The last thing this business needs is a screaming baby in the background.'

'But where could you go? Annie, you haven't thought this through. It's been a shock to you. You can't begin to comprehend the problems . . .' Alice looked down at her hands, remembering her own struggles when she had been abandoned in New York with a baby and no husband. In a flood, the loneliness, the grinding poverty, the terror she had often felt, swept back into her mind. And she was fearful for Annie. When she looked up it was to find that Annie had slipped from the room.

Harry looked sheepish when Alice later found him.

'But she turned me down, point blank,' he protested.

'Did you tell her that you love her as well as wanting to marry her?' Alice asked patiently.

His pause, though almost imperceptible, was nonetheless noticed by Alice.

'I can't remember if I said it at the time. But I've told her in the past. Of course I love her,' he blustered. 'I just don't understand why she's refusing. I'm quite prepared to face up to my responsibilities.'

'I'm glad to hear that, Harry. But don't you see, I doubt if Annie wishes to be regarded as a responsibility. She would only marry you because you love her, not because you feel you have to.'

'That's ridiculous. She knows I love her.'

'Maybe she does, but I think it's the future she's worrying about. Will a day come when you no longer love her, when you blame her because you were made to marry her because of the baby?'

'That's rot.'

'I fear not, Harry. Many men have short memories in such circumstances. Perhaps she will marry you after the baby is born. I could understand that.'

'You amaze me, Great-Grandmother. You should be shocked rigid by all this. You shouldn't be so understanding and trying to help.'

'The trouble with the young is that they think their generation is the only one that understands anything, that they alone discovered love, that they are the only generation who ever faced such problems. I tell you, my dear Harry, such problems have been with man since time began, and I assure you, I know about most of them.' She patted his hand. 'But in my opinion, Annie is wrong. The baby should be considered above everything else. Illegitimacy is an appalling burden even in this day and age. You must prevail upon her, Harry.'

'I will, Alice, I promise,' he said, knowing his great-grandmother was right and regretting it was so.

'I knew you would. And I've had a lovely thought, Harry. If it's a girl then we shall have another daughter of this granite land. That's a nice thought.' She smiled to herself.

To add to her joy at having Gertie staying, Alice received a telegram one morning from Juniper, saying she was arriving on the evening express from London. If she had been excited before it was nothing compared to her feelings now.

As she had the last time, she wanted bookings cancelled and those who were already staying with them to be moved out to other hotels after lunch. This time Annie was not alone to argue against such action – Harry and Gertie were there to back her up.

'Quite honestly, Alice, I don't think you are being fair to the young couple. They are both working so hard to make this business a success and you'll set them back goodness knows how much by these cancellations. It's too unprofessional, my dear. It just won't do. Juniper will just have to adjust to it, as we all have.'

Gertie's argument won the day.

Within an hour of her arrival Alice was downhearted and could wish the unthinkable – that her granddaughter had not come. Alice had had to endure a long, unpleasant interview with Juniper. She had had to face a Juniper she did not know existed. At the end, Alice felt she would never forgive Tommy for telling Juniper of her difficult circumstances.

'You should have told me, Grandmama,' Juniper said accusingly. 'I was appalled to learn you'd turned Gwenfer into a hotel. What on earth made you do something so stupid and undignified?'

'I didn't want to worry you when you had financial problems of your own.'

'What financial problems?'

'Hal stealing from you.'

'Good gracious, Grandmother, that was years ago. I've almost forgotten about it. I'm not poor. I was still left with plenty of money. Oh, how silly. Why on earth didn't you say you were worried about me? I'd have reassured you, helped you. What on earth gave you the idea I was broke? Can you imagine how stupid I felt when Tommy told me? I didn't believe her, I thought somehow she had got the wrong end of the stick. And I didn't enjoy having to defend myself in that way. And I gather you've been accepting charity from her.'

'I didn't regard it as charity, Juniper. She assured me she did not need the money and it was Lincoln's. She was right. Lincoln would have wanted me to have it. I was still his wife when he died, she wasn't,' Alice said, sitting upright with effort, for she felt immeasurably tired.

'Then you're to give it back. I'll get on to the lawyers in the morning and all this guest nonsense must stop. Oh, Grandmama. What a pickle you've made of everything.'

'I did what I thought best,' Alice said with quiet dignity.

'You didn't over Harry.'

'What on earth do you mean?'

'He and Annie – they sleep together, you realize?'

'Yes, I realized they did. I didn't condone it, I wouldn't. I tried to ignore it. There was nothing else I could do. These days the young do whatever they want. And for goodness' sake, Juniper, with my own past, who am I to stand in judgement on those young people.'

'Good God, Grandmama! This is your great-grandson we're talking about, not some stranger. You've allowed him to be at risk. His whole life could be ruined by that little gold-digger, Annie.'

'Juniper, that's a dreadful thing to say. Annie is not a gold-digger – what a spiteful way to speak of the child. She's a dear sweet person.'

'She's hardly a child. And far from innocent. I saw her the first time Harry came here, making sheep's eyes at him, chasing him. He didn't stand a chance. It's disgusting.'

'Juniper, I can hardly believe this is you talking. There's nothing disgusting in their relationship. In fact it's all been the other way round. It's she who is refusing to marry Harry at the moment.'

'Thank God for that then.'

'No, you're wrong. It's the baby they should be thinking of, not themselves.'

Juniper sat down with a jolt. 'The what?' she asked, her voice a mixture of shock and anger. 'So, the little bitch is pregnant?'

'Oh dear, of course, they wouldn't have told you. I should have been more discreet. Oh dear . . .' Alice was twisting at the pearls at her neck.

'No, no one has told me anything.' Juniper jumped up from her seat and rushed to the door. Opening it, she put her head out. 'You,' she said abruptly to Annie, who was in the hall arranging flowers in a vase on the table, beside the azure bowl. Annie looked up. 'You,' Juniper repeated.

'Are you speaking to me?'

'There's no one else around. Find Harry and come here.'

'Please . . .' Annie said with a quiet smile, but the door to the parlour had slammed shut. She went in search of Harry.

Five minutes later they were both standing in front of the fireplace in Alice's parlour and feeling shellshocked. Juniper did not mince her words. Alice could not believe what she was hearing. Juniper never lost her temper, never shouted. She was now. With distress Alice saw first Annie and then Harry's complexions whiten, saw the stiffening of their bodies, saw Annie fighting tears and Harry fighting anger.

Annie was finally galvanized into action when she was informed that she had become pregnant on purpose to trap Harry and by so doing would ruin his life.

'That my grandson should be a bastard . . .' Juniper shouted, her face distorted with anger.

'That's enough, Miss Juniper . . .' Annie said loudly emphasizing the Miss. 'How dare you. Don't you ever speak to me like that again. I have not tried to trap your son, I love him. I would do nothing to harm him. I'm sad we should both be in this position. I don't want a baby, but it's too late, it's happened.' Annie looked about her wildly. 'But you know, Juniper, I should be grateful to you, you've made me see things more clearly.' She turned to Harry. 'Right, Harry. I'm wrong. Yes, the child would be a bastard and at the mercy of intolerant people like your mother. I will marry you, Harry. Set the day.' And with head held high, Annie swept from the room before she said more.

'Mother, how could you speak to her like that?'

'It was the truth.'

'It wasn't. I seduced her, if you must know.'

'But don't you see, Harry, it's all a plan. It's always been a plan. When she came here as a tiny child, what did she do? She took my grandmother away from me, now she's taking you – the two people I love most in the world.'

'Mother!' Harry looked at his mother with disbelief. 'I have never heard such stupid rubbish in all my life. You're like a spoilt child talking. She's not taking anyone from anybody. You don't own us, Mother, don't you realize? You certainly didn't want to own me, did you? Not until it suited you. Grow up, for Christ's sake, before you do more damage.' And Harry stalked from the room in search of Annie.

'Juniper . . .' Alice said softly, putting her hand out to touch her. 'My poor darling, why are you so unhappy? What is it? Tell me.' Alice's distress at Juniper's reaction was boundless. She had always feared for Juniper, her wildness, her moods, but now she knew she had been watching the reaction of someone who was not normal. Juniper needed help.

'I can't.'

'You can tell me anything.'

Juniper looked angrily about the room as if searching for someone, or something, to attack. 'Okay, if you want to know, I'm sick to death of people whispering in corners " . . . what's wrong with Juniper?" I'll tell you what's wrong. Everyone deserts me, that's what. Everyone I love leaves me – they always have.'

'My dear Juniper, what did we do to you all those years ago? What damage did we inflict? You haven't lost anyone. You have me and Harry. He'll still love you even if you have made it difficult for him. You could have Annie and a grandchild to love and take pleasure in, if only you would see sense. You have always been like this, so jealous and possessive, so afraid. It has to stop, Juniper, you risk ruining your life with these delusions. I shan't always be here to reassure you, to turn to. You must learn to carry out your relationships with people in an adult way. You have to learn that you can't own people completely. I'm sure Harry loves you and needs you. He loves and needs Annie too, but in a different way. Can't you see? And he will love his child, and he or she will need him, and so the chain of life continues.'

'Don't say he loves that bitch. I can't bear it. You don't understand me, you never have. No one does . . .' Juniper began to cross the room to the door. She turned to face Alice, her face streaked with tears, her eyes full of fear. 'But there was one, he loved me, understood me, accepted me. But now . . . Oh Grandmama, help me. What is to become of me?'

Alice stepped forward to take hold of her, to comfort her, to bring reason into the sad turmoil of her mind. But Juniper did not stop for comfort, she raced from the room. 'Leave me alone,' she cried as she sped across the hall.

Gertie, who had been finishing the flowers for Annie, watched as Juniper bounded up the stairs. She heard a bedroom door slam. She crossed the hall and tapped gently on the door. There was no answer so she pushed the door open. Alice was sitting hunched over, her head in her hands.

Gertie gently took hold of her hands, 'My poor friend,' she said simply.

Alice looked up at Gertie and sighed deeply. 'My dear friend,' she said with her gentle smile. 'Too many dramas over too many years. Will it never end?' She shook herself as if to pull herself together. 'I need fresh air. Do you fancy a little walk? We have time before dinner.'

It was a beautiful evening. A slight chill in the air hinted at the autumn to come. The two friends walked slowly down the steps to the valley. There had been no question which way they were going, they both knew. Alice leant heavily on her stick, Gertie walked upright beside her. Once it would have taken ten minutes to reach the end of the valley, but with Alice's stiff joints it was nearly half an hour before they reached the beach. Gertie looked up at the sky and was concerned that it might be dark before they got back to the house.

'Let's rest just a moment before we return, Gertie.' Alice, with difficulty, manoeuvred herself on to the sand leaning her back against Ia's Rock. 'I'm getting too old to climb my rock and I know I'm getting too old for my family.' She laughed gently.

'Is the problem resolvable, do you think?'

'Everything always is, haven't you found? Look at us.'

'Ah,' Gertie said with a chortle. 'It was certainly time we pulled ourselves together.'

'It's Juniper I worry for. Harry and Annie have each other, I'm confident they will find their own happiness. But Juniper, I fear, used up all her happiness in childhood. Now there's nothing left to see her through the rest of her life . . . Do you know what she said to me, Gertie? "Help me. What is to become of me?" It was a cry of pain, dreadful to hear. And I did nothing, I did not follow her. I don't know any more how to help her.'

'You can't, Alice. She's a grown woman. You can't take on her suffering for ever.'

'I know, I know, my dear friend. But those words, the expression on her face will haunt me . . .'

They sat in silence, both thinking of Juniper, the child who had everything, the young woman graced with such beauty and charm that she'd been christened 'The Golden Butterfly', first by the press and then by everyone who met her. And that young woman had become this sad person who seemed doomed to unhappiness.

'Oh look, Alice. There's the most marvellous piece of driftwood.' Gertie slipped off the rock with ease. 'I must salvage that.'

'Dear Gertie, you never change, you're just like you were in the war. Do you remember what a scavenger you were?' Alice was laughing at the memories.

'Rats!' Gertie chuckled and made off across the beach to rescue the large lump of wood she had spied. She dragged it safely up the beach above the highwater mark. She stood hands on hip and looked out over the sea, pausing at the beauty of the sunset as the fiery September sun began to slip towards the horizon. As the red glow infused the great arc of the sky there was a momentary spurt of intense light, an incandescent green – the green flash.

'Alice, did you see that?' Gertie was pounding across the beach to the rock, shouting. 'Alice, the flash. At last. Did you see it?'

She stopped in her tracks a few feet from the rock. Alice sat unmoving, leaning against the rock, looking out to sea, a strange stillness about her.

'Oh no,' Gertie said softly. 'Oh no.' Slowly she approached her friend. 'Alice, my dear friend.' She took Alice into her arms. 'Did you see it, my darling? Oh, please say you saw it.'

Gently Gertie turned Alice's face to hers. She was smiling the sweet smile that had charmed people all her long life.

'You saw it, my dearest. Thank God you saw it.' And Gertie's tears fell on to Alice's face. As night approached Gertie sat holding her friend close to her. The lights began to shine from the windows. The great granite house stood warm and welcoming in the darkening light and watched. In the distance Gertie could hear voices urgently calling their names. She did not respond, she wanted these last few moments alone with Alice. She wanted to be close to her, this irreplaceable friend from the days of her youth. She wanted to hold her safe while her soul escaped to remain, she was certain, here in this cove, at Gwenfer, for ever.